The Killing Song

Lesley McEvoy was born and bred in Yorkshire and has had a passion for writing in one form or another all her life. The writing took a backseat as Lesley developed her career as a Behavioural Analyst / Profiler and Psychotherapist – setting up her own Consultancy business and therapy practice. She has written and presented extensively around the world for over 25 years specialising in behavioural profiling and training, with a wide variety of organisations. The corporate world provided unexpected sources of writing material when, as Lesley said, she found more psychopaths in business than in prison! Lesley's work in some of the UK's toughest prisons was where she met people whose lives had been characterised by drugs and violence and whose experiences informed the themes she now writes about. Deciding in 2017 to concentrate on her writing again, Lesley produced her debut novel, *The Murder Mile*.

These days she lives in Cheshire with her partner but still manages to lure her two grown up sons across the Pennines with her other passion – cooking family dinners.

Also by Lesley McEvoy

The Murder Mile

The Killing Song

Lesley McEvoy

ZAFFRE

First published in the UK in 2022 by
ZAFFRE
An imprint of Bonnier Books UK
4th Floor, Victoria House, Bloomsbury Square, London, WC1B 4DA
Owned by Bonnier Books
Sveavägen 56, Stockholm, Sweden

This is a work of fiction. Names, places, events and
incidents are either the products of the author's
imagination or used fictitiously. Any resemblance to
actual persons, living or dead, or actual
events is purely coincidental.

A CIP catalogue record for this book is
available from the British Library.

ISBN: 978-1-83877-655-8

Also available as an ebook and an audiobook

1 3 5 7 9 10 8 6 4 2

Typeset by IDSUK (Data Connection) Ltd
Printed and bound in Great Britain by Clays Ltd, Elcograf S.p.A.

Zaffre is an imprint of Bonnier Books UK
www.bonnierbooks.co.uk

Dee Logan 15.09.1955–18.03.2021
This one is for you my friend

'Whoever fights monsters should see to it that in the process he does not become a monster. And if you gaze long enough into an abyss, the abyss will gaze back into you.'

Friedrich Nietzsche

Chapter One

The horror was nameless, faceless – but I knew I was fighting for my life. I struggled, tried to free myself, but my limbs wouldn't move. I opened my mouth to scream but no sound came. My throat was tight, constricted as I fought to breathe.

Dark, grotesque shadows flickered across the walls, and the heat from a fire I couldn't see suffocated me. My heels pushed hard against the mattress to stop him pulling me back to where I didn't want to go; clawing hands held me down, hurting me. I pedalled my legs harder, desperate to get away, until my back was against a wall. I had nowhere to go – I couldn't escape. I was going to die.

I forced my eyes open as my breath came in sharp gasps, sending spasms of pain across my chest. My arms wrapped tightly around my body, squeezing me awake. I was pressed against the headboard of my bed, my legs drawn up in a tangle of damp sheets. Heart hammering against my ribs like a terrified animal banging against the bars of its cage.

I squeezed my eyes shut, then opened them again as sanity slowly returned, allowing me to make out the dim shape of familiar surroundings. Forcing myself to breathe more slowly, I willed my heart rate to descend from the heights of terror.

My hands were shaking as I untangled the sheets and put my feet on the floor. A sharp jolt of pain shot through my left thigh, and I cursed as my leg threatened to give way underneath me, forcing me to sit back down on the edge of the bed.

I gingerly massaged the ridge of scar tissue that ran from my thigh into my groin, gritting my teeth at the jagged shards of pain that threatened to send my muscles into a protest of cramp. The bedside clock said 4 a.m. Grief and hopelessness rolled all over me and I cried silently in the dark.

* * *

Kingsberry Farm, Fordley – Monday morning

'But it's the sixth time he's called.' Jen, my PA, peered at me over the top of her reading glasses and pursed her lips in that way she had when I was getting on her last remaining nerve.

'Tough!' My patience was already paper thin – a legacy of being woken by my recurring nightmares.

She handed me a mug of tea, reading my mood all too easily. 'Someone woke up grumpy.'

'Broken sleep . . . leg playing up, that's all,' I lied.

Jen sighed. 'There's no shame in admitting the last case got to you, Jo.' She indicated my leg with a nod of her head. 'If not psychologically, then physically. Getting attacked like that is enough to give anyone night terrors.'

I shrugged, trying to make light of it. 'You know me, Jen – hard as nails.'

'Hmm.' She didn't look convinced. 'It's *me* you're talking to, remember?'

I waved the message slip at her, moving the topic on to less uncomfortable ground. 'Anyway. What's the point in having a "gatekeeper", if you don't keep people away from my bloody gate?'

'I will and I do . . . but I really think you should talk to him.'

'Why?' I flipped through the messages while I perched on the corner of her desk. 'I'm not getting involved in police cases anymore.'

'Technically it's not a *live* case—'

'Death usually isn't.'

'Very funny.' She took the cup out of my hand and replaced it with the phone. 'Call him, Jo.' She raised an eyebrow as I looked down at her, trying to think of a plausible reason for not calling Charles Fielding. The father of a dead son, who continued to campaign for the case to be re-examined. The coroner's ruling that death had occurred under suspicious circumstances, meant an 'open verdict' – something the Fielding family had struggled to accept for years now.

'If for no other reason than to stop him mithering you,' Jen persisted. 'I've spoken to him, Jo . . . he's convinced *you* can help.'

'Why me? I'm a forensic psychologist, not a cop. West Yorkshire Police are looking at it, even if it *is* in the cold case files. Let them deal with it.'

She studied me for a moment before adding quietly, 'What if it was Alex?'

'Low blow, Jen.'

'You're a mother . . . you wouldn't give up either.' She raised an expressive eyebrow. 'Unless you speak to him, he's just going to keep on calling.'

'How did he seem? When you spoke to him?'

'Frustrated. Angry. All the things I suppose you'd feel if your son's dead and no one seems to care.'

The last sentiment did it – just as she knew it would. 'OK . . .' I said, resigned. 'I'll call him – but only to get rid of him.'

'Good.' She didn't even try to hide the smug look.

'But mostly to get *you* off my back.'

'Very wise.' She smiled sweetly, handing me the number.

* * *

Fordley – Later that morning

I pressed the button to crack open the window of my car and let in the early May breeze. I'd parked in a part of Fordley known as Little Italy. Named after the Italian immigrants who flocked to the city in the nineteenth century, to work in the booming woollen industry.

The huge warehouses and mills were being regenerated and many of the imposing buildings had been converted into trendy apartments, like the one I was about to visit.

Jen was right – Leo Fielding's father was no pushover. What I'd hoped would be a call to fob him off had ended with my reluctantly agreeing to meet him in the place where his son had died – or as he preferred to call it: 'The crime scene'.

'Just meet me there,' he'd said, 'then if you don't want to take the case, I won't bother you again.' The inference being that if I *didn't* come, he *would* keep bothering me. On balance, an hour of my time seemed a small price to pay.

I'd read the case file before I left – just to familiarise myself with the details, although I did remember it. Given the prominence of the Fielding family, it made the national as well as local news at the time and Charles Fielding had made sure it had stayed there ever since.

I looked through the windscreen, trying not to superimpose images of my own son, Alex, onto a scene that I knew haunted every waking moment of the Fieldings' lives – then taking a deep breath, I locked my car and walked across the street.

Chapter Two

Chapel Mills

Leo Fielding's name was still listed on the polished brass plate beside the door to Chapel Mills. I pressed the intercom for the penthouse apartment that his parents had held onto since their son's death.

'Yes?' A male voice, I assumed was Charles Fielding.

'Dr McCready.'

There was a 'buzz' and a metallic click as the chrome and glass doors unlocked.

The reception hall was impressive. A wide expanse of caramel-coloured oak floorboards, punctuated by ornate iron stanchions supporting the floor above. The space would have lifted the bleakest of moods had I not come here on such dark business.

But it was the smell that got me. Grabbing me by my olfactory senses and dragging me back to a childhood memory, of my mother's days as a burler and mender in a mill just like this one. The unmistakeable scent of lanolin from the wool. A pungent perfume that over two centuries had soaked into the woodwork – permeating both the fabric of these buildings and the clothes of the people who worked in them.

I took what had once been the goods lift, taking the time to gather my thoughts. The lumbering metal doors opened to reveal the entrance to the penthouse, which occupied the entire top floor of the two-storey building.

The eight-foot-high wooden door with a wrought-iron handle in its centre looked like something from Middle Earth. I pushed the bell – hearing its echoing chime coming from somewhere deep inside the place. The door swung open to reveal a tall, reed-thin man in his late sixties.

Charles Fielding took my hand in a firm grip that for some reason surprised me. 'Thank you for coming, doctor.'

He turned to the small, bird-like woman who was walking across the polished wooden floor towards us. 'This is my wife, Mary.'

Her hand felt cool when she took mine. Her grip delicate – like an imagined touch, half-felt. Her genuine smile conveyed a grim regret that we should be meeting under such circumstances.

I followed them to a pair of deep soft leather sofas, in front of huge windows that overlooked the city, where we sat opposite each other in an awkward silence. Although it wasn't a new experience for me, I was suddenly unsure of the best way to open a conversation about events that had undoubtedly destroyed both their lives.

'This is quite a place,' was the best I could come up with.

'Leo loved it here.' Mary's gaze followed mine. 'He took it because of the northern light – it was perfect for his studio, you see.'

The mill had a traditional slate-and-glass roof which faced north. A feature, I vaguely remembered reading somewhere, which was ideal for artists because it gave a consistent light throughout the day.

'Yes, I understand Leo was an artist,' I said.

Mary's eyes filled with pride. 'A very successful one.' She turned to her husband. 'We were so proud of him, weren't we, dear?'

Charles cleared his throat, obviously unused to voicing emotion, let alone displaying any. 'Yes, he did well for himself.' He waved a hand to indicate the space. 'Well enough to get this place. Didn't rent. Purchased it outright.'

His wife looked down at her fingers, which were twisting in her lap. *Her* pride obviously wasn't index linked. She stood up almost too abruptly. 'Can I get you some tea?'

'The doctor isn't on a social visit, Mary.' He sat forward, leaning over the files laid out neatly on the coffee table.

She shot an uncertain glance in my direction.

I smiled. 'Tea would be lovely, Mrs Fielding. Thank you.'

'Please call me Mary.'

'I'll give you a hand.'

Charles Fielding opened his mouth in protest, but closed it again as I followed his wife to the open-plan kitchen area.

'How long did Leo live here?'

'He bought it the year before he . . . before it . . .'

Her eyes were wet when she looked at me. 'I still can't go up there . . .' Her eyes flickered briefly towards the mezzanine floor. 'To where he . . .'

'I know. It's OK.' I looked into her eyes, forging a connection with her mental anguish. 'There's no manual for this. No rules to follow.'

Her eyes were almost imploring – reaching out to someone she hoped could give her answers. Take the pain away. I wanted to offer her something. But I knew that nothing I could say would end the waking nightmare she had lived since her son's cruel death.

'Just take it one day at a time.' I knew it was a cliché, but it was one way to get through crippling emotional pain. 'Breathe in and breathe out – one minute at a time – one hour at a time – until that day is done. Until one day you realise it isn't the first thing you think about when you wake up in the morning.'

She turned her face from me. Sniffing and wiping her eyes with the crumpled tissue.

'Well, I'm not there yet.'

The raw pain inside this petite, gentle woman was tangible.

How could any parent look at the brutalised, naked body of their child and not lose a part of their soul to the horror of it? It was incomprehensible. Yet it happened, and I walked all too often through the minds of the monsters who did these things and then somehow managed to justify it with their own brand of twisted logic.

She glanced over to where her husband was sitting, reading his notes. 'Are you married?'

'Widowed.'

'I'm sorry.'

I shook my head. 'It's OK. It was more than twenty years ago. He was in the SAS. Killed overseas.'

She touched my elbow, her eyes soft with emotion. 'So young. You can't have had much time together. I'm so sorry, my dear.'

Such a show of empathy from someone still trapped in the raw torment of her own pain was almost too much.

I always struggled to handle it when people were kind to me. I could take a punch easier than a compliment. Handle a fight better than I could a display of tenderness, which often left me struggling for a response. I knew it was a legacy of my upbring-ing. A tough Yorkshire-Irish father who valued endurance and

10

strength and an Italian mother who had impossibly high standards neither of us had ever managed to meet.

To the outside world my mother was the epitome of a doting Italian mamma. Behind closed doors, she employed the ceaseless dripping-water torture of negative evaluation and disapproval. A tactic that would have eroded my self-esteem, had it not been shored up by my father's unconditional love. We'd tackled my mother as a team. Coping with her since his death was proving more of a challenge.

My upbringing had forged an emotional armour that proved useful in my career but left me unable to cope when shown gentleness by others. Especially strangers – and always when it was unexpected.

Mary busied herself making the tea. 'You won't have had a chance for children then?'

'Actually, I have a son. Alex. He was just a baby when his father died.'

Her smile trembled as she wiped her eyes again. 'Does he live with you?'

'He went travelling after university. But he's in London now. Starting a new career.'

She poured boiling water into the teapot, risking a glance towards her husband. 'He wanted to sell this place after Leo died. I can't bring myself to let it go. It's all I have left of him. I come here – alone, mostly. To be near him, near the things he loved.'

I followed her gaze to a bunch of white roses in a vase on the counter.

'Were flowers something he loved?'

She went over and adjusted the stems until she was satisfied they were perfect.

'There were roses in the apartment when they found Leo. The police asked me if I knew where they'd come from.' She nodded to the window overlooking the private gardens below. 'He'd picked them from the garden out there. I've been replacing them for him ever since.'

I left Mary in the kitchen and went to join Fielding.

'It's been two years.' Fielding's tone was caustic as he launched straight into it. 'And still no progress because the investigators insisted on seeing this as some gay sex scene that my son was involved in.' His face flushed. 'My son was *not* a homosexual, doctor. The police are taking the path of least resistance and that shuts off any other lines of enquiry.' He strained his corded neck towards me like an aggressive cockerel. '*That's* why whoever killed my son is still out there.'

'I appreciate what you must be going through Mr Fielding—'

'Do you?' Fielding cut across me, his voice rising. 'You've had your son murdered too have you – and no one giving a damn about finding his killer?'

'I appreciate your *frustration*. Believe me your son's death has not been forgotten. The case is still open—'

'As a *cold* case file. The clue is in the name – *cold*. And it only *remains* open because I refuse to let it go.'

The tension was broken as Mary brought in the tea tray. 'The police officer who investigated Leo's death was very nice—'

'Nice!' Charles was contemptuous. 'Nice doesn't find my son's killer, Mary!'

My son.

I'd read up on Charles Fielding – high-ranking officer in Naval Intelligence, long retired but still well connected. Trotted out by journalists and news outlets whenever they needed a well-respected military strategist, now out of the game and free to comment.

I studied him. His whole demeanour screamed character traits forged by his background.

Dominance and control are your stock in trade, aren't they Fielding. Born of privilege and nurtured by arrogance and a sense of superiority.

Tinker, Tailor, Soldier, Prick.

'DCI Ferguson,' he was saying. 'They told me he was the best.' He tapped his notes. 'You know him . . . Ferguson.'

It was a statement of fact – not a question.

As if reading my mind, Fielding leaned closer – his eyes glinting. Confident in a knowledge he felt gave him power.

'They say you're in a relationship with him. Is that true?'

I was stunned at the directness of it – but didn't let it show. 'No,' I said honestly.

Ever since I'd been invited to consult on our first case together, almost two years before, Callum and I had danced around the edges of a relationship. The chemistry between us was undeniable. But we'd become distanced by events. By a killer we hunted down together – but at huge personal cost. Those events had changed me – changed both of us.

'Not that it's any of your business . . . or has any bearing on why I'm here.'

'Oh, but it has. Because this was *his* case and it was never solved.' He regarded me through narrowed eyes. 'If it turns out that he missed something . . . I need to know you can be impartial.'

I was at the end of my, already short, rope.

'Whether I can be impartial or not is irrelevant. I agreed to this meeting as a courtesy, but as courtesy seems in short supply, I'll make this simple for you. I'm not taking it on. I stopped consulting on this type of thing last year—'

'I know. I've asked around. Besides, after those murders last autumn, it was in all the papers. You were seriously injured' – he indicated my thigh with a nod of his head – 'and Ferguson got suspended. Nasty business. When you came out of hospital, the papers said you were going to take time out to concentrate on writing your books . . . making TV documentaries.' He tapped the notes on the table. 'Safer than doing it for real I suppose . . . if you've lost your nerve.'

As baiting tactics went, it was pretty blunt. It almost made me smile – almost.

I stood up. 'We're done here.'

'Please.' Mary lightly touched my arm. I'd almost forgotten she was there. 'Don't go . . .' She glanced at her husband. 'Charles didn't mean to offend you, did you, dear?'

He was still looking at me as he spoke. 'I don't need you to speak for me.'

I felt her gentle squeeze on my arm. 'We need you to help us . . . *I* need you to . . .'

'I'm not the only profiler around, Mary.' I put my hand over hers, returning the touch. 'I can give you the names of half a dozen competent ones who'd be happy to help—'

'Competent isn't good enough.' Fielding's voice drew my attention back to him. 'You're the best. That's why I chose you.'

14

'*Chose me!*' He made it sound like a done deal – I could feel my hackles rising already. 'And you'd know enough about my field of expertise to be the judge?'

'Not personally,' he conceded. 'But I've spoken to those who do.'

I'd calculated how much it hurt him to be humble. I wanted to hurt him some more.

'That's not enough to convince me.'

He took a long breath, indicating the seat opposite. Reluctantly, but for Mary's sake, I took it.

'In a previous life, I was an Intelligence officer . . .'

'I know . . . I've done *my* research too.'

'Then you'll know that I still have contacts in Government – in the police.' He rested his elbows on his knees, watching me over steepled fingers. 'I know what you did . . . what you've done before. I'm told you have a rare ability. To profile behaviours to the point you can predict an offender's thinking – what he's done . . . will do next. It's been described as "uncanny".' He indicated the files on the table. 'I *know* my son's death isn't as it first appears. For two years I've been trying to prove it – but they tell me that they need new evidence.' His eyes bored into mine. 'I *need* someone who sees beyond the physical evidence they already have . . . sees the things you do. What only *you* can.'

I considered him for a long moment – letting the silence stretch.

'And what if . . . after I've looked at it, I agree with DCI Ferguson's initial conclusion?'

He sat back, his breath leaving him in a long sigh. 'Then I'll accept your findings.'

Mary needed closure – some peace. Even if the result wasn't what she wanted to hear, it was better than the emotional purgatory her husband's relentless quest was putting her through.

She was pouring the tea into china cups, trying to restore normality to a horrifically abnormal situation.

'Leo had girlfriends,' she said, almost to herself. 'All through university. A parade of beautiful girls.' She handed a cup to her husband and then me. 'He wasn't homosexual. He would have told us if he was.'

I couldn't imagine Leo Fielding discussing his sex life with his parents, especially his father, who could barely say the word 'homosexual' without grinding his teeth. I took my cup. 'Did he have a regular girlfriend?'

'He was too busy moving in and then he had an exhibition to get ready for. Edward said he was painting all night sometimes, to get pieces finished before the opening in London.' Her eyes automatically went to the mezzanine, then flickered away again.

'Edward?'

'Morrison. The caretaker,' Fielding explained. 'He looks after the building.'

'The garden as well,' Mary said, sipping her tea. 'He showed me where the roses were. He lets me take them whenever I want.'

'The police suspected Morrison had something to do with it.' Fielding tapped the file with his finger. 'I still do. Not wholesome . . . people like him.'

'People like him?' I asked.

'Homosexual.' He almost spat the word. 'Leo wasn't involved in any of the deviant practices they say he was . . . he wouldn't have consented to . . . what was done. But Morrison – he *was* gay . . . probably *was* into all that. *And* he had access to the apartment. But your "friend" saw fit to let him go.' He glared at me. 'If anyone knows what really happened to Leo, it's Morrison.'

Mary gently cleared her throat, drawing our attention. 'Edward's always been very kind to me.' She somehow made it sound like an apology. 'Especially since Leo passed.'

'Well . . . he *would*, wouldn't he?' Fielding snorted his disgust at her naivety.

'He helped me organise the studio . . . to catalogue everything.' She looked at me over the rim of her cup – eyes shining with pride. 'Would you like to see Leo's paintings, my dear?'

'I'd love to.'

'She treats this place like a bloody shrine'. Fielding snorted. 'Won't change a damn thing – keeps everything just as it was the day Leo died. If she could bear to use the upstairs, I think she'd move in permanently and just bugger off and leave me to it!'

'Charles, please don't—'

'I'd love to see Leo's studio, Mary.'

'She can't open the shutters in there – they're too heavy,' Fielding said.

'I'm sure you can open them for us?' My smile was as thin as his patience.

Before he could object, Mary picked up the tray. 'Lovely. I'll join you when I've cleared away.'

Chapter Three

Chapel Mills

Fielding led me along a corridor, pushing open the wooden double doors to Leo's studio. We stepped into the dim interior and Fielding went ahead of me. There was a metallic sound as latches slid back.

A jagged shard of sunlight cut across the room as he heaved back the heavy wooden shutters that covered the floor-to-ceiling windows.

The space was full of canvasses propped in stacks several deep along the walls. The familiar scent of lanolin mingled with the oil paint and linseed. The studio had a warmth to it. It felt peaceful and I could see why Mary found it comforting to be there.

As if my thoughts conjured her up, Mary's heels clicked on the wooden floor as she came down the corridor to join us.

'Oh, it looks so much better in here when the shutters are open. I usually have to have all the lights on.'

I went to a stack of canvasses propped against the wall and started to tip them towards me. Many were scenes of the neo-classical architecture around Little Italy. Images that harked back to Fordley's industrial era. Cobbled streets populated by men in flat caps walking to work in the mills.

Mary came to stand beside me.

'He did portraits too.' She pulled back a dustsheet covering one of the easels.

It showed a beautiful woman standing beside a wall overlooking the ocean. I guessed the location to be the Mediterranean judging by the style of the buildings in the background.

'Commissioned by her husband the previous year,' Mary said in answer to my enquiring look. 'After Leo died, his wife didn't want it. They didn't want it to go into the catalogue to be sold– so they told us to destroy it. But I couldn't bring myself to do it.'

'It was that commission that bought this place.' Charles Fielding's abrupt tone carried no hint of pride.

Mary ignored his interruption. 'The paintings look so different in natural light, don't they?'

I studied a half-finished painting on the largest easel, by the window. There was a photograph pinned to the corner of the canvas. It had been taken down in the communal gardens, looking up at the studio.

'What do you know about this one, Mary?'

She came to stand beside me. 'It was different to anything he'd done before.' She lightly touched the photograph with a fingertip. 'It must have been experimental. A kind of self-portrait I suppose. He was working on it when he . . .' She swallowed hard, unable to vocalise the thought. 'Obviously he never got to finish it.'

The point of view was from someone looking up from the garden at night, into the lighted window of the studio. It showed the artist at his easel. 'That's Leo,' she said softly, 'he never painted himself. Maybe he was wondering what he looked like when he was working.'

I studied the painting – then glanced again at the canvasses against the wall. The more I looked at it, the more it jarred with every other piece. What I knew about art you could fit on a pinhead – but I knew this was at odds with the others.

As though Leo had inhabited a different mental space whilst working on it.

'Was this for the exhibition?'

'No.' She looked at the other half-finished canvasses. 'He should have been working on those. For some reason in the weeks before . . . well he seemed distracted.'

'He wasn't going to be ready in time.' Charles Fielding's tone was hard. 'Bloody idiot was messing about when he should have been completing the work for London.'

'Charles please—'

'It's a fact, Mary.' He waved his hand, dismissing his wife, in a way I suspected he did often. 'His agent was frantic. No good sugaring it up just because he's dead!'

Mary couldn't have flinched more if he'd slapped her in the face. For a second, I entertained the thought of slapping Fielding myself.

'His agent – Max Andrews – was the one who found the body,' he continued. 'He'd travelled up from London to meet Leo that Monday morning. When there was no answer, he got Edward to open the door. They found Leo upstairs.'

'Excuse me.' Mary's eyes were filling up again. She turned on her heel and walked out.

An embarrassing silence suddenly settled around us as Mary left. I turned my back on Fielding to look out of the window.

Down in the garden, a man I guessed to be in his mid-fifties was working in the flower beds, shovelling soil into a wheelbarrow.

'I think we've wasted enough time in here,' Fielding said abruptly. 'I'll show you the crime scene.'

* * *

We stood at the foot of the bed. Gone was the mattress which two years before had been heavily stained by Leo's blood and bodily fluids. His battered body had been discovered, face down, bound spread-eagled to the ornate iron bedframe.

'Do you have everything you need?'

'What . . .? Sorry. Miles away.'

Fielding's gaze followed mine, to the iron bedstead. He held out a manilla envelope. 'Crime scene photographs and post-mortem report.'

'How did you get these?'

'Some of it was made available for the inquest. The rest . . .' He shrugged. 'Contacts. Mary hasn't seen them . . . I'd rather she didn't.'

'Of course.'

'Because of things they discovered when they searched the apartment, because of the way he was found,' Fielding said tightly. 'The police worked on the theory that Leo probably picked someone up and brought them back to the apartment that night, to . . . indulge in this disgusting fetish. But whoever it was . . . took advantage. Once they had Leo tied up and helpless, they killed him.'

I studied his profile. He didn't turn his head. Couldn't look at me as he said the words he found so distasteful . . . so humiliating. 'The physical evidence seemed to back up the theory. Nothing has changed – nothing that means I can push for a fresh investigation.' He turned to look at me then – his eyes penetrating. 'But I *know* that's not what happened, doctor. I *know* Leo wouldn't just bring a stranger back here to . . . do these things. So, I need someone who can look at this in a different way.'

I took the envelope but didn't open it.

He hesitated as if he expected me to say more. When I didn't, he simply nodded. 'I'll leave you to it then.'

I waited, listening to his footsteps clanking down the spiral metal staircase.

The air seemed suddenly still as I stood there. The apartment below was silent and I realised I'd been holding my breath. I exhaled slowly.

The package seemed to weigh more than papers should, seemed to be getting heavier the more I stared at it.

The envelope fluttered with the slight trembling of my hand. Suddenly, unaccountably angry, I threw it onto the bed, the breath leaving me in a gust of annoyance and frustration.

Christ's sake, Jo – pull yourself together! This isn't your first crime scene. What the hell is wrong with you? Even as my inner voice posed the question – I knew the answer. I could feel it trickling in rivulets of sweat down my back.

Charles Fielding's goading remarks echoed in my head . . . *'Safer than doing it for real . . . if you've lost your nerve.'*

Bastard!

Last year's events had robbed me of so much – but I was damned if they were going to take from me the thing I did best. The sooner I did this, the sooner I could tell Fielding there was nothing I could add to the earlier investigation. Get rid of him and go back to my life.

I snatched up the envelope and tore it open, pulling out the glossy eight-by-ten photographs.

Taking a long breath, I turned them over.

They were brutal images. Coldly shocking to the senses – like being whipped across the face with barbed wire.

23

At thirty years old, Leo had a slim and athletic physique. Every muscle beneath his alabaster smooth skin clearly defined, like a Michelangelo carved in marble. His muscular arms had been stretched out – bound at the wrist by heavy leather cuffs which were buckled to the bedframe. His legs stretched wide and were shackled to the foot of the bed.

His once smooth back was marred by deep, bloody wounds that laid the skin open like gaping red jaws. His buttocks and thighs heavily smeared with his own blood, which looked like black molasses – pooling beneath his body to saturate the mattress.

I shifted uncomfortably as I tried to concentrate and began reading Callum Ferguson's own notes from the bundle presented to the inquest.

Leo Fielding – thirty years old. Found at 10.30 a.m. Monday eighth of May 2017. Pathologist estimates time of death somewhere between midnight and 4 a.m. Sunday morning. He'd been bound face down on the bed and repeatedly flogged with a heavy metal-tipped riding crop which was found at the scene – wounds in some places almost down to the bone. Some of the wounds were continually reopened in a prolonged and sustained assault. Pathologist thinks the attack might have begun as early as Friday night. A solid object, most likely the silver handle of the riding crop, had penetrated his anus multiple times, causing traumatic rectal haematoma. Further examination at post-mortem revealed pelvic damage and haemorrhage which could have resulted in death if left untreated.

The post-mortem had found chemical burns on the skin around his nose and mouth. There was a bottle of liquid amyl nitrate found beside the bed. A substance inhaled to heighten sensation during sex, which caused burns if it came into contact with the skin. The cause of death was listed as asphyxiation. Leo had been gagged with a leather ball-gag and choked on his own vomit.

There were also photographs of pornographic magazines, bondage paraphernalia and S&M clothing which had been found hidden in Leo's wardrobe. The magazines depicted homosexual sado-masochism, not unlike the crime scene – but without the same level of horrific injuries and gore.

I held up a photo superimposing the image over the room as it was now. Thankful that every trace had been scrubbed away by the crime scene cleaners. Sterile. Odourless. Unlike the harrowing scene that would have greeted the first people to find his body.

They would have smelled the metallic scent of Leo's blood. Maybe the faint residue of human sweat suspended in the warm air of the loft. I wondered fleetingly if they'd ever been given help to get over the trauma.

Looking back at the now empty bed, I tried to visualise the sequence of events that had ended Leo's life.

There were more images of the rest of the apartment.

In the kitchen, scenes of crime officers, or SOCOs, had photographed everything, even the contents of the bin. There had been an empty wine bottle and two glasses on the kitchen counter. All had Leo's fingerprints on them, but no one else's, and they tested negative for drugs.

There were shots of the items around the bed. The bedside table, with his watch and cufflinks neatly placed. His clothes and other belongings.

They'd photographed the door to the apartment, I assumed to determine whether there were signs of forced entry. There weren't. But my attention was drawn to the detail of the handle and locks. There was a silver Yale lock and a chain next to the black wrought-iron bolt that matched the door handle. On closer inspection, the holes that had been drilled to fit the chain and lock hadn't been varnished like the rest of the door.

I fanned the photographs out, like playing cards, and scanned them again. I stopped at one in particular, staring at it.

Shit.

My heels clattered down the metal stairs, alerting Fielding, who stood up from his seat in the lounge – frowning as he watched me heading for the door.

'Where are you going . . . Doctor—?'

His voice followed me across the hall to the emergency stairs beside the lift. I sensed, rather than saw him standing in the doorway to the apartment as I ran down the stairs, then crossed the hall to find the back stairs down to the garden.

Chapter Four

Garden, Chapel Mills

The man I'd seen from upstairs straightened up when he saw me. He leaned on the spade, wiping his hands on soil-stained jeans.

'Edward?'

His eyes narrowed for just a fraction of a second before he masked it. A micro-expression of suspicion. 'You've been to see the Fieldings . . . police?'

I raised my eyebrows slightly, as I smiled. The universally recognised sign of openness and honesty.

'Yes. I'm a doctor, though – not police.' I purposely didn't say what kind of doctor. If I left it, people often made their own assumptions and rarely asked more.

His gaze did a quick sweep. A swift reappraisal of who I might be and what I might want.

'Mary told me I'd find you here.' I was careful to say Mary – not 'Mrs Fielding'. Implying I'd known her for more than just a few hours.

He leaned more heavily on the spade, relaxing just a little. 'Nice lady, Mary.' He looked suddenly concerned. 'She's not ill or anything, is she?'

'Not physically, no.'

He nodded, silently understanding.

I looked past him to the flowers that bordered the garden. 'She said you let her take roses for Leo's flat.'

He shrugged. 'Why wouldn't I? Least I can do. If it gives the poor woman some comfort.'

'Did Leo come down often to get flowers?'

'I never saw him. But then I'm not in the garden all the time. Got lots of other jobs to do around the place.'

'I'm sure you're kept busy. The penthouse is amazing.'

He lowered his eyes and spoke to the ground. 'Suppose so. They should sell the place if you ask me. Move on.'

'Mary said you were the one who found him.'

'Hell of a thing that day.' His voice was hoarse. He cleared his throat, staring at his boots.

'Charles said you'd fitted the new lock for Leo?'

I was taking a chance. Guessing that the lock and chain had been done just before Leo's death because they'd never varnished the door afterwards. It was a fair assumption that Edward had done the work. But I didn't ask him outright. I needed to seem less like the police he was so obviously suspicious of.

He nodded. 'Couple of weeks before he died. Said he wanted extra security. I told the police that at the time.'

'Seems like a pretty secure building to me.' I kept my tone light, sensing that his defences had come down just enough for me to slip past them. 'Did he say why he needed the extra locks?'

Edward shook his head, pursing his lips. 'I thought maybe because he had so many paintings in there for the exhibition, he was getting more security conscious – like the shutters.'

I nodded, as if I already knew. 'Did you do those as well?'

He went back to his digging. 'I told him they wouldn't be cheap – size of those windows.' He hefted a spade full of soil into the wheelbarrow. 'But then money never was an issue for Leo, was it?'

'No. I suppose not.' I moved around, so I could see his face. 'So, the locks and the shutters were all done about the same time then? A lot of work for you – with everything else you have to do.'

'He was in a hurry. Poor bugger died just a few weeks later. Last jobs I did for him.' He glanced back up to the penthouse as he spoke. 'I'd see him painting up there, but eventually the shutters were closed day and night. Something changed – like his heart had gone out of it.' He shook his head again. 'Shame what happened to him.'

'Did you ever meet his boyfriend?'

Edward shot me a curious look. 'Leo didn't have a boyfriend.'

'The police thought so – you know, because of the way he was found?'

A reaction flickered behind his eyes, like an emotional flinch, and then it was gone.

'If Leo was gay, I'd have known.' He looked at me squarely. 'Leo knew I was gay. No reason to hide it from me.' He straightened up. 'Police knew it too – took DNA samples, after I found Leo.' Anger and pain jostled for position in his expression. 'I knew why they had to do it. I found him . . . they had to eliminate me as a suspect and I wanted to help . . . but still, bloody degrading.'

'I'm sorry,' I said and I meant it. The impact of a suspicious death touched everyone surrounding it.

He lifted the spade over his shoulder. 'Fordley's gay scene is a small one – the S&M scene is smaller still. I'd have known if Leo had been part of it. Police had me square in their sights because of my sexuality and because I lived in the building.' The muscles that worked in his jaw spoke volumes. 'His father treats me like a piece of shit. Still thinks I had something to do with it.'

'That must be tough.'

He shrugged. 'If Fielding lived here, I'd move on. Wouldn't be able to stand the way he looks at me. Thankfully, he doesn't come here much . . . and I like Mary. Like helping her to look after Leo's place.'

'Did you see Leo around town much?'

'No. We didn't exactly socialise in the same places. Saw him with a girl sometimes though. Think she was more of a friend – not his type. Bit rough, if you know what I mean?'

I tried not to sound too interested. 'Do you know who she was?'

He shook his head. 'Domino might know. She works at the café across the street – The Munch Bunch. Leo had breakfast in there most mornings.'

'Did you mention the girl to the police?'

'Told them what I just told you.' A chill crept into his tone. He really didn't like the police and I got the feeling he wouldn't volunteer anything he didn't have to.

I let him return to his digging and walked over to the roses lined up like colourful sentries in front of the shrubbery, their soft fragrance drifting on the warm air. I turned and looked up to Leo's studio – walking along the boundary until I reached the spot where the photo was taken.

Edward joined me. His gaze followed mine and I studied his profile. I knew he was replaying the scene when he'd found Leo's body. An image he would see for the rest of his life.

In the past, I wouldn't have been able to resist going there. Offering my hand to lift him out of his mental pain. Looking to offer respite from emotional trauma. But these days I wasn't as easily drawn to healing others. Maybe because I knew I wasn't in a position to help myself – never mind anyone else.

'He used a photo taken from here to do a self-portrait. Have you seen it?'

He shook his head. 'He came down one evening while I was working. Walked around the border, kept looking up at his window, then took the picture. He must've been here a lot – looking for this exact spot.'

'Why do you think that?'

'Because the flower bed had been flattened for a couple of weeks. I had to keep turning the soil. The rose bushes had been picked over as well. That's how I knew he'd been taking them. I told Mary. Suppose that's why she likes to have them in his apartment now. For comfort like.'

* * *

The oak bench felt warm as I sat in the sunlit reception hall, looking at the rough stone of the walls. As if by staring hard enough I could get them to speak to me and reveal all their secrets.

I was bracing myself to go back to Leo's apartment. To look again at those images – to see what I couldn't now 'unsee' no matter how much I didn't want it to be true.

31

Looking at those photos, I could see a killer as clearly as if they were still in the room. The presence of a monster. Ghostly. Ephemeral, like the kiss of cold air on the back of my neck. A fleeting shadow, shimmering on the edges of my vision but unmistakeable. I knew it would haunt me until I hunted it down, exorcised it. And to do that, I needed to 'walk the scene'.

For me that meant moving through the crime scene as the killer had. Seeing the same things he saw. Hearing the same sounds – breathing the same air. Getting into the mindset of a monster until I could profile his thinking and understand the drives that had built up inside him, before climaxing in the final scene of devastation that snuffed out a human being and crashed a wrecking ball through the lives of those loved ones left behind.

The police needed to look into the face of the offender. I needed to look into their mind.

Chapter Five

Leo's bedroom, Chapel Mills

I spread the photographs out on the bed, in a gruesome collage and leaned back against the railing while I read the notes.

I looked at pictures of the items around the bed. The riding crop. The amyl nitrate bottle. Leo's clothes folded in a neat pile with his shoes side by side beneath the chair.

I thought about the killer – standing where I stood now. Looking at Leo's body, stretched out and helpless. Gaping wounds, bleeding as he looked on.

You took pleasure in inflicting those wounds, didn't you?

My heart rate increased as his would have done, in the excitement and thrill of having a victim to dominate and control.

The torture that had ended Leo's life had gone on for days. This person was sadistic to a degree that was almost incomprehensible to most people.

I slowed my breathing and listened – straining to hear every sound the killer had heard as he stood where I was now.

You listened to Leo's muffled cries of pain – smelt the brassy tang of his blood and bodily fluids leaking onto the bed – watched the futile struggles of your victim and took pleasure in all of it.

I walked to the side of the bed and looked down, transporting myself into the mind of a sexually sadistic killer. Looking, not at an empty space but onto the image of Leo that I superimposed there. I could see it all – feel it all – just as the killer had done.

What did you say to him? Did you torment him with promises of eventual freedom? Even as the thought entered my mind, I knew the answer.

No – you told him he was going to die, didn't you? You kept reminding him of how helpless he was – that no one could hear him . . . no one was coming to help him. Maybe you even described what you were going to do to him in the coming hours . . . days.

A feeling suddenly swept through me – at first exhilaration. Then something I didn't expect – anger. It almost took me by surprise. Then I realised in that instant what this was. I was feeling what he felt. Rage towards his victim.

Pure, cold rage.

I gathered the pictures and the file together and went downstairs. My legs trembling from the adrenalin that had begun to course through my veins just as it must have done for the killer whose mind I was mapping.

I walked over and sat in the kitchen, looking again at the crime scene photographs. The wine bottle and glasses had been placed on the counter as if two people had faced each other, having a cosy chat over a drink. I looked up and had a clear view of the mezzanine – from my vantage point I could just make out the foot of the bed, as the killer had done two years before.

The sound of footsteps distracted me as Fielding came back, walking ramrod straight with his hands clasped behind his back – his whole demeanour as tense and buttoned up as his emotions.

'OK. I'm done,' I said.

'What do you think . . . now that you've seen everything here?'

34

I regarded him for a long moment – wanting to end it right then. But I couldn't.

'I'll put all of my findings into a report. Should have that with you in the next few days.'

'So, you're taking the case?' He rocked slightly on his heels – hands clasped behind his back.

'I'll be in touch.'

Chapter Six

Kingsberry Farm – Tuesday morning

The air was already warm when I went outside. I'd pulled on my Wellington boots and the old Barbour jacket that lived in my porch, before opening the studded oak door to allow Harvey, my boxer dog, to shoot out in a pent-up tangle of muscle and energy.

Standing in the shadow of an overhanging laburnum tree, I watched him run down the gravel drive and through the opening in the hedge. There were six acres of land that went with the house, adjoining the neighbouring farm that had belonged to my old friend George Theakston. But his place was empty since he'd died the previous year.

We were six miles from Fordley and four miles outside Kingsberry village nestled on top of the Yorkshire moors. I'd moved to the farm when I was appointed Head of Forensic Psychology at Fordley's psychiatric hospital – thankful in those days for the peace and isolation it offered.

Close enough for the forty-minute commute in the mornings and far enough away to feel like a tranquil refuge when I got back from the horrors of dealing with the tormented minds and damaged spirits that made up my working day. It all seemed a long time ago and far away from life in the private practice I'd built for myself over the years since then.

But now with Alex in London, I was alone and if it wasn't for Jen working from my office at the farm, I could go days without seeing anyone up here on the moors.

Harvey galloped back to me, skittish and playful, and I threw a ball for him. My boots crunched down the gravel driveway until I cut through the hedge to follow Harvey on our usual route into the woods.

* * *

Jen's car was parked in front of the farmhouse when we got back. I could hear her in the kitchen as I hung up my coat.

Harvey shot through the door and wrapped himself round her legs as she tried to reach the kettle whistling on the Aga.

'Daft dog – get from under . . .'

'Morning, Jen.'

She lifted the kettle and poured boiling water into the teapot as I sat at the long pine table in the centre of the room. Harvey came to me for a fuss, seeing as he was getting nowhere with Jen. I patted his silky ears as she busied herself making tea – the most important task of the day in my house. She put our mugs down and took a seat opposite.

'You look tired,' she said.

I knew she was worried about my nightmares – not a subject I really wanted to discuss. So instead, I took a sip of tea and watched the dust motes suspended in the sunlight.

She allowed me the silence, her grey eyes studying me for a while, before slipping her hand over mine with a gentle squeeze.

'Would talking about it help?'

I shook my head.

'It'll get easier, love. You know better than anyone how this process works.'

'Some psychologist I am, Jen,' I said quietly, my breath sending a plume of steam from the tea to join the dust motes. 'Getting screwed up by the job.'

'You deal with some seriously twisted people ... It takes its toll.'

I bit my bottom lip, not wanting to tell her the extent of it.

She absently patted Harvey. 'Time heals, Jo. You know that.'

'Yeah, of course it does. And God doesn't send us more than we can handle – and what doesn't kill us makes us stronger. Jesus! If I hear those clichéd platitudes from one more person, I swear to God ...'

She watched me over the rim of her mug – completely unfazed. This woman who knew me better than my own mother. 'Good job I haven't said any of those things then,' she said evenly. 'You finished? Or do you want another rant before we go down to the office?'

For a second, I just looked at her. Then couldn't help laughing. 'Oh God –sorry, Jen.'

She smiled at me, before pushing her chair back and gathering up the cups. 'It's OK. You're allowed to be a pain in the arse once a day. But that's your quota.'

'Did you call Callum?'

'Yes – he's coming at eleven.'

'What did you tell him?'

39

'Nothing. Just said you wanted to see him.' She turned to me, wiping her hands on a tea towel. 'He's not going to like it.'

'Understatement of the year, Jen.'

* * *

Callum stretched his long legs beneath my desk and nursed his coffee cup as he stared at the view across my fields. I caught the clean scent of his cologne and for some reason that caused a physical pain somewhere deep inside. Sitting here just inches away from someone I'd once been so close to made me feel more alone than ever.

I distracted myself from what was to come. 'Have you heard from the CPS?'

He ran strong fingers through his grey hair, which had earned him the 'Silver Fox' tag I knew he hated. It was an unusual feature for a man in his forties, but one that made his good looks even more striking.

'The IOPC passed their files on to them months ago. Still waiting for a decision.'

I knew the wheels of justice ground slowly in the Independent Office of Police Conduct and the Crown Prosecution Service. Especially if they were looking into an incident involving a police officer of Callum's rank – where public scrutiny would be unforgiving.

'I'm sorry,' I said, and I meant it.

The previous year he'd been suspended from operational duties after shooting a man. For an officer who wasn't licensed to carry a firearm it was about as serious as an incident could get.

Running projects instead of doing what he loved, which was working live enquiries, probably felt like exile to him.

'Don't be. I've gone over it a million times in my head and if the same thing happened tomorrow, I'd do it again in a heartbeat.' He shrugged. 'Anyway, the powers that be are fairly confident the IOPC will return a verdict of "no case to answer".' He was trying hard to sound convincing. Whether for my benefit or his own, I wasn't quite sure, but for his sake, I hoped he was right.

'Jen's worried about you,' he was saying in his soft Scottish accent.

I nodded – suddenly intensely focused on my notes.

'Would it help to talk about it?'

I finally looked up to be met by that steady gaze from startling blue eyes that made me feel he could see my innermost thoughts. 'Same question Jen asked.'

'And how did you answer her?'

'I didn't.' I looked down again. 'Shall we get on?'

'Jo.' He sounded exasperated as he raked his fingers through his hair. 'You really should talk about how you're feeling.' He reached across for my hand but I avoided his intended touch.

'My mother keeps telling me I should get a "proper job", with regular hours that don't involve dealing with serial killers.'

He was carefully gauging my reaction to a subject he knew strayed into dangerous waters. He tried a half-smile to soften the words. 'You had a legendary Irish temper at the best of times, but lately you've been on a hair-trigger. The slightest thing sets you off – Jen says you're not sleeping either.'

I studied him for a moment. Debating whether to say what I was *really* thinking, or play it safe? I decided to play it safe.

'I *will* talk to someone, OK?' I took a breath, trying to regain some equilibrium. 'It's just ... difficult to find the right person, given what I do for a living.' I could feel a pulse throbbing behind my eyes as I massaged my temples. 'Sometimes this job makes me feel like I want to take my brain out and scrub it under the tap. Not to mention the physical scars I've collected – a constant bloody reminder every time I take a bath.'

'I want to help.' His tone was tender – causing unbidden tears to threaten my undoing. I blinked them back. If he noticed he didn't let it show. 'We used to have something ...' I couldn't risk seeing the gentleness in his eyes, so I kept my head down – staring blindly at the words blurring on the page. 'But these days ...?'

I knew he was struggling with this as much as I was, but I couldn't help feeling an unwelcome coldness closing me off to him.

'You stick to being a copper and I'll be the therapist, OK?' My eyes flashed a warning that didn't need backing vocals.

He held his hands up. 'OK, just promise me you'll see someone.'

'I will. Now, do you want to know why I asked you here, or have you got all day to waste?'

He nodded.

'I've been reviewing the Leo Fielding case.'

He took a mouthful of coffee. 'Why?'

'Charles Fielding's been calling for weeks, wanting me to look into it. Jen persuaded me to meet with him yesterday if for no other reason than to get rid of him.'

'Good luck with that one. Fielding's been a complete pain in the arse for the last two years, to anyone who'll listen. It was one of my old cases.'

'I know – that's why I wanted to see you.'

'Same question: why?'

There was no way to soften this up. So, I didn't.

'Because you got it wrong.'

Chapter Seven

Callum paused with the cup halfway to his lips. 'Wrong?'

I nodded, saying nothing – just gauging his reaction.

'Christ, Jo. Why go poking around into one of my old cases? I need this like a hole in the head.' He put his mug down. 'Or do you think this is actually going to *help* with the IOPC?'

'They're unconnected, Cal. This won't have any bearing on their decision.'

'You know that for a fact?' He let his breath out in exasperation. 'Have you got any idea what it's like for an SIO to have an unsolved murder on their record, Jo?'

'No but—'

'Bloody embarrassing, that's what! Not to mention career limiting—'

'Doesn't seem to have held you back—'

'We'll never know, will we? Maybe I could have been a superintendent if I hadn't had that black mark on my copybook.' He raked his fingers through his hair – blowing out an exasperated breath. 'I didn't give up on it lightly, Jo . . . believe me. But I was working two other murders, a rape and a serious assault at the time. It's not like TV cop shows where the detective handles one job at a time, you know—'

'I know that, but—'

'We were overworked, short-staffed and under-resourced.' He leaned forward, resting his elbows on his knees as he glowered at me. 'But I *still* put everything into it. Every resource we had. But we came up empty. Sometimes – despite our best efforts – crimes go unsolved. When forensics drew a blank, too, there was massive pressure from above to box it off and move on. There's a limit to how long we can keep going, when we're getting nowhere. I couldn't justify the resources, and funding was short. That's not what the public wants to hear, and it's not how it should be, but that's the reality of it. The case is *still* open, it hasn't been buried or forgotten, despite what Charles Fielding thinks. And if new evidence comes to light that gives us a suspect, believe me, I'll be the first to go banging on the door of the CPS. But don't think it doesn't bother me to this day – because it does. Morally and professionally.'

He paused – out of steam – snatching up his cup to take a gulp of caffeine. 'What possessed you to get involved? And don't tell me Fielding bullied you into it, because that's impossible to do. I should know.'

'Mary Fielding, if I'm honest. Anyway, the point is I *am* involved. Question is, what do we do now?'

'Leave it alone – that's what.'

'You can't, Cal. Not now you know—'

'What I know is, all the evidence pointed to the fact that Leo had an interest in sado-masochistic sex. The search of his apartment found gay porn and bondage gear hidden away in the wardrobe. There were no other fingerprints on the porn magazines but his. Then there's the way he was found. The pathologist concluded he'd consented to being tied to the bed, then whoever he'd taken back to the flat, killed him.'

'I agreed with all of that . . . at first . . .'

'But now you don't?'

'No.'

'Why?'

I slapped a photograph onto the desk. 'This,' I said simply.

'The kitchen bin?'

Scenes of crime officers had photographed the contents of the bin. Apart from the usual waste, there was a bunch of white roses tied with ribbon – the petals days old, dried like crumpled tissue paper.

'The roses.'

'What about them?'

'Notice anything?'

'Apart from the fact they're dead?' I waited. 'And tied with ribbon . . .?'

'Exactly! Who picks flowers for themselves and then ties them with ribbon?'

'Your point?'

'Both Edward and Mary assumed Leo picked them for himself. He didn't. I think they were a gift – a gift he didn't want. So, he tossed them straight in the bin.'

'And that's enough for you to decide we got this all wrong?'

'Yes.'

He rolled his eyes. 'OK, if my whole team screwed this up, then what do *you* think happened to Leo Fielding?'

'That he was killed by his stalker.'

He stared at me for a long moment. 'Stalker?'

'Any mention of that in the original investigation?'

'No.' He took another mouthful of coffee. 'What makes you think he had a stalker?'

'Not one fact on its own. But putting everything together – including the flowers – points me in that direction.'

'Such as?'

'Leo bought the penthouse because it had a northern light roof.'

'So?'

'So, doesn't it strike you as odd that an artist who needs natural light for his work, gets the windows covered by shutters?'

'Leo had close to a million pounds' worth of paintings in his studio on the run-up to that exhibition. His insurance company had insisted on extra security. We checked with them at the time. Their letters and insurance renewals came in the month before he had the work done.'

'I went to speak to Edward Morrison. He fitted the shutters . . .'

Callum raised his eyebrows. 'Cold case or not, Jo, you can't go off half-cocked, speaking to suspects. If you'd told me, I'd have gone with you.'

'That's why I didn't tell you.' I registered the disapproval on his face. 'He resents the fact that he was treated like a suspect at the time . . .'

'That's because he was.' Callum shrugged. 'He lives at Chapel Mills. He had access to Leo's apartment and there was no sign of forced entry – so whoever was with Leo that night was probably invited in or had a key. Morrison had means and opportunity. He found the body. Was openly active on the gay scene, and given the circumstances of Leo's death, he was a person of interest. He didn't like the way he was questioned – but we wouldn't have been doing our job if we hadn't taken him in. He was swabbed for DNA samples and fingerprinted – if for no other reason than to eliminate him from the scene – after all, he'd been in the apartment regularly.'

'He felt he'd been treated unfairly because of his sexual orientation.'

'Tough. Given the circumstances, we couldn't overlook that fact.'

'If you'd been there, he wouldn't have opened up to me.'

'And did he? Open up to you?'

'A little, but he's guarded. Obviously doesn't like the police.'

'Suspects rarely do – it won't keep me awake at night. Besides, Morrison didn't exactly do himself any favours. He answered questions at the scene, but once we brought him in, he went "no comment" on us.'

'Told me he wanted to help . . . but didn't like the way he was dealt with.'

'Well, he was hardly tripping over himself to be the concerned and helpful citizen. He behaved like he had something to hide – how did he expect to be treated? I wanted to arrest him, but it was obvious we didn't have enough to meet the charging threshold – CPS would never have gone for it.'

Recalling all of this was just winding him up. I needed to change tack.

'So, to understand why Leo's behaviour makes me think he had a stalker – you need to put all the elements together. They can all be explained adequately on their own, but together they create a different picture.'

'Go on.'

'Before he died, Leo had new locks fitted – and shutters put on the windows.'

'Explained by the need to protect the paintings.'

'If it was security, Leo would only use the shutters at night. But just before his death, Edward told me they were closed all the time. He couldn't paint under those conditions.'

'OK,' Callum agreed tentatively. 'Still don't see how this adds up to a stalker?'

'He was concentrating on an odd self-portrait, instead of the exhibition pieces.'

I got up from my desk and went to the window.

'I don't know much about art, Cal, but that self-portrait was so different from his other work.' I turned to see him watching me, with that guarded look he had that wouldn't give me a clue to his thoughts. 'Why would someone as dedicated as Leo jeopardise his exhibition by wasting time on an experimental work?'

We both looked round as the office door opened and Jen came. 'Post,' she said, putting the pile on my desk.

She hesitated a fraction of a second, but long enough for me to catch the look she shot Callum before walking out. I followed his gaze, seeing at the same time he did, the single sheet of paper on top. I reached over and turned the pile face down.

I looked back at him. 'Where were we?'

'Stalker?' he said, not missing a beat. 'That's a bit of a leap, Jo.'

'Edward saw Leo in the garden ... taking the photo of his own window – he used that picture as the basis for his portrait.'

'So?'

'I think he'd seen someone out there, watching him when he worked at night. He was painting what *they* were seeing.'

'Why?'

'John Douglas was an instructor at the FBI Behavioural Sciences Unit in Quantico, back in the eighties. His work formed the foundation of criminal profiling. He used to say, "If you want to understand the artist, look at the painting." The criminal as the "artist" and the crime as his artwork – but in this case it fits with what I saw in Leo's studio, literally. A cathartic way of getting his fear out onto canvas? That painting is evidence of his state of mind just before he was killed. I believe he was terrified, and the only way he could express it was to paint it.'

He'd worked with me long enough to play along – up to a point. 'Go on.'

'Edward said the flower beds had been trampled for weeks. He assumed it was Leo . . .'

'Before he went "no comment", that's what he told the officers who interviewed him at Chapel Mills. By the time Leo's body was discovered, Morrison had repaired the damage. Which was another thing that made him a possible suspect.'

'I think it was a stalker who flattened the flower beds, watching Leo at night.'

'How can you be sure?'

'Because of the roses,' I said simply. 'Leo thought he was being watched. Had seen someone standing in the flower beds at night. Imagine then, he gets flowers from those rose beds delivered to his door – tied with ribbon like a gift. Leaving anonymous gifts is recognised as typical "stalking behaviour". Stalkers use seemingly benign gestures – especially those that a lay person would see as "loving" or "romantic" to intimidate victims.'

He pursed his lips. 'CCTV from Chapel Mills didn't show any deliveries being made. No images of Leo carrying flowers in either. So how *did* they get into the building?'

'I don't have *all* the answers. Finding the loopholes is your territory – mine is getting inside the head of the offender . . . And in this case, the victim.'

Callum tipped his head back – staring at the ceiling in thought. 'So, let's assume you're right. Leo's being watched by someone – he sees them in the garden at night. They pick the flowers – maybe leaving them outside his door – to send a message that they can get to him if they want to.'

'That would heighten his fear.'

'He's scared enough to have new locks and shutters fitted. So far so good . . .' He looked back at me. 'Why wouldn't he tell anyone? He never mentioned being followed or watched and he never reported this stalker to the police.'

'Look, there's a lot I'm not sure of in this case, Cal,' I conceded, sure now that my instincts were right. 'But one thing I *am* certain of is that Leo was terrified of something or someone on the run-up to his death. Maybe he *knew* the reason he was being watched . . . and had something to hide, which is why he didn't report it.'

'Such as?'

I chewed my pencil – a habit I had when I was thinking and one that drove Jen nuts. 'Don't know, but when we find that, it'll give us the motive.'

'There was no sign of forced entry to the apartment, so if we assume Leo let his killer in – why would he do that if he was in fear for his life?'

'You've checked CCTV from that night to see who entered and left the apartments?'

Callum nodded. 'Come down to the station and I'll show you the footage – probably worth going over it again in light of your stalker theory. But it shows Leo leaving around 8 on Friday night. We know he went to a local bar – "Calico's" –around the corner. He sat alone. Didn't speak to anyone but the bar staff. We've got footage of him returning at 11 p.m., obviously after one too many. He's being helped by a youth wearing jeans and a hoodie. No shots of the face. They help him into the Mills, but then reappear leaving by the main door a few minutes later and walk off into Little Italy.'

'Were they ever traced?'

'We flooded Little Italy with boots on the ground. Officers at the time circulated the image. There were reports of a rough sleeper in the area who fit the description, but we never found them. Besides, whoever it was, wasn't with Leo long enough to leave him in the state he was found in.

I tapped the pencil against my teeth as I went through the sequence of events I'd constructed at the scene.

I pulled out the crime scene photos. 'The bedroom looks like a BDSM scene.'

'Which is what we thought then. So what do *you* think?'

'Well, it wasn't suicide, Sherlock!'

He pulled a face which I ignored. 'There are different practices within bondage, discipline and sado-masochism and it depends on the relationship between Leo and his "partner" as to the dynamic at play before his death. Assuming it started off as something he consented to.'

I glanced up – Callum was looking at me like he wished he'd never asked.

'Who knew kinky sex was so complicated? I thought it was just jumping off the wardrobe, or having your bits whipped with a banana!'

53

'You worry me, Cal – you really do.'

'So, let's assume that we got the first part right, despite what Fielding thinks. Leo *was* into BDSM and met someone that night. He takes them back to his apartment. But he'd picked up a monster, and they killed him. Talk me through it.'

'BDSM is an erotic power exchange where the submissive gives mental or physical control to the dominant partner. What takes place, depends on what the participants are into. The fundamental principal is that it's carried out with the informed consent of all parties.'

He raised his eyebrows. 'How do you even *know* this stuff? Do they run classes on this in profiler school?'

'Something like that.'

'God, I wish I'd gone to your school . . .'

'Assuming it's consensual, it's important that the submissive can withdraw consent at any time if things get out of hand. When it results in death, it's usually because drink or drugs are involved and either the submissive doesn't realise they're in trouble until it's too late, or the dominant misses the signal that their sub is in trouble. Death can then occur through accidental injury or asphyxiation.'

'We found an empty bottle of amyl nitrate at the scene. It had Leo's fingerprints on it – no one else's.' He stretched knotted shoulders. 'That's used to heighten sexual pleasure, so I'm told. Doesn't that add to the possibility that Leo invited his killer back . . . that he was just expecting the usual fun and games?'

'Usually the stopper is taken off the bottle and it's placed near the bed so that both parties inhale the vapours.' I fished out the post-mortem photograph of the burn marks around Leo's nose and mouth. 'The nitrate was put onto a cloth and he was forced to inhale it – he wasn't taking it voluntarily.'

'If the killer wanted to torture him, why would they make him take it at all?'

'That's one of the things that bothers me,' I confessed. 'I think this whole scene was created to look like Leo consented.' I looked at the grim portfolio of a horrific death. 'Amyl nitrate, or "poppers", increases skin sensitivity. The attacker *could* have used it to increase Leo's pain while he was being tortured.'

'Lovely.' Callum grimaced.

'Directly inhaling it causes increased heart rate, dizziness and vomiting . . .'

'Which was the cause of death in this case.' Callum flicked through the photos. 'Rolex watch, gold cufflinks and cash all left in the flat.' He smiled as he looked at a photograph from the bedroom. 'He put his wallet in his shoe.' He flicked a photo across the desk for me to see.

'I used to put my purse in my shoe when I went swimming,' I said, recalling a memory from my childhood.'

'His bank account was never accessed,' Callum continued. 'So we knew robbery wasn't the motive . . .'

'I didn't think for one minute it was. If it had been robbery, the offender wouldn't have gone to the trouble of staging the scene to look like anything else. And make no mistake, Cal – this scene *was* staged.'

Chapter Eight

Callum had gone and as I walked into the kitchen, Jen was putting her coat on to do the same. I spoke to her over my shoulder as I washed our cups in the sink.

'You deliberately put that prison visiting order on top of the post for Callum to see.'

She fussed Harvey as she picked up her bag. 'Why would that matter if you thought he'd approve?' Her tone was matter-of-fact, but it wasn't something I would take lightly and she knew it.

'I don't need his approval to visit a client in prison, Jen. It's part of the job.'

She put her reading glasses on top of her head and turned steel-grey eyes on me. 'Maybe it was part of the job, when Dominique De Benoit was first sentenced, but that was four years ago.' She fished her car keys out of her bag. 'And besides, we both know she's more than just a client now, isn't she?' The disapproval in her tone was obvious.

I turned, wiping my hands on a tea towel. 'We've become friends. Is that a problem?'

'Not if having a convicted murderer and psychopath for a friend is regarded as normal.'

'Nothing about my job is *normal*, Jen.' I sighed, suddenly feeling weary. 'But it's what we do. What we've done for almost twenty years.' I draped the towel on the front of the Aga to dry. 'So why the sudden sensitivity about it?' I already knew the answer, but I wanted her to admit it.

She swung her car keys in displaced frustration.

'You helped defend De Benoit. She was an interesting case and you wanted to study her and I know you spent a lot of time with her when she agreed to be interviewed for your book – I understand all of that.' She expelled her breath in a short gust of frustration. 'But how you can call a woman like that a *friend* is beyond me!' She started to look around the table, distracted as she spoke. 'I was the one who typed up her psych report for the trial, remember . . . I've read all the transcripts – she's a psychopath for God's sake!'

'So what?' I said, watching her rummage through her bag. 'There are plenty of them about. They have jobs, wives, children. They go through life never committing a crime and get rewarded for their psychopathic traits in high-profile jobs. Surgeons. Hedge fund managers. Captains of industry. Psychopathic traits are highly valued in business.'

'But she's not in business, is she?'

'She was – a very successful one as it happens.'

Jen snorted indignantly. 'I'd hardly call running high-class escorts a reputable business.'

'I said it was successful . . . not reputable. But whether you approve or not is immaterial. She provided a service for some of the richest people in the world.' I regarded her calmly. 'You can sniff at the morality of it, but it made her a wealthy woman.'

'So, a wealthy psychopath is safer than a poor one then?' Jen glared – pissed off that I wouldn't concede the point.

'Her test scores for psychopathy were borderline– so technically she isn't one . . . '

Jen raised her eyebrows, 'A fine distinction!'

'Yes – actually it is. Nique loved her partner Yalena. That's what drove her to do what she did. She can be compassionate' – I hesitated before adding an important caveat – 'to those she cares about.'

'Tell that to the guy she murdered!'

'It was reduced to manslaughter – which is why she only got six years and not life.'

'Thanks to you!' she said, huffing.

That much was true. The psych evaluation I'd done as an expert witness for the defence had helped to get Dominique's sentence reduced. In many ways, I'd always felt she was as much of a victim of the events that led to her killing a man as her lover Yalena had been.

There had been massive media interest in the case and a lot of people were baying for Dominique's blood. Even sparking debates about reinstating the death sentence. The uproar that followed the verdict had led to appeals for it to be reviewed – but the courts upheld it and I'd been thrown into the public arena. Many accused me of making excuses for a killer. Of being part of a movement that was becoming too soft on crime and criminals. Nique had suffered too, and in some ways I'd felt responsible for what happened to her.

Jen disliked Dominique for all kinds of reasons, but over the past four years my visits to her in prison had become a routine thing. Something that started as professional curiosity, then developed into a friendship.

Nique, as her friends called her, was a fascinating character. Charismatic, erudite and amusing. Jen had never approved – but had never made such a fuss about it before.

'Why are you so upset about this visit?'

She regarded me for a moment before saying quietly, 'Because she's due for release soon, isn't she?'

'So?'

'So – having a psychopathic "friend" safely tucked away inside a high-security prison is one thing. Having her on the outside is something else entirely!'

'You don't fancy her calling round for tea then?' I couldn't help grinning at the look on her face.

'Don't even joke about it.'

'Jen, you're getting far too worked up about this, don't you think?'

'It's just that given the stress you've been under . . . I don't think – feel – that . . .' Her brow furrowed as she tried to get out of the knot she was creating for herself.

'You hoped Callum would see the visiting order and talk me out of it?'

She sighed, the anger suddenly leaving her. 'Something like that.'

I decided to put her out of her misery. 'It's fine, Jen.' My tone was gentle. 'Honestly, don't worry about me.'

She was majorly distracted now – hunting around the kitchen table.

'What are you looking for?'

'My bloody glasses!'

'They're on top of your head, hun.'

Chapter Nine

Fordley police station – Wednesday

After taking Callum up on the invitation to view Leo's last movements, I leaned forward to get a better look at the grainy CCTV footage on his laptop.

Callum sat on the corner of the desk, swinging one leg like a pendulum as he watched me patiently.

I studied the figure dressed in jeans, carrying a rucksack, helping a staggering Leo to the front of Chapel Mills.

'As you say – can't see the face,' I murmured, still concentrating on the images.

Seeing Leo alive made him real. A person with a life to live – hopes and dreams. A family and friends. Not a cold-case number, lying torn and battered on a bloodied mattress. Or as he'd looked on a mortuary slab – like a surreal mannequin that had been callously deconstructed.

As I watched the frustratingly short clip, Leo lowered his head to speak to his companion. The youth punched the code into the keypad, unlocking the door and with an arm around Leo's waist, they walked unsteadily inside.

'You can see from the time-stamp in the corner, it's only eleven minutes and forty seconds before "hoodie" reappears,' Callum said as he got up to pour strong black coffee from the percolator that dripped an endless supply into the pot on his bookshelf. He raised the pot in my direction, but I shook my head. I rarely drank coffee, unless I was absolutely desperate.

'Not enough time to get Leo into the apartment, overpower him and inflict the wounds he was left with,' I agreed.

'Pathologist said the attack was prolonged.' Callum sat opposite me. 'Not a "blitz" event.' He took a sip of hot coffee. 'Besides, we know Leo was six foot two and athletic. "Hoodie" is no more than five foot five or six. Slim build. No match for Leo if he'd put up a fight, even if he was drunk. Doubtful he'd overpower him. Not quickly anyway.'

I tapped the screen with a long index fingernail. 'You sure the hoodie who leaves is the same one who went in?'

Callum nodded. 'Same height and build. Gait analysis confirms it.' He flicked through the file on his desk. 'It's possible he simply took Leo home and has nothing to do with his death.'

I frowned – staring at the screen as if by magic it would suddenly show me the one clip that would explain it all. 'Maybe someone *already* inside killed him? If they lived in the building, Leo might have felt safe enough to let them in?'

'All the residents had alibis that checked out and were eliminated from the enquiry.' He pushed a sheaf of notes across the desk. 'Apart from Edward, who claimed he was out that night. He gave us a list of bars and clubs. Some people remembered him in one or two – but we couldn't draw up a consistent timeline that accounted for the whole night. Which is why we couldn't eliminate him entirely.' He stretched back in his chair, grinding the heel of his hand into tired eyes.

I pulled a file out of my briefcase. 'If Leo's watcher was the same person who killed him, then the stalking might have been a means to an end and not the endgame itself . . .'

'Meaning what exactly?'

'Sometimes stalking *is* the act of violence. Seeing the distress and the way it changes the victim's life is the end product.'

'Like leaving the roses as a calling card for Leo?'

'Exactly. Then you get the more common type – when a relationship ends. Aggrieved partner snooping on their ex to find out who they're seeing. If reconciliation fails, that can escalate to feelings of revenge . . .'

'Leo hadn't come out of a recent relationship. We checked at the time with everyone who knew him. He wasn't seeing anyone, at least not openly. Could his fame as an artist attract a celebrity stalker?'

'I considered that, but they don't fit. They're often delusional intimacy seekers targeting someone they know isn't ever going to reciprocate. But they rarely escalate to this kind of violence.'

'So which category does?'

'Only one fits. It's the rarest type but the most dangerous of all. The "Predatory Stalker" – if you have one on your patch, he'll have struck before and probably since. And one thing's for sure . . .'

'What's that?' Callum was studying me intently.

'If you don't catch him – he'll kill again.'

Chapter Ten

Callum considered what I'd just said. 'If you're right, what are we dealing with?'

'This type of attacker is a sexual predator. For them, stalking is foreplay. The real driver is the violent sexual fantasies they indulge in while they follow their prey. Watching their victim and seeing the terror as the person realises they're being stalked gives them a sense of power and control that feeds their sadism.' I indicated the crime scene photographs. 'Whoever killed Leo, played mind games with him. Letting him know he was being watched. Intentionally being seen down in the garden – then sending the roses. Terrorising him while mentally rehearsing every detail of what they were going to do with him when they finally got into that apartment.' I tapped my file. 'These offenders *only* get off by causing physical harm to their victim. Particularly when it's sadistic and non-consensual.'

'Well, that fits.' He began scribbling notes. 'What about individual characteristics of the offender?'

This was where profiling got its reputation as a 'dark art'. The almost clairvoyant listing of a person's behavioural traits. I looked through the notes I'd made after walking the scene in Leo's apartment. Getting into the mind of the offender. It was never an easy part of the job – but for me it was the only way I could map the motivations that lead to such brutal crimes.

'There's a cold callousness to this crime.' I tapped a fingernail against my teeth as I thought about it. 'I'd say he's above average intelligence with good social and interpersonal skills, evidenced by the way he could convince Leo to let him into the apartment. Or he came up with a way of gaining entry without force and got away without being seen either. He blends in easily. Possibly he lives or works around here. Look for someone between thirty and forty and physically fit. Might have a hobby that keeps him in shape.'

'Sounds a lot like Morrison, wouldn't you say?'

'Edward doesn't fit the profile of a predatory stalker – or a sexual sadist, for that matter. I looked over the notes made at the time. Nothing flags up that would make me think he would be capable of it. This type of offender doesn't just pop up in mid-life, commit a killing like this, then never offend again. He'd have had a history of offending – probably from adolescence. Minor stuff, working up to more serious things. It's not Edward, Cal.'

He nodded, without looking up from his note-taking. 'OK. Anything else?'

'I'd say this offender is meticulous in his habits. Maybe even has OCD type tendencies. Evidenced by the way the crime scene was left. Fastidious attention to detail, leaving no traces of themselves, which is very difficult to do, as you know. If you ever get to where he lives, it'll be well kept, almost clinical. This person likes order and neatness and that will extend to their surroundings as well as their appearance.'

I looked at the head of silver hair bent over the file opposite. Callum's looks sometimes caught me unawares. As if I'd just seen him for the first time.

He felt the silence and glanced up and I couldn't stand the scrutiny that might fathom what I was thinking. I looked down at my notes.

'We *did* find a single fibre from the rug in Leo's bedroom. The lab extracted a small amount of DNA from it. It didn't match anything at the scene, and forensics couldn't match it to anyone who had legitimate access to Leo or the apartment. But it wasn't in the system. So we didn't get a hit from it.'

'So, it'll only be useful if you ever get a suspect in the future?'

He nodded.

I went back to my notes.

'This is an "organised" offender,' I continued. 'He brought whatever he needed to control and subdue his victim. Anything left at the scene, like the riding crop and the amyl nitrate was done intentionally.'

I scratched my head with the end of the pencil. The more I thought about that staged murder scene, the more convinced I became that the props were clues to our offender's drives.

'It's almost as if those things were left as an homage – like a tongue-in-cheek way of showing us exactly why they committed the offence.'

'So, if we accept that it *was* all staged, could the manner of Leo's death be a clue as to why they chose Leo?'

'Yes, I think so. This is meant to look pretty straightforward. As Charles Fielding said – that takes you down a false trail.' I met his careful gaze. 'If he's right, you were being led there by the killer, and the deliberate markers left as to their *actual* motivation would be like two fingers up at the police. A private joke you weren't in on.'

'Hilarious.'

I scanned my notes. 'This wasn't a panicked attacker trying to make a quick exit. They spent from Friday night to Sunday morning in Leo's apartment. Inhabiting the victim's space. Not many people could do that.' I thought back to the wine glasses on the kitchen counter. I'd started to get inside his twisted psyche.

You sat there didn't you – whoever you are? Drinking wine and looking up at the bed above you. You listened to the sounds of suffering your torture had inflicted and you sipped your wine and savoured the moment before going back to your victim and doing it all over again. Leo was inconsiderate enough to die unexpectedly – ending your pleasure prematurely. He stopped the game early, didn't he?

'It takes nerves of steel to be able to stay put with your victim for so long.' I looked up to see Callum watching me intently. 'A lack of empathy to that degree means this person probably isn't in a long-term relationship.'

He watched me, thoughtfully chewing the end of his pen. 'Why did they stage the scene that way?'

'Because of the impact it would have on the people who found the body. Also, as I said – two fingers up to the police.'

Callum got up and took his cup back to the coffee pot. 'You said he'd kill again. This murder was two years ago and we've not had another one. Sexual predators don't commit one offence and then quit, do they?'

'Not as a rule,' I conceded. 'Only reason would be because they move away, in which case you'll see a similar MO cropping up in other parts of the country. Or they become ill, die or get caught.'

He sat on the edge of his desk, looking down at me as I gathered my notes. 'If I get you a list of the people we considered from the original enquiry, could you take a look? See if anyone matches your profile?'

'No problem.'

'Thanks Jo – appreciate it.'

Chapter Eleven

I stood up to leave Callum's office, when the door opened and Frank Heslopp stuck his head in.

Heslopp had been a DS when we'd first met. He'd actually interviewed me in connection with the death of one of my patients – and to say our first encounter had been a rocky one would be an understatement. I described him at the time as an arsehole and despite a grudging professional respect, my fundamental opinion hadn't changed.

Whatever our differences, he'd proved to be an invaluable member of Callum's team and had recently passed his Inspector's exams. Now he was 'acting up' as a temporary DI.

'Boss, when you've got a minute, we've got footage from that attack at the train station.'

Callum put his cup down. 'I'll come now, Frank; we're done here.'

Heslopp acknowledged me with a nod. 'Heard you were here, doc. Want to join us – see what you think?'

In another room officers were huddled round a computer, looking at CCTV footage. I recognised several familiar faces from Callum's team.

DC Beth Hastings turned as we walked in.

'Jo!' She beamed. 'Good to see you.' She nodded to my leg. 'How you doing?'

'OK, thanks. Limp a bit when it plays up.'

I'd had to have extensive surgery on my leg injury the previous year. Frustratingly it was taking its time to heal, aching like a bitch if I overworked it . . . or if the weather was cold. Reminding me of Mamma's clichéd tales about her arthritis in winter. *God – I hope I'm not turning into my mother!*

She nodded at the screen. 'You here to look at our train station attacker?'

I leaned forward to get a better look.

The images were from a station platform at Fordley Interchange. DS Tony Morgan rewound it so I could view it from the beginning. 'This was sent through by the train operator. British Transport Police have taken copies. One of their officers was assaulted in the incident.'

'When was this?' I asked.

'This morning – rush hour.'

The full colour images showed a white male in his mid-thirties, wearing jeans, trainers and a camouflage jacket, vaulting over the ticket barrier. He walked purposefully down the platform, weaving his way through the crowd waiting for the next train.

'Looks like he's strolling through the park, doesn't he?' Tony muttered almost to himself.

The member of staff he'd jumped past at the barrier, watched him for a second before disappearing.

Beth tapped the screen. 'A member of the gate staff thought he was just a "fare-dodger" and were going to challenge him on the platform.' She indicated his right arm. 'Then he spotted this and went back inside to get help.'

Everyone strained forward to get a look at the man's right hand – he was carrying a long blade, which hadn't been immediately obvious.

'Where the hell did *that* come from?' DS Hanson spoke for everyone.

'Inside his jacket?' Heslopp ventured. 'Or maybe the waistband of his pants?'

We watched as he walked calmly down the line of people crowding the edge of the platform. Engrossed in newspapers, or wired for sound with their earbuds in, all seemingly oblivious to the danger. Like bathers blissfully unaware of a predatory shark swimming around their legs.

The camera aspect changed– allowing us to see him from the front. His face was a mask – expressionless. But his lips were moving, as if talking to himself.

A small group of Asian men stood together. All dressed in traditional kameez tunics over baggy linen trousers. The group moved to let him pass, then realisation dawned on their faces.

Early morning sunlight glinted off the blade as he lunged into the centre of the group. There was a flurry of activity – bodies piling into each other as the men frantically tried to get away from their assailant. Arms flailing, as they clumsily attempted to block the attack and avoid the blade at the same time.

The attacker expertly aimed a roundhouse kick at the youngest man nearest to him. The blow landed squarely on his target's chest sending him staggering backwards to fall over the edge of the platform onto the rails below.

Almost in slow motion, as though activated by a single breath – the crowd began to move as one – backing away from the trouble.

Bizarrely, mobile phones were raised above the heads of the crowd as some onlookers began to film the drama.

A National Counter Terrorism security poster was clearly visible on the wall, advising the public to 'Run, Hide and Tell' in the event of a 'Marauding Terrorist Attack', which was the latest identified threat in open areas like shopping malls and railway stations.

'Should say, "Lights, Camera, Action".' Tony snorted in disgust. 'Bloody unbelievable.'

Although I knew the psychology behind it, people's voyeurism at tragic events never ceased to amaze me.

'People have become observers in their own lives through social media,' I said distractedly. 'Fight, flight and freeze are evolutionary mechanisms designed to keep us safe – these days, filming distances people from the trauma.'

'Doesn't keep them safe though, does it?' Beth observed, chewing the end of her pen as she watched.

I shrugged. 'No. But internally it makes them *feel* safer.'

'Should have the bloody posters changed then,' Hanson said. 'To "Fight, Flight, Freeze or Film"!'

'Don't knock it,' Callum said from behind me. 'Might be in bad taste, but it's invaluable to us. How many times have we relied on footage from witnesses?' He turned to Heslopp. 'Take it we've got these mobile phone images?'

'Yes, boss. BTP were first on scene, they're collating it all. One of their team – PC Yates – happened to be in the ticket office when this lot kicked off.'

We watched as a BTP officer appeared on the concourse. He ran onto the platform but his route was blocked by the sea of panicked commuters heading the other way.

Two of the Asians seemed to be trying to protect the older man in the centre of the group. But they were no match for the assailant, who was systematically taking them apart one by one.

'He can handle himself,' I said to no one in particular.

I could feel the warmth of Callum's breath on my neck as he looked over my shoulder.

PC Yates made it to the edge of the crowd. He drew his Taser in the same moment the man turned and saw the threat. Yates shouted a challenge as the red dot appeared on the assailant's chest. But before he could discharge the weapon, a member of the public broke through the crowd and ran across the front of him to go help the man down on the track.

'Helpful not!' Someone at the back chipped in.

The momentary obstruction was all the attacker needed. In just two strides he'd closed the distance. Pivoting on the ball of his foot, he swung a kick that knocked the Taser out of Yates's hand. They grappled and hit the ground and our view was blocked by the crowd. A second later the subject broke free and ran back the way he'd come.

'According to the incident log, Yates pressed his panic button while they were on the ground.' Heslopp provided the voice-over. 'BTP and local uniform responded, but it took two minutes before backup arrived.'

'That's what BTP stands for,' Tony said. '"Be There Perhaps".'

There was a ripple of laughter. 'When he kicked the Taser out of his hand,' Heslopp continued, 'Yates suffered a broken wrist and once matey had him down on the ground, he got in a lucky punch that broke his jaw.'

'What happened to the knife?' I asked.

'Dropped in the struggle.'

I looked back at the screen. 'Not sure our man's punch was that lucky. Looks professionally trained to me.' I turned to Callum who was at my shoulder. 'What do you think?'

'Think we've all seen enough pub brawls at chucking out time to know the difference.' He turned to Heslopp. 'What about the officer's body-camera?'

'He started recording as soon as he went through the barrier, boss. Footage was automatically uploaded onto the secure server. BTP are getting it over to us.'

'That'll hopefully get us a better look at matey.' He straightened up to go. 'You got everything you need, Frank?'

'The team are on it, boss. Yates is in Fordley General Hospital. Before he went into surgery, he said he'd be able to ID the attacker given the chance.'

'What about the victims?' I asked.

Beth scanned her notes.' The older man is Adel Abassi. He's the hafiz at the Madrasah – the religious school attached to Fordley Mosque. The one who got kicked onto the tracks is his son, Baahir Abassi. The others are students at the Madrasah.'

'How's the son?'

'Luckily for him, the guy who blocked Yates's Taser shot managed to haul him onto the platform, just before the express came through. Got a few bruises – and soiled underpants.' Beth grinned.

'Bet the adrenalin was running down his legs while he was trackside.' Hanson laughed.

I looked back at the screen. 'If this was a "marauding active terrorist",' I said, 'he would have stabbed and slashed indiscriminately as he went. But he didn't.' I looked at Heslopp.

'You're not dealing with a random attack here, Frank – this was targeted at that specific group.'

Heslopp ran a hand across the back of his neck. 'We've got officers at the hospital interviewing Abassi and the others. They're walking wounded – defence injuries to arms and hands mainly. We'll know more once we've spoken to them.'

'Can you get footage from the ticket hall and the concourse?' I asked. 'Anything that shows him *before* he jumped the barriers.'

'I'll get on it.' Hanson made a note.

Something about the attacker's demeanour didn't seem right. He had a look about him – an expression that bothered me. I'd come across something like it before but I needed to check my facts. If I was right, they were dealing with something far more bizarre than anyone could imagine.

Chapter Twelve

Kingsberry Farm – Thursday morning

Dark clouds scudded across a pewter-grey sky, pushed on by a stiff breeze that betrayed the promise of any warmth.

My boots crunched down the gravel drive behind Harvey, who was too excited about the prospect of a walk to give a damn about the weather.

Callum had emailed details of people questioned during the Leo Fielding enquiry, but no one had raised any flags for me. Edward didn't seem likely. He was certainly physically fit and his age was only just out of the range I'd given – but he didn't 'feel' right. I couldn't put my finger on exactly why. I knew Callum wouldn't discount him simply because of my gut feeling – but I knew we should be looking elsewhere.

I checked my watch. I'd have to get back to the farm to change for my trip to Manchester. Jen was still unhappy about my visit to Nique, but at least she was only deafening me with silence over it.

Harvey automatically turned down our usual path, but I called him back. He stopped in the gateway and tilted his head in a canine question.

'Not that way, boy.' I threw a stick by way of encouragement along the new route. The usual path was too far for my aching leg today.

As if my mind had triggered a resonant physical reaction, a splinter of pain jagged across my thigh. I rubbed the spot and caught my breath as my heart suddenly began to race and I felt the prickle of heat down my back.

I closed my eyes – letting the cold wind whip my face. Silently cursing the mind-traps my psyche kept setting – to spring unexpectedly and hold me in the iron teeth of the panic attacks I'd come to dread and despise in equal measure.

Harvey bounded back with his new stick, playfully dancing out of reach as I tried to take it from him, then running ahead as I limped along behind him, suddenly feeling bone weary. I hadn't slept for more than a few hours a night in months and it was beginning to take its toll. Even I couldn't kid myself that I was functioning at my best, because I knew it simply wasn't true.

The publicity from working high-profile cases had put an end to my private therapy practice in Fordley, so recently I'd put the office in town up for sale. I had enough work from the Crown Prosecution Service and barristers wanting me as an expert witness to keep me busy. I frowned as I thought about Charles Fielding and the problems of getting involved in one of Callum's old cases. That was a minefield I would have to navigate – but not today.

* * *

When I got back, Callum's car was parked in front of the house. I towelled Harvey off in the porch and let him run into the kitchen. I could hear the rumble of Callum's voice raised in greeting as Harvey jumped all over him.

Jen glanced up from her spot by the Aga, where she was sorting the post.

'You look windswept and interesting.' Callum grinned at me from his place at the kitchen table. Fussing Harvey and trying unsuccessfully to keep wet paws off his trousers.

The obligatory teapot and mugs were already laid out. I sat opposite him and poured myself a brew. 'Wasn't expecting you to visit today?'

'Spur of the moment. I got called over to Wakefield last night.' He paused, as if that explained everything.

'For what?'

'To see the Assistant Chief Constable. They got the decision back from the CPS . . .' He took a sip of tea, deliberately stringing it out.

Not wanting to spoil his fun, I played along.

'And?'

'They quoted section three of the Criminal Law Act . . . 1967 . . .' He paused for dramatic effect.

'And?' I said again slowly – grinning at him.

'Apparently, reasonable force was used. So – no case to answer.'

'That's brilliant news!' My grin was a mile wide. I squeezed his hand across the table. 'What happens now?'

'I've been reinstated with immediate effect. Back on the rota for the next case that comes in.'

'What about the Leo Fielding case?

'What about it?' He withdrew his hand and took a drink of tea. The chill obvious.

'I can't turn away from it now, Cal.'

'Never thought you would.'

'How do we handle it then?'

'*We* don't. Cold-case team are working it.'

'Fair enough.' I was damned if I'd be apologetic about it. 'Who do I need to contact there?'

'DS Pete Albright. I've already passed on your stalker theory.'

Subject closed. Just like that.

I nodded, making a mental note.

'Oh, while I remember,' he changed the subject. 'Frank Heslopp asked if you could give him some input on this station attacker?' He managed to look suitably embarrassed as he added, 'No budget for it though – as per . . .'

'As usual.' I tried to sound annoyed, but didn't quite manage it. 'I'll tell Frank to give you a call.'

I called after Jen as she went down the glass corridor to our office.

'Great news for Callum, isn't it?'

'I've already congratulated him.' Her disembodied voice drifted back. I shot Callum a pained look. 'Sorry about that. It's me she's pissed off with – not you.'

'I know.' He put his cup down. 'The visiting order from Dominique De Benoit was dated for today.'

I sighed into my cup. 'You saw it then?'

'Passed my "upside down reading course" with distinction.' He was smiling, but his eyes held a serious concern. 'She's worried about you getting involved when De Benoit gets out, that's all . . .' He paused for a second before adding, 'So am I, for that matter.'

I matched his steady gaze. 'Why?'

He shrugged. 'She's a psychopathic killer. How many reasons do we need?'

Considering the various ways I could answer the question, I decided to put him on the back foot.

'Nique doesn't pose a threat to me.' My exasperation was obvious. 'And if I'm not worried, why should you be?'

'She's dangerous, Jo. Simple as.'

'My evaluation also got the charges reduced from murder to manslaughter. Something she's always been grateful for. She's become a friend over the years, Cal – she's not going to hurt me.'

He didn't look convinced. 'Hmm, well, friendship aside, I'm not sure I ever bought the manslaughter angle, either.'

I raised my eyebrows. 'Just as well you weren't on the jury then, isn't it?'

'You argued a good case for her, Jo, no doubt about that. But to say it wasn't murder?'

The events surrounding Oliver Blackstone's death at his own thirtieth birthday party had sent the tabloid press into a feeding frenzy for months before the trial. The party had been organised by Oliver's billionaire father, Sir Neville Blackstone, and rumour had it that guests included glitterati from around the world. Oliver's friends were the children of the elite, who were keen to keep their names out of the scandal.

The decadent party, held in the seclusion of a private manor house – Boltby Hall, in the Yorkshire Dales – had been described as an almost bacchanalian orgy. Fuelled by illicit drugs and alcohol it was typical of the kind of event Nique's company was renowned for.

These parties were the stuff of legend among her privileged clientele, who paid to have whatever they wanted – no matter how outrageous. But the fee also came with a guarantee of anonymity that Nique would never break – even if it meant going to prison.

Yalena Vashchenko – Nique's lover – had been the events coordinator. Her client list included film stars, Russian oligarchs and millionaire entrepreneurs and her partnership with Nique combined their contacts, whose hedonistic requests were fulfilled by the stunning 'models' supplied through Nique's escort agency and nightclub.

It was a business model that made them a fortune – but ultimately ended with the death of the son of probably the most powerful man in the north of England. A property developer and philanthropist whose charity work had earned him a knighthood and whose private life and business dealings were a constant source of speculation and rumour, not always for the right reasons.

Nique's trial and conviction spawned a handful of TV documentaries. Eventually, frustrated by the inaccuracies and wild speculation, Nique had asked me to put the record straight and give her account of what had actually happened on the night that had changed the lives of everyone involved.

The book had caused a sensation – being written by the only person who had exclusive access to the killer. But even my account was missing key details. Pieces of the story Nique refused to give up, to this day, even to me. For one thing, Yalena, the other 'victim' that night, had been spirited away from the scene by Nique and her minder, Paul 'Edge' Brink.

Too traumatised by the attack and the injuries it had left her with, Yalena had been kept hidden by Nique and subsequently by Edge's underground network – ex-military from his days with the paras' Special Forces Support Group.

Word was that Edge and his mercenary contact had managed to get Yalena out of the country long before the case went to trial.

Despite the fact that her evidence could have strengthened the case for 'diminished responsibility manslaughter', Yalena had refused to come out of hiding. A decision Nique whole-heartedly supported – insisting on facing it alone to take her chances with the jury.

Her desire to protect Yalena – refusing to divulge her whereabouts, which only added to the charges against her – had impressed me. A depth of compassion and love that flew in the face of the coldly calculating psychopath the prosecution tried to portray.

Looking up to see Callum watching me, I took a long breath. 'Dominique got a panicked call from one of her girls at Boltby Hall to say Yalena had been badly injured and she should get there fast. Nique and Edge had no idea what to expect when they got there. While Edge got the other girls out of the house, Nique went to find Yalena. She didn't go armed that night, Cal. She used the victim's own knife on him. It was beside the bed where he'd dropped it. My assessment was that if Oliver Blackstone hadn't taunted her and bragged about what he'd done, while she was still in shock at seeing Yalena's injuries, he'd probably still be alive today.'

'But he's not, is he?' Callum couldn't keep the hard tone from his voice. 'Because your *friend* cut his cock off and left him to bleed to death!'

'She called an ambulance,' I reminded him. 'And when she passed his friend on her way out, she told him to go look after Oliver. If he had, Oliver might have lived.'

'That party was in chaos, Jo. Blackstone's Hooray Henry friends were all smacked out on drugs and alcohol. They were about as much use to him as a chocolate teapot! By the time the paramedics and police arrived, half his friends had scarpered to avoid being caught up in the scandal. There was so much "covering up" that we never did get to know the names of everyone at that party – it was a mess. Expecting them to stick around to stop him bleeding out and risk being part of the enquiry was a bit of a stretch . . .'

'He was no great loss,' I reflected. 'Nasty little shit by all accounts, with a history of abusing women. But none ever came forward because Daddy's wealth protected him and they got paid off – or warned off.' I wasn't sure which was worse.

'I didn't shed a tear for him either, but that doesn't make what she did right.'

'Maybe not right,' I conceded. 'But understandable given the circumstances. You make her sound like some rabid serial killer, Cal, which we both know she isn't. Until that night, she'd never committed a crime—'

'I'm not sure her business dealings qualify as never committing—'

'OK,' I interrupted. 'Never committed an act of violence then. Will you accept that?'

'Well yes, but—'

'But nothing!' I ran a hand through my hair in frustration. 'Given the right provocation we all have the capacity for violence,'

I added, perhaps unfairly. 'You should understand that better than most.'

He regarded me for a moment and then shrugged. 'Point taken.'

'Yalena was the love of her life. They'd been together for five years, and that night, Blackstone and his mates decided to take what they wanted just because they could. They beat her to within an inch of her life before raping her and Nique was the one to find her like that.' I took a mouthful of tea. 'If he'd done that to someone I cared about, I'd have cut his bits off as well!'

'Remind me never to cross you then.'

'Anyway, she paid the price, if that makes you feel any better?' I looked up at him, remembering the emotional devastation Nique had endured a year into her sentence, when news of her lover's death had come from the South of France. 'She never got over Yalena's suicide. I don't think she ever will.'

He ran fingers through his hair, finally giving up the argument. 'So, when does she get out then?'

'Should have been months ago. But Blackstone threw expensive lawyers at it. The parole date was put back while the appeal was considered.'

I'd submitted a letter in support of her application. Something which hadn't gone down well with Blackstone's legal team. They were used to getting their own way, so when the appeal was overturned, they must have been spitting nails.

He drained the last of his tea, pushing his chair back to go. 'OK – well Jen can't say I didn't try.'

I walked him to the door. He hesitated, looking down at me. Once he would have hugged me as he left, but now he just stood awkwardly in the doorway. Not really sure what to do around me anymore.

'Be careful, Jo. I know you think of her as a friend, but try to keep a bit of distance from this one – please?'

I said I would – but it didn't sound convincing, even to me.

Chapter Thirteen

Styal, Manchester – Later that morning

The sprawling estate of Styal women's prison in Manchester first opened its doors as an orphanage for destitute children in 1898. Some of the original outbuildings – large detached red-brick houses with white sash windows and high gable-end chimneys, known for some reason as 'Grey Houses' – stood in the grounds, away from the main block. They were home to women like Nique, who were considered less volatile and allowed more independent accommodation than those 'on the wing'.

The Grey Houses were imposing, even beautiful in their grand design, and could have commanded serious prices in any other part of affluent Wilmslow. Now they stood behind the high perimeter fence – peering out longingly at a world they were segregated from as much as the women incarcerated there.

I drove past the sign declaring that Styal was 'building hope and changing lives'. A bold claim considering that it had one of the worst suicide rates of any prison in the country.

Bullying and overcrowding, mixed with a deadly cocktail of drugs and a high incidence of mental health issues among prisoners, all contributed to the statistics. Although things had improved slightly in the four years I'd been visiting, four women had already died here in the past fifteen months.

Squeezing into the last parking space beside an old Mini, I hauled a carrier bag out of the boot and locked the Roadster. A large blue and white sign announced that under the 'Prison Act of 1952' it was a criminal offence to assist a prisoner to escape – as if you couldn't have guessed. Going on to say that if caught attempting it, you'd end up in a cell yourself for a minimum of ten years.

Various other offences such as supplying a prisoner with explosives, offensive weapons or drugs would also get you a ten stretch.

I joined the line-up of family and friends, familiar with the jaded routine of getting in to see their loved ones.

As the queue wound its way, families chatted to each other, almost oblivious to the electronic wand sweeping over them as they extended their arms to facilitate the search.

A toddler in a pushchair eagerly stretched out chubby hands to stroke the springer spaniel in a high-vis harness being led down the line by an officer, as it sniffed people, bags and baby buggies. Luckily the dog didn't indicate anything of interest, so the line happily moved along.

I put my handbag and the contents of my pockets into a locker and on production of photo ID was given a wristband and had my hand stamped. Reminiscent of the nightclubs I'd visited as a teenager, but without the anticipation of quite the same levels of alcohol-fuelled fun.

As I went to the kiosk where the magazines I'd brought had to be handed in and sealed into property bags, the familiar smell triggered memories of the institutions I'd spent most of my professional life in.

Hospitals, psychiatric units and prisons. No matter how colourful the walls, how modern the paintings or the modular seating – the smell was universal. An unmistakeable fusion of disinfectant, crowded humanity and the mustiness of a secure space denied the fresh air of open windows.

I passed my gifts through to a large female officer who had the expression of a woman sitting on a nettle and looking like she'd rather be anywhere else but here on this warm summer's afternoon.

Even in the room full of prisoners sitting expectantly at tables, I could have picked Nique out in a crowd of thousands with her distinctive brunette hair, falling in waves across her shoulders, and her meticulously applied make-up. The whole effect making her look far younger than her late forties.

Nique's standards of personal grooming remained the same in a prison visiting hall as they had been in her days hosting lavish parties at the most glittering venues in the world. If the freedom allowing prisoners their own clothes had extended to Louboutins and diamonds, I was certain she'd wear them. Even so, her tailored capri pants and fitted blouse looked incongruous enough in such a dreary place.

Her eyes lit up as I walked through the rows of tables. Her gloss-painted lips beamed the widest smile. 'Jo, *ma chérie!*'

'Nique – looking glam as ever.' She stood and we touched cheek to cheek in the typical Gallic 'air kiss'.

She sat holding both my hands in hers – eyes shining with genuine pleasure.

'It's so good to see you, *ma copine.*' Her French accent seemed even more pronounced than usual. 'I'm dying of boredom in this social desert.' She waved a hand around the room, long French-polished nails accentuating the elegant gesture.

I had to laugh – her sophistication was discordant in this place. Like a woman from a Renoir painting dropped in the midst of young girls with tattoos and face piercings.

I saw the other prisoners watching us. 'You don't exactly try to blend in around here, do you?'

'Why would I want to, *chérie*?'

'Oh, I don't know – maybe to make life easier for yourself?' I smiled as I said it – but it was a serious point. Standing out for all the wrong reasons in here was like sticking a target on your back.

Her large russet eyes twinkled with a mischief I'd come to recognise. 'An easy life would be so boring – complications are far more interesting, don't you think?'

Before I could reply, one of the women still waiting for her visitor, called out to the young female officer supervising the room.

'Oi, miss – you going for your dinner soon? Dominique can recommend the frogs' legs!'

There was a ripple of laughter and another girl chipped in, 'Think miss might have to go hungry – looks like those frogs' legs aren't open for business today!'

'That's enough, Jodie,' the female officer cautioned, shifting uncomfortably from one foot to another. I saw a faint blush creep across her cheeks just before she dropped her gaze.

Nique was smiling like butter wouldn't melt. I raised an enquiring eyebrow. 'Tell me you haven't, Nique?' I looked over at the petite, masculine-looking officer with cropped dark hair, watching us from her station by the door. Nique shrugged but didn't reply – which spoke volumes. I dropped my voice to a whisper. 'Don't you ever learn?'

Two years previously, Nique had been transferred to Styal from Durham after her affair with a female officer at HMP Low Newton had been discovered.

'There are ways to make life easier for myself,' she said, laughing at the look on my face, 'which are quite fun.'

'You must be mad, risking your parole at this late stage of the game – and for what?'

She grinned. 'If I have to tell you that, you're more naive than I thought.'

I looked again at the officer. 'Not your usual type,' I murmured.

'Beggars can't be choosers.' She shrugged. 'Besides, I'm *her* type . . . a "lipstick lesbian".' She laughed.

Lesbians at the more 'feminine' end of the spectrum, who wore make-up, and dressed in 'girlie' clothes, were referred to as 'lipstick'. Definitely Nique's category.

'She supervises the gym,' she was saying. 'Giving us plenty of opportunities to exchange contraband . . . in return for some affectionate considerations from me.'

Nique shot her lover a quick glance. The territorial stare sent my way was unmistakeable. I slipped my hand from beneath hers. 'I don't think you should flirt in front of her,' I cautioned. In the prison pressure cooker, covetous rivalry was a volatile ingredient.

Her expression was a mixture of devilment and indifference. 'Keeps her on her toes,' she said quietly. 'Sharpens the interest . . .'

'OK.' I sighed. 'I'm not your keeper . . .'

She held my disapproving look, a thin smile tugging the corners of her mouth. 'Are you *jealous* of Officer Harland, *chérie*?' she whispered seductively.

I'd long ago accepted Nique's flirting. With others, her flirting was a sociopathic tactic to manipulate, much as she probably used the female prison officer. To make her life easier – get special treatment. But over the years, with me I'd come to realise it was genuine on her part – or as close to genuine affection as she was capable of. It was definitely a complication I hadn't needed or encouraged. With the plan we'd come up with, I needed it even less now.

'Behave, Nique,' I warned. 'I'm serious. It's useless telling you not to take risks. I know it's the way you're wired. But right now? Your timing stinks.'

'It's not all about fun. Penny's possessiveness keeps the vultures at bay in here. She's tough . . . has my back,' she said with a slight raising of her shoulders. 'I needed a phone to conduct my business.' She risked a quick look at Harland. 'You understand, don't you, Jo?'

I slowly shook my head, feeling like a parent reprimanding a wayward child. 'Not when you're so close to release. Besides, I thought Edge took care of your business interests while you were inside?'

Edge was more than the minder she'd originally recruited him to be. In the fifteen years they'd been together, he'd become Nique's right hand. Her rock. The person she trusted most in the world to take care of her affairs as well as the girls who worked for her. He adored them all, like an overprotective big brother.

'He does ...' She glanced around, making sure no one was eavesdropping. 'But there are certain decisions only I can make.' She looked back at me with large hazel eyes. 'Certain people who will only speak to me – you understand?'

I understood – but it didn't make the risks she was running any less foolhardy. I decided to switch the topic onto safer ground. 'So, do you have an update?'

'Yes ...' She squeezed my hand across the table. 'The parole's been granted, but the issue of my "approved premises" has been delaying everything – the letter you sent really helped.'

Nique still owned a penthouse apartment in an exclusive district of Fordley, but the authorities hadn't felt it wise for her to go back there since Oliver Blackstone's father had made threats against her if she was ever released. She could be better protected from credible threats in a probation hostel, but there was a scarcity of places for women offenders and currently no vacancies in the north of England. Nique had refused to relocate to another part of the country and had taken the decision to go back to her apartment. The parole board had agreed, but only on condition that someone stood surety that she would observe her strict bail conditions. I had agreed to be that someone.

She ran elegant fingers through her long hair, flicking it off her shoulders.

'I know what this plan might cost you, Jo. I can't ever thank you.'

I studied her carefully. She was being genuine. 'You can thank me by staying out of trouble ...' I glanced across at Officer Harland who was watching us from the corner of the room. 'No more stupid risks, Nique – not if I'm sticking my neck out for you. Understand?'

Despite her soft femininity and gentle demeanour, which could lull the unwary into believing Nique's character was quite benign, I knew her better than most. The one thing guaranteed to piss her off was telling her what to do. She was looking down to hide the irritation I knew was on her face.

'I understand.' She lifted her head to look at me with a smile. Her expression changing in an instant – like throwing a switch – and I had the disconcerting reminder that I was dealing with borderline psychopathic behaviour.

'I come out at the weekend!'

I took a long breath. For someone who didn't want complications, I was about to run headlong into an almighty one.

Chapter Fourteen

The Munch Bunch, Little Italy – Friday morning

I sat at a table in the window of the Munch Bunch and looked across the road to Chapel Mills.

The café was bustling with punters. Some dashing in to get coffees 'to go', others enjoying a few minutes to themselves before joining the rush-hour madness of a nine-to-five existence.

The red letters painted onto the glass were distorted by rivulets of condensation running down the inside of the window blurring the view outside. I turned as I felt the young waitress at my elbow.

She smiled. 'Hi, what can I get you?'

'Just a tea.' I smiled back. 'Do you do a teapot?'

'This is Yorkshire, love – it's a sin to make tea in the cup round here.'

The Munch Bunch just went up in my estimation. 'Thanks.'

She walked away, calling a cheerful goodbye to a builder in a high-vis jacket.

'See ya, Domino,' he called back.

Through the window, I watched two students walking down the side of Chapel Mills to a sculpture set against the retaining wall of the gardens. It was a famous landmark in Little Italy. A life-sized padded armchair next to a grandfather clock, both carved from Yorkshire stone. The students took it in turns to sit in the chair and be photographed.

'Here you go, love.' Domino was back carrying a tray. As she set it down, I noticed her full-sleeve tattoos – brightly coloured images turning her arms into multi-coloured serpents.

'Domino, isn't it?' I swirled the teapot to mash the tea.

'Who's asking?' Her smile became fixed – guarded.

I nodded towards the Mills, not really answering the question. 'Edward said I should talk to you. Just need to pick your brains if that's OK? He says you know everyone round here.'

I kept my tone deliberately light – then looked down as I poured the tea. The less important it appeared, the more penetrable her defences would be.

'Sure,' she said after a second. 'I'll just serve this customer.'

I smiled as she went back behind the counter.

I watched her chatting to the customers. On the surface, a friendly, open character. But there was an air about her that I instinctively recognised. A light behind the eyes that hinted at a carefully concealed caution. An innate characteristic born of hurt.

I'd seen that look a thousand times before, reflected in the eyes of my clients. Some of whom had been victims of terrible abuse – most of whom, had gone on to inflict even worse brutality on others.

Eventually the customers thinned out. The old-fashioned bell above the door stopped chiming, the hissing of the coffee machine the only sound.

Domino wiped her hands on a towel and came to stand by my table. I glanced at the seat opposite. She took the unspoken invitation and sat down, resting her elbows on the table top.

'So, you know Edward?'

I put my cup on its saucer with a 'clack'. 'Actually, I'm a friend of Mary Fielding – do you know her?'

She shook her head, her brunette ponytail swishing from side to side. 'Everyone around here knows who she is . . . after what happened, you know?' Those cautious brown eyes studied me for a moment. 'You police?'

'No,' I smiled. 'I'm a doctor. A behavioural analyst. Mary's asked for my help with what happened to Leo.' It said a lot, without telling her much of anything.

'OK.' She nodded slowly, still unsure. 'So, what do you want to know?'

'Well, for a start, why do people call you Domino?' I smiled. 'Intriguing name.'

She grinned, pulling the front of her apron down to reveal three large black and white domino tiles tattooed across her chest. 'First ones I had done,' she said proudly. 'Fifteen. Too young really, but the artist was a friend.'

'Didn't have you down as a domino player.' She let the tunic go, re-covering her artwork. I caught a glimmer of something on her forearm – the light from the window revealing thin silver lines, barely discernible under the green and yellow tattoos.

'I'm not.' She shrugged. 'But they mean something, you know . . . to me.'

I nodded, watching her face closely. 'Your grandad, right?'

'How did you kn—'

I shrugged. 'It's what I do . . . read people.'

'Wow!' She leaned forward, resting her chin on her fists – like a child eager for a bedtime story. 'Like a psychic?'

'Not exactly.' I poured more tea. 'Edward told me Leo came here for breakfast most mornings?'

'That's right.'

'Apparently he used to spend time with a girl. Edward said you might know who she was?'

She looked across to an empty table by the window, as if the couple were still there – ghosts conjured up from the past.

'She started coming here in the mornings. Always sat by the window on her own. After a while her and Leo started sitting together.'

'Who usually arrived first?'

She frowned. 'What?'

'Once they became friends. Who would get here first?'

She pursed her lips and I watched as her eyes moved up, looking over my right shoulder as she recalled the memory.

Researchers had long ago found a correlation between eye movements and how a person recovers a memory. Domino was right-handed, so if she looked up and to my right, she was visually recalling a memory. If she'd have looked to my left, that could indicate a possible 'construct' – a fabrication. Not an exact science, but taken together with other body language cues, a fair indicator of how someone was thinking – though unfortunately for me, not *what* they were thinking, which would have made my life a whole lot easier.

'She did . . .'

'Always?'

Again, the flick of her attention over my right shoulder. Then the nod – 'Yeah always.' She grinned, like a kid pleased with herself for getting a question right at school. She'd been starved of praise and positive reinforcement in her younger years, our Domino.

'Any idea who she is?' I smiled encouragingly. 'You seem to know everyone round here.'

She preened under the warmth of the compliment. 'I overheard Leo calling her Thana.'

That got my attention. 'Thana? You're sure that's the name?'

'Yes . . . certain.'

'Does she work round here?'

'Don't think she had a job. Saw her sometimes when I finished work though. When I went for my bus.'

'Where?'

She jerked her head towards the door. 'At the bus stop over there – the one on the corner.'

'Which bus did she usually catch?'

'Never saw her get on one.'

I thoughtfully stirred my tea. 'What did she look like – this Thana?'

'Petite . . . short cropped dark hair. Plain.' She shrugged. 'Always in jeans . . . no make-up. Bit scruffy really. Got the feeling maybe she lived rough. Always paid in coins, like she was scratching for cash. After a while Leo started paying for her breakfast.'

'What did she eat?'

'What?' She looked puzzled by the question. 'No food. Just coffee.'

'What about her clothes?'

'Jeans, hoodies – street clothes you know?'

'Did she carry a bag? Handbag maybe?'

She snorted. 'Handbag? Not her. Scruffy rucksack some-times.' She leaned forward, chewing a fingernail. 'Tell me about this mind-reading then? How did you know about my grandad? I never told Edward that. What else do you see?'

'It's not a party trick.' I smiled. 'I'm a psychologist.'

'A shrink? My mum saw a lot of them when I was a kid.' She leaned in closer. 'Go on then – do me a reading.'

I couldn't help laughing. 'I'm not in a tent on the pier.'

Unaccountably, I suddenly heard Callum's voice in my head.

'*Witchcraft – that's what you do, McCready – bloody voodoo!*'

'I study people.' I hesitated to go where I was being invited. 'Sometimes I can tell things about them.' I looked into her eyes – to add weight to what I was saying. 'Things maybe they don't want to talk about.'

She rested her chin on her hand. 'It's OK – you can say any-thing. I'm interested.'

'Your grandad looked after you a lot when you were a kid?'

'Didn't know my dad. Mum drank, you know? Spent a lot of time with Grandad . . . he played dominoes.'

'Tough when he died?'

The statement caught her off guard. She nodded.

I indicated her art work. 'Great camouflage – no one sees you – they look at the tattoos, not at you – right?'

She chewed her lip. 'No one's ever said that before . . .'

'Bullied at school and when your grandad died it felt like you were alone again?' She nodded slowly.

'So, you invented a tough shell.' I concentrated on stirring the teapot – not watching her eyes, which had begun to swim with unshed tears. 'The kid who didn't take any shit – who broke all the rules. Smoked, drank . . .' I looked back up. 'Got tattoos underage – bet school loved that one?'

She smiled, despite the tears. 'Got suspended for the tats.'

With the tip of my fingernail, I gently traced the silver line than ran beneath the yellow ink. 'Great way to cover these up though.' She stared at me – suddenly going very still. 'You started cutting after your grandad died. To release the pain.'

She looked down – just nodding – unable to meet my eyes.

I felt the weight of her revelation and knew in that moment, she'd never shared it with anyone.

I smiled encouragingly, receiving a half-smile in return. 'You came through a lot and you survived it.'

She nodded and sniffed. 'Yeah . . . I'm good now.'

I felt relieved. I couldn't have left her lost in the wilderness of her childhood. Having opened that Pandora's box of pain, I would have had to help her navigate her way through and then close it again. And these days, I didn't want the responsibility.

She flicked the ponytail over her shoulder. 'I stopped getting the tats a few years ago . . .'

'Don't need them anymore?'

The self-harming scars were silver – old marks. She hadn't cut herself for a long time.

'Not these days.'

'Good – besides,' I said, aiming to lighten the mood, 'not enough skin left for any more.'

She laughed as we got up and she cleared the table. 'Do you have a card or anything?'

'I don't take private patients anymore.' I smiled.

She looked up, still wiping the table top. 'You should,' she said sincerely. 'You're really good at this stuff.'

'Thanks.' I laughed.

'If I needed . . . I mean, if I wanted to get in touch with you?'

I thought about it for a moment and then dropped my business card onto the damp table. She scooped it up and slipped it into her apron. 'Thanks.'

I stopped on my way out of the door. As though it was an afterthought.

'Did you ever mention Thana to the police?'

She shook her head – busy now behind the counter. 'They spoke to the manager, not me. I was off sick the day they came. They got my address from her and said they'd come to the house to see me – but never did. I didn't bother chasing it up. The manager said she'd told them everything. Besides, after Leo died, that girl never came back.'

Chapter Fifteen

Saturday morning

I clashed the gears for the third time and cursed the gearbox of the old Land Rover Defender. After driving my Roadster, the thirty-year-old vehicle felt like it was constructed from iron girders and handled like a tractor.

It had belonged to my old neighbour, George Theakston, until his death the previous year. His son had asked if I wanted it when he came to empty the property and sort out his father's affairs.

At first, I hadn't been sure, but it did remind me of my old friend. He drove it every day – it was a part of him. I'd found his old leather boots, flat cap and ancient Barbour jacket in the back. When I'd opened it up, the smell reminded me of him and from then on, I knew I'd keep it. It'd been in the barn behind my farmhouse for the last six months as I'd never had occasion to use it – until today.

As I drove into Fordley, I put in a call to the cold case review team and spoke to DS Albright.

'So, the girl at the café says Leo's breakfast companion was called Thana?' he was saying.

'Yes.' I pressed the earbuds in more firmly. No such luxury as hands-free Bluetooth in this old rattler.

'I obviously wasn't involved in the original case,' he said. 'Just came to it through the cold-case review, but I've read through everything from that time.' I could hear papers being shuffled. 'Edward told you he'd mentioned the girl when he was interviewed?'

'Yes.'

'Well, he didn't. Not when he was questioned at the scene. And once he was brought down to the station he went "no comment", so no mention of her then.'

'But she *was* brought to the attention of the investigation?'

'Uniformed officers doing door-to-doors spoke to the manager at Munch Bunch. She said Leo sometimes bought a girl a coffee if he was in for breakfast at the same time, but made light of it. Not like she was a girlfriend or anything. The manager couldn't give us a name. Said she looked homeless. Description was circulated but didn't lead to anyone. All the office workers were questioned but no one remembered ever seeing her and the rough sleepers in the area said she never showed up at any of their haunts. So it was treated as single-strand intelligence at the time. Seems like Domino got missed. It can happen.'

'Thana fits the description of this so-called rough sleeper and the hoodie on the last CCTV you have of Leo.'

'So-called?'

I stopped as the lights held me at red. 'Domino said Thana always arrived first. I think she made a point of waiting for Leo. But she never ordered any food – even though Leo picked up the tab. You ever know a rough sleeper who wouldn't take a paid-for breakfast first thing in the morning?'

'Maybe she ate at a hostel, before she went to the café?'

The lights changed and I pulled away. 'There are only two hostels in Fordley and both start serving breakfasts an hour after Leo's early morning visit to the Munch Bunch. Besides,' I added, 'I got a friend who's a counsellor for them to check their records and no one called Thana or anything resembling that name was resident at the time.'

'I'm impressed.' I could hear the smile in his voice. 'If you ever want a full-time job, just let me know?'

'But only if it's unpaid, right?' I said, smiling back.

'You really do know how it works round here, don't you? Any other thoughts on Thana, while I'm using my free credit?'

'Domino said she was often at the bus stop on the corner, but she never saw her get on a bus.'

'So?'

'That stop is directly opposite Calico's. Leo's regular watering hole. I don't think it was a coincidence that she was there to help him back to his apartment on the night he died. She wasn't waiting for a bus – she was watching Leo.'

'Watching him? Or stalking him?'

'You know the definition of stalking? Two people go for a walk together, but only one of them knows about it!'

He laughed. 'True. But does the MO of the killing fit with a young girl like Thana?'

'No, it doesn't.'

'If she *isn't* the predatory stalker, could she know who was? Be working with him?'

I thought about it for a second. The reflection of me with a furrowed brow looked back from the rear-view mirror. Predatory stalkers worked alone – rarely, if ever in concert with anyone else. I said as much.

'Think she's connected to Edward? Maybe setting Leo up for him?'

I shook my head. 'Edward put me onto her. If they were involved, he wouldn't have done that.'

I heard him sigh down the phone. 'Can't give me a name and address for her then?'

I smiled in the mirror. 'Sorry. That bit's up to you.'

'OK. Well, thanks for this anyway, Jo. I'll get someone to go out and talk to Domino. I'll let you know if anything turns up.'

Chapter Sixteen

I wrestled with the Land Rover for another ten minutes, relieved when I finally got out of rush hour traffic and on to the outskirts of town.

My old therapy practice on Laburnum Terrace was in an area that had been home to the wealthy wool merchants who dominated the West Yorkshire economy over a century ago. The imposing Victorian houses, a symbol of the boom of capitalism during the Industrial Revolution, had for the most part been converted into private practices for an army of dentists, doctors and therapists. It was the North's equivalent to Harley Street.

A mile from the city centre and bordered by the town's largest park, it was a leafy green suburb and a relatively tranquil place to do business. Street parking here was reserved for tenants, who paid a fortune for the privilege of an annual permit. I was careful to park further down the street – away from the practice – and displayed my badge on the dashboard before lifting the carrier bag of supplies off the passenger seat.

It felt strange seeing a 'For Sale' sign in front of what had been my office for almost a decade. I owned what would have been a basement flat of the larger house. The upper floors were occupied now by a physio who kept standard working hours, so the building was empty every night and at weekends – which suited my purpose perfectly.

I let myself in and walked down the hushed, cream-carpeted corridor to the kitchen, pushing the door open with my foot and depositing the heavy bag on the counter.

I leaned against the sink, recalling the endless times Jen and I had brewed tea or grabbed hasty sandwiches between client appointments. 'The end of an era,' Jen had said when I told her I was selling.

I mentally shrugged myself back to the task at hand and put the supplies I'd brought into the cupboards. I spent the next half-hour, checking the place over before locking up.

I drove the Land Rover back into town. The building I was looking for had an underground car park, accessed through a code-entry barrier. I checked the slip of paper before entering the code, bumping the Defender over the speed humps and parking in a bay in the quiet subterranean space.

I left the parking permit for Laburnum Terrace on the dashboard and put the keys for the office under the driver's seat before locking up and slipping the vehicle keys into the exhaust pipe.

As I walked towards the lift, I glanced back. The old Defender looked out of place surrounded by luxury vehicles – illuminated in the soft blue glow of this exclusive place. Like a grizzled old man trying to look inconspicuous among a line-up of beautiful women. George would have been highly amused. The thought made me smile.

Getting into the lift, I used the resident's code needed to access the floors above. As the doors swished open in reception, the concierge looked up from his post behind the sweeping glass desk – returning to the book he was reading when he realised I was simply on my way out into the sunlit street.

I was only fifteen minutes' walk from Little Italy and I decided to visit Chapel Mills to see Mary. She'd been on my mind the last few days and I wanted to see how she was doing. Besides, I told myself the walk would do me good.

* * *

Chapel Mills

I pressed the buzzer for the penthouse and waited. The intercom rang but there was no answer. I buzzed again. Nothing. Today was obviously one of the few days Mary wasn't coming.

I breathed in the soft warm air of what was shaping up to be a beautiful day, debating whether to visit The Munch Bunch and get a taxi to pick me up from there. But the place looked busy and it seemed too nice a day to spend behind glass. I checked my watch. It would take fifteen minutes to walk to the train station and get a cab from there.

I turned the corner and paused to admire the sandstone sculpture of the armchair and clock that had always fascinated me as a kid. It was so tactile – begging to be touched. I reached out and ran my hand across the back of the chair. Amazed that something that looked so soft and padded, was carved from stone – like a trick on the senses.

I glanced above, to the gardens I knew were on the other side of the wall and wondered whether Edward was there – digging over the flower beds?

As I walked, my leg began to ache and I questioned the wisdom of pushing it – but the physio had said I should exercise it more. As I got to the edge of Little Italy, waiting to cross the busy main road, my mobile rang.

'McCready,' I answered, distracted as I watched for a gap in the traffic.

'Is that Jo?'

'Yes. Who's this?'

'Domino.'

'Hi. You OK?'

'I saw you outside the Mills just now and, well . . . you're going to think this is nuts . . . but I thought I should warn you . . .'

The hair prickled across my scalp as the tone of her voice put me on high alert. 'Warn me? About what?'

'You're being followed.'

Chapter Seventeen

My first instinct was to turn and look behind me – but I squashed the impulse. Thankfully the traffic was nose to tail, with no opportunity to cross, so I could stand there while I processed what Domino had just said.

'What makes you think I'm being followed?'

'This guy looked like he was just walking along behind you, but when you stopped, he crossed over and came in the café. I waited for him to order, but he just stood by the window watching you. When you walked off, he hung back a bit and then followed you. I hope you don't mind? But he creeped me out.'

There was a gap in the traffic and I took the chance to cross.

'What's he look like, this guy?'

'Big guy – tall. Short blond hair. In his thirties I'd say. Wearing a dark suit and carrying a jacket over his arm.'

'Ever seen him before?'

'Not round here. Do you want me to call the police or someone?'

'No, it's OK, I'll deal with it – thanks, Domino.'

As the call ended, I glanced over, hoping that my 'follower' was a figment of Domino's imagination. But there he was – large as life.

I quickened the pace as my mind raced through possibilities. Who was he? Why was he following me, and more importantly, what should I do about it?

A right turn took me towards the station. I was desperate to look back – but decided against it. I needed to look like I wasn't so alone – isolated. My phone was still in my hand. I dialled Callum's number. I could tell he was in the car.

'Hi Jo.'

'Cal . . .' I hesitated as it suddenly occurred to me, I didn't know what to say – so I just blurted it out. 'Someone's following me.'

It was his turn to pause, then his tone changed – all business. 'You in the car?'

'No, on foot.'

'Where?'

'Walking down Shipley Road into Fordley – towards the station.'

Trying to hold a conversation and walk at the same time was making me breathless. I made a conscious effort to slow down. I could feel the familiar flush of heat creeping down my back – a forerunner to the anxiety that had begun tightening its grip on my senses at the most inconvenient times. The last thing I needed now was a bloody panic attack in the middle of the street.

'Any idea who's doing the following?' Callum was asking.

I shook my head. 'Never seen him before.'

'But you're sure you're being followed? '

'Yes . . . I think so—'

'Yes or no, Jo?'

'How the hell can I check? Want me to stop and *ask* him?'

'OK, OK. Want me to come get you?'

'No.' I wasn't sure exactly what I wanted.

'Stay where there are plenty of people. I can be at the drop-off point in front of the station in five minutes.'

'No, you don't need to come – I'll be fine.'

'I'll stay on the phone until you get there. Send me your exact location—'

'What! How the hell do I do *that*?'

'Share a link from the map on your phone.'

'Seriously?' I was incredulous. Callum of all people knew what a technophobe I was. 'You're shitting me! I haven't got time for that – I'll call you back.'

Callum was starting to say more as I ended the call.

Think – for God's sake, think!

There was a shop on the corner. I slowed as I got nearer – then stopped and pretended to look in the window. I stared past my reflection at Blondie still a few metres behind me. He stopped and began reading the menu outside a café.

A lorry rumbled past, causing his reflection to shudder as the plate glass vibrated and I suddenly realised I was staring intently at a display of fishing rods in an angling shop!

What an idiot!

Dragging myself away from the fascination of carp rods, I picked up the pace. The train station looked tantalisingly close, but I knew it was still a few minutes' walk away.

I left the shops and most of the pedestrians behind, heading towards the dual carriageway that stood between me and the safety of the station.

Reaching the busy road, I suddenly realised I had choices to make about how to get across. To my right, the dark mouth of a lonely, graffiti-stained underpass yawned open – almost daring me to go there. To my left, the steps to a metal footbridge offered a safer option.

My heels clanked against the steel steps, my breath coming in ragged gasps. I cursed again the ache in my thigh, which threatened to slow me down. As I reached the top, it dawned on me that I was alone.

Above the roar of the traffic thundering along beneath, I could hear the sound of heavy feet on the metal steps. I pulled the phone out of my pocket, just in time to see the battery die.

There was no one around and I could sense Blondie closing the distance between us.

Enough!

I'd had enough of being made to feel like a mouse to his cat. Impulsively, I stopped and turned to face him.

Chapter Eighteen

Blondie stopped dead in his tracks. For a second a look of surprise registered on his face, and then it was gone, replaced by the expressionless mask of someone confident with confrontation.

'Right,' I said, out of breath. 'I'm knackered, in pain and pissed off – so do you want to tell me what this is about?'

He stared at me, saying nothing and then we heard the sound of voices coming from below. He glanced behind him as a group of drunken football fans started up the steps.

Blondie turned back to regard me with cold blue eyes that gave nothing away. The jacket Domino mentioned was slung over his arm. He pulled it back with his left hand, revealing the handgun in his right. Leaning casually against the railing, he let the jacket slip back over the gun.

He seemed ice-calm, which was more than could be said for my heart rate, which had just gone off the scale.

I forced myself to look away to where half a dozen young lads were swaying onto the bridge. They were all wearing Fordley City shirts and carrying cans of lager, and somewhere in the back of my mind, I remembered something about a big match at Fordley stadium.

Blondie's full attention was on me. Imperceptibly he gestured with the gun, for me to move aside and let the fans pass.

I stayed put – frozen to the spot.

By this time the group had spotted me blocking their path.

I turned on my biggest smile. 'Hi lads – you off to the match?'

The one at the front leered, holding out the can of lager. 'Certainly are, love.' As if on command, they broke into a ragged chant and I took my chance to step into the middle of them. Making sure they were between me and Blondie.

'Fancy joining us, sweetheart?' He thrust his can into my hand. 'Make a change to have some nice totty to look at instead of this ugly bastard!' He punched his mate on the shoulder and they all laughed. I slipped my arm around his waist and took a swig from the can, as they almost carried me along to the other side of the bridge.

I glanced over the big guy's shoulder to Blondie. Whether it was sheer relief or something else – I wasn't sure – but for some reason I couldn't help smiling at him. If looks had been lethal, he wouldn't have needed the gun. He stared back for a second and then turned and calmly went back the way he'd come.

* * *

The fans were boisterous but good natured enough. I kept an arm round my rescuer's waist, out of pure necessity. As the adrenalin drained, my legs were shaking so much I'd have crumpled in a heap if I hadn't been holding on.

As we approached the station car park, I spotted Callum's BMW just pulling in.

'OK, lads.' I tried to sound more upbeat than hysterical. 'This is my stop.'

'Oh, babe – changed your mind about the match?'

I disengaged from around his waist. 'Just spotted a friend over there. Maybe next time.'

As I was enveloped in a drunken group hug, Callum stood by his open car door, staring in our direction.

The lads moved off and I found myself standing uncertainly in the car park, still holding a can of lager as Callum strode over to me.

'What the f—'

'You didn't need to come . . .' was all I could manage.

'Evidently.' His tone was a mixture of annoyance and relief. He took the can of lager out of my hand, arching a curious eyebrow. 'I just jumped every red light and triggered half a dozen speed cameras getting here – to find you swigging lager on your way to the match!'

'Cal don't—'

'Were they the ones following you? Good job I hadn't called it in – I'd have looked a right . . .'

'Cal, I . . .'

A tightness was spreading across my chest as my heart rate soared, the pressure making it hard to breathe. I could feel the heat trickling down my back and see a pulse throbbing across my vision. Knowing it was the start of a panic attack didn't make it any easier and I knew it was getting to a point where I couldn't stop it.

Not now – not in front of him . . . please not now . . .

I could feel myself swaying unsteadily and dots appeared in front of my eyes. *Shit I'm going to pass out.*

Callum's voice was coming from the end of a long tunnel. 'Jo . . . are you OK?'

I felt his arm around my waist. My legs responded sluggishly as he half walked, half carried me over to his car.

* * *

I sipped from the bottle of water Callum gave me – thankful that I hadn't actually passed out before he'd poured me into the passenger seat of the BMW. My attention focused on a spot on the dashboard, unable to meet those blue eyes that I knew were studying me as I willed my breathing to return to normal.

'Feeling better?'

I nodded slowly. He had his arm across the back of my seat, his other hand resting disconcertingly on my knee as he studied my face. 'Christ, Jo—'

'It's OK,' I said, not able to stand the concern that I knew would just unravel me further. 'I skipped breakfast this morning.' The lie came worryingly easily. 'Then the adrenalin . . . that's all it is.'

I felt his arm slide down the seat to rest across my shoulders. For once, his touch didn't trigger a flight response. I let his arm stay there, enjoying the old familiarity of it.

'This guy – Blondie?' He picked up the account I'd started to give him. 'You'd got to the part where you were on the bridge?'

'He threatened me with a gun.'

'What?'

'He showed me the gun . . . obviously wanted me to let the fans go past.'

'Then what?'

I saw the tightness of his jaw, as he thought through the implications.

'I used the fans as cover . . . got into the middle of them. I knew he couldn't do anything with them around. I just walked off the bridge with them . . .'

'That's it?' His tone implied he knew there was more to it. 'Did he say anything? Did you say anything to him?'

'No . . .' I hesitated, not really understanding what I'd been thinking, or why I reacted the way I did. 'No.' I finished lamely. But he could read me too well.

'Jo . . .?'

'As we walked off the bridge, I turned and . . . smiled at him.'

'What?' He was incredulous. 'Why didn't you just flip him the finger and have done with it! Jesus, Jo – what were you thinking?'

'I *wasn't* thinking! It was a visceral reaction to a bizarre situation.' I was trying to profile my own behaviour – make sense of something that looked foolhardy. 'I was pumped up on adrenalin and I'd just grabbed a lifeline. An automatic response to stress – like a nervous laugh when people hear bad news. It releases tension—'

'Bet it didn't do much to release *his* tension.'

I sipped more water and listened while he radioed in the report of a male, believed to be carrying a firearm in the city. As he relayed a description of Blondie and his direction of travel, I thought about my reaction on the bridge. The account I'd given Callum was plausible enough, but I knew it was more than that.

Lately I'd recognised a coldness creeping through me, like ice crackling across a surface. Freezing everything in its path. Transforming what was once soft and pliable into something brittle – threatening to fracture under the least amount of pressure. Shattering my composure at the most awkward moments and when I least expected it.

I also reluctantly recognised that this same phenomenon was making me more reckless. I'd avoided analysing that aspect too closely. Maybe it was time I did, before one day I paid the ultimate price.

Chapter Nineteen

Callum was driving me back to Fordley police station.

'A firearms officer will want to interview you – find out more about the gun.' He glanced across at me. 'You OK to do that?'

I nodded – still distracted by thoughts of Blondie as we drove.

'Armed Response Vehicles will conduct a sweep of the area.' Callum was saying. 'Hopefully they'll pick him up.'

'I'm not so sure,' I said quietly, sipping water as I looked out of the window. 'I think he's too good for that.'

I felt him look across at me. 'Why?'

'His expression – demeanour. Everything about him screamed "professional". He's not just some thug with a gun.'

'So why is a professional gunman following you?'

'No idea.'

Before he could say more, his phone rang.

'Ferguson.' He answered distractedly.

'DS Ross, Fordley CID. Force control gave us your number as the senior officer on call?'

'Yep – go on.'

'Uniform responded to a call from Argus apartments this morning. The manager was contacted by a concerned neighbour. They found the resident – Jacinta Williams – dead in bed. Looks like she's been strangled. Doctor attended and declared life extinct. Patrol have set up a cordon and local CID are conducting initial door knocks.'

'OK, show me on the log as attending.' He was already making a U-turn before the call ended.

*   *   *

The incident was in a part of town that had undergone 'gentrification'. Old warehouses converted into trendy apartments that commanded eye-watering prices, even though parts of the neighbourhood were still under construction.

The BMW was flagged down on a road, blocked by a police car and two uniformed officers protecting the outer cordon.

Callum twisted in his seat to look at me. 'I can't take you in with me – will you be OK?'

The situation reminded me of times as a kid when I'd be left in the car while my dad nipped into his local pub for a sneaky pint. 'Only if you bring me a bottle of pop and a bag of crisps.'

He stared at me nonplussed for a second before he finally got the joke, grinning at me. 'Well don't play with anything and don't talk to any strange men. I won't be long.'

I watched as he showed the officers his warrant card and signed the log before ducking under the tape. If my experience of these things was anything to go by, I was in for a long wait.

I searched the centre console until I found the phone charger I knew he kept there and plugged my phone in – then opened the window and breathed in the warm air.

A man, chatting to police at the outer cordon turned away, with a look of disappointment – which transformed into a grin as he spotted me in the car. He jogged over.

'Hello, Ron – you here to report the latest?'

The young crime reporter from the *Fordley Express* leaned on the edge of the open window. 'Unfortunately not. I've been frozen out.'

'By the police?'

'For once – no.' He flicked his floppy fringe back out of his eyes. 'Came down to interview the neighbour who tipped them off, but he's been signed up. My editor's well pissed off.'

'Signed up?'

'Yeah – national tabloid. Signed him up to an exclusive, so if he wants the big payout, he can't speak to any other journalists.' He shrugged. 'Guess that's what comes of working on a small paper without a big cheque book, eh?'

He looked at me with the sudden glint in his eye of a hungry predator, spotting a gazelle separated from the herd. 'You working this one then, Jo?'

'Afraid not – just getting a lift home when the call came in.'

'Well, it was worth a try. But if you *do* hear anything . . . ?'

The smile didn't reach my eyes. 'You just know *not* to wait in for my call, right?'

As he walked away, there was a 'beep' as my phone came back to life. A text from Domino asking if I was OK, and one from Heslopp saying he'd managed to get a budget code to actually pay for my consultancy time.

Wonders would never cease.

I replied to Domino, telling her I was fine and that my 'follower' had been a false alarm. No point inviting awkward questions that I had no answers for.

As I sat staring out of the window, feeling the adrenalin starting to drain away, my thoughts turned back to the attack at Fordley train station.

I dialled Jen.

'Where are you?' she asked. 'I called in for a cuppa. Your car was here, but you weren't?'

'Sorry, Jen, I had to take George's Land Rover in for some repairs – I was going to get a cab back.'

'Where's the garage . . . outer Mongolia?'

I glanced at the dashboard clock – it was mid-afternoon. 'Sorry, got a bit . . . distracted.'

'And why on earth are you bothering to fix the Land Rover anyway – we don't use it?'

I swerved the subject. 'I need you to check something for me.'

'Hang on.' I could imagine her pulling a pad across the desk, pen poised at the ready. 'OK.'

'Remember the case a few years ago, when that Transit van ploughed into a group of people at the Fordley Mela?'

'How could I forget? Awful.'

The Mela, held every August, was a festival celebrating South Asian culture, and the year of the attack was etched into the psyche of the people of Fordley. The city had come together in a show of unity – at a time when racial tension could have boiled over into something far worse. The driver of the Transit, an ex-marine veteran called Mark Nichols, had killed a prominent Muslim leader along with several others attending the festival.

'Get everything you can on the incident. You know the drill. Newspaper articles, TV coverage – whatever.'

'Anything specific?'

'Accounts of Nichols' demeanour before and immediately after the event – and anything in the psychological journals.'

Prior to his trial, psychologists had assessed Nichols. There had been few academic articles published after he'd committed suicide, while held on remand in Belmarsh prison. Taking his own life before the trial, had robbed us of the answers, but I was hoping the psych assessments might give me some insight.

'I'll get on it,' Jen said. 'Is Monday OK? Henry will have a fit if I work the weekend.' I smiled as I thought of Jen's long-suffering husband, who was very protective of their family time. 'What time will you be home?'

I thought about the interview I'd have to do at the station later. 'Late probably, I've got things to do.' I wasn't ready to tell her about Blondie just yet.

As I ended that call, the phone rang again.

'Jo? Frank Heslopp.'

'Hi, Frank.' I ran a hand wearily across my eyes, suddenly feeling bone tired. 'What can I do for you?'

'Just wanted to let you know we've got more footage of our station attacker. Including body-cam from PC Yates. There's another briefing scheduled for tomorrow morning, if you're interested?'

'Absolutely.'

'See you at seven then?'

'Oh, and thanks for the getting the budget code – appreciate it.'

I was surprised to hear a smile in his voice as he ended the call with an almost cheerful, 'No problem, doc.'

I was so deep in thought I jumped when the driver's door was yanked open and Callum got in.

'Just heard on the radio – they've got a firearms officer lined up to interview you. I can break off here and take you in?'

'No, it's OK.'

I'd thought about it while he'd been gone. He hadn't asked where my car was – or why I'd been on foot in Fordley. If he was with me during my interview, the subject was bound to come up and I didn't need any awkward questions right now.

'I'll be fine . . .' I saw doubt cross his face. 'Honestly.' I forced a smile and nodded towards the apartment block 'How's it looking in there?'

He leaned back in the driver's seat, flexing his shoulders.

'Like they said, young woman – strangled in bed.' He raked his fingers through his hair. 'No sign of a struggle. Lying on her back like she was sleeping.' He turned to face me. 'Bedding neat, head on the pillow . . . Who just lies there while being strangled?'

'No one,' I conceded. 'If you think I can be of any help, just ask.' I didn't really want to get involved – but it seemed fair, seeing as he'd just come running to my rescue.

'Thanks, I might take you up on that.'

I looked at the building, enclosed by fluttering blue and white police tape and thought about the scene unfolding inside.

'You need to get back in there.' I reached across and squeezed his hand. 'Don't need a chaperone you know.'

He held onto my hand, refusing to let it go. He looked like he was going to say something and then thought better of it – squeezing my hand before putting it gently back onto my knee.

'As long as you're sure you'll be OK?'

I nodded, relieved I'd averted any awkward questions. I already had enough trouble heading my way. I didn't need any more.

Chapter Twenty

Kingsberry Farm – late Saturday night

It was late by the time I'd finished giving my statement at Fordley police station and the officer on reception called me a taxi. I got the driver to drop me at the end of the lane so that I could get some fresh air and clear my head on the short walk up to the farm.

I loved the walk along this secluded lane that only went to my place and the farm a mile further along, which had belonged to my neighbour George. That had been empty since his death, so I'd come to regard this as my own private road.

I breathed in the still-warm air and revelled in the silence wrapping around me like a comforting blanket. No streetlights to pollute the darkness meant a clear view of the full moon and stars dotting the canopy above. An owl hooted somewhere in the trees ahead of me – the sound echoing across the valley as a territorial warning to unwary rivals.

As if in reply, another sound shattered the peace. It took a second to recognise the discordant electronic shriek, as a text alert.

I fished the mobile out of my pocket. The brightly illuminated screen flashed up the message which simply said *Call me now*

It was from my old teacher and the best psychologist I'd ever met, Professor Geoff Perrett – long ago retired and now living in peaceful seclusion just ten miles away from me in the village of Haworth. Not far as the crow flies, but a massive distance in the diversions our lives had taken since I'd last seen him – embarrassingly more than five years previously. But our relationship was one of those that could survive lack of contact. A 'go-to' colleague and friend who could pick up where we'd left off, as if time was a fluid element that refused to fade our affection or erode the bond we'd forged during my time as his pupil.

Although we hadn't seen each other, we had spoken over the phone in those intervening years. When I'd needed to run a theory past him before presenting evidence in court – or at times like this, when I needed to speak to someone I trusted implicitly. I'd messaged him earlier, asking for a chat.

I didn't want to go into the house just yet. The night was warm and I was enjoying the fresh air. I sat on the edge of the dry-stone wall and punched out his number.

'Your message said you weren't sleeping.' He launched straight into it with his usual curmudgeonly directness.

'Night terrors. Promised Callum I'd speak to someone . . .'

'And I drew the short straw?'

I smiled despite myself. 'Something like that.'

'Nightmares are understandable – after events of last year. What else?'

'Does there have to *be* anything else?'

'For you to call? Yes . . .'

I was beginning to wish I hadn't.

'It changed me, Geoff – last autumn.'

'Like I said . . . understandable.'

He let the silence drag out . . . knowing I hated it. Knowing I'd fill it if he left it long enough. Even though I knew the tactic, it still worked. After all, there was a good reason I'd reached out to the one person who understood my psyche.

'There's a darkness inside me. I don't . . . I can't . . .' I cursed under my breath, hating being on the other side of this figurative couch.

The silence weighed heavily down the phone as he waited.

I stared up at the moon. 'It scares me.' An admission I would never make to anyone else. Maybe not even to him if he'd been there in person. But somehow, sitting out here in the darkness made it feel safely remote. Like the Catholic confessional box of my childhood.

'You know what this is, Jo . . .' I could hear him shifting and imagined him sitting in his over-stuffed armchair. 'We talked about it back then, when you were my student. That darkness was there then . . . has *always* been there.'

'It's worse now. Dealing with these people . . . these crimes . . .' I tailed off, not knowing how to describe the spectre that had become my constant dark companion.'

'It's what makes you good at what you do,' he was saying. 'Gives you the edge. Take it away and you'd be diminished'

'I don't want to be able to see what "they" see . . . think like "they" do . . .'

'A curse or a gift,' he said quietly. 'Your choice.'

I watched the ghostly silhouette of the owl, gliding silently across the moonlit sky. 'A curse,' I said softly.

'Their minds are wired to inflict pain. You're using yours to make a difference, Jo. They can't hide from you. You see them and you use that to balance the scales. But there's a price – you know that.'

'What if I don't want to pay it anymore?'

'No choice.' I could almost hear him shrug. 'It is what it is. You're stuck with it, kid. The only choice you can make is what to use it for . . . light or dark. Hunter or hunted.'

'What if it takes me over?'

'That's what *really* frightens you, isn't it? That you'll lose yourself to it.'

Perceptive as ever.

'Maybe.' Even as I said it, I knew he was right.

'You won't let it. You're too strong.'

'Don't feel it these days.'

'Even on your worst days – you're made of girders. Besides, there's too many black hats already. We need you out there.'

I took a long breath. 'We need to sit down. Talk about it properly, when we have more time.'

'OK . . .'

'I've got something I need to run past you anyway . . . I'll know more when I get my head straight.'

'You know where I am.'

* * *

As I walked into the house, Harvey stretched and uncurled his huge body from his bed by the Aga.

'Hello, fella.' I rubbed his velvety ears and he pressed his wet nose against mine in a nuzzling kiss.

Opening the porch door, I let him out – listening as his paws crunched across the gravel before crashing through the hedge to startle whatever wildlife was careless enough to be there.

Filling the kettle was automatic – but even as I did it, I knew I didn't want tea. Instead, I reached for the bottle of brandy on the shelf.

Leaning against the open porch door, I sipped the warm liquid, enjoying the feeling as the heat of it coiled its way into my stomach and thought back over the events of what felt like an endless day.

The silence was shattered as my mobile shrilled – caller ID said 'Private Number'.

'McCready,' I answered cautiously.

'You OK, doc?'

'Paul?' The East London accent finally registered.

'Please, doc – it's Edge. Only my mother and the Magistrate call me Paul.'

I couldn't help smiling. 'Sorry. You came through as an anonymous number.'

'I'm using a burner phone – you should do the same whenever you call me – just to be on the safe side.'

I let that thought percolate. Burner phones were the province of criminals who didn't want their communications easily traced – and the stark realisation I was entering that world made me uneasy.

'I'll think about it. How's it going over there?'

He expelled his breath in a loud sigh. 'As we expected. Word on the street is Neville Blackstone's already got people out looking for Nique. There's been a couple of jokers hanging about the apartment building.' I heard him taking a drink of something. Knowing his preferences, it was probably an aged malt whisky. 'As surveillance goes, they were pretty amateur. Took me all of five minutes to spot them.'

133

Edge had moved into Nique's penthouse when she'd gone to prison, ostensibly to keep an eye on the place. A strategy that was paying off now that she was out, and we had the expected, but no less frustrating, complication of Blackstone's threats to deal with.

'Did everything go as planned?' I took another sip of brandy – wishing I'd made it a large one.

'Yep. Picked her up from Styal and came back here. Parked the Merc in the underground car park. I clocked one of Blackstone's goons then – made sure he saw us leaving the car and walking through the door to the lifts.'

Harvey appeared, walking more slowly now he'd run off some energy. I patted him distractedly, watching the darkness thickening over the trees.

Nique's penthouse was in a development that had once been a Victorian factory, with a warehouse next door. Both buildings shared a basement car park, with lifts to the apartments in a communal corridor. Once they'd gone out of sight, it was easy enough to walk down the corridor and into the basement floor of the sister building.

'So, you got her out OK?'

'Yeah. Sweet as a nut. One of the boys met us in the corridor and went up to the apartment with our bags – made a show of putting lights on – pulling blinds – just so they believed we'd gone straight up there, while me and Nique went next door and picked up your Land Rover. She wasn't impressed at having to lie under a smelly dog blanket in the back though.' He chuckled as he recalled it. 'She was cursing, all the way into Fordley.'

'I can imagine.' I grinned into the darkness. 'Did George's kit fit you OK?'

'Flat cap was no problem.' He laughed. 'Jacket was a bit tight across the shoulders – but it did the job.'

'Does Nique have everything she needs at my office?'

My therapy practice wasn't a stylishly appointed apartment – but it probably beat a shared cell in Styal prison.

'Your sofa is bigger than the bed she had in the nick and more comfortable – she's not complaining.'

I took another sip of brandy – realising it'd gone down far too easily. 'Blackstone's men today ... was one of them a big guy, blond, mid-thirties, by any chance?'

'No . . .' A note of caution crept into his voice. 'Why?'

'I was followed today by Blondie.' I hesitated, debating whether to tell him the rest, but then, I reasoned he'd need to know. 'He pulled a gun on me.'

His breath exploded down the phone. 'What? Bastard! What happened?'

Shrugging away from the door frame, I walked back into the kitchen and reached for the brandy – pouring a bigger measure this time.

'I managed to lose myself in a crowd. Got the impression he was a professional, Edge.'

'Should've called me.' There was more than a little venom in his tone.

'I can only imagine how *that* would have played out . . .'

'Don't know what you mean, princess . . .' I could hear his grin.

'The last thing we need is to draw attention to ourselves. Shock and awe on the streets of Fordley would hardly have helped, now, would it?'

'You're such a spoilsport.' I could picture the expression of mock innocence on his weather-beaten face. 'Where did you pick up your tail?'

'Not sure. Got tipped off about him when I was in Little Italy.'

'Has to be Blackstone looking for Nique – unless you're involved with anyone else who hires hitmen?'

'If he was watching Nique's apartment, he might have seen me after I put the Defender in the car park of the building next door.'

'Hmm. Anyway, Nique's safely tucked up for the night,' he was saying. 'So, let's see how it goes for the next day or so. Sleep tight, princess – oh and by the way . . .'

'What?'

'Anymore sightings of Blondie, you call me straight away, OK?'

'OK,' I promised – knowing that would be a very dangerous thing to do – very dangerous indeed.

Chapter Twenty-One

Fordley police station – Sunday morning

DI Frank Heslopp stood at the front of the room surveying the sea of faces. I'd slipped in at the back, sitting on the end of a row. My eyes felt gritty and a headache was beginning to nag.

Last night's brandy might have helped me sleep – and lately had proved effective at warding off the night terrors – but wasn't so helpful when I had to get up at stupid o'clock to make it in for a 7 a.m. briefing.

'Morning, everyone.' Heslopp launched straight into it. 'Sorry for the early Sunday morning, but think of the over-time!' There was a ripple of laughter around the room. 'You've all been involved with the station attack, so you're up to speed.' He glanced to where I was perched on my seat. 'Apart from Jo, who's joining us for today's updates.' He half smiled at me – I tried to reciprocate but in my sluggish state I wasn't sure I managed it.

He indicated the board which already had stills from the CCTV footage pinned to it.

'We'd have preferred releasing this in our own time, but social media beat us to it.' He tapped his finger on a close-up of the attacker's face. 'Fortunately for us, it resulted in an early ID of our suspect.'

I flicked through the folder I'd been handed and looked at the photograph. Intense brown eyes stared back at me as

I considered him. He looked like any other attractive, fair-haired man in his early thirties. Most women would probably have given him a second glance – if they didn't know he'd just attempted a vicious knife attack.

That was the thing about violent offenders. If you met them in a bar or waiting for a bus – you'd never know what lurked beneath the surface or what they might be capable of. We took people at face value – trusting that all-powerful first impression.

But I knew from experience that the most dangerous – the psychopaths who walked among us – could project an almost foolproof initial impression. Reflecting back to us with practised ease those qualities they instinctively knew we liked, or respected, or trusted. Reading their prey like the most proficient predators they were.

The truth is, we never really know anything for certain about the people we meet. Apart from the story they told about themselves. I shuddered as I thought about how terrifyingly deadly some chance encounters could be.

Heslopp was directing his comments towards me. 'Several people called the incident room – all giving the same name. Josh Stamford. Thirty-six years old. Ex-army. Served tours in Iraq from 2005 to 2008. Discharged with PTSD. Once in Civvy Street, he ended up sleeping rough. Got into a fight in a kebab shop in 2015. Seriously assaulted another customer. He got six months custodial in Armley prison.'

'Anything since then?' I asked.

'No. On release his offender manager got him a place at a Sangar residential unit. He was there for twelve months and they managed to get him onto an apprenticeship. Then a job as a brickie with Tillie Construction in Leeds. Been with them ever since.'

Sangar, named after temporary military fortifications, was a charitable foundation set up to help ex-service personnel suffering with mental health issues who had also served time in prison. The organisation had a unique programme of signposting service users to vocational courses and getting them jobs in industry and construction. I'd read about their cutting-edge treatments for post-traumatic stress disorder.

'We've put out appeals,' Heslopp continued. 'But so far, no reported sightings – so our man is in the wind.' He turned back to the photos on the board. 'Press officer is arranging a news conference for us tomorrow morning.' He looked at a young officer on the front row. 'Raf, any more from his employer?'

DC Rafiq Sabir glanced at his notes. 'Lads he worked with all say the same thing, boss. Friendly enough but no one felt they really knew him. Kept to himself. Didn't socialise much out of work – just went on site, did his job and left.'

'Mike' – Heslopp turned to his DS – 'anything on antecedents?'

Hanson shook his head, chewing the end of his biro. 'Not much to go on, boss. Stamford has no living family – no girlfriend in the last couple of years. Like Raf says, bit of a loner.'

'What about his regiment?' I asked no one in particular as I studied his military record. 'Lot of ex-service personnel stay in touch with mates from the old days.'

'We're on it.' Hanson twisted in his chair to look over at me. 'They're scattered to the four corners though – so not easy to track down.'

'Stamford's got to be sleeping somewhere, eating some-where,' Heslopp said, tapping the board. 'Sofa surfing with a mate – or even sleeping rough – he's done that before, so he might go back to the anonymity of the streets to lay low. We'll be putting his picture out at the press conference tomorrow and boots on the ground will be showing his picture at hostels, homeless charities – the usual drill.'

'Any affiliations with far-right groups?' I asked. This was being treated as racially motivated but I couldn't see anything on his file that would point to it.

'His computer was seized but doesn't look like he accessed far-right websites or researched anything along those lines, and the people he worked with say he never expressed any racist ideology,' Raf said.

Heslopp indicated a young female DC on the front row. 'Kerry's been pulling together all the footage and putting it into chronological order.'

Kerry turned on the TV. 'OK,' she said as the picture flick-ered into life. 'We collected footage from the concourse outside the station . . .'

Stamford's figure was indicated by a red arrow, marking him out among other pedestrians. 'He enters the ticket hall.' Kerry ran the commentary. 'Everything's normal – until *this* happens.'

Chapter Twenty-Two

Stamford was standing in the queue – two young school girls carrying violin cases were behind him, chatting and laughing. It looked like a normal early-morning scene.

Then Stamford started fishing for something in his jacket pocket. We watched as he produced a mobile, and simply stared at it.

'Why doesn't he answer?' Heslopp asked, distractedly hitching his pants up over his bulging stomach.

Kerry consulted her notes. 'The girls in the queue said the ringtone was a piece of classical music – "Ride of the Valkyries" by Wagner, to be precise. It was loud and went on for a bit. He didn't answer the call . . . just let it ring. Then this . . .'

He suddenly stepped out of the line, paused for a second, staring straight ahead, and then took a run at the barriers. Clearing them in one leap.

The footage cut as we followed his progress onto the platform. Kerry had edited the film, splicing the action so that it worked chronologically. The next shots were from the BTP officer's body camera, as he went onto the concourse.

The footage bobbed around as PC Yates pushed through the crowd, finally making it to the front. The crush opened up to create a surreal arena with the two combatants facing each other.

We all shared Yates's view, looking down his outstretched arms to the Taser held in both hands. The red dot of his aim clearly marking the centre of Stamford's chest. His shouted command – to stand still and drop the knife – interrupted as a member of the public ran in front of the officer to help Abassi who'd been kicked down onto the tracks.

I concentrated on Stamford's face. Completely devoid of emotion, as he moved with the practised grace of a professional fighter – swinging the kick that took the Taser out of the officer's grip.

Just before Yates grappled with him, there was a brief glimpse of the knife in Stamford's hand before he dropped it. Both men closed the gap, coming chest-to-chest for a second – obscuring the camera.

Then we saw from Yates's view down on the ground a close-up of his attacker's face as Stamford delivered the final blow. There was a collective groan around the room as the sickening crack of the officer's jaw was picked up on the recording.

The next shots were of Stamford running back into the ticket hall and out into the street where he slowed down to a brisk walk.

'That's the last sighting of him.' Kerry flicked off the film.

I chewed my pencil and thought about what we'd just seen. 'Any chance I could have a copy of that?'

'No problem.' Kerry beamed me a smile and made a note.

Stamford was muttering something as he headed for Abassi – I turned to Heslopp.

'Any idea what Stamford was saying as he made his way through the crowd?'

'Witnesses said it sounded like "Vanger", or "Vager".'

I looked back at the now empty screen.

'Wagner,' I said under my breath.

Chapter Twenty-Three

After Heslopp's briefing, I wanted to get back to the office and do some research. Something about Stamford's demeanour was bothering me, but I needed to check my facts before saying anything to the team.

My concentration was shattered as the mobile rang.

'Jo?' Callum's voice crackled over the speakers. 'Where are you?'

'Driving back to Kingsberry – why?'

'Remember you said you'd take a look at the scene from Argus apartments if I needed you to?' He exhaled down the phone and I could imagine him raking fingers through his hair. 'Well, I need you to.'

'Want me to come back to the station?'

'No . . .' He paused – enough for me to know there was something he wasn't saying. 'Better if you meet me at the apartment. If that's OK?'

A thousand reasons why it might *not* be OK tumbled through my mind and he either sensed my hesitation or realised what my concerns would be. He immediately took hold of my silence.

'The body's been removed.'

I exhaled slowly. 'I can be there in . . .' I glanced at the dashboard clock. 'Twenty minutes?'

'Great. Park by the outer cordon – I'll tell them to expect you.'

* * *

As I parked my car on the roadside, I half expected the street to look different to the day before. It didn't. But somehow, I felt it should. That the horrific act of murder should leave an indelible and visible mark on a place in the same way it marked those individuals touched by it.

Family, friends, the loved ones left behind who had to pick up the pieces of a life cut short. Of events that wouldn't happen for the one they had lost – birthdays, Christmases. Family milestones that would never be shared and celebrated and the anniversaries that would torment and haunt the people left to get on with their lives with a huge piece missing.

Callum walked over to the blue and white tape – his figure unmistakeable to me, even though he was wearing the anonymising white scene suit, the hood covering his silver hair and the mask over his face – until he pulled it down, leaving it dangling round his neck.

'Thanks for coming over on a Sunday morning, Jo.'

'No problem,' I said distractedly as I signed the scene log and took the protective suit offered to me.

Callum leaned against the side of a SOCO van and watched as I pulled on the suit, overshoes and latex gloves.

He led me through the outer cordon and up the stone steps. The glass doors to the entrance hall had been propped open to facilitate the comings and goings of scenes of crime officers and their equipment.

We walked down a short corridor, careful to only walk on the metal stepping plates that had been laid out by SOCO to establish a 'common approach path' into and out of the protected crime scene.

Another officer guarded the door to the apartment, which was surprisingly hushed given the amount of activity that inevitably surrounded a sudden death.

Eventually we were alone in what was once the victim's bedroom. For most people a tranquil and safe space – but for this girl, the scene of a terrifying end to her life.

Callum distractedly handed me a photo of the corpse, lying as she had been found, in bed, with the covers pulled up neatly across her chest.

'It bothers me,' he said. 'The way she was found.'

I looked at the picture of a woman of mixed race, who had undoubtedly been stunningly beautiful in life, but whose face had been contorted during a brutal strangulation. Her glassy eyes stared unseeingly at the ceiling – her tongue, discoloured and swollen, protruded grotesquely between her teeth. The harsh line of a ligature around her neck could be seen just above the bed covers.

'When the pathologist turned her over, the ligature was tied at the back of her neck and there were bruises along her spine, the back of her thighs and calves, so looks like she was strangled while face down on the bed . . .'

'And then turned onto her back and "arranged" like this?'

He nodded. 'She would have put up a struggle. The bedding would have been messed up – but the killer's gone to the trouble of straightening the bed, pulling the covers neatly over her.' I sensed him looking at me. 'Talk to me, Jo. What do *you* see when you look at this?'

'Any other physical evidence?'

He shook his head. 'I'm waiting for Tom to come back to me with the results from the post-mortem.'

Tom Llewellyn was the Home Office Pathologist. He was a nice guy and I liked him – but more importantly he was thorough. If he was handling the case, it was in good hands.

He followed my gaze. 'Obviously they moved the body – with the ligature. Tom wanted to untie that during the post-mortem to preserve any evidence on it.' He flicked through the photographs in his hand. 'The clothes she'd been wearing that night have been taken in for testing, but they photographed them first. You can see from these, everything else is in exactly the same place.'

'She was naked in bed though?'

He nodded. 'Looks like she was undressed and on or in the bed when the attack took place.'

The room was stylish – opulent even – with exclusive upholstered furniture and cushions in muted greys and silvers. There was a large chair in one corner. I looked at the crime scene photo. It showed her clothes – presumably those she'd taken off – neatly folded on the seat. A pair of designer shoes with impossibly high heels were side by side beneath the chair next to a Gucci handbag. A diamond bracelet and matching earrings were on the bedside table.

'Expensive taste, our victim,' I said. 'What did she do for a living?'

He was standing so close; I could feel the warmth of his body and smell the scent of his cologne. But for the first time in a long time, I didn't feel the need to move away.

'Pole dancer at a club in Fordley.'

I looked up at him, raising a sceptical eyebrow. 'Really? Who knew there was *that* much money to be made as a pole dancer?'

'There isn't,' he conceded. 'It's not your low-rent type of place. Private gentlemen's club, high-end, exclusive. Members only.'

'Even so . . . this is quite a lifestyle.'

There was that slight hesitation again. I gave him the silence, waiting for him to finally tell me the piece I knew instinctively he was holding back. His expression was giving nothing away. 'She had a sugar daddy who picked up the tab,' he said simply. Then sensing I was waiting for more, added, 'I'll tell you more about him later. For now, I need to know what *you* see here?'

There was a cabinet against the wall opposite the bed. The top drawer was open and various items of underwear dripped over the edge – some lay scattered on the floor – as if they'd been pulled out and discarded as someone rummaged through.

I went over to the drawer and studied it. I felt Callum at my shoulder. 'The ligature used to strangle her was a silk stocking from the drawer.' His soft Scottish accent was barely discernible.

I turned and looked around the room again – trying to picture it as the killer had seen it. 'Any idea on time of death?'

'She was seen by a neighbour when she returned to the flat around midnight on Friday. Said he heard a row going on between midnight and half past. Heard a woman's raised voice – so we can assume she was still alive until about twelve-thirty. Pathologist's initial estimate is between midnight and 4 a.m. on Saturday morning.'

I slowly began to 'walk the scene' – tracing our steps out of the bedroom to the short, carpeted corridor that led into the lounge. The apartment's external door led directly into here.

I stood with my back to the door and surveyed the room.

Callum leaned against the wall facing me – the eyes above his mask were all I could see, but the body language leaked his impatience.

'Witness said she entered the building with her boyfriend – so we assume they walked in here together,' he said.

Callum's fast pace was legendary and when we'd first begun working together, he did little to hide his frustration when I wouldn't give him the quick answers he needed. But over time, he'd begun to value my way of working, appreciating that it got the results we both wanted. Besides, he knew it was pointless to push.

I took a few steps forward and stopped. Taking in the room through all my senses.

The killer had been here – seen it, smelled it, felt the things I was feeling now. I needed to get inside his head – to think like he did – feel what he did that night.

The coffee table had been shoved out of line, away from the sofa, dents in the thick carpet marking its original location. I walked around it and stood with my back to the sofa.

On the door into the corridor that led to the bedroom, there was a yellow evidence marker. 'What's that?'

Callum shrugged away from the wall and went over to the door. 'SOCO think it might be a blood spot on a handprint. Size of the print would suggest its Jacinta's.'

'OK,' I said finally, taking a long, slow breath. 'I think I've seen enough. Now do you want to tell me what *you've* got?'

Chapter Twenty-Four

'The neighbour heard a car pull up. The couple were arguing in the street, so he looked out of the window. He gave us a description of the car and a partial number plate.'

'Observant.'

'It was obvious that he didn't approve of Jacinta's lifestyle – he'd reported disturbances before when she'd had parties.'

'And he saw them walk into the building together?'

He nodded. 'The row carried on. He heard some of it. Apparently, she was screaming at the boyfriend, so it wasn't difficult. Then after about half an hour it went quiet and he saw the boyfriend leave. He said he thought he heard a noise coming from the apartment just as he was about to turn in – an hour later – so he came down and knocked on the door to see if she was OK. But there was no answer, so he went back to bed.'

'I take it you've traced the boyfriend?'

He was about to answer when his mobile rang. It was a different ringtone to his usual one. 'Hang on a minute, this is Tom,' he said before he'd even reached his phone. 'Hopefully he'll have something from the post-mortem.'

As he took the call he walked out of the flat. I took a last look around the room and followed him, half listening as the conversation drifted back to me from down the hall.

'That's useful.' He was saying. 'OK, thanks Tom. Let me know when you get the rest.'

Out in the street, we both leaned against the SOCO van, peeling off our protective clothing. 'So, you have Saint-Saëns' "Danse Macabre" as Tom's ringtone?' I grinned at him as I slipped off the overshoes.

'Lets me know who's calling before I answer – comes in handy sometimes. Besides' – he grinned – 'it's appropriate for what he does, don't you think?' He peeled off his gloves. 'He's sent the ligature off for further tests. The handprint on the door matches Jacinta's but the blood spot isn't hers. She had skin and blood under her fingernails. Hopefully those will be a match for our killer.'

'As you say, she put up a fight.'

He straightened up to watch me. 'What do you think, Jo?'

We were walking towards his car which was parked opposite mine. I hesitated. 'You know I don't like reading a scene on-the-fly like this, Cal. Better if I take some time to think about it.'

'Fancy a coffee while you're thinking?'

I smiled. 'No. But tea would be great. By the way – what ringtone do you have for me then?'

He grinned across at me as we climbed into his car. 'What makes you think I have one for you?'

I arched an eyebrow at him. 'Answering a question with a question, Chief Inspector, is classic evasion ... so that means you do.'

He shrugged and pulled away from the kerb. As he drove, I pulled my phone out and dialled him. A track I knew well began to play. 'Trouble' – by Elvis.

I shot him a look. '"Trouble" . . . *really*?'

* * *

Five minutes later, we were sitting in a quiet corner of a Costa.

He'd asked again for my first thoughts and I'd hesitated a second time – uncomfortable at having to speculate.

His tone was coaxing. 'But you'll have an initial impression, right?'

I took a sip of scalding tea, wishing it had been made in a teapot. 'Well, it looks pretty cut and dried I suppose – that she rowed with her boyfriend and he killed her.'

'I sense a "but" coming . . .'

'I'm not saying he didn't,' I hedged. 'But when I analyse the behaviours that fit the scene, the sequence of events is a bit odd – you'd have to clarify it when you interview him – but a few things jar.'

'Such as?'

'When she walks into the apartment with the boyfriend, they're already in the middle of a heated row and the lounge is the first room they come to.'

'OK.' He sipped his coffee, watching me over the rim of his cup.

'They argue and it gets physical – that's when the coffee table gets pushed away in the struggle. She had skin and blood under her fingernails. So, the row escalates and she lashes out at him. She catches him with her nails – then she heads for the bedroom and leaves a handprint on the door panel when she pushes it open.'

151

I paused to let him contribute, but he just carried on watching me. He really didn't want to give me anything and I couldn't shake the feeling that it was because there was a piece of this jigsaw he was deliberately holding back.

'She's drawn blood – so the fight's already physically violent. I don't think she would walk into the bedroom, take off her jewellery, calmly undress . . . folding her clothes on the bedroom chair and lie down on the bed?' I raised my eyebrows at the unlikelihood of it. 'Presumably with the argument still raging, he then walks over to the cabinet, pulls out a silk stocking, goes over to the bed and strangles her?'

He considered for a minute. 'Not likely – I agree. What if, while she's getting undressed, he gets the stocking from the drawer, starts to strangle her from behind? Forces her face down onto the bed and finishes the job there?'

'That's more likely – but it still doesn't explain the bizarre behaviour of her getting undressed in the middle of a violent row, does it?'

'He could have torn the clothes off her – then *he* could have folded them and put them on the chair after she was dead.'

'Possibly. Check to see whether any of the clothes were torn? Or forcibly removed in a struggle – they'd leave marks on her body.'

'I'll check with Tom.'

I blew the surface of the hot tea, enjoying the warmth on my face.

'You asked why he would put her into bed and tidy up.'

'Yes. It bothers me.'

'Killer's remorse,' I said simply. 'It indicates a level of care. Not a brutal attack by a stranger – or a blitz attack against

152

someone he hates. Once the rage passes, he wants to care for her.'

'So that would fit with the boyfriend then?'

'That depends on *his* character. On what type of person he is? Whether he would feel remorse. You'd need to establish the nature of their relationship – get their history as a couple. I can help you assess that once you have him. Which goes back to my original question – do you know who he is?'

He nodded slowly – looking into his empty cup rather than at me.

'Have you got him?'

'Oh, we've got him.'

'So? What do you know about him?'

'Everything.'

I couldn't shake the feeling something bad was coming.

'Who is he?'

'Sir Neville Blackstone.'

Chapter Twenty-Five

Kingsberry Farm – Monday morning

I was sitting in my office with my chair facing the window but wasn't seeing the view. I was too preoccupied thinking about Callum's little bombshell.

Sir Neville Blackstone!

Knighted by the Queen. Respected businessman and philanthropist – father of the deceased Oliver Blackstone – and now, taken in for questioning over the suspected murder of his mistress.

This hand grenade exploded so many dangerous questions, the deadly shrapnel from which had implications I was struggling to calculate.

Jacinta Williams was murdered in the early hours of Saturday morning. The same day Nique was released from prison. The same day that I'd been followed by a gunman presumably employed by Blackstone.

How the hell did all this fit together?

My thoughts were interrupted when the office phone rang. I answered distractedly and was pulled back to the present by Callum's voice.

'Just wanted to give you an update on Blackstone.'

'He's in custody, right?'

'Err, not exactly.'

'What do you *mean* – not exactly?'

'He didn't make any bones about the fact that he was with Jacinta that night – or that they'd argued. He had scratch marks on his neck and when questioned about it, he admitted she'd clawed him during the row and when he couldn't calm her down, he said he left . . .'

I was stunned. 'And you just accepted that?'

'No, of course we didn't.' He was trying hard to hold onto his patience. 'When he was brought in for questioning, his hot-shot lawyer was already at the station . . .'

'Obviously.'

'He gave us a pre-prepared statement. Blackstone, predictably remained "no comment".' There was a pause as he took a drink I presumed was his usual treacle-thick coffee. 'He's cooperated fully, Jo. Giving DNA samples, surrendering the clothing he was wearing that night . . .'

'But you *are* going to arrest him – right?'

'For what? It doesn't meet the charging threshold . . .'

'Even if the skin and blood under Jacinta's fingernails turn out to be his?' I couldn't hide my exasperation. 'The time of death matches him being there – he admits they argued – he's got claw marks on his neck – what more do you need, Cal?'

'Well, a written confession would be nice, but I'm not holding my breath.' He gentled his tone to soften the blow. 'Look, I'm as frustrated as you are. There's nothing I'd like more than to lock him up – but there's no point running the clock down prematurely. I could only hold him for twenty-four hours before I'd have to charge him or let him go. His story fits the evidence. He's cooperating with the police and he says she was alive when he left her and until we've got more, there's nothing to hold him on.'

'So, what now?'

'Still waiting for DNA evidence from the ligature. We've checked ANPR from the area. It shows Blackstone's car in the vicinity at the right time. Unfortunately, the street doesn't have CCTV. Nor does the building. But what we've got matches the times given by the neighbour and Blackstone himself . . . oh and his driver . . .'

'He has a driver?' Even as I said it, it was obvious he would have.

'Yeah – a guy called Myles Lawson. Word is, he's Blackstone's protégé. Actually, went to school with Blackstone's son, Oliver – played rugby together – were thick as thieves. Lawson went to work for Blackstone once he graduated university and after Oliver's death stepped into his shoes as the father's right-hand man.'

'Sounds like he'd alibi him anyway.' Lawson's name rang a bell, but I couldn't place it. 'Wouldn't exactly call him an impartial witness.'

'No,' Callum agreed. 'But he *was* with him that night. Waited outside by the car while Blackstone took Jacinta inside. Apparently, they'd gone to a restaurant for dinner – we've checked that out. But Jacinta was drunk and in a bad mood, so Lawson drove them back. Blackstone wasn't planning on staying the night – just long enough to see her inside. One thing *does* bother me though . . .'

'Just one?' I didn't try to hide the sarcasm.

'Blackstone's phone.'

'What about it?'

'He told us Jacinta was alive when he left her, so we checked to see if she contacted him after he left – but there was nothing. Let's face it, if they'd argued like that and he'd walked out, what normal woman wouldn't have been ringing him or sending vitriolic texts?'

'I wouldn't . . .'

'You're not a normal woman.'

'Thanks.'

'Anyway, he's put it down to the fact that she was too drunk. Said she probably just went to bed after he left.'

'OK, back to the driver – Lawson. Does he say anything about Blackstone's state of mind when he returned to the car?'

'Says he seemed annoyed that she'd scratched him, but nothing to indicate he'd just killed his mistress. Would Blackstone have committed a murder, with Lawson waiting outside?'

I shrugged. 'If it wasn't premeditated, would it make a difference? Depends on what kind of a character Blackstone is, how calculating he is . . .'

'Which brings me to my next question . . .'

'Which is?'

'Before you knew who the boyfriend was, you said the way the body was left, could indicate killer's remorse. That you'd know more if you could analyse what type of character he was. Now you know it's Blackstone . . . ?' He left the question dangling.

'I know the way he's portrayed in the popular press . . .'

'Which is a misogynistic, arrogant, ruthless bastard.'

'That's on a good day . . .' I couldn't help smiling, despite the subject matter.

'And I know that given his threats against your "friend" Nique, you'd love to see him go down for this . . .'

'True.'

'Do you think you could appraise him impartially?'

'Yes – if I got the chance.'

'You have. His solicitor's been in touch. Blackstone wants a private meeting with you in his office.'

'What?' The implications of that were stunning.

'Apparently he rates you. His legal team were impressed by your evidence at Nique's trial, even though you *did* get her sentence commuted to manslaughter.'

'Then why do I smell a rat?'

'Oh, I don't know.' I could hear the scepticism in his voice. 'Perhaps because Nique is out on parole. Maybe that's why he wants to see you?'

'Maybe. But she refused a bail hostel. If Blackstone wants to find her, he could. Why would he need to see me?'

He paused for just a second and I wondered in that moment if he knew Nique wasn't at her apartment.

I steeled myself to lie to him, but he simply said, 'His brief says he's adamant he didn't kill her and he wants you to talk to him. To see him as a behavioural analyst and give a report to us via his legal team. Suits me if you want to do it?'

'Not an official psych assessment?'

'No – nothing so formal.'

'OK,' I said cautiously.

'Great. Tuesday afternoon, at his office in Leeds. I'll send you the details.'

Given that I believed Blackstone had hired a gunman to follow me and that he would have Nique killed if he got the chance, walking into the lion's den felt like an insane thing to do.

But I knew I'd do it anyway.

Chapter Twenty-Six

Kingsberry farm – later Monday morning

'Alex! It's so good to hear your voice.'

He laughed down the phone. 'Blimey – I've not been gone *that* long.'

I suddenly felt the prickle of unexpected tears and blinked them back. 'I know, but I got used to having you around over Christmas.' I stared out at the bright blue sky above the treeline, revelling in the sound of him. 'The house doesn't feel the same without you.' Harvey lifted his head from his paws and started to stretch up from his place on the rug. 'The boy misses you, too.' I laughed as Harvey planted his front paws on my knees and strained his nose towards the phone.

'Hi boy!' Alex teased him from two-hundred and fifty miles away.

'How's the job going?' I asked as I heaved five stone of solid boxer off my lap. 'Have you met "Q" and got your Aston Martin and exploding pen?'

'I keep telling you, Mum, I'm just a junior analyst – no big deal.' He laughed. 'Maybe the gadgets and beautiful girls come later, when I've passed my probationary period.'

The sense of pride I'd felt when he'd begun working for the UK's Internal Security Services had jostled with an overwhelming relief that he'd decided to take that route – rather than following his father's footsteps to operate at the more brutal end of counterterrorism.

'I'd ask what you're working on – but if you told me, you'd have to kill me, right?'

He laughed. 'Something like that. Right now, I'm on training courses. When they're finished, I've got a week's leave to take. Thought I'd come back then? I'll send you the dates.'

'Can't wait.'

'Anyway, just wanted to call and make sure you're OK … and staying out of trouble?'

I stared out of the window as I considered answering that question honestly – then decided against it.

'Of course. I've got Jen watching me like a hawk.'

'And Callum I'll bet. How's he doing?'

'He's fine.' Why did my innards tighten when I thought about Callum? Regret? Longing? I couldn't afford to analyse my feelings right now and pushed them away.

I stared at the phone for a while after the call ended. Harvey suddenly looked up from his place on the rug and growled softly, then left the office to trot down the corridor to the kitchen. A second later I heard the commotion as Jen arrived.

Five minutes later, she appeared with two mugs of tea and a bundle of papers under her arm.

'That dog should be listed as an official trip hazard,' she said good-naturedly, putting a mug down on the corner of my desk and giving me a peck on the cheek. 'Good weekend?'

I debated what I should tell her, finally stretching back in my chair to ease my knotted shoulders. 'Well, it was eventful.'

She raised a curious eyebrow as she opened the post – my cue to tell her about seeing the CCTV footage from the train station and about the Jacinta Williams murder. She was incredulous when I told her about Blackstone's request for a meeting.

'You're going to do it?' She regarded me with those insightful grey eyes.

'Why not?' I shrugged.

'I can think of a million reasons why not.'

I hadn't mentioned Nique's release over the weekend, but she was too sharp to miss the connection.

'De Benoit's out on parole – you don't think that's why Blackstone wants to see you?'

'I think he's got more to worry about than Nique right now, don't you?'

'Still . . . What does he have to gain by meeting you?'

I took a sip of tea. 'People like Blackstone think they're above the law. Their wealth and privilege give them a sense of entitlement, that they can throw money at a problem and make it go away. Pay off witnesses, make evidence disappear – bribe officials, or even the police. He's used to people doing what he tells them to do.'

'Doesn't know *you* very well then, does he?'

'Probably arrogant enough to think that all he has to do is tell me he didn't do it, then order me to run along and tell the police the same.' I smiled at the next thought. 'You never know, he might even try throwing money *my* way to pay for a psych assessment he can use to strengthen a case for his defence, if it ever gets to court.'

'That's another reason I'm worried about you going.' Jen's frown deepened. 'You helped his son's murderer; he's hardly your biggest fan, is he?'

'No,' I agreed. 'But I'm curious to see what he does.'

'What is it with you?' she said, exasperated. 'Best way to get you to do anything is tell you not to. Or worse, warn you it's dangerous.'

I laughed at the look on her face. 'You know what they say, Jen. If you're not living on the edge, you're taking up too much room.'

'Remind me to buy a shark dive for your next birthday.'

I was glad I hadn't told her about Blondie. I knew she'd draw the same conclusion as Edge – that the two events were connected and I didn't need the grief right now.

'So, Callum's first murder case is Neville Blackstone's mistress?' She couldn't keep the salacious tone out of her voice. 'Love to be a fly on the wall when his wife finds out. The tabloids will be salivating.'

I thought about the journalist from the *Fordley Express*. Interestingly there hadn't been anything in the media about the murder.

Jen finally turned her attention to her notes. 'Anyway, back to business. I researched the Mela attack.' She peered at me over the top of her reading glasses.

'Thought you weren't working weekends?'

'I wasn't.' She scratched her head with the end of her pencil. 'But Henry went to watch bowling in the park, so I took the chance to do something less geriatric.'

'Careful, Jen,' I laughed. 'Don't let Mamma hear you say that – the girls at her bowling club will have your guts.'

She was already lost in her notes. 'I dragged up everything I could find on Mark Nichols, the ex-marine who carried out the attack – including the assessments done on him while he was on remand. I've emailed the file over.'

"There's a press conference this morning on the station attack – we should watch that.'

'OK. What else?'

'Get on to DC Kerry Bellingham at Fordley nick. She's sending us footage of the station attack. Suppose now we're actually getting paid for it, we should prioritise that.'

The rest of our morning was lost in companionable silence. At eleven, Jen nudged me from the depths of Nichols' psych reports as she switched on the TV.

The red and white 'Breaking New' banner scrolled across the bottom of the screen as Heslopp sat in front of the West Yorkshire Police backdrop. A young Asian man I didn't recognise sat to his right. Heslopp looked about as uncomfortable as it was possible to get, as flashes from the assembled cameras flickered across his pale face. A patina of sweat glistened across his bald head, and despite knowing I should feel sorry for him, I somehow couldn't quite manage it.

'Josh Stamford, is a person of interest and we urge anyone who might know of his whereabouts to get in touch with the incident room here at Fordley CID.' The number for the inquiry team flashed up on the screen as Heslopp went on to introduce the man beside him as the Imam of Fordley's largest mosque and a local community leader.

'This was a serious and unprovoked attack on a group from our local community. We are requesting any information that will help the police to bring Mr Stamford in for questioning so we can have a peaceful conclusion to this matter. In the meantime, I am appealing for calm from the Asian and Muslim communities within Fordley.'

There was a barrage of questions from the gathered press pack.

'Is it true,' shouted one journalist, 'the intended target was Adel Abassi – the controversial preacher at Fordley Mosque?'

Heslopp held up his hand to stem the questions. 'At this time, it's not helpful to speculate. Mr Abassi's son, Baahir, was kicked onto the train track – obviously we're thankful that didn't result in an even more tragic outcome. A BTP officer was also seriously injured and is recovering in hospital.'

Another journalist shouted from the floor. 'Are the police treating this incident as racially motivated?'

Heslopp was struggling to control the interview. 'Investigations into the circumstances surrounding the attack are still ongoing.' His tone betrayed the stress he was under. 'It's urgent that we trace Josh Stamford as quickly as possible. Members of the public are urged not to approach him, but to call the incident room number if they spot him.'

'Adel Abassi has been accused of inciting racial hatred,' another journalist unhelpfully pointed out. 'Is there a connection between that and this attempt on his life by a veteran of the Iraq war?'

Heslopp held up his hand as the press pack bayed for more. Eventually the press officer stepped in, announcing that the interview was concluded. Jen flicked off the TV.

'Well, that went well,' she said with more than a hint of sarcasm.

'Hmm – Heslopp just got his first taste of leadership under fire,' I mused, turning back to the psych reports.

There was something about Josh Stamford's demeanour at Fordley train station that bothered me. It reminded me of something I'd read after Nichols' arrest for the Mela killings five years before.

As I scanned the reports from his assessments in Belmarsh prison, the similarities resonated even more.

Nichols had driven into Fordley with his fourteen-year-old son Charlie on the day of the Mela. Just before the attack, he made Charlie get out of the van with no explanation. Charlie had heard the sirens and turned up at the scene minutes after his father's arrest.

Jen found news footage from the time. CCTV showed the van slowing down at traffic lights, then suddenly swerving onto the pavement. It crashed the barriers and went through the gates into the festival, running down several pedestrians before crashing into the Fordley Mosque's marquee.

In the aftermath, mobile phone footage captured the moment Nichols was attacked by outraged survivors. I watched it through several times, before rewinding and pausing it.

His face was an unemotional mask as he was dragged from the van. The crowd began punching and kicking him to the ground. The ex-marine made no attempt to escape or defend himself, though he was more than physically capable.

Footage from the body-worn cameras of police who arrived almost immediately showed a bruised and bloodied Nichols being led away in a confused state. Officers reported he seemed dazed and simply said he didn't know why he'd done it. That line continued throughout subsequent interviews – either that, or he said nothing at all.

During his imprisonment in Belmarsh, his behaviour became more bizarre, leading to spells on the hospital wing. He'd been moved back onto the cell block just two days before his suicide.

I looked at photographs of his cell – graffiti scrawled across the walls in the hours before he died, echoing the only word he'd muttered over and over for weeks.

'*Back . . . Back . . . Back . . .*'

Chapter Twenty-Seven

Offices of Blackstone Enterprises – Tuesday Afternoon

The Blackstone building was a towering edifice of glass and steel, dominating the Leeds skyline. From a deep leather sofa in the dazzling reception area, I watched the stream of people entering and leaving – each one lost in their working-day worries. There was a frenetic energy about the place – this cathedral to commerce, that I was relieved I wasn't a part of.

The nine-to-five existence had never appealed to me, but then, I reasoned, my erratic working hours in grim locations like psychiatric units, prisons and mortuaries wouldn't suit everyone either.

I always believed my job provided freedom from a stifling existence I really couldn't see myself sticking to for more than a week. Then I thought about the psychopaths I'd interviewed – the killers I'd met and the dead eyes of their victims staring out at me from forensic photographs, or worse from their bloodied surroundings at crime scenes. And reflected that maybe I was the one who was out of step with everyone else.

My watch said two-fifteen. The huge skeleton-clock suspended above the curved glass reception desk said the same – confirming that Neville Blackstone had kept me waiting for fifteen minutes past the time he'd scheduled for our meeting.

Despite his secretary saying that I should be prompt as he had a very busy schedule.

Time was power. The higher up the hierarchy, the more valuable an individual's time was deemed to be. Theirs mattered – yours didn't. This, like everything else about Neville Blackstone, was designed to put people at a disadvantage. To elevate his status and diminish mine. A power play that no doubt served him well in negotiations in the cut-throat construction industry that had made him a billionaire.

Before coming here, I'd done my research. One surprising source of insider information was my publisher, Marissa. She'd called to say I'd had mail delivered to her office in London and she was forwarding it.

My address wasn't in the public domain – given that most of my clientele were serving life sentences thanks to me – so readers of my books often sent letters via my publisher.

I'd mentioned during our call that I was scheduled to meet the great man and Marissa told me her husband had worked for Blackstone Enterprises as a press officer.

'He's a complete bastard to his employees.' She hadn't sugared it up. 'Bullying and intimidation are his stock in trade, but he's protected by his money and his lawyers. When Marcus worked for him, stonewalling the press was a full-time job. He had a production line of injunctions on the go, to silence his accusers. He's got "Catch and Kill" down to a fine art.'

'"Catch and Kill"?'

'Yeah.' She exhaled loudly and I could picture her vaping – disappearing in a sweet-smelling cloud as she clacked her polished fingernails together, a nervous habit she had. 'Used by the great and the good to stop damaging stories coming out in the press. He's got powerful allies in Fleet Street. The old school tie and all that.'

'Never heard of it.'

'That's the idea – you're not meant to. His detractors get signed up to an exclusive, in exchange for a big payout which comes with a gagging order. Then they never publish, so the story's "caught" then "killed".'

'And presumably, Blackstone foots the bill – so the news-paper's not out of pocket?'

'Exactly. In the past, Blackstone paid people off directly but that didn't stop stories appearing in the press. The last one cost him over a million quid.'

'Nice work if you can get it,' I murmured, thinking about the damage Jacinta could have done to Blackstone.

'After that last scandal, MPs called for the Queen to strip him of his knighthood, so he changed tactics. These non-disclosure agreements make sure it's kept out of the public domain forever.'

'What's to stop someone selling to a newspaper who *won't* squash the story? That way they get the money *and* the satisfaction of ruining him?'

She exhaled loudly again. 'That's the thing. They don't realise the story's going to be buried. As far as they're concerned it's a legitimate deal. They've sold exclusive rights to a paper they trust will print it. By the time they realise it's not going to happen, it's too late – they're up to their kazoo in a legal contract that would bankrupt them for the next four generations if they breached it.'

'Clever,' I said – thinking about what Ron, from the *Fordley Express* had said about the key witness in Jacinta's murder being signed to an exclusive.

'Friggin' slippery more like.' She oozed contempt. 'Be careful, Jo – the man's a complete snake.'

* * *

My thoughts were interrupted as a woman came through the security barrier and headed towards me. A vision in a pale pink skirt-suit. Her smile broadened as she extended a perfectly manicured hand. 'Doctor McCready? I'm Kim – Sir Neville's PA.'

She spoke with an almost breathless quality that was designed to make her sound calm and professional but missed the mark, making her sound more like a sexual vamp in a bad porn movie.

The VIP lift only went to the executive suites and we travelled in silence until the doors opened with a whisper to reveal an impressive outer office – Kim's domain. Gatekeeper and guardian to Sir Neville.

She handed me a clipboard and pen. 'If you could just read through our standard confidentiality agreement and pop your signature on the bottom, I'll inform Sir Neville you're here.' She smiled with saccharine sweetness before disappearing through huge double doors to the inner sanctum.

I scanned the document, noting the legalese that camouflaged threats of lawsuits and prosecution for anyone in breach of its stifling restrictions and decided against 'popping' my signature on any of it. I dropped the clipboard back on the desk just as she reappeared.

'Sir Neville will see you now.'

The man whose image I'd seen on the front of countless newspapers was standing in front of panoramic windows overlooking the city. He was shorter than I imagined, but the collar-length silver hair and permanent bronzed tan gained from spending half the year on his super-yacht was the same as his tabloid images. Apart from four deep, red claw marks running down his neck, to disappear beneath the crisp white collar of his shirt.

He stepped forward offering his hand.

'Dr McCready – we finally meet.' His handshake was firm, but the smile superficial – almost wary – as he appraised me with steel-blue eyes that lacked true warmth.

Although I'd appeared as an expert witness during Nique's trial, Neville Blackstone and I had never actually met. He'd been absent from court the day I appeared.

He gestured for me to take a seat opposite the huge desk. As he went to sit down, there was a gentle knock on the door and Kim appeared, wielding the clipboard. Without a word, she put the offending item on his desk, shooting me a look that was as aggressive as she could manage – which was about as intimidating as a kitten chasing a butterfly. I stifled a smile and watched her leave as Sir Neville scanned the form.

'You haven't signed this.'

'Clearly.'

'No matter.' He tossed the form aside. 'What we say here is covered by doctor-patient confidentiality anyway.'

'Except that you're not my patient and you've already given consent to my sharing this conversation with the police.' I raised an enquiring eyebrow. 'Or have I got that wrong?'

He tilted back in his leather chair. 'They said you were a girl who could be difficult to deal with.' His eyes glinted with the challenge that belied the smile. 'I can see they were right.'

I crossed my legs and brushed an imaginary speck from my skirt, resisting the urge to wonder who 'they' might be.

'I think you'll find I'm not a "girl", Sir Neville – and your dealings with me can be as easy or difficult as you choose to make them.' I looked back up and gave him an equally insincere smile.

'Fair enough . . . So how do we do this?'

'This isn't a formal psychological assessment, Sir Neville. Just a meeting.'

'Of course – I understand that.' He leaned back, appraising me across the desk. Seeming to decide whether to elaborate. Eventually he nodded. 'My legal team were impressed by your evidence in court . . .' His eyes narrowed. 'Even though it went against us. Your credentials are impressive. I decided that if we met you'd be able to form an impression, a professional opinion. To know whether I'm telling the truth.'

Being able to map behaviour and read body language – though a good indicator when someone was being deceitful – didn't make me an infallible polygraph. A lot depended upon the skill of the deceiver. Often, I could tell, but some people could get past my radar. I decided now was not the time to disabuse him.

I produced a notebook. 'In that case, I'll ask some questions and we'll see where it takes us?'

He nodded. Watching me over his steepled fingers.

I wanted to cut to the chase and ask him directly whether he'd killed Jacinta Williams, but I needed to get baseline responses from him first. See how he reacted to unimportant questions. Then when we got to more thorny issues, I'd be able to spot body language that might reveal the lies. The micro expressions and 'tells' that everyone has and no one can completely control all of the time.

I gestured towards a table with a collection of silver-framed photos. 'Your family?'

'Yes, my wife Talia and daughter Sophia.'

I picked up the picture of Blackstone on the deck of his super-yacht arm in arm with his wife – a stunningly beautiful younger woman. Others showed him standing proudly with his daughter at a polo match as she raised the winner's trophy.

'Your wife lives in the Cayman Islands, I believe?'

I already knew, but I wanted to keep it non-confrontational for now. Which was why I didn't mention the fact that I also knew all of Blackstone's companies were registered in his wife's name and as a resident of the Caribbean tax haven, they avoided paying UK taxes.

'The family's scattered these days. My daughter moved over there when she married – splits her time between the Caymans and the UK. My wife comes back several times a year.'

One picture showed Blackstone standing beside his wife as she sat at a grand piano.

'Nice photo.'

'She's an exceptionally talented classical musician. Could have played professionally . . . But then Sophia was born and she didn't want to travel so much.'

'And you? Where do you call home?'

'We have a house in the country, just outside Fordley. I stay there when I'm over here on business. But I prefer Monaco – I have residency in the principality.'

Another tax haven, I thought – but kept it to myself.

'Who wouldn't prefer Monaco?' I kept my tone non-judgemental. 'Better weather for a start.'

He came to stand beside me. I could smell his expensive cologne as he took the picture of his wife, standing looking out over a clifftop scene in Monaco.

'Personally, I enjoy the changing seasons.' He replaced the picture. 'It's not about the weather. Fordley's where I started out – the city's been good to me and I like to pay it back.'

I'd walked to one wall, adorned with framed photos – mainly of Blackstone receiving awards or posing with the great and the good. Various members of the Royal family, British icons of film and music, supermodels. Even one of him being received by the Pope – the only one where he had a bowed head and an expression approaching anything resembling humility. Catholic boy from the back streets made good.

I tapped the award for 'Yorkshireman of the Year'.

'For outstanding contribution to the County,' he said. 'There were incentives to move the business south, once we got big.' He straightened up to his full five foot nine inches. 'Stayed in Yorkshire – where it all began with my first property development in Fordley.'

'Mill conversion, wasn't it?'

'The old woollen mills had been left to rot. Beautiful architecture – built to last. I scooped them up for peanuts, then started to regenerate the areas from being the haunts of druggies and down-and-outs to places people actually wanted to live.' He was

176

warming to his favourite subject. 'People thought it was mad to try to sell luxury apartments in edge-of-town ghettos. But I knew, if we invested in the infrastructure, people would come. Sank a fortune into reviving artisan shops, trendy restaurants and theatres. And now look . . .' He stretched his arms out to encompass his empire.

He gestured for me to look at a scale model of an impressive development.

'The jewel in my crown,' he said immodestly. 'Eight hundred apartments. A fitness centre, restaurants, shops. Even a cinema complex.'

I bent down to get a closer look. Like the eyeball peering through a window in the *Land of the Giants*, I looked at the tiny figures in tree-lined avenues. A glass dome on the roof of the mill protected an impressive swimming pool – complete with tiny model swimmers ploughing their plastic lengths before going to their imaginary offices.

'This is huge.'

'In its day, it was the biggest textile mill in the world. The floor space in the factory was twenty-seven acres.' He pointed with a fat finger. 'That's not counting the land around it. The park that we're planning will be bigger than all the current natural open spaces in the city combined.'

'Impressive.'

'We broke the ground last month. It will be my legacy. "Oliver's Court" – *his* legacy really.'

I followed him back to our seats.

'Blackstone Enterprises own most of the mill developments in Yorkshire. And we helped a struggling construction industry. Sub-contracted to smaller firms as we got bigger.

Those companies have gone on to be some of the biggest in the country thanks to the work we gave them in those days, and we still work with them now.'

I was looking at a picture of Blackstone with Prince Charles at the opening of a new building. A group of workers in the background attracted my attention. Their hardhats bearing the logo of the construction company.

'Tillie Construction – in Leeds?'

'We run an apprentice scheme helping ex-offenders find work in construction. Tillie takes some from our charity every year.'

My brain froze momentarily as the connections fired.

'The Sangar Foundation . . . that's your charity?'

A look of surprise crossed his face – and something else that I didn't expect to see.

Fear.

Chapter Twenty-Eight

It was fleeting – but unmistakeable.

Fear.

It flashed across his eyes for a fraction of a second – then he masked it, clearing his throat and composing himself.

'I'm not directly involved. I just bank-roll it. These charities get very little core funding. My father fought in the last war and my brother served – so I have a connection. My son-in-law's the Chief Executive. He's in the Cayman Islands most of the time – my daughter is more involved in running things.'

Why fear?

I deciding to file that nugget away until I could use it to best effect.

'Tell me about Jacinta Williams.'

'She worked as a dancer at a private club I visited in Fordley. My wife lives abroad most of the year, so things just . . . developed.'

He seemed relaxed speaking about this extra-marital affair, as if it really was of no consequence.

'Jacinta was a lot younger than me – she liked being around the kind of people I could introduce her to . . . the lifestyle I could give her. '

'You paid for her apartment?'

'I paid for *everything*,' he snorted. 'She might not have come from a wealthy background, but she developed a taste for the finer things in life soon enough.' He shrugged. 'I own the building – so the apartment cost me nothing in real terms.' He glanced at me, then added coldly, 'But on a cost-to-benefit basis, I came out ahead on the deal.'

I played dumb. 'I don't understand?'

'Jacinta used to be a high-class escort. In fact, she used to work for your friend De Benoit, back in the day. I didn't know her then, but she was one of her highest-earning escorts apparently.'

'I didn't know that,' I admitted.

'She was a friend of Yalena Vashchenko – they met at the gym. Pole dancers have to train hard, upper body and core strength. Vashchenko had been a gymnast as a kid in Russia. She introduced Jacinta to De Benoit.'

'Was Jacinta at your son's thirtieth birthday party the night he died?'

'No. She told me she was in Paris entertaining another client that weekend. As I said, I didn't know her in those days. When De Benoit went to prison, Jacinta left. She blamed De Benoit for her friend getting hurt, said Vashchenko should never have been there that night . . .'

'She blamed Dominique? Not your son?' He didn't answer the question – staring down at his clasped hands. 'Didn't it bother her, having a relationship with you . . . after what Oliver did to Yalena?' I pushed.

He regarded me with cold eyes. 'No one could prove that Oliver did *anything* to Vashchenko . . . as you know, she vanished before the police arrived. We only have De Benoit's version of what my son told her before she murdered him.'

He spoke quietly, but the undercurrent of barely suppressed aggression was unmistakeable. 'I for one don't believe a word to come out of that whore's mouth and nor did Jacinta.'

'And after she left Dominique's club . . . ?'

'She went to work at Leather and Lace – the private members' club. That's where we met a couple of years later. She wanted to be a model . . . a film star . . . who the hell knows, but not to put too fine a point on it – she charged for sex. What it cost to buy her trinkets and keep her in that apartment was cheaper than paying her going rate as an escort.'

He might as well have been talking about the cost of running a car.

'I have a simple philosophy,' he added. 'If it flies, floats or fucks . . . rent it.'

'What does your wife think about that?'

The question didn't faze him – he simply lifted his shoulders in an attitude of indifference. 'I met my wife when we were teenagers, when neither of us had a pot to piss in.' He shot me a look – gauging whether his crudity had shocked me – it hadn't, but I had the sense that he said and did a lot of things just to shock people.

'In those days, you met a girl, got married, had kids. That was the way of things. Talia's grandparents came over from Poland. They escaped the Nazi Holocaust and arrived with the clothes on their backs.' He regarded me and I made sure my expression gave nothing away. 'She understands survival – understands the nature of the life we have now . . .'

'Did she know about Jacinta?'

'I didn't rub her nose in it, if that's what you mean.' He toyed with a letter opener. Displacement activity. The first indication

181

he was becoming uncomfortable. He wasn't used to having his behaviour questioned. 'I didn't take Jacinta to public events or places where the paparazzi would be. I move in circles of trusted intimates, doctor. People who respect the privacy of their friends. The rest of the time, I saw Jacinta at her apartment, or at the club. It's owned by a friend of mine. He knows the value of discretion . . .'

'What about the girls who work there – how can you rely on their discretion? They could earn quite a fee for dishing the dirt on a knight of the realm.' I was being deliberately provocative.

'It wouldn't happen.'

'Does Kim get them to "pop" their signatures on an non-disclosure agreement?'

He turned ice-cold eyes on me and held my gaze just long enough for it to be threatening. 'Agreements like that are commonplace in private clubs where influential people go to relax, doctor. There's nothing unusual in it.'

'Tell me what happened on the night Jacinta died?'

'We'd booked a restaurant in town. Myles Lawson, my assistant, picked Jacinta up and drove her here—'

I suddenly remembered why Lawson's name was familiar.

'Lawson – he was a key witness at Dominique's trial, wasn't he?'

'Yes.' His eyes narrowed, suddenly suspicious. 'What of it?'

I shrugged. 'No reason. So he became your assistant?'

'Yes, after he graduated.'

'A reward for being your man in court?'

Blackstone toyed with the pen on his desk in an attempt to hide the anger in his eyes.

'Myles graduated Cambridge with a first in business and economics.' He lifted his head to look back at me – eyes hard as flint. 'I'm not sentimental, doctor. Nor do I create jobs for people who don't deserve them. Myles got the job on merit. The fact that I knew him through Oliver is irrelevant.'

'And the fact that his evidence was crucial in convicting Dominique De Benoit? Is that an irrelevance as well?'

Blackstone's breath left him in exasperation as he barely controlled his anger. He really wasn't used to being questioned and his patience was wearing thin.

'De Benoit came out of Oliver's bedroom as Myles was going in there. She was covered in my son's blood.' His words were ground out through clenched teeth. 'She *told* him what she'd done, for Christ's sake!'

'She also told him Oliver was still alive and that she'd called an ambulance. Myles let your son down when he passed out on the bathroom floor, too far gone on drink and drugs to help him.'

'I don't see how making me relive my son's death is relevant to what happened when Jacinta was murdered.'

'It helps to establish the credibility of your main alibi that night.' I broke eye contact to make a note; when I looked back, he was regarding me with undisguised loathing. I rewarded him with a thin smile. 'Seems like Myles is making a habit of giving witness statements for you, Sir Neville.'

He opened his mouth, but before he could say anything, I switched topics. Shifting gears to keep him off balance. 'So – you were saying that Myles drove Jacinta over here to pick you up for dinner?'

'I was held up in a meeting, so I said I'd meet them at the restaurant. By the time I arrived Jacinta was drunk and in a nasty mood . . .'

'Was that usual?'

He was becoming annoyed as he thought about it. 'She often drank too much, but that night it was different. She had an edge to her . . .'

'An edge?'

'Myles said she was OK when he picked her up. They parked outside and Myles came up to see how long I'd be. When he got back to the car, he said she was different – moody. He asked what was wrong, but she snapped his head off. He took her to the restaurant but said she seemed to be on a mission to get drunk – ordering a bottle of champagne, which she'd downed before I even got there.'

'Did she say anything to explain her mood?'

'When I tried to talk to her, she launched into her favourite gripe.'

'Which was?'

He twisted the letter opener between his fingers, his anger from that night bubbling up with the memory. 'She wanted me to leave my wife – stupid bitch thought I'd be willing to divorce and throw everything away for her. We didn't even finish the meal. She was spoiling for a fight, so after the first course I told her we were leaving.' He dropped the letter opener with a clatter. 'Myles drove us to her apartment. She was embarrassing, shouting the odds in the street.'

I'd read the neighbour's statement Callum sent me. I quoted from it.

'The neighbour said he heard her scream, "Your ghosts are coming back to haunt you – just like they have for your son." What did she mean?'

'I have no idea – like I say, she was drunk . . . I've told the police all this . . .'

'But I'm here for you to tell it to me again. If you had to guess what she meant?' I pushed.

He washed a hand across his face. 'She'd said if I didn't leave my wife, she would go to the papers, have my knighthood stripped away . . .'

'And the reference to Oliver?'

He shook his head, his breath escaping him in a gust of frustration. 'How the hell would I know? Maybe that the circumstances of Oliver's death . . . could threatened my knighthood.'

'But it didn't . . . because you paid off witnesses at that party – to keep quiet and disappear?'

He slammed his fist on the desk. 'Christ!' He glared at me. 'You really know how to push it, don't you, McCready?'

'Yes, I do,' I said quietly. 'Want to strangle *me*? Did you lose it like that when Jacinta brought Oliver into it, too?'

He bit his bottom lip – finally exhaling. 'I did lose my temper when she mentioned Oliver . . . I admit that. I slapped her and called her a calculating whore – that's when she flew at me – clawed my face.' His fingers went to the marks on his neck. 'That shook me up I suppose. I realised it was getting out of hand, so I walked out on her.' He regarded me silently for just a second before adding quietly, 'She was alive when I left her, you have to believe that.'

'You had every reason to want to kill her – she could have ruined you.'

'You think so?' His laugh lacked humour. 'It wouldn't have ruined my marriage, despite what she thought. As for my knighthood . . . I would have paid her off. When I walked out that night, I'd already decided we were done – she'd crossed a line and I'd had enough. She was a mercenary whore – in it for the lifestyle and the money. If I'd made her an offer, she'd have taken it. End of.'

I found it interesting that he was more willing to pay to protect his knighthood than his marriage.

'Were you planning to get one of your news editor friends to do a "catch and kill"?'

He glared at me. 'Maybe – there are no laws against it . . .'

'Or did you catch and kill this one, literally?'

'Better opponents have pushed me to lose my temper and for higher stakes in business. Christ, if I strangled everyone who got me into a rage, I'd never get out of the boardroom for bodies! If her revelation would lose me everything I valued, then committing a murder certainly would! You think I'm that stupid?'

'Well, if *you* didn't kill her who did?'

'If I knew that, we wouldn't be sitting here, would we?'

'So, you're saying after you left, someone else went to the apartment that night? Who else would have a motive . . .?'

'That bitch De Benoit maybe?' His eyes spat venom.

'That's a non-starter and you know it. Nique wouldn't attack an enemy's loved ones to get at them—'

'And you'd know that for a fact?'

'Yes . . . actually I would. She's a psychopath . . .'

It wouldn't hurt for you to remember that, is what I wanted to say – but I didn't.

'Her thinking is really not that complicated. If she hated you that much, it's *you* she'd kill, not your mistress. Besides – she was still in prison that night.'

'But that minder of hers wasn't.'

I knew he was clutching at straws and said so.

'Edge Brink wouldn't risk jeopardising his freedom or Nique's on the eve of her release. Besides, she wants to get on with her life. She wouldn't do anything to feed this vendetta.'

I studied him across the desk and knew he didn't believe it was Nique. Not for a minute. This was a diversion away from his *real* fears.

'So, if not her, then who?'

He shook his head, but his eyes held an almost haunted look.

Time for me to cash in that valuable nugget he'd inadvertently given me at the mention of Sangar.

'Josh Stamford maybe?'

Chapter Twenty-Nine

His mouth opened, then closed again. I knew I'd said out loud something he was too terrified to vocalise.

'You know Josh Stamford?'

He was rattled and I wanted to leverage the advantage.

'I've seen him on the news, like everyone else.'

'But you've considered the possibility he might have killed Jacinta?'

He looked like he was going to deny it, but as his eyes met mine we both knew the truth. His breath escaped him in a ragged sigh and he sat back in the chair.

'Not really. But when I heard he'd come through Sangar, I thought ... maybe?' I'd mapped his baseline responses. He was lying and I wasn't about to let it go.

'Why would he kill a woman he'd never met because of Sangar?' I kept up the pressure. Still nothing. I let my breath out in a gust of frustration. 'If you know something – tell me *now!* Because otherwise the police only have one person of interest for this and that's *you!*'

He raised his head slowly – and when he looked back at me his eyes were as hard as iron. He'd pulled back from that cliff edge of weakness he'd stepped unwittingly close to before realising his mistake. He wasn't going to go back there now – no matter how hard I pushed. The advantage was lost and I knew it.

'It was stupid. But when they said he'd been through Sangar – I just thought, maybe there was a connection. That perhaps he was hitting back at a system he felt had wronged him somehow?'

'How could he feel wronged by a charity that rehabilitated him?'

'I don't know!' He raised his voice in exasperation. 'He's ex-military – wanted for attempted murder and he's been through a charity I fund. Then my mistress turns up dead!' He shook his head again. 'And I know I didn't kill her, so he came to my mind . . . That's all.'

'What are you so frightened of?' I asked quietly, watching him steadily.

'Isn't that enough?'

No – not enough to account for the visceral fear in your eyes.

I knew I wasn't going to get any more out of him. The shutters were firmly down. I stood, packing my notebook, ready to leave. He came round the desk and walked me to the door. Stopping with his hand on the doorknob.

'You don't like me do you, McCready?'

'Liking or disliking requires emotion and I really haven't invested any,' I lied.

'Not even where De Benoit is concerned?'

'I'm seeing you in a professional capacity, not a personal one, so my feelings don't enter into it.' It was my turn to hesitate – just a heartbeat – before adding, 'But as you've raised the subject, I *could* ask you to call off the hounds.'

'I really don't know what you mean.' His smile was humourless. 'But supposing I *did*, you know how pointless that would be, don't you?'

I studied him, sensing his enjoyment at the game-play. Like a predator toying with his prey before devouring it, just for the sheer amusement at the cruelty he could inflict. Payback for making him lose his composure.

'Even if it affects the content of my report?'

He tilted his head – weighing me up. The smile that slowly formed was irritatingly sardonic. 'You wouldn't do that, McCready – you're too much of a straight dealer.'

'You think so?'

'You work with DCI Ferguson – you're invested in that . . . relationship. Firmly on the side of the law. The moral code you live by would never allow someone like you to cross that line.'

His words resonated inside me. Awakening that dark spectre and the memory of something a sadistic killer had once said to me – that I understood the minds of monsters because in some ways I was wired the same. That it would be easy for me to cross the line into the dark abyss they inhabited, given the right motivation.

His threats towards Nique had already meant I'd bent the rules. Helping Edge to hide her – breaking the terms of her probation. But I justified it to myself because I was protecting her life. On the scales of justice, I felt just fine about the balance. But would I go much further – to prejudice my report? To actively manipulate a police investigation?

As if he read my mind, he added quietly, 'You have a son, don't you?'

Even as he said it – almost before the words were out of his mouth – I felt something tug deep inside me. His words triggering a visceral reaction that told me he'd unwittingly just

191

scored a dangerous bullseye on a primeval target. *This* was per-
ilous ground. I could almost see the rim of that predicted abyss
getting terrifyingly closer.

I nodded, not liking where this might be going.

'Then I hope you never feel the agony of losing him.'

'Is that a threat?' I could feel a pulse behind my eyes.

'I'm not in the business of making threats, doctor. I'm just
one parent explaining to another the raw emotion that such
a loss causes. I hope you never experience it. But if you did,
you might appreciate my feelings about that woman and why I
regard it as a personal insult that she's out there drawing breath,
while my son is dead.'

The last thing I wanted him to see reflected in my eyes was
the chilling image he'd just conjured in my mind. But as I left,
the feeling I'd glimpsed the soul of the deadly reptile Marissa
warned me about was one I couldn't shake.

Chapter Thirty

Kingsberry Farm – Wednesday morning

'So, do you think he killed her?' Callum's voice came over the loudspeaker in my office.

I was looking at my notes. 'I'll send the report later today . . .'

'I tried patience once, it's crap . . . Just tell me?'

I tapped the pencil against my teeth. 'I'd love to say yes . . .'

'But?'

'I want him for it, just like you, Cal. But . . . I don't think he did.'

'Why?'

'Blackstone's everything his reputation says he is, but worse. He's a malignant narcissist. Perfectly capable of killing someone who crosses him and sleeping at night.'

'So why not his mistress then?'

I watched my reflection on the computer screen purse thoughtful lips at me. 'He had motive. She'd threatened to tell his wife about the affair and ruin his reputation in the press, and that's just for starters – but she wasn't worth the risk. Self-preservation is a major consideration for Blackstone. He won't do anything that would jeopardise his freedom. More than that, like a lot of narcissists, he's a coward. He knew he could deal with her an easier way . . . and one that was safer for him.'

'Such as?'

'Pay her off. He's made it his stock in trade – there's even a name for the way it's done – if you have a friendly newspaper editor in your corner.'

'Catch and kill . . .?'

'You're just showing off now, Ferguson.'

He laughed. 'Not really, only recently heard the term myself. When it became obvious there was no press coverage, I put out some feelers.'

'And?'

'A national newspaper's got exclusive rights, but nothing's appeared. Call me cynical, but it's my guess it's been killed.'

'What about TV coverage?'

'Local news picked it up briefly, but only to say a woman's body had been found. Major networks won't run it – unless they make the connection to Sir Neville. And that's unlikely as his legal team have applied for a privacy injunction to keep his name out of it. So, unless we charge him, he's safe for now.'

'Well, he *has* got a violent temper and a short fuse, wrapped up in a thin skin. At one point, when I pushed him, he wanted to strangle *me* . . .'

'*That* I can understand.'

I pretended not to have heard. 'If he'd lost it that night, in the heat of the moment, he would have strangled her with his bare hands. Why use a ligature? Also, the killer's remorse doesn't fit. He wouldn't know remorse if it bit him on the arse. If he killed Jacinta, his one and only concern would be self-preservation. He certainly wouldn't give a toss about his victim – about how

194

she would look when she was found, preserving her dignity. None of that would enter his thinking. He would have made a hasty exit. None of which fits the scene I looked at.'

'How can he see a woman for best part of two years and not give a damn?'

'Because Blackstone saw her as an object, not a person. He loves himself first and foremost. His daughter probably comes somewhere between that and his wealth. His wife . . . Well, I'm guessing the only reason he hasn't divorced is because he'd lose too much in the settlement – to avoid tax all his companies are registered in her name. She turns a blind eye to his affairs, in return for the lifestyle.'

'Cosy arrangement.'

'There's something else too . . .'

'What?'

'Blackstone told me Jacinta was a friend of Yalena Vashchenko. She used to work as an escort for Nique . . .'

There was silence as he digested that little nugget. 'Was she there the night Oliver died?'

'He said she wasn't. That she left Nique's agency after the trial.' I listened to his silence for what seemed an age, before adding, 'Jacinta was killed before Nique's release.'

'Edge was on the outside though.'

That was the leap I'd been afraid he would make. I knew Edge wasn't involved, but I couldn't tell him why. Knowing I was keeping things from him caused a thrum of discomfort deep inside – a longing for the openness and transparency we once had, but which I'd forfeit to protect a friend.

'That's not feasible. What's his motive?'

'Blackstone's made no secret of the fact that he wants Nique dead . . . Jacinta's his mistress – pre-emptive strike maybe? Send a shot across Blackstone's bows?'

'Why wait until now?' I reasoned. 'If Edge wanted to do it, he could have, anytime.'

'The timing makes it obvious – sends a clear warning to Blackstone.'

'I'm telling you, Cal, it's not her – or Edge. All they want is to be left to get on with their lives. Nique wouldn't do anything to make this situation with Blackstone worse . . . not now.'

'Hmm – you're biased.'

There was no point in trying to dissuade him. In fact, I knew the more I tried, the more he'd pursue it. I changed tack. 'Did you know that Blackstone's the money-man behind the Sangar charity?'

There was a pause. 'No – does Frank Heslopp know?'

'Not sure. But when I made the connection, Blackstone's reaction was one I didn't expect. He was scared.'

'Of what?'

'He said he'd considered Josh Stamford might have killed Jacinta to get at him, but when I pushed him for more, it was obvious he'd regretted admitting that much and shut down.'

'Stamford? Why would he link him to Jacinta's murder? I think you'd better send that report over now. I'll ring Frank. We need to talk about this once I've made some calls.'

He was right. If there was a connection, we needed to find it – along with Stamford – sooner rather than later.

Chapter Thirty-One

Fordley police station – Wednesday afternoon

Callum and Frank Heslopp were sitting opposite me in a small conference room on the top floor of Fordley nick.

I nursed a disgusting cup of vending machine tea and listened as they discussed the possible links between their two cases. Apparently, that morning, Intelligence had uncovered Blackstone's connection to the Sangar charity by 'following the money trail'. Which led them to the tax haven in the Cayman Islands.

'But what makes Blackstone suspect Stamford of Jacinta's murder?' Heslopp was saying.

They both looked at me.

I shrugged. 'His explanation was as fractured as his thinking – all he said was he knew *he* hadn't killed her. Stamford was the only person he could think of who might have. But he wasn't convincing. He's lying through his teeth.'

Callum stretched long legs out under the table. 'De Benoit and her minder have more of a motive. I've got officers going round to question them later today.' He shot me a challenging look, but I didn't rise to the bait.

'I know one thing,' I said.

'What's that?' Callum asked.

'Whatever else was fake – Blackstone's fear was real. And whatever he's terrified of, it's got something to do with Sangar and Stamford.'

Callum took a mouthful of coffee. 'I'll have him brought in again. Can you come up with some questions we could use in our interview strategy? Put him under pressure?'

I made a note. 'While I remember, Frank, did you manage to review the Mela attack?'

He pulled notes from the bottom of a pile. 'Nichols went through Sangar when he left the army.' He frowned. 'We've already looked into this and there's no other connection between Nichols and Stamford.'

'Frank's right, Jo,' Callum added. 'The charity helps thousands of veterans every year – it's one of the leading treatment centres for ex-service personnel in the UK. Their clients have all served in the military and done time in prison. Eighty per cent of their referrals come from probation officers or offender managers. If we cross referenced veterans with Sangar on our offender database, we'd get hundreds of hits.'

'True,' I agreed. 'But only a small percentage get a place in the residential units.' I tapped my notes. 'Both Nichols and Stamford were long-term residents.'

'Both got employment through the scheme, at companies associated with Blackstone Enterprises,' Heslopp added. 'And both went on to carry out random attacks – stretching coincidence a bit far.'

'Maybe Blackstone's made those links, too?' Callum said. 'And maybe he knows something about Sangar that he won't or can't share with us – something that terrifies him into thinking

Stamford might have killed Jacinta?' He looked across at Heslopp. 'Let's get the team to dig some more.'

I held back, knowing I wasn't sharing everything with them, but I needed to be sure of my facts before I went any further.

* * *

I'd waited until I was in the car and on my way back to the farm before I made my next call.

'You even have to ask me that, princess?' The hurt was obvious in Edge's voice.

'Sorry. But yes, I do.' I sighed. 'You've got to see it from Callum's point of view.'

I listened to his breath, heavy down the phone, and rode out the silence. I wished we'd been able to meet in person, but we'd agreed it was too risky.

'I've never killed a woman, doc. God knows I'd do anything for my girl, but even if she'd asked me to do that . . . I wouldn't have. Besides what motive would we have?'

'To warn Blackstone off?'

He snorted down the phone. 'You're the profiler, not me, but even I'd guess that topping his woman would piss Blackstone off and make him even more likely to go after Nique. We need to keep things calm until I can get her out of the country. I'm not going to stir up the hornets' nest, am I?'

'That's what I thought.' I paused as I negotiated a flock of sheep in the narrow lane across the moors. 'But just so you know, you'll be getting a knock on the door sometime today.'

'Thanks for the heads-up. I've got to smuggle Nique back to the apartment later – her probation officer's coming round – she needs to be at her approved address. Won't hurt if Blackstone's men see probation and police coming in and out. More convincing that she's here. I'll get her back to your office later.'

'It's not an ideal place to be cooped up, I know . . .'

'It's perfect for what we need, princess. She's meeting people there to make final arrangements – the guy who's sorting our passports is going there tonight – so in the next few days we should be out of your hair. Once she's out of the country, I'll breathe easier.'

I was already complicit in breaking Nique's bail conditions – now I'd compounded my guilt by leaking information about the direction of Callum's enquiry. So much for being a morally incorruptible 'straight dealer'.

I shuddered to imagine what Callum's reaction would be if he even knew the half of it. If he ever found out, it would fracture what little remained of our tenuous relationship forever.

Chapter Thirty-Two

Kingsberry Farm – Wednesday night

'Thank you for taking my call, Charlie.'

Charlie Nichols was nineteen years old now and living in Australia where he and his mother had emigrated after his father's death. I'd emailed in advance and he'd agreed to speak to me. I'd allowed a few days to give him time to get used to the idea of speaking about the day that had changed his life forever.

'No problem.' His voice held the hint of an Australian accent. 'But I haven't got long – leaving for work soon.'

'It's just a quick question about the Mela attack.'

'Not something I like to think about.' He sighed heavily. 'But go on.'

'How did your dad seem when he was driving the van into Fordley?'

'Fine– until he changed . . .'

'Changed how?'

'Looked kind of distant and then just pulled over. Leaned across – opened my door. Didn't even say he wanted me to get out, but it was obvious that he did.'

'Did you ask him what was going on?'

'Yeah, of course. But he just stared at me – freaked me out, like he was looking straight through me. So, I jumped out. Then he pulled the van back into traffic and drove away. Just left me there in the road.'

The pain and confusion still echoed in his voice – the distant sound of a hurt child, resonating down the years.

'I'm sorry, Charlie.' I meant it. 'I know it must be painful to think about it after all this time, but you have to know how valuable this information is.'

'It's OK.' He sounded resigned. 'If it helps get an idea of what was going on in his head, because we never got any answers back then. It nearly destroyed my mum.'

I hesitated before asking my next question – so much hung on the answer.

'I know this might seem like a strange question – but just before the change came over your dad – did anything happen?'

'Like what?'

I had to be careful not to lead him, but I also knew it wasn't going to be easy for him to remember every small detail from five years ago.

'Take yourself back to that morning. Picture it for me. Try to recall as much detail as you can. What you could see . . . hear . . . smell.'

'OK . . .' he said slowly, humouring the unhinged.

'What was the weather like?'

'Sunny . . . a nice day – we had the radio on.'

'Can you remember what was on?'

'"Crazy Stupid Love" . . . Cheryl Cole. We were both singing along.' He laughed at the memory. 'Dad was pretending to play the sax bit in the song, then . . .' He paused for so long, I thought I'd lost the connection.

'Hello? Are you still there?'

'Yeah . . . um . . . I'm still here.'

'Then what, Charlie?'

202

'That's when he kind of froze – I mean his face went blank. He stopped playing about and just stared straight ahead. Then it all got weird.'

'Nothing else. One minute you're singing along and the next he just changed?'

'No, something did happen. Now I remember . . . yeah just before . . .'

'What?' The silence seemed to go on forever. I held my breath and then he said it.

'His mobile phone rang.'

* * *

A theory was forming – but before I dare present it as anything workable, I needed to run it past someone with first-hand experience, someone I trusted implicitly. I fired off an email to Geoff Perrett to arrange the meeting I'd hinted at when we'd spoken on Saturday.

Then I looked again at the Fordley station attack. I'd watched the CCTV footage so many times, every second was ingrained.

I'd been drawn to one section over and over. Taken from PC Yates's body camera and it showed the moment Stamford kicked the Taser out of his hand.

At first, it seemed Stamford dropped the knife before grappling with the officer. But as I watched it back, it became clear to me that he'd deliberately thrown the knife away.

Why would a well-trained soldier give away such an advantage? Why risk arrest – when he could have used that knife so efficiently to help him get away?

203

I tilted my head to relieve the crick in my neck that was close to becoming permanent. I could still see images of Josh Stamford playing on the back of my closed eyelids.

I was just turning off the lamps in my office when the phone rang.

'McCready.'

'Frank Heslopp.'

'Hi Frank – I've just emailed you about Stamford.'

'That's timely – we've found him.'

'Where?'

'He turned up at Sangar House. Staff called it in. He was armed with a handgun and barricaded himself in with Michelle Briggs, his therapist. By the time officers arrived, he'd stolen her car and fled the scene.'

'Is she OK?'

'That's the problem – he's taken her with him. We've pinged her phone to track their location and I've now got a surveillance team who've got eyes on her abandoned vehicle on Norland Moor. I'm headed there now. Incident commander has deployed a police negotiator and a full firearms team have been briefed and are en route. Given Stamford's history, they've asked us to gather intelligence on his mindset. Potential behaviour in a dynamic situation . . . You know how it works.'

I did know, and the dangers of a man with Stamford's background being faced with armed officers while holding a hostage were enormous.

'They've set up a rendezvous point at the pub on Moorbottom Lane,' he was saying. 'Can you meet me there?'

'I'll set off now.'

Chapter Thirty-Three

Norland Moor – Wednesday night

The Moorcock Inn was a hive of activity by the time I arrived. Police vehicles cordoned off the area and, ominously, an ambulance was on standby outside the perimeter.

A tactical command post had been set up in the pub car park, which was where Heslopp met me. Hands jammed into the pockets of his waterproof jacket.

'He abandoned the car and took his hostage on foot, onto the moors. He's in an old quarry over the ridge.' His breath plumed on the chill evening air as he looked towards the rolling hills covered in purple heather.

I knew the place well, having often explored the two-hundred-and-fifty-acre nature reserve on long walks with Harvey. Beautiful in summer and desolate in winter. Dotted with the scars of eighteenth-century quarrying. Dips and hollows that would provide ample cover for Stamford to evade his hunters – particularly now as darkness was falling.

Heslopp took me to a van where communications had been set up.

The 'silver' commander wasted no time in making the introductions to the team. The crisis negotiator was introduced to me simply as Bill.

There was also a TAC advisor – tactical firearms commander. The 'silver' commander and his TAC would have to make the final decisions on which way this would go, with authorisation coming from a 'gold' commander over the phone from headquarters.

'Stamford has a mobile phone.' Bill launched straight into it. 'But he's not answering. We found *her* mobile in the abandoned car.' He indicated an officer at another desk. 'We're in radio communication with the armed officers. They've got eyes on the subject and his hostage. They've created a containment area around the quarry. We need any information you can give us about Stamford's likely reaction to the environment or the way we approach him.'

'OK. Where is he exactly?'

The silver commander walked me over to a map laid out on another table. He tapped with his finger. 'Here – in the bottom of the quarry. Obviously, our objective is to contain him and neutralise the threat he poses, without using force. But it's a rapidly evolving incident so as things develop, we're evaluating our tactical options. These things run from "green" status through to "amber" and then "red".' He glanced at the map. 'We're already at "red".'

'Which mean's what, exactly?' I asked.

'That firearms are authorised to use lethal force if necessary.'

I turned to Bill. 'Obviously, you're aware that Stamford's ex-military.'

He nodded. 'And now he's under stress and on the run.'

I talked fast. 'He's going to do what he knows best and that's rely on his training.' I nodded towards the moors. 'That's why he's gone for open ground, headed out on foot. He was a top graduate of SERE training before he was deployed overseas . . .'

'SERE?' Heslopp asked.

'Survive. Evade. Resist. Extract,' Bill explained. 'Techniques in evading capture by a hunter force and resisting interrogation. Stamford's an expert.'

'Great.' Heslopp rolled his eyes heavenward.

'He operates best out there. Under cover of darkness.' I was thinking out loud. 'Tell your armed officers, if they get into dialogue with him – try to use military language – it's what he's used to.'

'Might he respond to orders?' Bill asked.

'If he's regressing back to incidents that created his PTSD, he may believe he's back there. If he thinks you're an enemy force, he might not respond well to being commanded . . .'

Bill nodded – his face showing no signs of strain – a testament to *his* training.

I went to stand in the doorway of the claustrophobic van, looking out over the moorland. Out there, just a few hundred yards away, a deadly scenario was playing out.

I took a lungful of night air – trying to order my thoughts. The clatter of a police helicopter overhead caused me to look up into a powerful search light that swept over the car park and then headed out over the moors. I quickly ducked back inside.

'I don't think that's a good idea.' I looked over to Silver. 'If he *is* having a psychotic episode, he might believe he's back in a warzone. Having that flying overhead won't help.'

Silver nodded and reached for the radio – a minute later the helicopter flew back towards Fordley.

The radio crackled into life and we all fell silent as the firearms officer in charge of the inner cordon relayed an update.

'*Subject on the move with his hostage.*'

I listened as instructions were given while Stamford moved around the edge of the quarry – to keep a mobile containment around him.

Bill swivelled round to face me, his arm resting along the back of his chair. 'What do we know about Stamford's mental health?'

'Not as much as we'd like.' I had to be honest. 'Treated for PTSD in 2016 at Sangar House.' I nodded in the direction of the moors. 'By Michelle Briggs and her team. But the incident at Fordley train station would indicate a potential psychotic episode.'

'There's nothing on his medical records about drug or alcohol abuse, or medication he might not be taking.' Bill ran a hand across the stubble on his chin. 'Anything to indicate he was on drugs during the attack at the station? From your observation of the video?'

I thought back to that expressionless face – those dead eyes lacking all emotion at a time when any normal person would be flooded with adrenalin and cortisol and every aspect of their appearance would scream a heightened emotional response.

'He was in an altered state,' I admitted, adding cautiously, 'but we have no way of knowing whether that was due to substances or . . . something else . . .'

We were interrupted by urgent transmissions from the firearms team.

'*Subject dragging the hostage. Situation deteriorating. Advise?*'

The TAC liaised with Silver as map co-ordinates were barked across the radio as to the current location. I went to the map and looked at it uselessly, until Silver traced his finger over an area I knew well.

'He's moving on to more open ground – good for us . . . bad for him.'

'Why would he break cover?' I frowned. 'He knows what he's doing – where's he going?'

'Looks like he's heading here.' He tapped the map.

As I looked at the spot, my stomach churned with sickening realisation.

'Shit – that's not good.'

Chapter Thirty-Four

Ladstone Rock stood at the top of Norland Moor.

'It's believed that rock was used by Druids for ritual sacrifices,' I explained quickly. '"Ladstone" is a kill stone.'

The commander looked down at me, with the expression of someone dealing with a dimwit. 'But our man wouldn't know that, surely?'

'Why not? He's a local lad, from Halifax—'

The radio burst into life with an update from the firearms team.

There was a slight pause that seemed to still the air. Then the calm voice came over the radio – echoing through the heavy silence in the room, four of the deadliest words in the English language . . . '*I have the shot.*'

There seemed to be collective intake of breath.

Silver took the radio. 'You have authority from Gold – take the shot.'

'*Subject dropped down into gulley . . . taking hostage with him. I've lost sight.*'

'Confirm – have you eyeball?'

'*Negative.*'

No one moved. Everything froze in those vital few seconds – the silence broken only by the gentle hiss of the open radio frequency.

A woman's primeval scream splintered the silence – followed by the crack of a gunshot.

'Sit rep?' the commander asked.

'*Shots fired . . . no visual.*'

TAC looked across at Silver and simply nodded.

'All units, be advised shots fired. Move into position – get visual on subject – assess situation with hostage.'

I stared at the radio as if by willing it, I could see what was happening out there on the moors. My nerves were taut as piano wire, making me jump when the voice came over the radio.

'*No visual on subject. Hostage has been shot. Repeat . . . Hostage has been shot.*'

A tinny sound could be heard faintly in the background, like the small sound from an old transistor radio. Then barked commands deafening . . . filling the small space we were in.

'*Armed police . . . stand still! Drop the weapon!*'

I jumped again as the crack of a pistol rang out . . . once, twice. Then a louder volley of shots. Then . . . silence.

Chapter Thirty-Five

Fordley police station – Thursday morning

'Provoked shooting.' Heslopp leaned back in his chair.

'Suicide by cop,' I translated, watching as the detective pulled his tie down and undid the button of his collar.

He nodded. 'Once he'd killed his hostage, he came out shooting . . . They didn't have a choice.'

'That sound we heard – just before they shot him. Sounded like music?'

Heslopp leaned forward to check the record on his laptop. 'Stamford was out of sight, but they all heard a phone ring.'

'Stamford's phone?'

He nodded. 'Then a second later he appeared from around the outcrop and opened fire.'

'Do we know whether he took the call?'

'The phone's being analysed – but it appears he didn't.' He smiled across at me. 'Think he had more important things on his mind than chatting on the phone, doc. Call came from an anonymous number. We're trying to trace it.'

'Any idea what he wanted with Michelle Briggs?'

'Staff say he turned up demanding to see her. They didn't realise he was armed. Thought they could contain him until the police arrived, so they tried to calm him down.'

'That went well then.'

'Stamford was ranting – saying she had to "fix things . . . and . . . undo it." As soon as he saw her, he produced the gun. By the time officers arrived, he'd stolen her car and taken her. We know the rest.'

On my way out of the door, I paused and looked back. 'One more thing. Find out from the firearms team what the music was?'

'What?'

'The ringtone . . . on Stamford's phone. See if they can identify what it was.'

He nodded but had the expression of a man humouring me.

* * *

As I was leaving– Callum stuck his head round his office door.

'Got a minute, Jo?'

I walked into the familiar space, dumping my briefcase before dropping into the chair. He gestured with the coffee pot, which I usually declined.

'Actually, this morning I need the caffeine.'

He handed me a mug. 'Tough night I heard – not the most pleasant thing to witness.' He sat down opposite, sipping from his cup.

'I didn't actually *see* anything. Just heard it.'

'Still stressful.'

I sipped some of his disgusting coffee as I tried to think back to the last time I'd felt the grip of that suffocating anxiety. Apart from the meltdown after my encounter with Blondie – I couldn't recall it happening recently.

'Did you interview Edge yesterday?' I tried to make it sound unimportant. 'About the night Jacinta died?'

He nodded, studying me in a way I found suddenly disconcerting. Or maybe it was just my guilty conscience.

'He was out with some of the ex-military lot who work with him ... Or is it for him?' He shook his head. 'Anyway, they played pool until the small hours at a club in Fordley. Staff and a few customers corroborated that. Edge crashed at a friend's place until he went to collect De Benoit from prison.'

I glanced across the desk. 'He couldn't have killed Jacinta then?' I couldn't keep the triumph out of my voice.

'Unfortunately, not.' He couldn't keep the disappointment out of his.

I nodded, shifting the topic back to safer ground. 'Shame we couldn't interview Stamford. He could have given us valuable information about Sangar.'

'Convenient though. If Blackstone was in fear of Stamford – for whatever reason – his problem got taken care of last night.'

Convenient indeed, I thought.

'Got this back from Tom.' He was flicking through the post-mortem report. 'Toxicology confirm no drugs in Jacinta's system – apart from alcohol. With levels like these, she'd be too drunk to stand up ...' Callum scanned the report, running his finger down the columns of facts. 'Petechial haemorrhaging of the eyes – bursting of the blood vessels to you and me. Cause of death was compression of the jugular vein leading to asphyxia and cerebral hypoxia ...'

'Strangulation to you and me.'

'Was Stamford left or right-handed?'

I thought back to the video footage I knew frame by frame. 'Right. Why?'

'No DNA on the ligature, except Jacinta's. But the way the knot was tied on the stocking can indicate "handedness" of the attacker – but it's not foolproof . . .'

'And?'

'Left-handed . . .' He shot me a look. 'Blackstone's right-handed.'

I took a long breath. 'Suppose we can hope he just ties his knots in a cack- handed fashion.'

'Tom analysed the clothes Blackstone was wearing that night and found traces of Jacinta's hair and DNA, but they had what he euphemistically refers to as "legitimate access to each other" – so transfer of fibres from one to the other isn't damning evidence.'

'Any indication that Jacinta's clothes were ripped off?'

'Looks like she was undressed without a struggle – no marks on her body to suggest otherwise.'

I peered over, trying to read upside down. 'Anything else?'

'I was saving best till last. There was bruising along Jacinta's spine – consistent with a knee in her back. Appears the killer strangled her face down on the bed, while kneeling on her. The toe of his right foot was pressed into the back of her right calf leaving a partial footmark.' He pushed an autopsy photo across the desk. It showed a pinkish circular pattern on the skin. 'Tom says it's consistent with the pattern of a trainer.' I looked up to see him watching me. 'Blackstone was wearing formal shoes that night – not trainers. Tom's made a comparison with the toe print . . . it's not a match.'

'Shit!'

Chapter Thirty-Six

Kingsberry Farm – Thursday evening

There was a chill in the air as I walked Harvey across the fields. I breathed in the fresh scent of grass and warm earth and turned my face towards the last warming rays of the sun.

Harvey lolloped across and dropped a stick at my feet, then crouched down ready for the throw. I tossed it as far as I could and watched him thunder across the meadow.

With the immediacy of Jacinta's murder and the station attack, Leo Fielding's case had been pushed down everyone's priority list. It was a cold case, after all. But I'd been dreaming about crime scenes for the last week and I realised it wasn't Jacinta's case that was niggling me . . . it was Leo's.

I'd woken in the early hours over the past few days – prodded awake by the insistent nudging of my unconscious mind. The scenes that repeated night after night were a jumbled collage of two places, two bedrooms. Jacinta's and Leo's. A torn kaleidoscope of confusing impressions that had me staring into the darkness – wondering what it was that my subconscious was trying to tell me.

I turned down the track and headed back to the house with Harvey lagging behind – less enthusiastic now he knew we were on our way home.

The unconscious mind communicates in images. If it was trying to tell me something, the answer would be in the crime scene photographs – but I couldn't see any connection between Leo and Jacinta. The only similarity was that both victims were killed in the bedroom. Maybe that was all it was? There couldn't *be* any more of a connection than that.

Could there . . . ?

* * *

I sat on the floor of my office, in mellow silence only broken by the hollow ticking of the grandfather clock in the corner. I couldn't help smiling as I watched the slowly swinging pendulum measuring out each passing moment. Another legacy from my old friend George – gifted to me by his son. Now it was standing sentinel in my work space. Giving me comfort – as though George himself was watching over me.

The floor was covered in a carpet of photographs, spread around me like the jumbled pieces of two jigsaw puzzles that I was trying to fit into one coherent picture.

I scanned the crime scene images from Leo's apartment – laid out in batches according to the rooms they'd been taken in. My hand hovered over the pictures from his bedroom. His battered body on the bed . . . close-ups of the bindings on his wrists and ankles. The contents of his pockets, spread across his bedside table. His clothes folded and on the chair with his shoes underneath.

I crawled across to the pictures from Jacinta's room and scooped them up, taking them to Leo's. Silently introducing them to each other as I laid them side by side.

Jacinta looked almost peaceful beside Leo. His body was stretched out naked, tortured and scarred.

She could have been mistaken for asleep, rather than dead.

Leo's room was cluttered with the mechanics of his torture and death. No attempt made to clean *him* up. No consideration for how he would look to those who found him. No thought or concern for his dignity.

Jacinta's room, by comparison, was neat and tidy – apart from the underwear spilling out of the cabinet drawer. Her make-up and perfume bottles were arranged artistically on the dressing table. The jewellery she removed before bed laid out on her bed-side table. Her handbag and shoes on the floor beneath the chair.

The ligature was hidden under the neatly arranged duvet. Her hair had even been arranged across the pillow. Care for her and how she would look in death were evident.

The jewellery on the bedside table was stunning.

With typically feminine interest, I picked up the photo and held it close to get a better look. The bracelet sparkled with the unique grey-white brilliance that only emanates from true dia-monds. The clasp had the unmistakeable entwined double 'C' of the Cartier logo, which was replicated on the diamond earrings on the table.

'Great taste, Jacinta,' I muttered thoughtfully, picking up a picture of the Gucci sandals and matching handbag underneath the bedroom chair. Just as I was about to drop the pictures – the shoes caught my attention. I looked again.

Something was reflected in the photographer's flash. Glinting in the open toe of one of the sandals.

I hunted around the floor for more images of the shoes.

Harvey was sprawled in his usual spot on the Chinese rug in front of my desk, snoring contentedly, his big body lying on a few stray pictures. I rolled him over as he lifted his head, grumbling sleepily.

'You're not very helpful, are you?'

He stretched and yawned, managing to lick my nose, before slumping back down.

I found the image I was looking for. There – nestled inside one of her shoes – was a matching Cartier watch.

I sat back on my haunches and stared at it for a second, before crawling across the floor to the area I'd designated as Leo's bedroom. I picked up a picture of the chair where he'd neatly folded his clothes – his shoes side by side beneath the chair – and stared at the image of his wallet pushed inside the toe of one shoe.

A memory flashed across my mind – a younger self. The school swimming champion, representing Yorkshire County.

The 5 a.m. training sessions at Fordley university pool. The chlorine smell of the poolside changing cubicle with the constantly wet floor that I had to avoid dropping dry clothes onto.

Putting my watch and purse inside my shoe, with a sock stuffed in behind to keep my valuables hidden and safe while I trained.

An adolescent habit carried into adulthood. A signature behaviour. Habitual and unconscious – just like the way we fold our clothes.

Two bedrooms of seemingly unconnected murder victims – two years apart.

Two piles of clothing – neatly folded in exactly the same way and stacked on the seats. Shoes placed side by side underneath.

Two locations.

Two victims.

One killer.

Chapter Thirty-Seven

Kingsberry Farm – Early Friday morning

It was almost 1 a.m. I stared at the notes I'd made, my fatigued mind not really taking them in anymore. There was nothing else I could do now until the rest of the world was awake.

I was about to leave the office when my phone rang. I'd have ignored it, but caller ID said it was Callum.

'I wasn't sure you'd still be awake,' he said.

'You and me both – what's up?'

'There's been an incident.'

His tone sent a tingle of apprehension prickling across my skin. 'What kind of incident?'

'A fire. Major incident . . . the whole of Fordley centre has been closed off while they try to tackle it, but it doesn't look good. Probable fatalities . . .'

The roof of my mouth was dry. I could sense something awful was coming. I swallowed hard before finding my voice. 'Where?'

'Nique's apartment block. Looks like it started in the penthouse – it's been totally destroyed. I'm sorry, Jo.'

* * *

I switched on the small TV in the corner of the kitchen – brewing tea and watching the breaking news bulletins. There was sparse information, as the city was only just becoming aware of it. My phone proved more useful, as residents nearby hit social media, streaming real-time images of the blaze with amateur commentaries.

I'd tried ringing the last number I had for Edge – no answer. It was the same when I tried Nique's mobile and my therapy practice.

Edge was smuggling Nique back into the apartment for a meeting with her probation officer on Wednesday. The blaze started late on Thursday. She should have been back in my office by then – I hoped to God she had been.

But if they were safe, why couldn't I reach either of them?

There was no doubt in my mind this fire was deliberate and it didn't take the deductive reasoning of a genius to guess who might have planned it or why.

Harvey whimpering at the door to go out made me look at the clock. It was 6 a.m. already. I was still wearing the clothes I'd had on yesterday and hadn't eaten or slept.

I stood in the porch, teasing fingers through my hair to untangle my thoughts, as I tried to shake off the mind-numbing fatigue.

Keeping things from Callum meant I couldn't enlist his help in tracking down Nique and Edge to make sure they were safe.

He knew about Blackstone's threats against Nique and, like me, would suspect he was behind this attack. He was pulling the businessman in for more questioning this morning and I wanted to be there.

As always when faced with a challenge, inaction was the thing that stressed me the most. Doing *anything* was better for me than doing nothing. An antidote to feelings of impotence and helplessness.

I let Harvey back in and went upstairs to shower and get dressed. I had things to do.

* * *

Laburnum Terrace – Friday morning

I sat in the Roadster outside my old office and stared at the front door – as if by sheer force of will I could make Nique appear, safe and sound. But I'd already been inside to look for her and knew the place was empty.

A mile from the centre of Fordley, the area was just at the edge of the road blocks that had been set up to keep people away from the scene. The unmistakeable acrid smell of burning hung in the air and a fine flurry of white ash was falling like snow, dusting the rag-top of my car. A reminder, if one were needed, that a scene of total devastation was so close by.

When I'd gone into the office, I'd expected to breathe a sigh of relief at the sight of Nique sitting on the sofa in my old treatment room. Instead, I found cups stacked neatly on the draining board – her clothes and books still there – all looking as though she'd just got up and walked out. But no sign of the woman herself.

I jumped when my mobile rang.

'Jo – it's me.' Jen's voice crackled through the Bluetooth. 'Have you seen the news?'

'Callum called me in the early hours. I've been up all night trying to get more information.'

'Where are you?'

'I couldn't stand watching it unfold on the news. So, I drove down here. But I can't get near. They've cordoned off the whole area.'

There was a pause and I knew she was struggling to say something that didn't sound hypocritical. 'You know how I felt about you being involved with that woman, but if this turns out to be bad news, I'm sorry, Jo. I wouldn't wish this on anyone.'

'I know,' I said wearily, rubbing a hand across my tired eyes.

'I care about *you* . . . you know?' Her voice faltered slightly and I knew she was regretting being so distant lately. Her disapproval of Nique had created a void between us that she desperately wanted to breach now.

Despite my crippling fatigue – or maybe because of it – I decided to cut her some slack. Besides, I didn't have the energy for recriminations.

'They're reporting fatalities. I hope to God she wasn't in there, Jen.'

'I know, sweetheart . . . What about Edge? Have you heard from him? I mean, he lived there as well, didn't he?'

'Yes, he did . . .'

I'd been about to say that Edge was more likely to have been in there than Nique – but deceit meant I'd cut myself off from my closest ally. The gaps in what she and Callum knew meant I had to guard what I could disclose – and that made navigating a way through this so much more difficult.

The ache of complete isolation at a time when I needed the companionship of my closest supporters ran through me like a physical blow. The ice-cold loneliness of separation from everyone I would have reached out to made me actually shiver as I sat there – frozen in an emotional quarantine of my own making.

'You think Blackstone's behind this?' Jen asked.

I stared blindly out of the window. 'Bloody big coincidence if he isn't.'

'Anything I can do, Jo, just let me know?'

'Listen, Jen, I'm going to see Callum. I'll get more information there than sitting at home. Take today off and make a long weekend of it. Let me know if there's anything I need to be dealing with, otherwise I'll see you on Monday.'

'Oh, there is actually. Marissa emailed to say she's lost her mobile.' My publisher was renowned for losing things. Car keys, diaries. It wasn't the first time. 'You need to call her about the book promotion, can you ring the office landline?'

'Will do. Enjoy the time off.'

I stared at the empty street for a while. With road blocks in place, it was pointless trying to drive into town. I got out and began to walk.

Chapter Thirty-Eight

Fordley police station – Friday morning

As I walked up the wide stone steps and through the double glass doors into the reception area of the station, my mind was already making the connections between Jacinta and Leo Fielding that I wanted to run past Callum.

I was so deep in thought, I almost bumped into two men coming the other way. An automatic apology died on my lips as I glanced up to see Neville Blackstone. Despite the early hour, he looked like he'd just stepped out of a board meeting – immaculately dressed in a sharp suit, crisp white shirt and silk tie.

'Well, well, Doctor McCready, what an unexpected pleasure.' The sardonic smirk made me want to wipe my knuckles across his teeth. He tilted his head. 'You look tired . . . Stressful night?'

The rage that had simmered beneath the surface ever since I'd watched the images of the blaze bubbled up inside. The man beside him, put a hand on Blackstone's elbow.

'We need to go, Sir Neville.'

'Judging by the images coming out of Fordley, looks like we *both* had an eventful night.' I was surprised at how calm I sounded.

That thin smile didn't reach his eyes. 'I really don't know what you mean.' He nodded towards his companion. 'My solicitor was with me all night. We had an excellent dinner, while discussing this morning's interview. I really didn't have time to concern myself with anything else.'

He made to leave and I side-stepped – blocking his path. 'Hope and pray she isn't dead, Blackstone,' I said quietly, through clenched teeth.

He reached out to push me aside. 'Get out of my way.'

Reflected light glinted at his wrist. I stared at the gold cuff-links for a split second as an image from last night crashed through my mind.

'Nice.' I tapped his wrist with my finger.

Blackstone pulled his hand away. 'They belonged to Oliver.' He almost spat the words in my face, tucking his cuff back beneath the sleeve of his jacket.

His solicitor was attempting to steer him towards the door. 'Sir Neville . . . please . . .'

Blackstone angrily brushed him away, regaining his composure as he smoothed down his tie. 'Personally, I hope De Benoit burned in the hell she deserved last night—'

White-hot fury streaked across my vision and I took a step towards him. I was rewarded by the shock flickering across his face as he stumbled back in an attempt to create space between us.

I don't know what I intended – whether I intended anything – but my half-formed objective was halted as a broad chest suddenly got in my way. Like a predator fixed on its prey – my eyes looked past the obstruction. Glaring at Blackstone, I stepped to the side to move again, but annoyingly the chest moved with me, blocking the route. Frustrated, I looked up into penetrating blue eyes.

Callum frowned down at me. 'A word, Jo – in my office.'

I was vaguely aware of the solicitor almost man-handling his client past us as Callum cupped my elbow in a firm grip and steered me towards the lift.

* * *

'Just what the hell did you think you were doing?' He was barely holding onto his temper as he glowered at me.

'Think you'll find, he pushed me first,' I offered lamely, like a kid caught fighting in the playground.

'Oh, that's all right then.' He paced in front of the desk. 'That'll make all the difference when his lawyer makes accusations of threats and intimidation from the police's own profiler!' He slammed his mug down on the desk – spilling coffee. 'Do you deliberately *plan* on making my life difficult or does it just come naturally?'

'OK, OK.' I washed a hand across my eyes, exhausted. I looked up as he glared at me. 'I've not slept since Wednesday – I'm all strung out and then that bastard goads me.' I was struggling to keep the volume down. 'All I did was take a step towards him—'

'And what would you have done if I hadn't got in the way?' he snapped.

'Luckily, we don't need to find out now, do we?'

'Jesus!' He sat down heavily in his chair, running fingers through his hair. 'Of all the people you could square up to!' He looked at me like a parent, exasperated by a wayward child. 'And in front of his solicitor . . . In a police station!'

I had no defence to that, so didn't offer one.

'Have you heard anything more about the fire?' I asked – as much to distract him away from his anger as out of a genuine need to know.

He stared at me for a moment, then sighed. 'The fire started in the penthouse. They managed to evacuate the building, so all the residents in the lower floors got out.'

He hesitated.

'What?' I needed to know but at the same time, didn't want to hear him say it.

'The blaze was so intense; the penthouse floor gave way – collapsing into the apartment below which was vacant.' He studied me before adding quietly. 'There's a body in the wreckage, but it's not safe enough to recover it.'

'So, if the flat below was empty ... whoever's down there must have been in the penthouse?'

He nodded slowly and his expression softened. 'Looks that way ... I'm sorry, Jo.'

I took a ragged breath to compose myself – then tried to get my mind back to the reason for my visit.

'I was hoping to see you before you interviewed Blackstone. Obviously, I was too late.'

He took a mouthful of coffee. 'He had early meetings scheduled, so we accommodated him.'

I was struggling to concentrate – my mind conjuring up unwanted images of a burned corpse lying broken in twisted wreckage. I wanted to ask him whether he knew if the body was male or female. But it was a pointless question. If they couldn't get near enough to recover it – they wouldn't know.

'Blackstone gave us the same line about Stamford that he did with you,' Callum was saying. 'We pushed him on it but he didn't budge. Besides, he's more relaxed about it all now Stamford's dead.'

'Did you ask him about his threats against Nique? About the fire?'

'His solicitor advised "no comment", as you'd imagine. It's a minefield to walk into, given who he is. We can't accuse him out of hand.' He looked across at me. 'And there is no solid evidence.'

'Apart from the fact that he threatened Nique's life if she ever came out of prison.' I tried to keep my tone calm. Not sure I managed it.

'So do a lot of grieving families. Lots of things are said in the heat of a murder trial, but most of the time, that's all it is – talk. Majority of people don't act on it. Besides, his solicitor is his alibi for that night.'

'Blackstone wouldn't have done it himself. He'd pay someone, just like he paid—' I could have bitten my tongue off – too late.

'Who?' His eyes narrowed. 'Blondie?'

I berated myself for the slip – fatigue had a lot to answer for. 'Maybe.' I shrugged as if it was of no consequence. 'I couldn't think of anyone else who would have me followed on the day Nique was released . . . Too much of a coincidence.'

'Is there something you're not telling me?' he asked in that deceptively quiet way he had.

'Of course not.' I rummaged in my briefcase to break his uncomfortable eye contact. I would usually have talked him through my findings – explaining the rationale and my conclusions – but my brain felt like mush. Lack of food and sleep were taking their toll.

I pushed two photographs across the desk. He stared at them and then looked back at me, his expression begging the questions.

'This was why I wanted to see you . . . I was looking at these last night. Two chairs with neatly folded clothing on them,' I said. 'One in Jacinta's bedroom and one in Leo's.' I selected two more pictures and slid them across. 'Two pairs of shoes, both beneath the chairs.'

Two more photographs slid across to join their partners. 'Valuables safely tucked into the toes of both . . .'

He moved the photographs around with an index finger, before looking across at me.

'The signature of the same killer,' I said. 'And here's the best bit . . .' I took the picture of Leo Fielding's bedside table and slapped it down in front of him.

He stared at it.

I tapped the image of the gold cufflinks on the table. Leo's gold cufflinks in the distinctive shape of a pair of golden acorns.

'The same cufflinks Blackstone had on just now.'

Chapter Thirty-Nine

Kingsberry Farm – Friday Afternoon

Callum was going to liaise with DS Albright on the cold-case team. Somewhere there would be a link between Leo Fielding and Blackstone. But until he came back to me, there was little more I could do.

I brought the post in from the box by the porch, then brewed tea and switched on the TV to catch up on the latest from the fire. I watched the scrolling banner along the bottom of the screen as I made a sandwich with whatever I could find in the fridge.

The towering block of steel and glass looked like a smouldering scene from a disaster movie. Fire appliances grouped around the building, hoses snaking along the street which was slick with water and foam. Fire fighters looking exhausted, the strain of the long night showing in white eyes that looked out from blackened faces.

Reports confirmed at least one person had been trapped in the wreckage, but the structure was too dangerous to recover the body. Only residents from the penthouse were unaccounted for. Unconfirmed reports said the body was believed to be that of a woman. No names were being released.

I stared at the screen not knowing what to think or feel, not wanting to accept that, somehow, my friends were in there.

I started to go through the post and found the package Marissa had forwarded. The padded envelope contained a thin bundle of letters from readers. One of them caught my attention. It had 'Private and confidential' on the front in red ink. Distractedly I ripped it open. The single sheet was folded once – the neat handwriting simply said: '*Stay away from Nique.*'

I sat and stared at it – then checked the postmark. It was dated the Monday after Nique's release.

Whoever was warning me off obviously didn't know where I lived and had no other way to reach me.

I studied the four simple words – trying to squeeze as much information as I could from them. The author referred to her as Nique. Only people close to her called her that.

Could my new pen-pal be Blackstone? But even as the thought occurred to me, I dismissed it. Such an amateur approach really wasn't his style.

My mobile vibrated a message alert. As if I'd conjured her up, it was a text from Marissa's mobile asking me to call. I dialled but it went straight to voicemail. I tried her landline number, surprised when she answered it almost immediately.

'You found your mobile then?'

'What?' She sounded confused.

'Jen said you'd lost your phone . . . but I just got your text.'

'Oh that. No . . . I still haven't found the damn thing.'

'So how come you just texted me from it?'

'I was working late in the office on Thursday. Was going to call you but it was after midnight.' She vaped noisily. 'Knew I'd forget if I left it, so I set a task on my mobile to send you the text. Then I went and lost the bloody phone. But at least the automatic message did its job.'

'You can do that?'

She laughed. 'You're such a technophobe, yes, you can do that. Anyway, get your diary. I need some dates.'

*　*　*

For the first time in months, probably due to complete exhaustion, sleep came easily, which made waking up with a sudden start even more shocking. I sat bolt upright and squinted at the digital display on the clock – 1.20 a.m.

Harvey was howling and throwing himself against the kitchen door. I swung my feet out of bed and pulled on a robe as I headed for the stairs. As I reached the kitchen, my hand hovered over the light switch, then hesitated as I thought better of it. I knew the layout of my house in the dark – a potential intruder didn't. Best to have the advantage.

Harvey's hackles were raised as he growled softly and looked at the door, tilting his head at a sound inaudible to human ears.

'What is it, boy?' I whispered, walking barefoot across the stone floor. I peered out of the small side window onto the gravel drive outside. The security light hadn't come on. The whole area was eerily dark. I took a breath to steady myself. Other than the blood thundering in my ears I couldn't hear anything.

Instinctively, I pulled open the tall pantry door and bent down to reach the recess under the very bottom shelf – my fingers closing around the barrel of my father's old shotgun. It contravened all the rules of my licence to store it out of the gun cabinet and to keep it loaded – but given what I did for a living, it was a rule I was willing to break.

I checked the cartridges were loaded, slipped off the safety catch, then put my hand on Harvey's collar to hold him back. Still nothing moved outside, but he continued to growl, straining to be let out.

'If this is just a fox, you're in big trouble,' I warned as I eased open the door. The porch was cold after the warmth of the kitchen and I shivered as I moved to the oak door and slid back the lock. As soon as it opened, Harvey bolted out, his baritone bark splitting the silence as he crashed through the bushes.

The security light burst on and I stood in the pool of ice-white illumination – my back braced against the oak door, the shotgun half raised – listening to the commotion as Harvey found whatever was lurking in the undergrowth.

Cursing the light for ruining my night vision, I slid my finger inside the trigger guard and raised the shotgun just a fraction.

'Harvey!' I called.

A sudden sound from behind, caused me to swing around to the right, as a figure stepped out of the darkness and strong hands ripped the shotgun out of my grasp.

Chapter Forty

I looked up, terrified, into flint-grey eyes that looked back with a mixture of amusement and grudging admiration.

'Careful, princess. You can put a serious hole in someone with that!'

'Edge!'

I threw myself at his chest and held him. It felt like hugging a boulder.

'You scared the living shit out of me!' Anger jostled with relief that he was alive.

His response was cut short as Harvey thundered out of the bushes and ran towards the house, carrying what looked like a bundle of cloth in his mouth. He slowed for a second, taking in the scene, then dropped the rag and launched himself at Edge.

'Harvey . . . Stand!' I shouted, only just in time. He put his front paws straight out, digging into the gravel before sliding to a shuddering stop, his bared teeth just inches from Edge's groin. 'Here, boy.'

Reluctantly he came to me – careful to keep his body between me and the threat. I grabbed his collar with a shaky hand as he growled softly, not yet sure about letting this intruder go un-chewed.

'Great welcome.' Edge managed a thin smile.

'It's not funny,' I snapped as the adrenalin surge finally began to ebb away. 'You nearly gave me a friggin' heart attack! What's wrong with knocking on the door like normal people?'

'I had to make sure you were alone.' He broke the gun and slid the brass cartridges out of the barrel, before snapping it shut and handing it back to me.

'And what's *that*?' I nodded to the scrap of shredded material Harvey had dropped.

'Well, it *was* my jacket. I rubbed it around the doorway and then laid a trail through the hedge as a diversion, just in case Hound of the Baskervilles came out first.' He looked me up and down and managed a tired smile. 'Can't say I was prepared for the sight of you in nothing but a dressing gown and toting a shotgun though.'

I pushed Harvey through the porch door, then turned back to him, hugging him again. 'Thank God you're OK. Where's Nique?'

My stomach dropped when he didn't answer the question.

'One thing at a time, princess. There's a lot I need to tell you. I left the Land Rover down the lane till I knew it was safe. Can I bring it round?'

'Yes.' A million questions jostled for position – but I knew now wasn't the time to ask. 'Park it round the back in the barn.'

By the time I'd reloaded the shotgun and returned it to its hiding place, I could hear the lumbering engine of the Defender as Edge swung it round the back of the house. I turned as he came in – followed by a figure I'd prayed for, but never expected to see again.

'Nique!'

Her hair hung in a tousled mess around her shoulders. Her eyes were sunken into deep sockets ringed with dark shadows. She looked pale and hollowed out by shock and fatigue. The pair of them looked like a couple of refugees fleeing some natural disaster – which was closer to the truth than was comfortable.

I looked from one to the other, then automatically began filling the kettle.

'They've firebombed my apartment, *ma copine*.' Nique's shoulders slumped. 'One of my girls is dead!'

Edge nodded towards the kettle. 'If it's all the same to you, think we need something a bit stronger than tea.'

*   *   *

We sat around my kitchen table, nursing glasses of brandy as Edge brought me up to speed.

'We'd both fallen asleep on the sofa.' He ran a weary hand across his face as he recounted events of that night. 'I woke up when the smoke alarms went off, but Sandra had gone.'

Sandra Hayton had been one of Nique's girls and worked at her club in Fordley. Against all the rules, Edge confessed he'd been seeing the girl for the past few months.

He took a sip of brandy, staring at a spot in the distance. 'She'd covered me with a blanket, probably tried to wake me, then gave up and took herself off to bed. The apartment was full of smoke.' He glanced at Nique who had listened in complete silence. 'I ran out to the hall, but it was already ablaze. I could see through the open door into the bedroom . . .' He shook his head slowly, looking down, unable to meet our eyes. 'I could see

Sandra on the bed – but it was already on fire. She wasn't moving . . .' He held up his hands to show blackened skin. 'I tried to get in the room, burnt my hands on the door frame. Got a couple of paces in and the floor started to give way.' He looked at Nique, his eyes imploring. 'I couldn't get to her, Nique . . . I tried . . .'

Nique sipped from her glass, her eyes steady as she regarded him. There was no emotion, but then I hadn't expected any.

There was only a simmering anger behind those eyes – whether directed at Edge or at whoever started the fire, I wasn't sure. Nor was he, which is why he shifted uncomfortably in his chair. Taking a final swig that emptied his glass.

'The only way out was down the hall to the front door – but it was an inferno.' His hand went for the glass, suddenly realising it was empty. I reached out and topped it up.

'You were lucky to get out alive.' I saw the torment on his face and wanted to say something that would ease the guilt and pain I knew he was feeling – but no words would do that.

He took a ragged breath. 'Only way was up onto the roof garden. Thank God we were in the penthouse. There's an external fire escape from there that goes down to the balcony of the flat below.' He sipped from his glass, but I doubted he was tasting it. 'Went down each one till I got to the ground floor apartment. That's got a security grill on the balcony, accessed from the outside by a key code, to stop people getting onto the fire escape from the street. The woman who lives there has a cat. At night she props the grill open so the bloody thing can get out rather than crapping all over her balcony. That's how I got into the street.'

Nique turned to me. 'He went to your office on foot to check I was OK. But once I'd heard what happened, I didn't feel safe there. We left in the Land Rover.'

I took a drink to give myself some thinking time. Firebombing Nique's apartment put this into a whole new league.

I looked at Edge. 'Do you think they knew it was Sandra in there with you?'

He shook his head slowly. 'I'd arranged to meet her at the club. Blackstone's men had the apartment under surveillance. When they saw probation coming to visit, then the police, they would've been convinced it was Nique in there. Sandra wanted to come back with me at the end of the night, but if I'd just walked her through the front door they'd have smelled a rat. Everyone knew the strict house rules about seeing the girls. I'd never have taken her back with Nique there.'

Nique watched him across the table – sipping from her half-empty brandy glass.

'I got one of the lads to smuggle Sandra in through the under-ground car park from the block next door.' His eyes never left mine, his tone tight with anger as he said softly, 'They must've waited till they were sure I was in there.'

'Jesus,' I said softly.

'We spent last night in the Land Rover down in your woods,' Edge went on. 'I needed to make sure Blackstone's men weren't staking this place out too.'

I went to the counter and got the warning letter, pushed it across the table. 'This was sent via my publisher. Do you recognise the writing?'

Nique studied it, then shook her head, pushing it back.

'Who would warn me away from seeing you?' I searched her face for answers. 'It's someone close to you . . .'

She suddenly looked exhausted and I felt bad for putting more on her than she already had to deal with. 'I've no idea, *ma copine*.' She ran a hand across her eyes and reached for my hand across the table. 'Can we stay here tonight?'

'Of course.'

I tried to sound unfazed, but my mind was already racing through the tangle of implications. I'd have to keep Jen away from the farm for a start, not to mention Callum.

Nique drained the last of her brandy, setting the glass gently down on the table, before looking up to meet my eyes with a calmness undeserving of the situation.

'I heard on the radio they can't recover Sandra's body yet . . .' Something about those words made me want to shiver. 'Until they do, Blackstone thinks I'm dead. That gives us a window of opportunity.' She looked at Edge. 'If we bring our plans forward, we can be out of the country before he realises I'm not.'

He simply nodded. 'Leave it with me.'

As I showed her upstairs, I couldn't escape the feeling that the decisions I would make from now on might mean the difference between life and death – for someone.

Chapter Forty-One

Kingsberry Farm – Early Saturday morning

I tossed and turned – my unquiet mind tormented by images of burning buildings and tortured bodies. Finally, I gave up and swung my legs out of bed. The clock said just after 4 a.m.

The past week was beginning to take its toll. Lack of sleep and the pressure of contributing to two live cases meant I was running on empty.

I knew now that Leo Fielding and Jacinta Williams had been murdered by the same hand. But the scenes had very different characteristics. I needed to understand the psyche of a killer who could commit crimes that were the same, but different – and why that might be.

Then we had Blackstone's charity – Sangar – and the connection to random attacks carried out by seemingly unconnected individuals. At least for that, I had the makings of a theory. I just needed to organise my fractured thinking.

'Get your act together, McCready.' I scolded my reflection in the bathroom mirror. Pulling on a robe I went downstairs. The kitchen was warm and I flipped the lid on the Aga, wondering where Harvey was.

As if I'd conjured him up, the door nudged open and he padded across the kitchen. The long tail wagged his whole body as I crouched down to wrap my arms around him. 'Morning, fella.'

He licked my nose, then buried his head against my neck, the weight of him almost pushing me over.

Preparing the teapot, I noticed Harvey had gone back the way he'd come. I left the tea to brew and went to investigate.

With sunrise still an hour away, the lounge was in darkness, but I could just make out Harvey on the sofa in front of the huge stone fireplace.

'Hey you, 'I scolded, only half annoyed. 'You know you're not allowed on there.'

'He's not on the sofa.' The unexpected growl of a deep voice made me jump. 'He's lying on me!'

'Christ, Edge! Are you determined to give me a heart attack?' The shadowy figure sat up. 'Sorry, princess . . .'

I snapped on a lamp. 'What's wrong with the spare room?'

He ran a large hand over his shaved head. 'Nothing, darling.' He managed a weak grin. 'Just wanted to stay downstairs.' He ruffled Harvey's ears. 'Like my mate here – on guard duty.'

He was trying to make light of it, but the strain showed on his face and I knew he was thinking about Sandra.

He unfolded himself from the sofa and stretched.

'You must be stiff as a plank,' I said.

He scratched the stubble on his jaw. 'Beats a drainage ditch in County Omagh.' He grinned. 'Or sleeping up a tree in the jungle, getting bitten to death by mozzies.'

'Put like that, you're in the lap of luxury then.'

He'd slept in the clothes he'd been wearing ever since the fire. The dark silk suit and white shirt looked incongruous given the circumstances.

'All I need is a mug of tea and a shower,' he said grinning. 'Bit of scran wouldn't go amiss either – if that's OK?'

We went into the kitchen, with Harvey fussing around Edge's heels.

'You've made a friend. He's usually cautious around new people.'

Edge sat at the table, pulling Harvey's head onto his knee.

'Me and animals have an understanding. Part of the gypsy heritage.'

'I didn't know your family were travellers,' I confessed, putting a steaming mug of tea in front of him. On reflection I didn't know much about his life.

He sounded wistful. 'Learned to look after myself . . . Independence the hard way.' He watched as I began cracking eggs into a bowl. 'Stood me in good stead though when I joined the paras. Sergeant was like a pussy cat compared to my old man. As for sniper training, I was a natural. My dad taught me to shoot when I was a nipper. Could take the hind legs off a bee at forty yards. Could live off the land for weeks by the time I was fourteen.' He winked at me. 'If you know what I mean?'

'Poaching?'

He laughed. 'I prefer calling it a redistribution of natural resources.'

'Why the army?' I asked as I put bread in the toaster and beat the eggs.

'I was a fighter for the travelling community.' He put up his fists. 'You know – bare knuckle . . . pretty good, but I ran with shady company. Probably would've have ended up in the nick if I'd stayed. I was young, wanted to travel, have some adventures.'

When I'd first met him during Nique's trial, the thing that struck me most was his immaculate appearance. Expensive handmade suits, the lining of his jackets in coloured silk, matching handkerchief in the top pocket. Shoes, polished like mirrors – which I'd attributed to his time in the military. The grooming complemented by perfect manners and a respectful air, especially around women. Many of whom gave him more than a second glance during the trial. His quiet capability – a silent menace – acting like a pheromone to the opposite sex. Reminding me of a throwback to the sixties gangsters – like the Kray twins. A savage in a Savile Row suit.

These days he was Nique's legitimate business partner, but with an undercurrent of carefully concealed aggression that sounded a warning bell to the unwary.

'I'd have served at Her Majesty's pleasure one way or another.' He continued to fuss Harvey, who was loving all the attention. 'Decided it might as well be in the army.' He sat back and poured more tea from the pot. 'Did my twenty years – would have stayed on longer if I could.' He watched as I put a pile of scrambled eggs onto the toast and set the plate in front of him. 'The Falklands happened when I was sixteen – that's what made my mind up.' He dug into the food, like a man who hadn't eaten for a week. 'Two years later I was in uniform – First Battalion, Parachute Regiment.'

'Is that where you got your nickname?' I asked, as I watched him eat.

He grinned round a mouthful of toast. 'My sergeant thought it was hilarious, given my surname. That's where nicknames usually start. Still – could have been worse. My mate's surname was Day. He served twenty years being called Doris!'

I laughed as I topped up his mug.

'But as a sniper, it took on another meaning. The lads use to say having me along, gave them a certain "edge".' He shrugged. 'It stuck.'

I watched him eat as my mind trawled through the sparse database of facts that existed on Edge's military career. 'You were attached to the SAS in Sierra Leone, weren't you?'

He thoughtfully chewed his food – as though debating whether to talk about it. Finally nodding. 'Nique said your old man was in the SAS. Heard he didn't beat the clock?'

The names of the SAS who died on operations were inscribed on the plinth of the Regimental clock tower at the barracks. To survive and come back alive was known as 'beating the clock'.

'No,' I said quietly. 'Pete was killed in '96.'

He concentrated on his plate. 'Sierra Leone – Operation Barras, to release British soldiers from an ugly militia group . . .'

'The West Side Boys?'

He shot me a look. 'You know about that?'

I shrugged. 'I take an interest – you know, because of Pete's service.'

He pushed his plate away and swilled the remaining tea round his mug, as though contemplating a fine wine.

'Some of the guys who work with you now are ex-special forces aren't they?'

His slate grey eyes regarded mine carefully. 'Some.' His tone was cautious and it was clear that any credit I had being an SAS widow had its limits.

'So how did you meet Nique?' I moved onto safer ground.

'After I came out – considered taking mercenary jobs. Money was good – but I'd just come back from Iraq and to be honest,

I'd seen enough. Was up here with a few mates, went into a club after the pubs emptied out. There was a bit of trouble with some drunks. The boys on the door couldn't cope, so we gave them a hand.' He looked up at me, grinning at the memory. 'Turned out it was Nique's place.'

'You think the world of her, don't you?'

He paused for a second, then looked down. 'Love that girl like a baby sister, you know that.'

I squeezed his hand across the table. 'She'll come round. She loves you too . . .'

He looked up. 'You and I both know she's loyal to the people she *does* care about – but she's not wired quite the same way we are, is she?'

'The feelings she has for you run deep. That's love, Edge. As surely as it is for any of us. She cares for you as much as she did for Yalena.'

'The way she was with Yalena,' he said, reaching for the teapot and finding it empty. 'That *was* the closest thing to true love I've ever seen in her.'

I took the teapot and went to the Aga. 'What was she like?'

'OK, I suppose – if you like that kind of thing.'

'What "kind of thing"?'

'She'd been a gymnast as a kid in Russia,' he said, as if that explained everything. 'Tipped for the Olympics, before she got an injury that ended it all – but she was an athlete . . . muscular.' He sculpted the air with his hands. 'No curves, you know? Not her usual type.'

Maybe Nique's tastes had changed? I thought, as I recalled Officer Harland in Styal. But kept the thought to myself.

248

'Yalena was childlike in some ways,' he was saying. 'Could be endearing when she wanted to be . . .'

'But?'

He shrugged. 'She had a tough childhood in Russia – came from poverty and that made her hard. Her family were on the wrong side of the law. I heard her old man did business with some seriously bad boys. She was a hustler. Her event management company had a lot of rich punters, mostly from the Soviet and the Eastern Bloc. But they weren't as "exclusive" as Nique's clients.'

'In what way?'

'Our clientele were lords, MPs and society names. Yalena organised over-the-top parties for Russian gangsters, corrupt oligarchs. She saw a chance to elevate herself to the next level.'

'You think she used Nique?'

He hesitated. 'Wouldn't put it quite like that.'

'Can't imagine Nique being manipulated that easily.' I baited the hook to get him to open up.

'She wasn't.' He was guarded.

I wanted to know more.

'What then?'

He shrugged. 'In every relationship there's a lover and a beloved. Yalena was the beloved. Wrapped Nique round her little finger. Nique's no fool . . . She knew exactly what was happening but indulged her anyway – besotted with her.'

'But the partnership worked?'

'Oh yeah – it worked. I never knew Nique happier than those five years they were together. They made each other rich too, let's not forget.' He shook his head. 'But after Yalena's suicide, I watched my girl come crashing down so far that I never thought I'd get her back. She blamed herself for Yalena being at the party that night, but what made it worse . . .'

'What?'

'Yalena blamed Nique, too.' His eyes turned to flint at the memory of it. 'After we got Yalena out of the country, I'd travel over to see her. She had to have surgery for some of her injuries—'

'I didn't realise . . .'

'Hmm – Blackstone and his mates beat her pretty bad. Broken cheekbone and eye socket, she was a mess. Nique arranged for it all to be done in private clinics. We'd got Yalena a new identity – passport, papers. If she was cold before, she was bloody glacial afterwards. She wouldn't let Nique off the hook for making her go to the party that night.'

'Did she? Make her go?'

'Not exactly.' It was obvious he didn't want to say too much.

Nique's relationship with Yalena was something she never talked about – but I'd always felt those missing pieces were key to deciphering the enigma that was her personality. And Edge was probably the only person who could fill in the blanks.

'When I interviewed her for the book, Nique told me Yalena never got involved with the escort side of the business. She just organised the events.' I refilled the teapot while I waited for him to pick that up – or not. I'd long ago learned that the most powerful question was a silent one.

'On the night of Blackstone's party, Nique had agreed to support a fundraiser in Fordley,' he said. 'She asked Yalena as a one-off – to go with the girls and make sure everything was OK. It caused a row, but eventually Yalena agreed.' He looked heavenward. 'God knows, Nique did enough for her and never asked for anything in return. So, when it went bad . . . you can only imagine . . .' He ran a hand over his eyes. 'Yalena refused to come back for the trial. I told Nique it was because of her injuries and then the treatment – that she was too sick to travel, too traumatised.'

'But that wasn't true?'

He slowly shook his head. 'How could I tell her that the reason the so-called love of her life wouldn't come back to testify was to hurt her. Bitch wouldn't lift a finger to help Nique – just left her to it. That night at Boltby Hall changed everything.' He glanced up at me. 'Funny thing is, before all this happened, Nique loved that place. Even talked about buying it.'

'Really?'

He took a mouthful of tea. 'When they first went to check it out as a venue, they fell for it. Steeped in history – been there since the Reformation or something.' He managed a thin smile. 'You know how Nique loves all that stuff. The owner gave them a tour. She came back like an excited kid, telling me about a priest hole in the cellar that went down to the chapel in the village. They both came back with cobwebs in their hair after exploring it all. Think maybe she would have gone ahead and bought it . . . if it hadn't all gone so bloody sour. After what happened the owner couldn't even give the place away. Derelict now – damned shame.'

His tea was going cold, but he didn't seem to notice. 'When the news came that Yalena had died, Nique knew then she'd never be able to put things right between them.' I felt my throat constrict at the sight of such raw pain in his eyes. 'She blamed herself for Yalena's death . . . It changed her.'

251

'How?' I asked quietly – not wanting to break this spell of intimate disclosure that seemed to have settled around us.

'She was in prison in Durham then. Just pressed the self-destruct button. Risky behaviours, trouble with other prisoners. I thought she'd end up killing someone in there . . . or getting killed herself. Just didn't seem to care – like she had nothing to get out for. That's when she started the affair with that prison officer, the one that got her sentence extended.'

An unexpected voice suddenly shattered the atmosphere.

'Very cosy.' Nique wasn't even trying to hide her annoyance. 'Please, carry on – don't mind me.'

Chapter Forty-Two

She was standing in the doorway to the kitchen – I wanted to ask how long she'd been there, but that felt like reaffirming our guilt.

'Can I get you something to eat?'

'A portion of loyalty would be nice – with maybe a side-order of discretion.'

Edge looked like a scolded schoolboy. He scraped his chair back and got up. 'I'll get that shower now.'

Nique glared after his retreating back as I dug my rarely used cafetière out of a cupboard.

'Cut him some slack, Nique,' I said quietly. 'He's hurting enough.'

'Heaven forbid I should hurt *his* feelings.' Her tone was a mix of contempt and sarcasm that she had down to a fine art. It could sting more than a slap across the face, but over the years I'd become immune.

She sat at the table, raking long fingers through her tangled hair. As I put a cup in front of her, her eyes locked onto mine. 'I don't appreciate you both discussing my business.'

I was leaning close across the table and I met her gaze – unflinchingly.

'I think you'll find, when you enlisted my help, Nique, you *made* it my business.'

She held my stare for a moment, before lifting her shoulder slightly in that Gallic gesture of indifference. As her gaze slid away, I couldn't help feeling like I'd scored a point.

'He shouldn't be telling you those things – they're personal.'

I poured hot water into the cafetière and put it in front of her. 'Bullshit!'

She stared at me, but I saw the beginnings of a smile tugging at the corners of her mouth. 'What?'

It was my turn to employ the indifferent shrug. 'You don't have personal boundaries with me that you care that much about and we both know it.'

'Fair enough.' She pouted.

'How much did you overhear anyway?'

She leaned back in the chair. 'I didn't know that Yalena refused to testify, just to punish me.'

'So how does that make you feel?' I already knew the answer, but wanted to see how honest she'd be.

She opened her mouth to trot out the formulaic response she'd give to someone who didn't understand her. Then smiled slightly. 'Disappointed . . .' Her eyes met mine with a penetrating look that we both understood, before adding, 'But honestly? Angry. *Really, really* angry.'

I depressed the plunger of the cafetière. 'Tell me about when she died?' I didn't soften the request – that was a social nicety I didn't need to employ with her.

I'd learned over the years that applying the social norms suggested a lack of understanding of her very nature. Abandoning them, signalled that she didn't need to put on a mask for me – it was a coded way of communicating that we both understood.

'Thought you'd heard it all from Edge?'

'You interrupted before he got to the interesting bit,' I said and smiled.

She concentrated on pouring the coffee.

'She was on the yacht of a friend– Dimitri Chernov. They'd known each other since childhood. He was the son of a Russian client she did a lot of work for. His family were involved with Russian organised crime – the Bratva. Anyway, they were sailing off the French Riviera to Tunisia with a party of his friends.' She held the cup, delicately blowing the surface. 'Edge wasn't happy – he'd told me she'd been doing drugs since leaving the clinic a few months before and we both knew the kind of company Chernov kept . . . that drugs would be around.'

'I didn't know she had a drug habit?'

'She didn't when we met,' she said simply. 'But after her surgery, she became addicted to prescription painkillers. Edge got suspicious when he was settling the bills, that's when we found out. Then when she was alone so much back at the villa, it got out of hand.'

'Did Edge talk to her about it?'

'Of course, but you had to know Yalena . . . Headstrong. Besides, once Chernov came back on the scene, he supplied whatever she wanted.'

Nique sipped her coffee thoughtfully. 'Technically, Yalena hadn't committed a crime. *She* was the victim in all this. Though you'd hardly know that. Blackstone's legal team barely gave her a mention at the trial.'

She had a point. Blackstone's lawyers had worked hard to distract the jury from any mitigation for the offence, which I'd tried to rebalance when presenting my evidence.

'Chernov was Yalena's suggestion when we had to get her out of the UK before the trial,' Nique continued. 'She needed a new identity, Dimitri had people who specialised in that kind of thing and she trusted him. He lived near her on the south coast of France.' She frowned. 'But the lifestyle he led . . . the drugs – I wasn't happy about her being around that. But what could I do? I was in prison and Edge could only go over occasionally. She left a note the night she died, saying she just wanted the pain to stop.'

Contrary to popular belief, most suicides never leave a note. But if there was one, it could provide clues to their state of mind and motivation.

'She meant the pain in here.' She tapped the side of her head. 'The physical injuries healed, *ma copine*, but not the mental damage those bastards did. I tried to get her to see someone – but she was a strong person. Prided herself on being able to deal with things alone, fight her own demons. But you know more than anyone, sometimes people just can't. They need someone to help.'

I shifted uncomfortably in my seat – her words hitting a painful target she was oblivious to.

'When I saw what they'd done to her, that night at Boltby Hall . . .' Her jaw bunched as she tried to control the anger. 'That's why I did what I did to that bastard and if I'd known then who the others were . . .' Her voice trailed off.

'Did you ever find out who else was involved?' I asked quietly.

'Myles Lawson was one . . .' Her knuckles blanched white around her coffee cup. 'But she only told me that later. I'd supplied girls for them that night – but she was out of bounds – they

256

knew that. But they were spoiled, privileged brats who thought they could do whatever they wanted, as long as they paid for it.' Her jaw tensed. 'Lawson spiked her drink. Then when she couldn't even stand up – he got her into Oliver's bedroom. They held her down on the bed and watched while Blackstone raped her, beat her, then they took it in turns. They laughed, said they'd show her what it was like to have a man. Told her she should enjoy it.' She shook her head slowly. 'And because she wouldn't testify, they got away with it.'

'Did she ever give you the names of the others?'

'No. She was too sick and I didn't want to press the point. It didn't matter anyway. What mattered was getting her through it. But in the end, I let her down . . .'

Her words trailed off as she sat, lost in thought. I held her hand across the table – knowing there was nothing I could say, that would ease her pain.

Chapter Forty-Three

Fordley police station – Saturday morning

Acting DI Heslopp scratched his bald head as he read my file. I'd told him about my call to Australia.

'Charlie said when his dad's mobile rang, it was a ringtone he'd never heard before. His dad didn't answer, but that's when he seemed to change.'

'Nichols' phone was examined at the time,' Heslopp said. 'A call *did* come in from an unknown number on a pre-paid sim. Caller was never identified. He didn't answer the call either.' He rocked back in his chair. 'And you think there's a link between *these* killings in 2014 and Josh Stamford's attack?'

'Stamford was fine – until he heard the phone ring.'

I waited for him to say something, but he just continued to study me – like an alien life-form had invaded his office.

'In Stamford's case, the ringtone was a piece of classical music. Witnesses said he was muttering something as he made his way towards Abassi . . .' I was fishing in my briefcase for some photographs I'd brought along.

'Something like *venger* or *vagar*,' Heslopp said.

'I think it was "Wagner".' I began to spread the photographs across his desk.

'So did Charlie say it was Wagner playing when his dad's phone rang?'

'No. Didn't know what it was, but he remembered it being used in a commercial, so I looked it up . . .'

I tapped the photographs of the graffiti on the walls of Nichols' cell after his suicide.

'This was all anyone could get out of him. He just repeated this one word over and over.'

He looked at the photographs of the graffiti.

'"Back . . . back . . . back". So?'

'I think he was spelling it phonetically – because he'd only ever heard it, never seen it written down.'

'So, what do *you* think it was?'

'Bach . . .'

'The composer?'

I nodded. 'Two phone calls – two classical pieces of music.'

He stared at the photographs, before adding, 'We found another connection between Nichols and Stamford.'

'What?' I was distracted, packing my briefcase.

'Michelle Briggs, the therapist.' He glanced up at me as I got to the door. 'Also treated Nichols while *he* was at Sangar, but that was in Birmingham – before she moved to Yorkshire to take a post here.'

'Too much of a coincidence.'

He shrugged. 'She'd worked with Sangar for over a decade. Not unlikely that she should have patients in common.'

'True. But how likely is it that hers just happen to be the ones who commit murder?'

'You're singing to the choir, doc. I've already got the team digging further into her background – see what else comes up.'

I paused, half out of the office. 'Did you find out what the ringtone was, on Stamford's phone before we shot him dead?'

260

He stared at me for a second before nodding.

'Something by Mozart.'

*　*　*

'Hi Cal.' I answered his call as I drove out of Fordley and headed up onto the moors.

'Got a message to call you.' He sounded distracted – I could hear papers shuffling. 'What's up?'

'In Blackstone's office, I saw a photograph of his wife. She looked familiar, but I couldn't place where I'd seen her before. But it came to me last night – I've seen the same picture of her.'

'Where?'

'In Leo Fielding's studio. It's the portrait they said a husband commissioned – then never collected.'

There was a pause as he digested the implications. 'The commission on that painting bought Leo's apartment . . .'

'I know. A husband who pays a couple of hundred grand for a portrait has to have a pretty good reason *not* to collect it don't you think?'

'Mary said the wife didn't want it after the murder.'

'Now I know it's Blackstone, I don't believe that.' I took the road for Haworth, putting my foot down to take advantage of the thinning traffic. 'He measures his relationships on a profit and loss sheet. If he'd paid that much, he'd want a return on his investment.'

'Maybe his missus has more heart than him?' he reasoned.

'Maybe, but knowing him he'd have sold it.'

'So why didn't he?'

261

'Because he didn't want anything connecting him to Leo Fielding. There were news articles about how much Leo's work increased in value after his death. Collectors and galleries were interested in what paintings were still held by the family and how much they would be worth. Talia's portrait was a private commission. Leo's agent hadn't had time to list it in the catalogue, so it slipped under the radar. If Blackstone had taken possession, it would have attracted unwanted attention.'

'Hmm . . . Like you say, high price to pay for privacy. Intelligence found something else, thanks to you spotting the cufflinks.'

'Go on.'

'We knew Myles Lawson and Oliver were at Cambridge together. But apparently they were also in the same year at Oakleigh.'

Oakleigh was an all-boys boarding school in Ryedale, North Yorkshire. One of the leading independent public schools in the UK. Children of the wealthy and elite were sent there to benefit from a first-class education – and from connections that opened doors to privileged society. Yorkshire's equivalent of Eton, it was a feeder school for Oxford and Cambridge. I could visualise the school emblem – a green oak tree on a black background – with a Latin inscription I seemed to remember translated to 'Men of Oak'.

'And Leo?'

'He was at Oakleigh too, but didn't attend until he was sixteen. Myles and Oliver were two years older; they'd already left for university by then. When we were investigating Leo's death, we weren't looking for a connection to Lawson or Blackstone, so it was never picked up.'

'So where did their paths cross?'

'Oakleigh's rugby club. Quercus . . .'

'The scientific name for oak.'

'How do you know so much random shit, McCready?' I could hear the grin in his voice.

'What can I say? I'm a pub quiz dream.'

'And the emblem for Quercus is the golden acorn. Members who play for the first team, are awarded gold cufflinks . . .'

'Bit of a step up from my comprehensive – had to borrow my first hockey stick when I made the team.'

'Terrifying thought – you wielding a hockey stick! Like something out of St Trinian's.' He laughed.

'You can only imagine.'

'Quercus association remains strong long after pupils leave the school.' I could hear papers shuffling. 'Social events and matches are often attended by politicians and Fortune 500 CEOs, members of the British establishment – the old boys' network. They must have all known each other, either during their days playing rugby or from social events.'

'So now we know there's a definite connection between Sir Neville, Oliver and Myles, to Leo Fielding.' I silently cursed the fact that I was driving instead of sitting at my desk where I could be making notes on all of this.

'And you think that Leo and Jacinta were murdered by the same killer, two years apart?'

'Definitely . . . same signature behaviours at both scenes. What are the chances, Cal, that two people are killed by the same hand and *both* of them knew or were in some way involved with Blackstone?'

'But to be fair to Sir Neville —'

'Oh, let's not.'

'He's never been questioned about Leo Fielding. Until now we never made the connection. But we can pull him in on it now.'

'The more we find, Cal, the more I'm convinced this all goes back to that night at Boltby Hall.'

'We have no way of knowing whether Leo was a guest at that party. Blackstone had security at the event, and they obviously had a guest list so they could prevent the paparazzi gate-crashing. But those lists were secret – Blackstone made sure the names never came to light. A lot of guests disappeared before the police arrived and, for obvious reasons, never came forward. Yalena Vashchenko's little black book disappeared when she did – so no joy there.'

'Where was Sir Neville that night?'

'In Monaco with his wife and daughter.'

'OK. So what now?'

'We pull Blackstone and Myles Lawson in for more questioning – shake them up and see what falls out.'

Chapter Forty-Four

Haworth – Saturday afternoon

I drove across rolling moors of purple heather, taking advantage of one of the rare occasions I could put the roof down on the car, to feel the warmth of a glorious summer's day.

I was driving to meet Geoff Perrett in Haworth.

The picturesque Airedale community, just a few miles west of Fordley and set in stunning countryside, was a literary mecca made famous by the Brontë sisters and more recently brought to the attention of a different audience as part of the Tour de Yorkshire cycle race.

Before reaching the village, I put in a call to Jen.

'Sorry to bother you on a weekend.' There was a screeching of childish laughter in the background.

'That's OK.' She sounded a bit out of breath. 'I'm shepherding the grandkids while Henry's watching football. What's up?'

'Need some research doing?'

'This weekend?' I could hear the panic in her voice.

'No – Monday's fine – may as well work from home for this one, Jen.'

I heard the sounds of her shooing small people from underfoot and could imagine her going in search of a pen.

'Hang on a minute.' Her voice was more distant as she held the phone under her chin. 'OK, fire away.'

'Can you look into a Russian – Dimitri Chernov? His family are connected to the Bratva . . .'

'The Russian mafia?'

'You're better than Google.'

'Always. Any period or event in particular?'

'See what comes up. He was a friend of Yalena Vashchenko in Russia going back to childhood.'

'De Benoit's girlfriend?'

'Yes.'

'Why does *that* not surprise me?'

I ignored her disapproval. I also didn't tell her about Yalena's death. It would have been recorded under the false name in her new passport and I didn't want Jen's search complicated by that. Or perhaps clouded by it? I wasn't sure which.

I could hear her making notes. 'No problem – I'll go through my "back-channel" sources. If he's Bratva, there won't be much in the public domain – they'll be our best bet.'

Over the years, and because of the nature of the work I did and the agencies we'd been involved with, Jen and I had built up a network of information sources, including the FBI Behavioural Sciences unit in Quantico and a host of useful connections in the UK's National Crime Agency.

It had proved an invaluable two-way street of strategic allies and non-partisan information sharing that had given us a vital 'edge' more than once.

'Don't suppose you've checked your emails today?' she asked.

'No. Why?'

'Alex emailed. He's getting the train to Fordley, Tuesday afternoon. He needs collecting from the station.'

I wondered when Sandra's body would be identified. Nique should be out of the country by the time the news broke – before Blackstone found out she was still alive.

My mind was still racing through all those complications as Jen's voice dragged me back. 'You still there?'

'Yes – sorry. Just trying to work out where I'll be. The police briefings are all being scheduled this week.'

'I don't mind doing it. Haven't seen him since Christmas.'

'Thanks, Jen, that'd be great.'

I made a mental note-to-self as we ended the call – to get Nique and any evidence of her stay out of the house by then.

* * *

As I left the Roadster in Haworth's museum car park, I was greeted by one of my favourite rural sounds – the cawing of rooks in the surrounding trees. Their ebony silhouettes lined the branches and the old Victorian street lamps to peer at the people below like curious choristers.

Walking down the iconic cobbled street, I could never shake the feeling that I was stepping back in time. No matter how many tourists filled the place on sunny summer days, walking dogs and pushing baby buggies, it still managed to retain a vintage charm that spoke of a bygone era.

I stopped at the bakery halfway down Main Street to pick up the obligatory sticky Yorkshire parkin that had always featured in our tutorials and usually served to soften the gruff welcome Professor Perrett was fond of. Making a visitor feel like a complete nuisance in his busy day.

'Oh, it's you,' he said as he pulled open the front door to his cottage. The expression in his sharp hazel eyes betrayed his pleasure. But it was customary that we played the game.

'Getting an appointment with you is harder than seeing the Queen,' I said straight-faced as I walked into the cosy living room.

'Well, she's not as important, or as busy, is she?'

I handed him the paper bag. 'Payment for your time.'

'Should think so.' He called over his shoulder as he took the spoils into the kitchen. 'Had to make time in my hectic schedule for you. Least you can do is provide the cake. Make yourself comfy – there's a brew by your chair.'

I sat in the overstuffed armchair beside the stone fireplace and sipped my tea.

'How you keeping?' I called to the kitchen.

'So, so. Bloody arthritis slows me down these days, but other than that . . .'

He appeared with the parkin on two plates. Putting one on the arm of my chair, he settled himself down opposite.

'So, gracing me with your presence and taking a day out from chasing serial killers and psychopaths, eh? I'd like to think you're here just to hide away from the madness and let me unpack these nightmares you've been having, but you hinted at a bigger reason for the visit.'

I stifled a smile. I'd always found his challenging directness amusing– never missing the twinkle in his eye when I picked up the gauntlet. It had become a hallmark of our sessions. A mental sparring we both knew was a perverse display of affection between two Type 'A' personalities.

'You got my email?'

He nodded, taking a bite of parkin. 'Something about the work I did with Sargant a thousand years ago?'

William Sargant was a British psychiatrist, running a teaching and research unit at St Thomas' hospital in London until his retirement in 1972. His book *Battle for the Mind* made him a controversial figure in the world of psychological research. As a graduate, Geoff had been one of his research assistants.

'Yes . . . More specifically, the MK-Ultra programme.'

He raised his eyebrows. 'Talk about going back into the mists of time.' He licked the sticky ginger from his fingers, his eyes never leaving mine. 'What are you involved in, Jo? Don't tell me it's anything to do with that?'

I took a sip of tea. 'That's why I wanted to talk to you – see if my theory is totally wide of the mark, or not.'

'Hope for your sake it is. I know the world's going to hell in a handcart, but God help us all if anyone ever resurrects that dystopian nightmare.'

Chapter Forty-Five

Geoff Perrett's cottage – Saturday afternoon

'MK-Ultra was a dark period in the history of psychological research.' Geoff shook his head. 'Of course, as a young graduate, I was flattered to be chosen by Sargant, but I seriously questioned the morality of it.' He glanced at me with a wry smile. 'But then, anything funded by the CIA in those days was hardly likely to be whiter than white, was it?'

'But you didn't know that?'

He shook his head. 'Minions like me weren't in the know. But later, as I learned more . . . that's when I left the programme. I assumed it was shut down. Amazed when the *New York Times* exposed it as late as 1974!'

I remembered studying the details of it at university. Thrilled that one of my lecturers had actually been a part of the CIA's secret experiments into mind control and conditioning.

To a young student, it seemed like a glimpse into a clandestine world of spies and espionage that were the stuff of fiction. Movies like *The Ipcress File* or *The Manchurian Candidate*, which I'd watched on a Sunday afternoon with my dad. Made real by my favourite lecturer, who had worked alongside the British scientist recruited by the CIA to conduct classified experiments in the UK.

'We called Sargant the "Mindbender General",' he recalled with a humourless smile. 'Working closely with that taught me a valuable lesson at the start of my career. Whether it's a doctor, lawyer or second-hand car salesman – if they suffer from evangelistic certainty, don't trust the bastards.'

'Present company accepted, of course?'

The hazel eyes twinkled. 'Of course.'

I took a bite of cake and considered how best to frame my questions. Now that I was sitting with the man who could validate my theory or blow it out of the water as ridiculously far-fetched, I almost didn't know where to start.

'I've researched his work,' I started tentatively. Geoff raised his eyebrows, giving me the silence to find my own way. 'The CIA recruited Sargant to experiment – without patients' consent?' It was a statement of fact, that I framed as a question – hoping he'd lead me by the hand. Typically, he didn't. I ploughed on – feeling suddenly self-conscious. Reminiscent of sitting in his study, waiting for his faint praise or cutting damnation of my theories.

'Patients attended clinics for anxiety or depression and under the guise of treatment, he carried out the MK-Ultra experiments?'

Geoff nodded. 'Initially back in the sixties, subjects volunteered to have mind-altering drugs administered, like LSD. But when that resulted in long-term mental disorders or in some cases suicides, volunteers dried up. That's when they started to experiment without their consent. Sargant discovered that inducing a state of deep sleep – narcosis – meant a patient had no memory of the treatments used on them. As you know, narcosis breaks down resistance to suggestion, which is what the CIA were originally interested in.'

'I know they were studying interrogation techniques, to use on Korean prisoners of war, so why did it continue so long after the war ended?'

'Because America was so bloody paranoid. Fear of communism during the cold war was at its height. The Agency spent millions on studies into manipulating the mind during interrogation. They used psychoactive drugs, searching for the perfect truth serum . . .'

'But then it became something else?'

He nodded, remembering those dark days. 'They realised a combination of chemical and psychological methods such as hypnosis broke down a person's resistance and created an amnesiac state to such a degree that the individual had no recollection of what they had done or why.'

'It never really worked though . . . I mean, wasn't as effective as they'd hoped. Was it?'

He sat back in his chair, resting his legs across an overstuffed footstool.

'Is that what you're hoping? That it was one of those crazy projects the CIA came up with, like developing exploding cigars to kill Castro?'

'If anyone can demolish my theory, it's you.'

He smiled. 'I seem to remember as a student, you were never that thrilled whenever I managed to knock down one of your theories.'

'That wasn't real-world,' I said quietly. 'This is.'

He studied me, as though trying to come to a decision. 'You've heard of Sirhan?'

'The guy who assassinated Bobby Kennedy?'

'He claimed to have no memory of committing the murder, even forty years later. His parole was turned down fourteen times – as recently as 2011 – because they said he'd never shown remorse. He said that was because he had no recollection of committing the crime, though he accepted he obviously had.'

'You're saying that's connected to MK-Ultra?'

He regarded me silently for a moment, before taking a long breath. 'In 1968, when I saw the footage of Kennedy's assassination, it seemed probable that Sirhan was in some kind of altered state. When I saw the interviews stating he had no recollection, I believed he was telling the truth. And then I worked with Sargant . . .'

'And?'

'I thought it highly likely Sirhan had been programmed to commit an assassination he had absolutely no memory of.'

Chapter Forty-Six

I sat for a moment, letting the noises from outside wash over me. People talking – children laughing. The everyday sounds of a busy village on a sunny afternoon.

Normality.

Safe and secure. Everyday life.

A universe away from the Gothic horror of human experimentation and terrifying mind control we were discussing.

I looked up to see Geoff watching me intently over the rim of his glasses.

'So, they *actually* used it . . . successfully?'

He nodded, his eyes never leaving mine, and I suddenly realised he was still conscious of the Official Secrets Act he must have signed, which prohibited him from disclosing anything about his work – even now.

'I'll understand if this conversation has to end right now.' A part of me almost hoped it would.

'Ordinarily I'd say it probably should.' Then he shrugged, his look as perceptive as ever. 'But at my age, what can they do to me now? Besides, we're only discussing a hypothesis, right?'

'Right.' I took a sip of tea, before saying quietly. 'But let's just say, hypothetically, if someone wanted to replicate that today, how long would it take?'

'Hypothetically?' He paused – choosing his words carefully. 'Depends on the subject being conditioned.' He poured more tea from the pot. 'The CIA had an endless supply of servicemen during the Korean War. Many were in treatment for months, so they could work on them for intense periods under the guise of trauma therapy.'

'Plus, the use of drugs,' I added. 'Which would break down resistance and speed up the process.'

'Yes. And don't forget, the drugs they were using were pretty crude, compared to the substances we have now. Even prescription drugs available from a GP these days would do an adequate job.'

He got up from his chair and went to the bureau in the corner. He dropped the lid and began rummaging around in the small drawers inside. I thought about the ex-servicemen going through Sangar. Not dissimilar to those CIA guinea pigs in the sixties.

He came back and pressed a small packet into my palm.

'What is it?'

'A souvenir,' he said, watching me from his armchair.

I unrolled the protective plastic.

'A relic of the Cold War.' He nodded to the medical vial. 'A prototype drug designed by Sargant – to induce the narcosis he needed for his guinea pigs to accept their conditioning. Of course, it didn't have a name then, just a number. You'll recognise it from the generation of drugs it went on to become. Flunitrazepam.'

I rolled the glass tube around in my palm. 'Rohypnol?'

He nodded. 'One of the earliest benzodiazepines. Initially developed to induce deep sleep in hospital patients.'

'Better known these days as the "date rape drug",' I said quietly.

'Because of its qualities as one of the most powerful hypnotics, with the interesting side-effect of causing amnesia.' He settled back in his chair. 'Keep it – as a memento of the madness.'

I slipped the bottle into my briefcase.

'Of course, these experiments have been replicated since, for "*entertainment*".' He drew quotation marks in the air with his fingers. 'A student volunteering for an experiment into how hypnosis improved concentration was programmed, without his knowledge, into shooting a famous personality on stage in a theatre. Obviously, the gun fired blanks, so the celebrity didn't get hurt – but the kid couldn't have known that. He was doing it for real. Afterwards he couldn't remember doing it. The programme attracted huge audiences and a lot of discussion about the ethics of it.'

'Yes, I remember it,' I recalled. 'With that in mind, there's something I need you to look at.'

I balanced my laptop on the small table between us. Geoff leaned forward to get a better view as the video of Josh Stamford's attack at Fordley train station flickered into life.

'I've seen some of this on the news . . .' Geoff watched it through, then jabbed the screen with a thick finger. 'Play that bit again.'

He was interested in Stamford, before he jumped the barrier. That footage had never been released to the media. He watched it several times before sitting back in the chair and slipping his glasses off to polish the lenses with the corner of his shirt.

'Interviewed after the Kennedy assassination, Sirhan said he believed he was firing at a target on a rifle range and not at a real person. He called it "going into marksman mode".' He slipped his glasses back on. 'Just before the shooting, a woman in a polka dot dress bumped into him and spoke to him – but he could never remember what she actually said. The combination of the visual and auditory trigger sent him into the "marksman mode".'

He watched me in silence – letting what he'd said percolate for a moment, before adding. 'Stamford was an ex-serviceman being treated for PTSD – he's already in a vulnerable state. Already trained to kill in the service of his country.'

I nodded.

'A subject like that makes this easier. They've already been pre-qualified.'

'I need you to talk me through the process for installing this kind of conditioning, if someone wanted to replicate the experiment – hypothetically.'

'You already know the techniques, Jo. It's nothing you haven't come across before. You suspected it when you saw that video.'

'I was hoping you'd tell me I was wrong.'

'I'd love to . . . but I can't.'

Chapter Forty-Seven

Kingsberry Farm – Sunday morning

I stared at the computer screen in my office, listening to Harvey crashing around the garden outside my half- open window, chasing some rabbit unfortunate enough to cross his line of sight.

'Breakfast?' Nique startled me as she stuck her head round the door.

'No thanks . . . I'm fine.'

She pushed the door wider and came in, taking a bite from the slice of toast in her hand. She was wearing a bathrobe, her wet hair falling in coiled tendrils around her face as she padded barefoot over to my desk.

'All work and no play.' She leaned over to hug me from behind, her hair damp against my cheek. 'What's so important that you can't eat?'

'An attack at Fordley train station.'

She nudged me playfully. 'Crime fighting needs energy,' she teased. 'You should eat, *ma copine.*'

'I know . . .' I ran a hand wearily across my eyes. 'Five more minutes.'

I was vaguely aware of her moving over to the window to watch Harvey, laughing at his antics, as I replayed the images that continued to bother me.

When the BTP arrived, Stamford appeared to abort the attack. A logical thing to do when threatened with a Taser. But

I didn't believe he'd dropped the knife. As I studied it, I became convinced he'd deliberately thrown it away.

What if Adel Abassi hadn't been the intended target at all? What if Stamford had been after someone else entirely?

I'd run the film to the moment Stamford lunged at the group, just as Nique turned to me, laughing. 'Harvey is so—' She stopped mid-sentence, leaning over my shoulder to point to a figure on the screen. 'I know him!'

I twisted round to look at her as she stared at the laptop, a thin frown creasing her forehead.

'Adel Abassi?'

'Don't know his name.' She tapped the screen with a long fingernail. 'But I never forget a face.'

I looked back at the laptop. 'Who?'

'Not the old man . . . *him*. I saw him at Boltby Hall. At Oliver Blackstone's party.'

* * *

I'd asked her to look again – but Nique was adamant that she'd seen Baahir Abassi, the cleric's son, at Boltby Hall.

I swivelled my chair round to face her as she perched on the windowsill, still eating her toast.

'Are you certain, Nique?' I knew I sounded like a defence barrister on cross-examination, but this was too important. She had to convince me before I could rely on it. 'There were a lot of people there that night – how can you be so sure?'

She waved the remains of the wholemeal slice.

'Because that wasn't the *only* time I'd seen him,' she said simply, oblivious to the importance of what she was saying. 'Yalena and I went to Blackstone's house to make final arrangements for the party. His wife took us into the study and we walked in on Blackstone and that guy.' She pointed again at my laptop. 'When she realised her husband was in there, Talia apologised and took us into the sitting room instead. When we left, Blackstone was standing by the guy's car. They exchanged a file and shook hands.'

I turned and looked back at the image of the hafiz's son. 'And then you saw him at the party?'

She nodded. 'When Edge and I went to look for Yalena. I walked through the house – he was there, and I recognised him from before. He's good-looking, don't you think?'

'Yes, I suppose so.'

She grinned, slipping off the windowsill to nudge me out of my chair.

'I teased Yalena about him after we'd met with Blackstone's wife. Told her if I was ten years younger and into men, I might have gone there myself. She was jealous . . . It made him memorable.'

I allowed her to tug my hand and pull me away from work. 'Try twenty years younger,' I teased as she ushered me towards the kitchen.

'Bitch,' she laughed, hugging me as we went.

*   *   *

I left Nique and Edge making their plans. The previous evening Edge had returned to the farm with a motorbike in the back of the Defender, along with a Bergan – military rucksack – full of what he mysteriously referred to as 'essential gear' and changes of clothes.

They now had new passports and fake papers and Edge's contacts had arranged for a boat to pick them up somewhere along the south coast for the first leg of their journey. They were moving back into my practice in Fordley, as I couldn't keep visitors away from the farm for much longer.

For the rest of the morning, I decided to do what I always did when my head was too full and I needed to think. Walk. Aimlessly and for as long as it took to restore some equilibrium.

I was getting no argument from Harvey, who loved these endless hikes over the moors. I threw a stick for him as I contemplated the latest developments and the new problems they were creating for me.

Heslopp and Callum needed to know about the connection between Baahir Abassi and Blackstone. But how to tell them without creating more complications for myself?

That train of thought was derailed when the shriek of my mobile shattered the rural stillness. Callum's name flashed up on the screen.

'Hi, Cal.'

'Sorry to bother you on a Sunday, but I just heard from one of the team working the arson case. They'll be recovering the body, or bodies, from the penthouse later tonight.' He hesitated for a second, his tone becoming gentler. 'I didn't want you hearing it on the news.'

'Thanks . . . that's . . . good of you.'

'You OK?'

I silently cursed the fact that he knew me so well – every nuance of my voice, every hesitation could betray the secrets I'd been keeping from him. The news had caught me off guard and

282

my reaction wasn't quite as it should have been. After all, I knew Nique was very much alive and kicking.

'How long . . . before they release the news?'

'Obviously they'll have to confirm it's her. *We* know it is – but they'll still have to formally identify the body—' He stopped as he suddenly realised he was talking about someone I considered a friend. 'Sorry, Jo.'

'No . . . that's OK.'

'They won't release anything to the media until they've notified next of kin.'

'Her parents are both gone. She has an older sister, living in Paris now I think.'

'They'll contact her, before it's made public.' He paused. 'There's another thing . . . Investigating officers heard from the fire service about someone hanging about the scene. Apart from the usual morbid onlookers, she's there every day.'

'She?'

'No one from the building knows who she is – but we've got a partial image on CCTV. Description similar to Thana. If she shows up again, we'll pick her up. Wouldn't be the first arsonist to revisit the scene.'

'I got a letter in the post,' I said cautiously. Not wanting to invite too many awkward questions, but unable to ignore the possible connection. 'Warning me to stay away from Nique. The handwriting's female, I think.'

'When?'

'It arrived the morning after the fire.'

'Have you still got it, and the envelope?'

'Of course.'

'Bring it in next time you come down.' There was a shuffling of papers. 'There's also been a development on Jacinta's case.'

'Oh?'

'When Lawson drove Jacinta to the office, CCTV picked up his car. He parked on double yellows.'

'Of course he did.'

'After he's gone, she gets out of the car and calls over to someone.'

'Any idea who?'

'No. Whoever it was is out of shot. We're trying to get CCTV from a different angle. If we turn anything up, I'll let you know.'

'Whoever it was changed her mood and caused the row with Blackstone.'

'You still OK for the joint briefing tomorrow morning?'

He'd arranged for a briefing with all three SIOs running the cases we agreed had connections, along with members of the different teams involved. It was scheduled for first thing in the morning.

'Yes, of course.'

'OK, see you then.'

I stared at the phone for a long time after the call ended before turning back to the house. I had to get my notes into some kind of coherent order. It was going to be a long night.

Chapter Forty-Eight

Kingsberry Farm – Sunday night

I'd told Nique and Edge about Sandra's body being recovered during the night, which meant they'd have to bring their plans forward before Blackstone found out.

Nique had insisted on cooking dinner as a 'thank you', endearingly remembering all my favourite French dishes, and had gone to the effort of getting fresh scallops and making a faultless crème brûlée for dessert.

Sitting around my table, I'd experienced a sudden feeling of tremendous loss for two people who, inadvertently, had become a big part of my life over the past few years. If things went to plan, I would never see them again.

Sensing my mood, Edge held my hand across the table.

'If you ever need me, princess, I'll come running – you know that. Once we're safely away, I'll get a mate from the Regiment to get in touch. If you need to reach me, he'll know how.'

After dinner, he'd taken Harvey for a walk, leaving Nique and I alone. As I poured brandy, she came up to hug me from behind, slipping her arms around my waist. I felt her cheek against my shoulder and turned to face her.

'Thank you, my friend,' she said quietly, her eyes suddenly moist. 'For everything you've done for me . . . everything.' Her accent was noticeably more pronounced, heavy with emotion. 'I will never forget.'

My throat constricted and, in that moment, I didn't know what to say – how to vocalise the feelings that hijacked me. I turned my cheek, expecting the usual Gallic kiss, but she'd cupped my face in both her hands – looking into my eyes – and planted a lingering kiss on my lips. Then turned away and went upstairs, leaving me to watch her go.

Now, alone again, I sat back in my office chair and stretched aching shoulders. The silence broken only by the ticking clock and Harvey's snoring as he lay contentedly on the rug.

As the printer hummed into life, producing my notes for the next day, I realised I'd been staring at the words but not really seeing them. My mind was occupied by something else.

Something Edge had said the night he and Nique had turned up at my door had begun to chime in my mind. I reached for the phone and dialled a familiar number, hardly surprised when it was answered on the third ring.

'Cal? It's me. Are you busy?' I could hear what sounded like a TV in the background.

'No. I'm off duty . . . for once. But why do I get the feeling that's all about to change?'

'I've been reviewing the CCTV we've got of Leo.'

'That Friday night, on his way home?'

'Yes. I want to test a theory.'

I assumed he muted the TV as the background noise stopped. 'What do you need?'

'Could you meet me at Chapel Mills . . . tonight?'

He paused for just a second. 'Can't it wait until tomorrow?'

'Not really. It might come to nothing once I walk the scene again . . .'

'Pete Albright's running the Fielding case now, Jo. It should be him you're talking to.'

'I know, but you're used to the way I do things . . . And besides, I'll feel like an idiot if I present it and it doesn't stand up.'

He didn't say anything – the silence stretched out for what seemed an eternity. Either he really wasn't comfortable stepping on Albright's toes, or he was just buying more thinking time. As an extrovert who hated empty space in conversations, his habit of doing this drove me nuts.

'OK.' He sighed heavily down the phone. 'I'll call Edward Morrison, get him to open up Leo's apartment.'

* * *

Callum looked me up and down – amusement seeping out of every pore.

'Nice outfit.'

'Cut the sarcasm.' I hefted the straps of the rucksack over my shoulder. I was wearing black jeans and trainers, a black windcheater was unzipped over my dark sweatshirt.

'Didn't even know you *owned* a hoodie?' He barely stifled his laughter, tracing an outline of the 'Hollywood Vampires' logo with his finger. 'Or that you were into heavy metal.'

'It's Alex's,' I said, slapping his hand away. 'Borrowed it from his wardrobe.'

'If I'd known we had to dress for the occasion, I'd have dug out my old Judas Priest T-shirt.' He was still grinning as we walked across the street to Chapel Mills. 'What *is* the occasion anyway?'

I looked up at the building, then turned and walked along the street. He fell in step.

'Like I said, I want to test a theory.'

'And we need to dress up for that?' He was still smirking.

I pretended not to have heard as we stopped opposite Calico's wine bar. For a Sunday night, the place was still busy. Through the windows we could see maybe a dozen customers around the bar. The street was empty.

'I've been through all the witness statements from the time of Leo's murder,' I said, trying to picture this spot as it had looked two years before. 'It was a busy Friday night. Staff said Leo sat at his favourite table by the window.'

Callum followed my gaze to that same table now occupied by a middle-aged couple. 'We know,' he said. 'He ordered his usual bottle of Merlot and sat drinking alone.'

I went to stand by the bus stop. Callum followed me and we both turned to look across to the bar where Leo had unknowingly spent the last peaceful hours of his life.

'This is where Domino from the café said she'd seen Thana, waiting for buses she never caught.' I looked up at him. 'She wasn't waiting for a bus, she was watching Leo.'

'Watching him or stalking him?'

'Same question Albright asked.'

'What answer did you give *him*?'

I leaned back against the wall, looking across the street to the couple at Leo's table, perfectly framed in the window. Callum followed my gaze. 'What do *you* think?' I asked quietly.

'So, what now?' he asked, looking down at me.

'Wait here.'

I didn't wait for the questions I knew he was about to ask but pushed off the wall and walked across to the bar. When I got to the door, I paused for a second to zip the jacket up, covering the distinctive logo on Alex's sweatshirt, and stepped into the warmth of the interior.

The smell of cooked food and beer hit me as I slipped inside and took the first seat in a booth by the door. The staff were occupied, serving customers along the length of the dark oak and brass bar. No one looked my way.

To my left, the couple we'd seen through the window were engrossed in conversation. Other couples stood around upturned oak casks dotted about the limed-oak floorboards.

A minute later the door opened and two lads came in, laughing and chatting loudly. As they passed in front of my booth, blocking my view of the bar, I stood and passed quietly behind them to walk to the toilets that were on my right.

There was no one in there – so I stood for a moment, looking at my reflection in the mirror above the sink – blonde hair scrunched into a tight ponytail.

Beneath the unforgiving scrutiny of the harsh strip lights, I noticed the dark rings under my eyes. My skin looked paler too. Not enough sleep. I grimaced at my reflection, then pulled open the door and left, careful to avoid eye contact with anyone as I went through the bar and back out to the street.

Callum was studying me as I unzipped my jacket.

'What was all that about?' he asked.

'I'll tell you later – come on.' I turned and began walking back towards Chapel Mills.

When we reached the glass-fronted entrance, I slipped my arm around Callum's waist, replicating the footage we'd both seen from our victim's last known movements.

'Time check?' I said simply.

By now he'd realised what I was doing and looked at his watch. 'Nine-oh-six exactly.'

'OK. Tell me the door code.'

Playing the game, he slid his left arm across my shoulders, leaning against me, just as Leo had done when 'hoodie' had helped him back home. 'One-nine-six-zero.'

I reached over and entered the security code to unlock the door with a gentle click.

The reception was quiet. Soft golden lights lit the space from discreet angles as we walked towards the goods lift. Neither of us spoke as we rode to the top floor. As the metal doors shuddered open, Edward was standing awkwardly in the hallway opposite Leo's apartment.

Callum was still leaning heavily against me as I walked him out of the lift.

'Everything OK?' Edward looked completely confused.

'Fine,' I said breathlessly, struggling now with Callum's weight. He was enjoying this a bit too much.

'Doors unlocked, like you asked.' Edward looked quizzically at Callum, who said nothing. 'Is he OK?'

'That's a matter of opinion.' I hefted Callum's almost dead arm a bit higher. 'We can take it from here.'

He nodded, calling over his shoulder as he walked towards the service stairs. 'Drop the latch when you leave then.'

I fumbled with the iron handle and leaned our combined weight against the huge doors which helpfully swung open. Without closing them I walked Callum to the metal stairs leading up to the mezzanine. He swayed against me, almost making me lose my balance.

'You're getting a little too into this,' I managed through gritted teeth.

'Thought you wanted realism?' I could feel the warmth of his breath against my skin as his cheek rested on mine.

'An approximation will do,' I grunted as we climbed the first steps. 'You're not up for a bloody BAFTA.'

I could feel his grin, but he obliged by not leaning on me quite so much and cooperated with the last few stairs.

When we reached the top, it was two paces to the edge of the bed. I dipped my shoulder and tipped his weight forward – catching him off balance to send him sprawling heavily across the iron bedframe. The shock registered on his face for just a second, then he was back in character. Slumping back in an ungainly spread-eagled position, eyeing me with amusement.

'Could get into this role-playing.' He grinned. 'Is this the bit where you tie me to the bed?'

I pulled a face, then turned on my heel and headed back downstairs. 'No time . . . come on.'

His polished shoes clanked down the spiral staircase as I headed out of the door and across to the stairwell beside the lift. I heard him drop the latch as Edward had asked, and then he was behind me as we ran down the few flights of stairs that took us back into reception.

I crossed the space and found the door in the corner that led down to the garden. There were a dozen steps to the fire door at the bottom.

Callum watched in silence as I unzipped my rucksack. I pushed the bar to open the door just a fraction, then slipped an item out of the bag and used it to prop the door open.

'A rubber dog bone?' Callum laughed. 'Really?'

'Borrowed it from Harvey,' I said distractedly, making sure the door couldn't close over the heavy red bone. 'It does the job.'

I pushed past him and took the steps two at a time. We crossed the hallway at a jog.

As I pulled the main door open to let us out into the street, I nodded towards his wristwatch. 'Call it.'

He glanced at the time. 'Nine-eighteen.'

'Twelve minutes,' I said breathlessly. 'One minute longer than hoodie took but shows it's doable.'

He jerked his head back towards the door. 'What's the idea with the dog bone?'

'You'll see. On the CCTV, hoodie comes out of the building, turns right and walks back down the street.'

He nodded. 'Takes a right, past Calico's, and we lost him.'

'OK. I'm knackered . . .' I absently rubbed the ache that was beginning to jag through my left thigh. 'So, you can do the next bit.'

'Which is?'

I indicated the route with a nod of my head. 'Walk back towards the bar. Keep turning right – around the block and back here. Once you get past the area covered by CCTV, run the last bit.'

I watched him walk down the street – waiting until he turned the corner, before I turned left – walking round the side of the building to the stone sculpture of the armchair and the clock.

I leaned against the cool stone of the artwork, taking the chance to catch some breath, gritting my teeth as the dull ache in my thigh became sharper – a reminder if I needed one that I wasn't as fit as I should be.

The sound of Callum running up the street a minute later was my cue to climb up onto the seat of the stone chair and wait for him to reach me. Infuriatingly he was hardly out of breath, just raising that eyebrow of his in an unspoken question.

I looked up at the wall high above my head, then put my hand on his shoulder. 'Give me a leg-up.'

He cupped his hands, providing a stirrup for my right foot, boosting me up high enough to reach the wall that bordered Edward's garden. Gripping the top of the wall, I scrabbled my feet against the stonework, gritting my teeth at the effort.

'Need to work on your biceps . . .' came the unhelpful suggestion from below.

Struggling to take in enough air didn't leave me with enough to swear at him, as I heaved my hips level with the top and swung my leg over the side. Determined not to make a complete idiot of myself by failing to make the final pull over the edge, I went sprawling in an unladylike heap into the rose bushes.

I lay for a second – gasping and gripping my left thigh that now felt like it was on fire. 'Shit!' I cursed under my breath, forcing my leg to move as I half rolled out from under the bushes and onto the gravel path.

Standing shakily, I limped towards the door to the apartments – retrieving Harvey's bone as I went inside. The door closed behind me and I then made my way back upstairs into the silent reception hall.

Callum was propped against the doorway waiting for me when I went back outside. I leaned against the cool stone, guessing from his expression what I must look like.

He grinned, reaching to pull a twig out of my hair and holding it up like an exhibit. 'Suppose it's feasible . . .'

I began to brush myself down, spilling crumbs of soil onto the marble step.

'One way to look like you've left the building and walked away, only to get back in to Leo's apartment unseen. Climbing the wall also gives the stalker access to the gardens at night – to watch Leo. That's probably how they left the roses outside his door.'

I started to walk back towards the wine bar, failing to hide my limp. His expression was concerned. 'You should've let me climb the wall.'

I shook my head, dismayed to see more crumbs of soil drop out. 'I couldn't have boosted you up there. Besides, you're not dressed to scramble up walls and crawl around flower beds in the dark.'

'Think this could have been two offenders, working together?' he said. 'I mean, to get over that wall, like we just did?'

'Possibly.'

'What gave you the idea?' he asked as we walked.

'Something someone said about a woman propping open a balcony door, so her cat could get out at night. I knew Leo wouldn't have opened the door to a stranger, given the mental state he was in before his death. The door to the apartments isn't accessible from the garden without the code, but if it had been propped open from the inside . . .'

'And our hoodie on the CCTV was carrying a rucksack, which contained something to prop open the door?'

I nodded. 'An organised offender. Brings everything they need to the crime scene – and takes it away afterwards.'

294

We'd reached the bus stop opposite Calico's.

'Have you got your warrant card?' He shot me a look that said of course he had. I looked across the street. 'Go in there and ask whether anyone saw me earlier? Bar staff, customers.'

He studied me for a moment, then walked across the street. I kept my place, leaning against the wall. I could see through the windows as he walked up to the bar and flashed his ID. Just a copper asking questions – nothing unusual in this part of town.

The barmaid leaned across to get a better look at the warrant card – then slowly shook her head. She turned to speak to the young barman who was busy pulling a pint. I watched him shake his head too. But the biggest test came as Callum moved to the group of lads standing by the toilets, nearest my old booth, and asked the same thing. I could tell from his gestures that he was describing what I'd been wearing.

I didn't realise I'd been holding my breath, until it escaped me in slow relief as I watched them all giving the same response: 'No'.

I took a deep lungful of cool night air as Callum came out and walked over to me.

'I take your point.'

'Didn't think I'd stated a point.' I was trying hard not to look smug. 'But now you mention it . . . I went in less than an hour ago and no one remembers me. No surprise then that Thana could go in there on a Friday night when the place was even busier. Hide in the crowd – dressed the same as me, staying inconspicuous. I think she stayed out here watching Leo through that window. Waiting for him to go to the loo before slipping in there to spike his drink. If I'm right, she'd be in and out in under a minute. Even less chance of people recalling her, especially if they were questioned days or weeks later.'

He looked at me, then back over to the bar. Nodding slowly. 'He usually drank a bottle of red. He'd have a tolerance for that amount of alcohol. Unusual for him to be as drunk as he appeared on the CCTV . . . too drunk to walk straight.'

'And all she'd have to do was wait out here for him to leave,' I said. 'Then go over and offer to walk him home. He knew her – trusted her. She'd been grooming him for months in the Munch Bunch. He'd go back with her and let her help him into his flat. "Hoodie" wasn't any match for Leo if she'd tried to overpower him . . . and the time lapse on the CCTV wasn't long enough for her to tie him to the bed and inflict his injuries.' My eyes met his and I held his attention. 'But she didn't have to. If he'd been drugged, it could all have happened the way we did it tonight. He'd be totally incapacitated until she returned. Once she's back inside that flat, she has all the time in the world to do whatever she wants with him.'

'So, Thana *could* have murdered Leo Fielding.'

I nodded. 'I'm certain now that she did.'

Chapter Forty-Nine

Fordley police station – Monday morning

DI Frank Heslopp regarded the joint teams assembled around the conference table in the briefing room. He'd brought everyone up to speed on the connections made between Stamford's attack and Nichols' killings at the Mela.

'Intel have also been looking into Michelle Briggs' background, as she treated both men.' He tapped the photograph on the whiteboard. 'She was ex-military. Her CV is in your folders.' There was a shuffling of papers as everyone scanned the notes

'A captain in the Community Mental Health department at Catterick Garrison. Served five years before being dishonourably discharged for assaulting an officer. Other allegations from service personnel in her care involve bad experiences during therapy, or questionable outcomes. One tried bringing a case for mental and emotional trauma, but it couldn't be substantiated.'

DS Mike Hanson raised a hand. 'Any record of her coming into contact with Stamford or Nichols during their service?'

'No. As far as we know, they met through Sangar when they'd all left the military.' Heslopp hitched his pants up, before pacing the front of the room.

'So, the theory is,' DC Shah Akhtar asked tentatively, 'that Stamford and Nichols were ordered to carry out these attacks by Briggs?'

Heslopp ran a hand across his bald head. 'Not "ordered" exactly . . .' He shot me a look. 'Think this is where I hand over to the doc.'

I looked at the sea of expectant faces – many of whom weren't even a twinkle in daddy's eye when Sirhan Sirhan aimed the gun that changed political history.

'OK, for most of you, what I'm about to say will feel like a story from ancient times – but bear with me.'

I'd put together footage from various documentaries on the assassination of Bobby Kennedy and the claims Sirhan's law- yers had made about the MK-Ultra programme. I turned on the TV and as the images flickered into life, I sat on the corner of the desk and watched the faces of my audience.

* * *

Stunned silence greeted the end of the presentation. A few shifted in their seats; no one wanted to be the first to speak.

Heslopp cleared his throat. 'The doc has a theory about how this fits in with Stamford and Nichols . . .'

'Thank God for that,' DS Ian Drummond chipped in. 'For a minute there I thought we'd fallen down a rabbit hole.'

There was a ripple of uneasy laughter. I slipped off my perch on the corner of the desk.

'That video explains how to condition a subject to go into "Marksman Mode" and carry out an attack but have no recol- lection of it. The same claim made by Nichols after the Mela killings. The experiment has been replicated since, for a TV documentary – using the same techniques and with a successful result. It's completely feasible using hypnosis and conditioning.'

'And you say your old professor was involved with this MK-Ultra programme back in the day?' said Hanson.

'That's right. He's viewed the footage of both Stamford and Nichols. He agrees that both offenders appeared to be in an altered state.'

I pointed to Nichols' mugshot pinned to the board. 'He was never the same after that day – his mental health deteriorated, culminating in a total breakdown and eventual suicide – but when he *was* lucid, he said he had no memory of those events. I've studied his psych evaluations. He had no real motivation. He wasn't radicalised and, in my opinion, what happened at the Mela *wasn't* a racially motivated attack.'

I pulled forward the flip chart I'd drawn up in preparation.

'For this to work, you have to carefully pre-select your subject. Both our offenders were highly trained combat veterans, so the concept of killing under orders is one they've already accepted.'

'And you think that during these sessions for PTSD, Briggs did this *thing* to them?' It was Hanson.

I nodded. 'This *thing* – as you so aptly put it – is to accept embedded commands and carry out behaviours – in this case the attacks – after receiving a "trigger" signal. On the night Stamford took Briggs hostage, he was shouting at her to "undo it". I believe he was referring to the programming.'

It had haunted me ever since the hostage situation on Norland Moor. 'He *did* remember . . . maybe not entirely, but enough to know that Michelle Briggs had done something to him during his therapy sessions. And he knew she was the only one who could "undo" it. That's why he went back for her that night. But it all went wrong when the police turned up and he didn't have enough time with her . . .'

'And they're triggered by the ringtone on a mobile phone. Maybe they don't even have to answer – just hearing it ring is enough?' Heslopp asked, although he already knew from our earlier discussions that was the premise.

Hanson's mobile was on the table. He regarded it suspiciously. 'Could *you* do that, doc?' he said, prodding it with a hesitant finger, as if it was coiled to spring any minute. 'Hypnotise us into doing something when the phone rings?'

Everyone suddenly jumped as his mobile shrieked.

'Bloody hell!' He nearly swept the phone off the desk as he fumbled to switch it off. His hand was trembling slightly as he looked at the screen. 'Just the missus.'

The team broke into nervous laughter.

'Well, she's certainly got *you* programmed.' Callum grinned.

As the banter subsided, I returned to the business at hand.

'To answer your question, Mike, yes I could. It's only the same as a stage hypnotist. You've all seen how *that* works. Members of the audience programmed to act out on stage on a given command. Then after they've made total prats of themselves, they have no memory of it.'

'How long would it take?' Callum watched me from his place across the table. 'Assuming you've picked the right subject. I mean are we talking weeks, months?'

'A stage hypnotist can do it in a matter of minutes. Get someone to behave like a farmyard animal . . .'

'This lot do that after a few lagers on a Saturday night,' Hanson joked.

I scanned my notes. 'Using certain drugs speeds up the process, so something similar *could* be achieved quite quickly.

Triggers to external stimulus are the way any subconscious behaviour is created – the habits we can't control.'

'For example?' Callum asked, tipping his chair to rock on the back legs.

'People with anger management issues.'

'Plenty of them round here,' Shah said.

'Phrases that people use or certain situations trigger their emotional explosions,' I explained. 'Once we identify their "triggers", we can replace their negative responses with more "helpful" ones.'

'A form of reprogramming then?' Callum asked.

'Yes, exactly. During MK-Ultra, subjects were given drugs to break down latent resistance and help embed the commands. I think that was done with these two, but we'll never know for sure now all the players are dead. Then the trigger is set.'

'How do you stop it triggering accidentally?' Callum asked.

I took my seat back at the table. 'The combination of audible and visual triggers in the right sequence. If it was just a typical ringtone on a mobile – the subject could hear that passing someone in the street and trigger a random attack.'

'That'd get you barred from Sainsbury's,' someone joked.

'Like Mike shitting himself when his missus rings?' Heslopp laughed.

'Something like that.' I smiled. 'That's why I think they went for pieces of classical music that weren't so common.'

'And the visual trigger?' Callum asked, taking a mouthful of coffee.

'Probably an image that flashed up on the phone when it rang – most likely a picture of the target. But the audible trigger would be enough on its own. The visual would just be a bonus.'

There was a silence as everyone digested the information. Then Callum leaned forward, raking his fingers through his hair. 'How do they set them on the right target?'

I'd run that question past Geoff Perret. The answer he gave me worked – I went with the same one.

'We think it's the piece of music used for the ringtone. A different piece indicates a different target.'

Callum regarded me intently for a moment as he considered the implications of that. 'So they can be programmed to hit multiple targets?'

I held his gaze. 'If you have the luxury of time with your subjects – which Michelle Briggs would have had at Sangar – why not install multiple targets triggered by different pieces of music?' I paused for a heartbeat before adding, 'It makes your "weapon" far more flexible, and valuable.'

'Jesus,' Heslopp muttered, almost under his breath.

Chapter Fifty

'So . . .' Heslopp ventured tentatively, 'what's Briggs's motive?'

'She was ex-military – served in Iraq and Afghanistan,' Shah offered. 'Maybe wanted to get rid of controversial figures preaching anti-British propaganda?'

I hesitated, knowing I was straying into potentially dangerous waters, dangerous for me. I had to provide the next piece of the jigsaw without betraying my sources. Easier said than done in a room full of professional interrogators.

'That's if we accept these men were the intended targets in the first place.' I needed to halt this line of thought before it took us down a false trail.

Everyone turned to look at me. Callum shot a look that said, *'And this is the first I'm hearing about it?'*

'I don't think Michelle Briggs was acting alone. She was doing the programming on behalf of someone who had the real motive for these attacks.'

I walked over to the TV screen.

'Identifying the right targets gives us the motive. And that in turn gives you your suspect.'

I'd queued up the footage from both the attacks to demonstrate my point. I flicked the remote to bring up Stamford's attack.

'If you look closely,' I said, slowing it to run one frame at a time, 'he's lunging into the group.' I froze the image. 'Follow his eye line.'

Heslopp got up and came to stand beside me, squinting at the image. 'He's looking at the son,' he said to no one in particular.

'And the knife is aimed into the middle of the group – not directly at Adel Abassi,' I said, tracing the arc of action with my finger. 'He's using the knife to separate the group – scatter the others away from Baahir . . .'

'Separating him from the herd,' Heslopp agreed.

I advanced the footage frame by frame.

'As the group splits, Baahir is left alone at the edge of the platform. But the BTP officer is already on the scene and has shouted a warning – there's not enough time to close the distance to attack Baahir at close quarters with the knife, so . . .' I froze the action to show Stamford's expertly aimed kick, sending the man onto the railway tracks. 'That was the best he could do in the circumstances – and it could have been enough . . .'

'The blow or the fall could have killed him,' Hanson chipped in.

'If the train had been on time,' Callum said. 'That would have done the job.'

'He's not aborting the attack,' I said. 'He's done what he came to do.' I tapped the TV screen. 'Look at his expression. No vacant stare like before.' I turned back to face my audience. 'There's sanity in his eyes – he's snapped out of that altered state and realised what he's doing – but he's not about to kill a police officer, so he drops the knife. Only using sufficient force to get away.'

There was silence for a second, before Heslopp took a long breath. 'Looks like we need another little chat with Baahir Abassi, then.'

I changed the image on the TV to show the carnage after the Mela attack four years earlier.

'You might want to review this one too. Look into the other victims,' I said.

Heslopp frowned. 'He was going for the Imam . . . the guy he killed.'

I regarded him steadily. 'It was never established as fact. I reviewed all the assessments on him at the time. His demeanour was one of remorse. A man ripped apart by regret and guilt – not a racial bigot who's just pulled off an attack he was proud of. The knowledge of what he'd done caused a total mental break-down. He was barely coherent from the day of his arrest. There was never any evidence of radicalisation. Like Stamford – no connection to right wing groups, no affiliations or history of expressing racist views.'

'If Briggs was doing this on behalf of someone else, who else *is* there?' Heslopp said.

'Look at who else was killed that day – their backgrounds. You could have been looking at the wrong victims all along. And if I'm right,' I said slowly, 'identifying the *right* victims will give you the key that unlocks everything.'

Chapter Fifty-One

Fordley police station – Monday afternoon

Heslopp and his team left to gather more information and set up an interview with Baahir Abassi. Everyone else had taken the opportunity for a break and I'd made a hasty exit to the ladies' room. As a strategy for avoiding Callum, it was short lived.

He was waiting for me in the corridor when I came out. His arms casually folded as he leaned against the wall, but from his expression I could tell he wasn't happy.

He pushed off the wall and fell in step beside me as we walked.

'What are you *not* telling me, Jo?'

I kept my head down, focused intensely on the blue carpet. 'Don't know what you mean?'

He stepped in front of me, bringing me up short as he blocked the way. 'Cut the crap. I know you too well.'

I looked up at him, meeting those sharp eyes with an intensity that matched his. I raised my eyebrows – mirroring the silent technique he was so fond of.

His breath left him in a gust of frustration. 'You've been off-kilter ever since De Benoit's release. So, come on, Jo. Talk to me.'

I looked past him to where the others were starting to drift back into the briefing room.

'We've both got a lot going on, Cal. I'm just distracted that's all.'

'With De Benoit's body being recovered?'

I shot him a look. 'Was it?'

He studied me for a moment as if by looking hard enough he could read my thoughts. 'Yes, early hours of this morning – but no formal identification yet.'

My mind was racing a million miles an hour. *How long would it take for them to realise that body wasn't Nique's? When would the announcement go public?*

'It's Edge Brink, isn't it?'

Whatever I'd been expecting him to say, it wasn't that.

'What?'

He kept his voice low – barely audible above the banter coming from the end of the corridor. 'They pulled *one* body out of the wreckage this morning, not two.' His blue eyes seemed to get darker as he studied my reactions. 'They're still looking, but we both know they're not going to find him. Because he's not in there is he, Jo?'

I became suddenly still – working hard to control my body language under his unforgiving scrutiny. 'I don't know what you're talking about.'

'I think you do.' His large hand was warm on my shoulder as he moved me aside to let someone pass in the corridor. His touch unnerved me. 'Edge hasn't been seen since the fire. I think you've known all along that he's not in there.'

'What makes you think that?' I was impressed at how calm I sounded.

'He's dropped off the grid and you know where he is.' He ignored my question, relentlessly pursuing a theory that was a little too close to home. 'That's what you've been keeping from me, isn't it?'

I looked him square in the eye. 'No,' I said firmly. 'You're way off the mark, Callum.'

'Really?'

'Really.'

I made to move past him, but he side-stepped, blocking my way again. 'I don't want to have this conversation on the record, Jo. But if I have to I will.'

The inference that he would put me in that position felt unexpectedly shocking – though when I reflected on it later, it shouldn't have.

'You'd *do* that?' I asked. 'Despite our friendship?'

His expression remained ice cold. 'Not despite of it . . . *because* of it.' He glanced around making sure weren't overheard. 'If we've got the relationship I thought we had, you wouldn't force me to. But if you did . . .' His eyes flashed me an unmistakeable warning. 'So, tell me?'

'There's nothing to tell!'

'Edge Brink is out there and if you know where he is, you're withholding vital information.'

I leaned my shoulder against the wall, my frustration boiling up to meet his.

'I didn't realise being a missing person was a criminal offence?'

'He's a witness to what happened on the night of the fire, but right now I'm more worried about what else he might be up to.'

'Like what?'

'If he suspects Blackstone or someone who works for him of starting that fire, he could be out there looking to get even for De Benoit's death, and the last thing I need on my watch right now is a vigilante.'

I'd heard enough. I made to walk away, but he grabbed my arm. 'Aiding something like that would drop you in serious shit, Jo.'

I shook his hand away. 'Don't treat me like a suspect.'

'Then stop behaving like one!'

People walking into the briefing room shot us curious glances. I turned my back to avoid more attention.

'Look,' I hissed, lowering my voice. 'If Edge isn't in that wreckage, then I don't know where he is or what he's up to. If I did, I'd tell you.'

'I bloody well hope so,' he said through barely gritted teeth. 'Because if I find out you *are* obstructing an investigation, Jo, I swear—'

'Ready?' We both stopped dead as DS Albright came up on our blind side, smiling as he indicated the briefing room door with a nod of his head.

'Yes.' I flashed him the broadest smile I could manage and gratefully walked with him. I could almost feel Callum's eyes boring into my back as we went.

* * *

Callum and Albright brought everyone up to date on their two cases, then opened it up to questions.

Beth raised a hand. 'Valuables were pushed inside the victim's shoes at both scenes. Could it be coincidence that Leo and Jacinta just had the same habit?'

'Unlikely,' I said. 'I've asked Mary Fielding if that was something Leo did, she said not.' I looked around the team. 'These are the type of habits we develop in childhood – or maybe during early teenage years. If it was something he did routinely, his mother would probably be aware of it.'

'The girls who worked with Jacinta at the club said she never did that either,' Callum added. 'They shared a dressing room back stage, so they would have noticed something like that.'

'Also, the way the clothes are folded.' I went to the board and tapped the photographs. 'They look like the precisely folded items in a shop window display – they're almost too perfect. Clothes at both scenes arranged in exactly the same way.' I turned to face the team. 'If I gave each of you a shirt to fold, you'd all do it differently. What are the chances of getting two like this, so identically carried out?'

'What about the differences though?' Albright asked. 'Leo was tortured, brutalised. But care shown with Jacinta's body afterwards. Different MO surely?'

'I still believe we're dealing with the same offender. But different motivations behind the killings would account for the way the victims were treated.'

I walked over to where the gruesome gallery of crime scene photographs was pinned up.

'In Leo's case, the killer felt rage.'

I transported myself back to Chapel Mills. Almost smelling the tang of fresh blood that would have hung in the still air of the loft as the killer inflicted Leo's injuries. The sounds in the briefing room replaced in my imagination by Leo's muffled cries of agony.

'To want to torture the victim for no material purpose,' I said almost to myself. 'Not to extract information or break their will, but just for the pleasure of meting out such pain and watching the suffering.'

'What about the stalking?' Callum said.

I turned back to the board. 'Leo's killer undoubtedly stalked him. To terrify him, play mind games with him. But primarily to learn enough about his routines, to get into that apartment with the aim of killing him in a prearranged way. Every detail carefully planned and executed.'

'Just like Leo himself.' Albright grimaced at his own pun.

Chapter Fifty-Two

Callum explained the theory for how Thana could have returned to Leo's apartment, based on our visit the previous night.

'We always assumed Leo's killer was male,' Albright said.

'Not unreasonable, considering the rarity of females who kill this way,' I said. 'Plus, we had no DNA evidence to the contrary.'

I was staring at the gruesome images of Leo's battered body.

'Leo's murder is a one-off, not part of an escalating series. The driving force behind his torture and murder was rage ... not erotic gratification. That's why there are no offences like this on your database. This offender hasn't been in the system for similar attacks, as I'd first thought, because the motivation isn't sexual.'

'If that's not the motivation,' Albright asked, 'then what *is*?'

'Hatred,' I said simply.

'Personal hatred of Leo? For what?' Callum addressed me from his place at the table.

'That's the million-dollar question,' I said. 'Get that and it gives you your killer.'

'An ex-girlfriend?' Shah offered.

'Maybe someone in the art world?' Beth offered. 'A business deal that went sour?'

Albright made a note. 'Thana is still a favourite for it. She was never identified. No sightings of her after Leo's death. Her trail is well and truly cold.'

'Well,' I sighed, sitting back down to look at my notes. 'My original offender profile still applies. I haven't changed my stance on any of that. We can tell a lot about her from her signature behaviours at the scene.'

I flicked the remote to put the notes up on screen. 'She's an organised offender – which means this was planned, well in advance. She stalked him to learn his routines, then engineering a meeting at the Munch Bunch. Having breakfast with him most days, getting under his defences, earning his trust.'

'Watching him at night from the gardens? Terrorising him as a stalker, then meeting him in the morning like nothing's happened?' Albright sounded incredulous. 'That's one sick puppy . . .'

'A cold and calculating puppy,' I agreed. 'You're looking for someone between thirty and forty years old. Above average intelligence. Good social and interpersonal skills.'

'We know Thana presented herself as a rough sleeper,' Albright said. 'But that could be so she didn't look out of place hanging around the area early mornings and late at night.'

I glanced round the team. 'This type of profile fits with someone who is probably employed in a professional job.'

'We checked businesses in the area.' Callum raked his fingers through his hair as he stretched back in his chair. 'Nothing came up that matches, but we'll keep looking.'

I thought about what it would take to stay with her victim over a period of days. 'Sadistic and cruel . . . goes without saying.' I closed my eyes for a moment, pinching the bridge of my nose to ward off a headache. I wearily opened them and glanced across to the whiteboard and its gallery of death. 'But she still couldn't resist planting clues, for her own amusement. She believes she's too clever for you, so you'll never see them for what they are.'

'Anything else?' Albright asked. He'd been scribbling notes as I spoke.

'Yes,' I said. 'Her name – she probably thinks that's amusing too.'

'What about it?'

'It's Arabic . . .'

'So?'

'It *can* be translated as "thankfulness". But in its original form, it means "Death".'

There was a pause as that fact rattled around the room. Someone cleared their throat.

I took advantage of the silence. 'Another important detail is the timing of Leo's death – it was prearranged.'

'He choked on his own vomit,' Callum cut in. 'The killer couldn't have planned that.'

'They didn't,' I said. 'Leo robbed the killer of the climax to this carefully prepared murder, by inconveniently dying on the wrong date. He died a day early.'

'He died on the 8th of May 2017.' Albright checked his notes. 'What's so important about the 9th?'

'That was the date of Oliver Blackstone's death.'

Chapter Fifty-Three

Albright shot me a look. 'You're saying that Leo Fielding's murder is connected to Oliver Blackstone's death two years before?'

'I'm just pointing out a fact that could be coincidence.'

'But you don't think it is?' Callum said.

'I'm convinced that whoever killed Leo Fielding, also killed Jacinta Williams. The date of Oliver's death and Leo's is a coincidence we shouldn't ignore.'

'The obvious connection to Oliver is the party where he died,' Callum said, his eyes suddenly looking weary. 'Jacinta wasn't at Boltby Hall that night. We checked – she was in Paris. There's no evidence that Jacinta ever knew Leo, and Pete's team can't find any evidence that puts Leo at that party either.'

I stood up and went over to the coffee percolator in the corner. An inveterate tea drinker, it was unusual for me, but my brain felt like it was trawling through sludge. I needed the caffeine.

'Quercus is a solid link between Oliver and Leo,' Albright offered.

'I've arranged an interview with Myles Lawson for tonight,' Callum said, watching as I poured my coffee. 'He knows all the people involved – maybe if we push him hard enough, he'll give us something?'

Personally, I didn't think Myles Lawson would give us the steam from his tea, but I kept that thought to myself.

'Could I get the crime scene photos from Boltby Hall?' I asked.

Callum frowned. 'Didn't you see them when you gave evidence at the trial?'

'All I saw were the photos in my bundle. The ones they thought I'd need to prepare my evidence. Mainly the bathroom – Oliver's body in-situ and at post-mortem. Not everything.'

Callum made a note. 'OK. I'll email them to you. You said the motivation for the killing of Jacinta and Leo was different.' He was still writing. 'Even though it was the same offender?'

'Yes,' I said, walking back to my seat. 'That would account for the differences in MO.'

'If the drive behind Leo's murder was hatred, what was it in Jacinta's case?'

I slowly sipped from the mug, grimacing at the strong taste.

'As I said from the beginning. The killer showed consideration with the body.'

'Which means what?' Beth frowned.

'They cared about her.'

Callum flicked on the TV monitor – putting up the image of Jacinta as she was found, lying on her back in bed, the covers carefully pulled up.

'We know from the post-mortem report that she wasn't killed in this position,' he said, changing the image to show her face down in the mortuary. The bruises clearly visible along her spine and the partial footprint on the back of her calf.

'Imagine the room is pitch black. She's lying face down on the bed. The killer takes a stocking out of the drawer – walks over and slips the ligature round her neck. Kneeling on her back, they strangle her. Leaving the footprint on her leg and the bruises on her back where they knelt to pin her down. Talk us through it from there, Jo.'

'It's then that we see classic displays of "killer's remorse". Jacinta is turned over, "put to bed" like a sleeping child. We see behaviours like this in mercy killings or someone killing a loved one in the heat of the moment and becoming overwhelmed by guilt or regret immediately afterwards.'

'Do you think *this* is heat-of-the-moment?' Beth asked. 'With the killer then regretting what they'd done?'

I shook my head. 'They show remorse at having to do it. But no guilt.'

'Surely they're the same thing?'

'Not necessarily. You can be sad that it came to it, but not feel guilty about having to do it.'

'Like they had no choice – a mercy killing?'

'Yes. Jacinta's killing was necessary as far as they were concerned, but one they took no pleasure in.'

I flicked up the image of the bedroom – the clothes on the chair and the shoes placed neatly side by side with the jewellery hidden inside.

'This was no blitz attack carried out in anger. There's no panic here. Instead, they took their time. Arranging her body. Then they tidied up, folded her clothes.'

'Why didn't they tidy the cabinet where the stocking came from?' Beth asked.

'Because they were disturbed. By the neighbour from upstairs knocking on the door,' Callum said. 'That would fit with the time he said he heard noises coming from Jacinta's flat. An hour after Blackstone left. Also, according to toxicology Jacinta was so drunk she wouldn't have been able to fold her clothes with such precision.

'The killer did that,' I said. 'Habitual behaviour– an unconscious act. Thankfully for us, one that's become a "signature" that we can identify at both scenes.'

'Forensics estimate a size five trainer from the partial print.' Callum consulted his notes. 'That would fit with a woman of Thana's estimated height and build. And the use of the stocking' – he glanced around at his team – 'would explain a female who needed the extra leverage a ligature would give her to strangle the victim.'

'If she knew Jacinta, that would account for how she got access to the apartment,' Beth added. 'No sign of a forced entry – points to someone who knew the entry code.'

I'd been doodling on my notes as the team kicked around the possibilities. I stared at the words I'd absently circled, almost without conscious thought.

'*Boltby Hall*'.

'It's the party,' I said – to no one in particular. 'Everything goes back to that one night . . . everything.'

Chapter Fifty-Four

Fordley police station – Monday evening

I don't know why I'd expected Myles Lawson to look any different to the way he had during Nique's trial four years previously, but he didn't.

I sat in the observation room, watching the interview across the corridor on-screen, as Callum prepared to put his questions to the man reputed to be Blackstone's trusted right hand.

We had instant messaging set up, so that anything I typed on my keypad appeared on Callum's tablet.

'Thanks for coming in to see us, Myles.' Callum smiled slightly. 'OK if I call you Myles?'

Lawson nodded, leaning nonchalantly as far back as the rigid plastic chair allowed. His arrogance hadn't diminished during the intervening years.

I recognised the same sardonic twist to his lips, the same shrewd brown eyes that reminded me of a bird of prey eyeing up his quarry.

'You've agreed to this recorded interview, without your solicitor present,' Callum noted.

'That's because I don't need one.'

Arrogant little shit, I thought, tapping my pencil against my teeth.

'We're just trying to make sense of a few things,' Callum was saying, minimising the importance of the interview. 'Relating to the night Jacinta Williams was murdered.' He paused, but Lawson said nothing – studying him with an attitude bordering on disdain.

'You collected Jacinta and drove her to Sir Neville's office earlier that evening?'

'Yes.'

'But Sir Neville was running late?'

'That's right. I went to see what was keeping him.'

As Callum took him through the sequence of events, I watched Lawson's body language. The buttons of his expensive suit jacket were undone – I could see the rise and fall of his chest beneath the silk shirt. I calibrated his breathing. He seemed relaxed.

'Did Jacinta say anything when you got back to the car?'

'No. But she was edgy. When I asked what was wrong, she snapped my head off.'

'She didn't say she'd seen or spoken to anyone while you were gone?'

'No. I've already told the police all of this.'

'Does the name Thana mean anything to you?'

Lawson frowned. 'No. Should it?'

'She never mentioned a friend by that name?'

'No.'

'*Ask him about his relationship with Jacinta?*' I typed.

Callum posed the question. I watched Lawson's body language. He simply shrugged, but there were displays of tension. He sat up straighter.

'I didn't know her that well.'

'But you knew she was Sir Neville's mistress?'

Lawson's eyes narrowed slightly, suspicious about where this was going.

'Who the boss screws is his business.'

'*He's avoiding the question.*'

'What was she like as a person?'

Lawson sat up straight, leaning his elbows on the table. 'Chief Inspector, once and for all, I didn't *have* an opinion of her as a person. She was a whore, till the boss started paying for exclusivity. If he was happy . . .' He shrugged again.

'He *wasn't* happy though, was he?' Callum challenged. 'He told us he was going to end it. She'd crossed a line, the night she died. He'd had enough.'

'Good for him,' he said tightly.

I watched his hands, under the table where Callum couldn't see them. He was unconsciously twisting his signet ring.

'*Leaking anxiety signals,*' I typed.

'Did he talk to you about the row they'd had?'

'Sir Neville wasn't in the habit of discussing his love life with me.'

'So that night, he gets back in the car – he's angry, his neck is bleeding and he doesn't say *anything* to you about why?'

'He called her a stupid bitch. Said she was raging as usual . . .'

'A neighbour heard Jacinta shouting, "Your ghosts are coming back to haunt you – just like they did for your son."' He glanced at Lawson. 'What do you think she meant, Myles?'

His breathing was becoming more rapid as his pulse rate quickened. I watched the signet ring being twisted more.

That habit with the ring was a 'tell'.

'I've no idea.'

His body language said otherwise.

'*Ask him about Blackstone's wife?*'

'How well do you know Lady Blackstone?'

323

'We've met once or twice.' Twisting the ring again. 'She lives in the Caymans.'

'Have you ever been to the house there?'

'No.'

'*A lie.*'

I saw Callum glance at my message.

'You're his right-hand man. Involved in every aspect of his business, and he's *never* taken you to his place in the Caymans?'

'He keeps that part of his life private. I work with him; I don't live in his pocket.'

More pressure signals.

'What do you think of his wife?'

His body became still. His chest expanded as he took a slightly deeper breath. 'She's OK.'

Watching him, something suddenly occurred to me.

I typed – Callum read the note – then asked, 'But you like her? Lady Blackstone.'

'I suppose so . . . yes.'

'It didn't bother you that Sir Neville was cheating on her with Jacinta then?'

'I'm his business associate, not his moral compass.'

The ring was twisting faster.

Callum suddenly changed tack, taking him back to the moment Blackstone left Jacinta's apartment.

'He said she'd been raging as usual? What did he mean? What did she usually rage about?

Lawson's breath left in frustration. 'How the hell would I know?'

'You knew them both – worked closely with him. You must have some idea?'

'Divorcing Tal . . . Lady Blackstone I suppose. That's what the serious fights were always about.'

I typed, '*Leo?*'

'Sir Neville commissioned a portrait of his wife,' Callum said – switching gears again, keeping him off balance. 'I believe you knew the artist – Leo Fielding?'

Lawson hesitated. His eyes widening in genuine surprise. Whatever question he'd been expecting, this wasn't it.

'Leo . . . yes. I mean no, not really.'

'Which is it?' Callum smiled disarmingly. 'Yes, or no?'

'We attended the same school, not at the same time.'

'But you knew him through Quercus?'

'Quercus? That's ancient history. What's that got to do with anything?'

I watched as his body, previously still, became more animated as the stress hormones surged. His knee began to bounce restlessly. He brought his hands onto the table – unconsciously twisting the ring.

The 'tell' wasn't missed by Callum this time.

'You must have met him at Quercus events?' He took hold of the silence that followed. 'Easy enough for us to check, Myles.' The disarming smile didn't quite reach his eyes.

'Yes. OK,' he finally conceded. 'But I barely knew him. Oliver had more to do with him. He suggested Leo when his father wanted the portrait as a present.'

'Pretty extravagant present, considering he never collected it.'

'*Huge anxiety*', I typed, watching Lawson's body language. Perspiration was breaking out on his forehead. He wiped his top lip with a finger.

I was about to type the question – but Callum beat me to it.

'Was Leo at Boltby Hall?'

Lawson stared at him for just a second, before seeming to deflate.

'Yes,' he said quietly, as if he'd suddenly run out of steam. 'He was at the party. What of it?'

Callum let the silence linger for a painful moment. 'Was Leo's name on any guest list?'

Myles shrugged. 'Printed invites weren't sent out, if that's what you mean? Security had lists of who could get in, but that wasn't even released to them until the night. These events were . . . discreet.'

'You mean secret?' Callum pushed.

'I prefer "discreet". These guests value their privacy. We never wanted the press to get wind of where the party was going to be held or who was attending.'

'How did the security company vet the guests who arrived?'

'People were invited over the phone by the event organisers. A barcode was sent to their smartphone that would be scanned by security on the night.'

Lawson was leaking adrenalin with every animated gesture – every rapid rise and fall of his chest. 'Oliver was inviting people all the time. On the run-up to the party. He had the code on his phone – he just sent it to people. He didn't consult the events co-ordinator . . . just did it.'

'The events co-ordinator?' Callum sat a little more forward in his chair. 'Yalena Vashchenko?'

Lawson had mentioned her without prompting. A mental slip that Callum seized on – probably at the same moment Lawson realised his mistake.

326

Lawson became suddenly very still. Hands clasped tightly before him on the table. He didn't say anything.

'Oliver beat and raped her that night. That's why Dominique De Benoit killed him.'

Lawson shook his head. 'Vashchenko never gave evidence. No one knows what happened between her and Oliver.'

'*You* know though, don't you, Myles?'

His eyes narrowed as he stared at Callum – a snake in front of a mongoose.

'I wasn't in Oliver's room,' he said tightly. 'I only went in there after De Benoit appeared, covered in his blood, telling me she'd called an ambulance. That was the first I knew . . .'

Callum hadn't asked whether he'd been in Oliver's room. His mind had made an involuntary leap to information he was trying to conceal.

I typed again.

'Was Leo in Oliver's room?' Callum asked. 'Did *he* rape Yalena Vashchenko that night?'

No response, but the unconscious twisting of the ring.

Lawson shifted in his chair. Gone was the arrogant, over-confident appearance he so often projected. He looked at a spot over Callum's shoulder, absently running a finger along the inside of his collar.

He was a man standing at the edge of a chasm. I could see the cogs turning as he debated what to say next. No doubt he regretted the arrogance of agreeing to this meeting without a solicitor present. He was probably considering asking for one now, but he knew how that would look.

I didn't need to type – Callum could see the signs as clearly as I could.

327

Finally, Lawson splayed his hands out in a gesture of conciliation.

'Look, I don't know for sure what went on in that room . . .' He let the sentence hang in the air.

Callum picked it up. 'But you *do* believe that Leo had something to do with the attack on Yalena?'

He dropped his head – staring at the table top – trying to take himself out of this arena. But he had nowhere to go.

'Is your association through Quercus the reason you've kept Leo's name out of it, Myles?' Callum waited. 'Quercus members look out for each other. A brotherhood. "Men of oak" – isn't that the motto?' Callum raked his fingers through his hair, a sure sign he was losing patience. 'Leo's dead, Myles. Why carry on protecting his reputation now?'

'OK. OK,' he said finally. 'Leo left before the police arrived. He begged me not to mention his name. Said it would end his career if he was ever associated with the scandal. But he never admitted anything to me. I just assumed he didn't want to get caught up in it. It was the best I could do for him.'

Callum referred to his notes. 'Leo's phone was recovered from the scene when he died. We had it forensically examined. There were no messages relating to the party on there and no barcode. So how did he get in?'

'Oliver invited him when they spoke and told security to let him in when he arrived. He never had the barcode sent to his phone, so there was no record of him having been there. The barcode scanners we provided to the door teams that night were all recovered after the event and destroyed. That's the way these things were done.'

'Was Leo there when you went into the room to help Oliver?'

'No,' he said emphatically. 'Oliver was alone . . . on the bathroom floor.'

I believed him on that point. It tallied with what Nique had told me.

'Everything I know about that night is a matter of public record.' His voice was calmer now. 'From the evidence I gave at the trial. The only reason Leo wasn't mentioned is that no one asked at the time and I just thought he was like a hundred other guests who panicked that night and wanted to get away before the shit hit the fan.'

'Do you only give information you're specifically asked for?'

He sighed, crossing his legs to flick an invisible speck from his trousers. He was regaining his composure. His eyes were shrewd as he studied Callum. 'As far as I'm aware, he wasn't a person of interest to the police that night or during the trial . . . so why are you asking about him now?'

'Because he's dead,' Callum said bluntly. 'Two years after the party, he was tortured to death.'

'And?' Lawson raised an imperious eyebrow, as though this whole thing was of no importance.

'And now Jacinta's dead. Did *she* know Leo Fielding?'

Lawson shook his head slowly. 'Not that I'm aware. Why don't you ask Sir Neville?'

'We will. Was Jacinta involved in Oliver's party in any way?'

'No. She wasn't one of the girls supplied that night – she didn't even know Sir Neville then.'

I typed a note. Callum glanced at it. Then hesitated, before looking back at Lawson.

'Apparently Dominique De Benoit has alleged that *you* were one of the men who raped Yalena Vashchenko that night, along with at least one other. Was it you and Leo? Is that why you covered for him? And he did the same for you. Men of oak . . . having each other's backs?'

'Complete bollocks!' he spat, his eyes glittering more with fear than indignation. 'When? When did she come up with *this* accusation?'

'Since her release.'

Lawson's thin smile was more scornful than humorous. 'She's a lying bitch, who'll say anything to deflect what *she* did. Besides, I heard she died in a fire – so unless you can communicate with the dead, Chief Inspector, I doubt anything she said, to sell a book or an interview, will matter a damn to anyone now. Will it?'

'Two people connected to you have been murdered, Myles. You might want to think about that before withholding information.'

Lawson sat up and pushed his chair back. I noticed his fingers were trembling slightly as he straightened his cuffs.

'If you have new evidence to support these wild accusations, I suggest you arrest me and we'll conduct any further interviews in the presence of my solicitor.' He raised his eyebrows. 'If not, then I think we're done here.'

* * *

'When *exactly* did De Benoit tell you that Lawson was one of the men who raped Yalena?' Callum rounded on me as soon as we

330

were back in his office. The muscles bunched in his cheek as he tried to control his temper.

'After her release from Styal.' I suddenly felt washed out and bone weary at having to juggle half-truths and deceptions. It was exhausting. Part of me almost sympathised with the way Lawson must have felt doing the same.

'But *before* the fire?'

'Obviously!'

He threw his suit jacket over the back of his chair before turning on me. 'Not *so* obvious. Seeing as these days I'm never sure exactly what you know and what you're keeping from me.'

I dropped my briefcase on his desktop, scattering papers. 'I'm not keeping anything from you.'

'Really? So why did it feel like an ambush in there? You didn't think to tell me about Lawson before now? Not exactly unimportant, is it?'

I ran a hand across my eyes – struggling with a headache that felt like it was gnawing through my eyeballs. 'I didn't know what to make of it when she told me.' I looked across his desk, which felt like an expanse of no-man's land, but less inviting. 'She said Yalena told her the morning after the party. But she was out of it on painkillers at the time. And by Nique's own admission, Oliver was alone in the bathroom when she went in. She said she didn't see Lawson until she was leaving. That all tallied with his evidence at the trial.'

'You should *still* have told me.'

'It was hearsay, from someone who's now dead,' I reasoned. 'It can't be corroborated. It was only when I was watching the

331

interview that it occurred to me again. I wanted to see how he'd react when you put it to him.'

'He terminated the interview, that's how!' Callum raked his fingers through his hair – pacing behind his desk. 'A reaction I could have done without!'

'His body said far more than his mouth did,' I countered. 'He's *scared*, Cal. And for what it's worth . . . I believe he *was* there. I think he *did* rape Yalena along with Oliver and Leo, and that's why two of them are dead!'

'So, what's he so scared of now, exactly?'

'That he's next.'

Chapter Fifty-Five

Tuesday morning

Jen's call came in as I was driving into Fordley.

'Where are you?'

'On my way to meet Heslopp. He's asked me to attend when he talks to Baahir Abassi.'

'OK.' Jen's tone was all business and I could imagine her adjusting her reading glasses as she looked at her notes. 'I started looking into Dimitri Chernov yesterday – interesting character.'

'I can imagine.'

'The family have connections to the Bratva.' I could hear her shuffling papers. 'Dimitri's the new generation – tasked with making the family business appear more legitimate. He fronts several genuine companies in Russia and Europe. Has properties in London and Rome but lives mostly in the South of France.'

'Criminal record?'

'Minor offences as a teenager. Possession of cannabis, a few brawls in nightclubs. The usual stuff for a playboy with too much privilege and not enough responsibility. At nineteen, after the last run-in with the law, Daddy jerked his leash. Word is he threatened to cut off the boy's allowance unless he reined it in.'

'Lucky he didn't threaten to cut off more than that.'

'Anyway, after that, he calmed down. Got involved with his father's enterprises and been clean ever since. Interpol's been sniffing around for years into drug running between the cartels in South America and Africa he's reputedly responsible for, but they can never get enough evidence.' I heard the turning of more pages. 'The family are Teflon. International agencies struggle to make a case. Witnesses refuse to talk. Hardly surprising – people who cross them seem to conveniently disappear.'

'Anything else?'

'There was a death on his yacht on a trip to Tunisia. Anastasia Petrov – went overboard after overdosing on drugs. Her body was recovered by the coastguard. Verdict was suicide. I've got copies of the report.'

I couldn't help marvelling at how simple she made that sound. 'Can't have been easy, Jen,' I said, smiling. 'From Tunisian authorities?'

'Filing clerks and indexers are an undervalued breed.' I could hear the grin in her voice. 'The invisible people everyone overlooks.'

'Except you, right?'

'It helps that in some countries the red tape is a little more, err . . . negotiable. I'll email it all over to you.'

'Thanks, Jen. You're worth your weight in gold.'

'From your lips to God's ears. When are you going to be back?'

'Not until late. I'll be tied up with Heslopp, then an interview Callum's conducting.'

He'd arranged to interview Neville Blackstone. I was surprised by the invite, given the way he'd been with me yesterday. But then he'd never been one to let personal feelings get in the way of the job. Besides, I'd provided him with suggestions for an interview strategy that hopefully would give us some leverage.

'I'll pick Alex up from the station and bring him to the farm.' She sighed heavily down the phone. 'Working from home is driving me mad.'

'Most people see it as a perk, not a punishment.'

'They don't have Henry underfoot all day, do they? Keep nagging him to get a hobby. Remind me never to retire.'

'Don't worry – you're far too valuable for me to allow that.' I meant it.

I could hear her tapping her pen on the desktop. 'Think we've got kids hanging about the garden at night – he's like a man on a mission. Turned into a complete pain trying to catch them out. I'll be glad to get back to murderous psychopaths.'

'Kids? Doing what?'

'Nothing serious. But you'd think we had Al Qaeda lurking in the bushes the way he's carrying on.'

'Causing damage? '

'A bit – nothing serious. Tipped over the bin ... rubbish strewn all over the garden. Then the garage lock was broken.'

'Did they take anything?'

'Only my old car in there and who'd want *that*? So, no – just a broken lock. I left him chaining the bin to the fence-post this morning.' I could almost hear the rolling of her eyes. 'He'll be planting anti-personnel mines in the petunias by this afternoon.'

I laughed. 'Better get yourself back to my office at the farm then.'

'Can't happen soon enough,' she ended cheerfully.

* * *

As soon as I cleared that call, the phone rang again.

'Princess.' Edge's voice rumbled through the car's speakers. 'Where are you?'

'Driving. Is everything OK?'

'Yes – sorry we missed you yesterday.'

'Tried to catch you before I left.' I'd gone down to the kitchen, expecting to find him eating breakfast, but there was no sign of him, or Harvey. 'Thought you'd stolen my dog,' I joked.

'Didn't have a choice.' He laughed. 'He's been coming along when I go for my early run . . . Think he's getting to like it.'

'You still run every morning?'

'Legacy of army life – train hard, fight easy.'

I'd been tied up at the station all day and they'd moved out to the Fordley practice by the time I got back the previous evening. I'd walked in to find a single white rose in a stem vase on the kitchen table – with a note in Nique's handwriting. '*To my precious Yorkshire rose.*'

'Well, Harvey better not get too used to it,' I said grimly. 'I won't be going running any time soon.'

'Anyway – just wanted to let you know everything's OK at your office. We'll be shoving off tonight. Nique's just tidying the place . . . make sure we don't leave any evidence that we've been here.'

'Thanks, Edge.'

'No problem.'

'Listen, I know this was never the plan, but when I'm finished today, I want to come to the office. I need to see you before you leave.'

'Thought we'd agreed . . .?' He sounded cautious.

'I would have spoken to you last night, but you'd gone when I got back.'

'So, what's up?'

'We interviewed Myles Lawson again yesterday. Some things came out I need to speak to you about, but not over the phone.'

I wanted them in front of me when I asked my questions. To see Nique's reactions.

'OK, princess.' He sighed. 'Usual precautions though – make sure you're not followed.'

'I will.'

'We'll be here till midnight.'

Chapter Fifty-Six

'There's been a change of plan.' Frank Heslopp's call came in when I was almost at Abassi's address. 'Whereabouts are you?'

'What is it with everyone today? You're the third person to ask me that.'

'Baahir called asking us to meet him at the Madrasah. Doesn't want us at the house. Wants to see us in private.'

'Sounds ominous.'

'He's in an emotional state. I don't do emotion.'

Why did that not surprise me?

'It's next to Fordley Mosque. I'm already here.'

I glanced at the dashboard clock. 'OK, I'll be five minutes.'

* * *

Heslopp was leaning on the bonnet of his car, smoking a cigarette when I pulled into the almost deserted car park at the back of Fordley's 'Grand Mosque'.

The building's huge green dome dominated the city skyline. The magnificent two-million-pound construction, entirely funded by its two thousand regular worshippers, had become a focal point for the local community and the base for its most controversial teacher – Baahir's father.

Heslopp took a final drag on his cigarette, annoyingly blowing smoke in my direction. 'The boss asked me to let you know,' he said. 'The body in the penthouse . . . the one they recovered yesterday? It wasn't De Benoit.'

How much had Callum told him, about the impact that bomb-shell might have?

He squinted at me through the grey smoke, watching for some kind of reaction.

I paused – as if letting momentous news register. 'Oh.' I put my briefcase down and took a ragged breath. 'That's, err . . . that's good news. Any idea whose body it is?'

He watched me for a moment before shrugging. 'Not my case. You'll need to speak to the boss.'

I nodded, trying to look as though I was struggling to get my mind back to the job at hand.

'OK . . .' I glanced over to the mosque. 'Any idea why Baahir was so emotional when he called?'

Heslopp dropped his cigarette, ground it underfoot. 'If I had to guess? I think he believes we know more than we do and that we're here to confront him with something.'

We began walking towards the door. 'So how do you want to play it?' I asked.

'Let him talk,' Heslopp said simply. 'If he wants to tell us more than we already know, then I'm happy to let him.' He pulled open the door and held it for me. 'You chip in as and when, doc – but let him drive the conversation. I don't want him clamming up before he's got whatever's bothering him off his chest.'

As we walked into the corridor, we were met by the man I'd seen at the press conference. The community leader who had appealed for calm after the attack. He smiled, extending a skeletal hand.

'Mr Patel,' he said simply by way of introduction. His skin was cold against my palm despite the warmth outside. He shook Heslopp's hand. 'Detective Inspector, pleased to see you again.'

He turned and led the way down the corridor – pushing open a door at the far end, to usher us inside.

The room was lined with bookshelves, all neatly arranged with beautiful leather-bound volumes. Seated at the desk opposite the door was the unmistakeable figure of Adel Abassi – the contentious preacher, whose image usually stared out at me from the front pages of the tabloid press.

Beside him, his son Baahir sat rigidly in a leather-backed chair. I noticed the dark rings beneath his eyes. His hollowed-out cheeks creating the gaunt expression of a man who hadn't slept much in days.

Mr Patel quietly closed the door as he left us.

Adel Abassi indicated the chairs opposite. 'Please, sit.' His face was a mask, but I could sense the tension he was holding inside, taut as fine wire.

A strand of tasbeeh – prayer beads – were wrapped loosely around his fingers. He absently moved the amber stones back and forth with his thumb as he watched us.

'My son,' he said in a soft voice, 'has something he wants to say.' He half turned his face towards Baahir, who shifted uncomfortably in his seat.

Baahir looked down at the fingers twisting in his lap. 'I'm a biologist. The senior environmental assessor for the Council . . .' He paused, swallowing hard under the unrelenting gaze of his father.

'We were so proud of you.' Adel Abassi's voice was deceptively quiet. He tutted against his teeth. 'Now, to bring such shame upon our family . . .'

'Please,' Heslopp said quietly. 'If you could let your son speak?'

The old man shrugged, his dark eyes glittering with barely concealed contempt.

'I carry out reports on land quality, for planning applications.' When Baahir looked up, his face was a mask of anguish, his eyes imploring. 'I never intended to get involved like this . . . never meant for things to go this far. You've got to believe me—'

'That's OK – just tell us what happened.' Heslopp's tone was surprisingly reassuring.

'Will I go to prison?' Baahir almost wailed.

I shot Heslopp a look, wondering if he was going to pursue *that* one. He'd been right: Baahir thought we knew more than we did. He believed Heslopp was here to arrest him for something.

'You're a witness to the attack at Fordley train station.' Heslopp was choosing his words carefully. 'The purpose of our visit is to speak to you as a victim of what was essentially attempted murder.'

'I-I never thought they'd go that far,' he said haltingly. 'They said they'd kill me. I never really believed it . . .'

'Everyone thought *I* was the target!' His father raised his voice. 'You let them think that.'

'That's what we originally believed, yes.' Heslopp addressed the old man.

'You brought shame on our family to protect yourself!' Adel hissed.

Heslopp turned back to the son, who was visibly shaking – either with emotion or fear, I couldn't quite decide. 'I've come to hear what you have to say. Just start at the beginning, Baahir.'

'I'll pay all the money back, I still have most of it. The house . . . I can sell my house, can't I?' He leaned forward, his voice pleading.

Frank sat back in his chair and began to take notes. 'Just tell us what happened.'

'Most of the countryside around Fordley is protected green-belt. Majority of building taking place is on brownfield sites.' He washed a hand across his eyes, taking in a ragged breath as he calmed himself. 'Land that was once industrial.'

'Like the factories being renovated along the canal banks?' I asked, trying to put him at ease.

'Yes. But often the land doesn't meet current standards.'

'In what way?' Heslopp asked, still taking notes.

'Mostly it's soil contamination. What was acceptable to pour into the ground or the drains two hundred years ago isn't now.'

'So, you test the soil?'

'Yes. Then prepare reports for the council, the land owner or construction companies. We make recommendations on the clean-up operation and they can do a cost analysis. But on some sites the contamination is so severe that the cost of cleaning it up is more than the land would be worth after redevelopment . . .' He stopped, his eyes going from one to the other of us, as if that explained everything.

'And that's what happened?' I asked. Hoping the ambiguity of the question would do all the work.

He nodded, dropping his head into his hands – the breath escaping him in a shuddering sob.

Heslopp looked up from his note-taking, hoping the young man would compose himself. But Baahir didn't move.

The old man finally shifted in his chair. 'The attack at the station was reported as racist.' He adopted the commanding tone I suspected he used when he was preaching. 'Everyone pointed the finger at *me*! The police, the press,' he spat. 'They said that crazed soldier was an avenger.' He slowly turned to look at his son, who was sobbing quietly. 'When it was *greed* all along.' He prodded Baahir, the prayer beads clacking in his hand. '*Tell them!*' He commanded.

Baahir looked up, tears streaking his face. 'I have a young family, a mortgage—'

'Greed!' his father shouted. His chair scraped back as he jumped up, raising his fist.

For a man his size, Heslopp moved faster than I expected. He was suddenly on his feet – his shoulder between the two men, blocking any intended blow. Adel glared at him, breathing hard. A drop of spittle appeared in the corner of his mouth.

'I think it might be better if we spoke to your son alone,' Heslopp said calmly.

For a second it seemed as if the old man wasn't going to move. Then slowly he straightened his robes, walked around the desk and left the room without a word.

Heslopp sat back down. Reaching out, he gently touched Baahir's shoulder. 'Go on.'

'It was seven years ago, the first time I did what they wanted . . .' His voice trailed off.

I watched his hands twisting more tightly. When he looked at me, I could see in his eyes, the visceral battle between conscience and fear.

344

'You altered a report?' I guessed.

He nodded. 'It was just minor things. Playing down the severity of contamination that wasn't too bad. They paid a lot for what seemed so little . . .'

'But then it got more serious?' I ventured.

He was watching me for any sign of judgement. I gave a slight smile of encouragement.

'I got promoted. My reports were key to some of the bigger developments getting approved.'

'And you took bribes?' I kept my tone non-judgemental.

He just nodded. His head down as he stared at his feet.

'What led to the attack?' Heslopp asked.

His breath left him in a slow sigh. 'The huge mill complex, just outside Fordley. A massive project.'

'The "Crater"?'

It was the name locals had given to the huge half-derelict pile of rubble and deep exposed foundations that had once been the biggest woollen mill in the North. A blot on the landscape that had been there since my teenage years – sitting on the edge of the city on greenbelt land, known romantically as the 'Gateway to the Dales'.

He still spoke with his head down. I had to strain to hear the words, barely above a whisper.

'It's been undeveloped for decades. They couldn't go ahead unless they secured investment. But no businesses would commit to investing unless they knew it would succeed.'

'A catch twenty-two,' Heslopp said, still taking notes.

'The developers got it cheap. Then about four years ago, they secured the money from a European fund management company and began to have the plans drawn up. Local Government got behind it. The Prime Minister even made a speech about it, saying it heralded the city breaking away from its industrial past.' His laugh was humourless. 'All very grand . . . it became hugely political and there was massive pressure for it to go ahead. I was called in to assess the site.'

'What did you find?' Heslopp asked.

'The worst of everything.' Baahir hunched forward in his seat, his elbows on his knees as his leg bounced nervously. His words pouring out in a torrent. Now he'd started, he couldn't seem to stop.

'Underground storage tanks had leaked and contaminated the soil with deadly toxins.' He shook his head. 'Not just the usual poisons from the dyes they used in the mills back in the day, but mercury, lead, some really deadly carcinogens.' He sat back, tilting his head to look at a spot on the ceiling. 'I should have listed it on the Contaminated Land registry . . .'

'But you didn't?' Heslopp asked.

'They paid me not to. I altered the report and the planning was approved.' He looked at us and his face crumpled as tears ran down his face. 'They told me they would clean it up, but I knew they were lying. Otherwise, they could have let the report go through. But I knew the cost would be astronomical. The clean-up would take years. The clock was ticking. If they didn't start building soon, investors would pull out. Some already had penalty clauses written into their contracts. Delay would bankrupt the developer and if businesses began to pull out – they'd lose everything.'

He looked at us both, agonising as he relived what he had done. 'They paid me to keep quiet.'

'How much?' Heslopp asked.

'A hundred grand,' he groaned. 'But then, it got more serious and I couldn't . . . I just couldn't. If they build on that land with that level of contamination, it's a serious health risk. Breathing problems, cancer. People might die!'

'So you told them you were going to report it?' I asked.

He nodded. 'That's when they threatened me. They've put everything into this development. It's going to be their flagship. They've got two-hundred million invested!' His eyes were wide. 'Two-hundred *million* for God's sake! If this gets out, they're finished . . .'

'Who's "they"?' Heslopp finally asked.

I waited, almost holding my breath. But I already knew the answer. Blackstone himself had shown me the model for this vast development in his office.

The reason Blackstone had invited Baahir to his home to conclude their business. Then invited him to Oliver's extravagant birthday party. A sweetener to seal the deal. To give an impressionable young man a glimpse into a lifestyle he could have if he played the game. An entrée into another world. A world of corrupt financiers and tainted opportunities.

And then he said it.

'Blackstone Enterprises.'

Chapter Fifty-Seven

Fordley police station – Tuesday morning

'So, Blackstone used Josh Stamford to eliminate Abassi? To stop him blowing the whistle?' Callum twisted his pen between his fingers as he listened.

'Looks like it,' Heslopp said.

'It explains why Blackstone was so terrified of Stamford when I met him in his office,' I said. 'Stamford's attempt to murder Abassi went wrong, he's on the run, maybe expecting Michelle Briggs or Blackstone to help him. And when they didn't . . .'

'That would explain why he thought Stamford killed Jacinta – to hurt him, or send a warning shot that he was next?' Heslopp said.

'It's a workable theory,' Callum agreed. 'So how did you handle Abassi's confession to bribery and corruption?'

'Told him that we were there to investigate the more serious crime of attempted murder, but we couldn't ignore the fact that during his statement, he'd alluded to misconduct in public office and we were duty bound to bring that before the CPS.'

'Did he implicate Blackstone directly?'

'No,' Heslopp said. 'Blackstone stays at arm's length – too clever to get his hands dirty. But he implicated Myles Lawson. Baahir said Lawson was the one who told him what they needed in the site reports, and paid him.'

'Have we got anything linking Lawson to the money trail between them and Abassi?'

'Not yet, boss, but Intel are on it.'

Callum nodded, taking a mouthful of dubious looking coffee. 'And he made a full statement to all this?'

'Yep – the whole thing. He's shit scared, either of his father or going to prison. Seemed relieved to get it off his chest.'

'I almost feel sorry for him,' I said.

'Well don't!' Callum put his mug down on the desk like a full stop. 'He was happy enough to take the money until Stamford tried to turn him into ragu in front of the 8.15 from Leeds!'

'But his conscience got the better of him,' I reasoned. 'Even though it cost him his family. The father's disowning him.'

'That's rich.' Callum snorted. 'With a charge sheet as long as his father's! Getting disowned by that lot is doing the son a favour, if you ask me. But it puts Blackstone in our cross hairs now.'

'You pulling him in, boss?' Heslopp asked.

Callum nodded. 'Tony and Beth are already on the way to Leeds to bring him and Lawson in.' He dropped a sheaf of papers onto a lopsided pile on his desk. He glanced at Heslopp. 'Get Intel to expedite the info on the Mela victims. We need to know if any of them could have been targeted because of an involvement with Blackstone – like Abassi.'

'On it, boss.'

As he left, Callum turned to me. 'There's something I want you to see.'

He went to his laptop. 'Initial image of our voyeur at the penthouse fire.' He turned the screen towards me. 'Know who she is?'

I stared at a face I knew.

'She's a prison officer at Styal. Her name's . . . Harland.'

He didn't seem surprised.

'You already knew?'

He nodded. 'Penny Harland. We went to interview her but she'd disappeared.'

'Disappeared?'

'Didn't report for her shift the day after Nique's release and no one's seen her since.'

'They were having an affair,' I said almost to myself. I looked up to see him watching me, his face as dark as his mood.

'And you didn't think to mention that?'

'Why would I?' I snapped. 'Nique was out – what she'd done inside didn't seem to have any bearing.'

'Might have a bearing on the arson,' he said tightly. 'Or be the person who sent you the warning note?'

I thought back to the jealousy Harland had displayed that day at Styal.

'We've got people looking for her,' he said. 'Meantime – this is the CCTV from outside Blackstone's office building. It shows Lawson's car pulling up outside the day Jacinta died. She's sitting in the back.'

He fast-forwarded the images and stopped at the point Lawson got out of the car and ran up the steps and into the building.

I leaned closer to watch the tinted glass of the rear passenger window slide down. Jacinta looked out, squinting in the bright sunlight.

It was the first time I'd seen her alive and I was struck by how beautiful she was. It always affected me when I saw the brutal remains of a once vibrant, animated human being, laid out like so many dissected pieces on a mortuary slab.

Seeing video or film of them alive just made the juxtaposition of such a vital, complex person with the cadaver they became even more horrifying. Perhaps the day it didn't, was the day I gave up the job.

She was calling out to someone. Then she opened the door and got out, taking a step forward and calling out again.

'We managed to find CCTV from the bank across the street,' Callum explained, pulling up another clip.

It showed Jacinta from the back. Callum used the tip of his pen to outline a figure in the shadow of the office block.

The person – dressed in jeans and a dark jacket – turned to look directly at Jacinta for just a fleeting moment, then stepped around the corner and out of sight.

'Techies have cleaned the images up as best they can, but not enough to identify any facial features. They *can* tell us approximate height is about five foot five or six. Short cropped dark hair, Caucasian.'

'Male or female?' I asked.

'Probably female. Harland?'

'Could be . . .' The fact that she'd disappeared was compelling and I was convinced that she'd sent the note warning me away from Nique. 'Or Thana?'

He nodded. 'Height and build the same.'

'Harland and Thana could be the same person,' I said.

He thought about it for a second. 'Maybe she's been taking care of business on Nique's behalf?'

Could Nique have got Harland to kill Jacinta? My mind raced through the possibilities. *If she had, then that meant Nique had been behind Leo's death as well.*

I looked again at the image on the screen. Harland? I couldn't discount it.

He switched to more video. 'I got the team to look for any CCTV down that side street. Unfortunately for us, nothing close to where the figure was standing. But Beth tracked this down. From the opposite end of the street.'

We could see a speck in the distance.

'That's too far away.'

Callum tapped his pen against the screen. The camera was on the roof of a building, looking down onto a line of parked cars. He followed the grainy spec as it moved down the row and got into one of the cars. As they pulled away, it came towards us.

'A blue Mini,' Callum said. 'The team are checking CCTV and ANPR, to see if we can track it. With any luck we might get the number plate.'

'Whatever passed between that person and Jacinta changed her mood for the worst,' I said thoughtfully.

'And was possibly the reason she died that night,' he said quietly.

* * *

'Frank's told you that it wasn't Nique in the wreckage of the penthouse?' Callum said, once we'd viewed the CCTV.

I nodded. 'Have they ID'd the body yet?'

'A girl called Sandra Hayton.' He continued to watch me for some kind of reaction. I felt as though his eyes were drilling into my head.

'So Nique's still alive.' I didn't have to work hard to sound relieved.

'Which begs the question,' he said, watching me intently. 'Where's she been since the fire and why has she dropped off the grid? By doing a Houdini she's broken the terms of her parole. Which means if we *did* find her, she'd be sent back to finish the rest of her term inside.'

And whoever helped her wouldn't come out of it too well either, I could almost hear him thinking.

'I'd guess she's lying low to stay out of Blackstone's way.' I met his eyes. 'We both know Blackstone was behind the arson, Cal – it was attempted murder for Christ's sake!'

He pursed his lips, his dark eyes never leaving mine. 'Unlucky for Sandra then,' he said quietly. 'Wrong place, wrong time.'

I took a long breath, not rising to his bait. 'When are they going to release the news . . . that it was Sandra?'

'As soon as next of kin have been notified.' He leaned back in his chair, stretching his legs out beneath the desk. 'I would have thought De Benoit would contact you after the fire – if she wasn't in it?' He wasn't even trying to disguise his suspicions.

'Me too.' I looked him square in the eye. 'Suppose I don't have the relationship with her I thought I did.'

'I still thought she'd come forward,' he pushed. 'If only to help the arson investigation? Sandra worked at her club and from what I understand, she's protective of her girls. I mean, look what she did to the person who seriously hurt the last one.'

'This is different,' I said. 'She wasn't in a relationship with Sandra Hayton.'

'How do you know?'

'Because Sandra was seeing Edge.'

354

He raised an eyebrow. 'Really? You seem to know a lot, considering you haven't seen either of them since Nique's release . . .'

His words and the way he delivered them, were an attempt to push me and we both knew it – and I was just strung out enough, on stress and lack of sleep, to happily take the bait.

'Oh, for God's sake!' I snapped. 'Just because I haven't *seen* Nique, doesn't mean we haven't spoken.'

'When?' he probed – watching me with an intensity that was deliberately designed to poke a pissed-off tiger with a sharp stick.

'When I went to visit her in Styal,' I said, my patience for this game of cat and mouse evaporating fast. 'Then later, when she was holed up in the penthouse – we spoke on the phone. And before you ask, I had conversations with Edge as well, that's how I know he was seeing Sandra.' I raised my own eyebrow. 'Does that answer your question, Chief Inspector?'

We were saved by the bell when his phone rang. He listened, frowning. 'OK. Thanks for letting me know.'

'Well?' I asked when he hung up.

'Blackstone and Lawson have disappeared.' He stood up, snatching his jacket from the back of his chair, already shrugging into it as he brushed past me on his way out.

'When officers got there, the press pack were already outside the office. Apparently, news has broken about the development.'

'The Crater?' I grabbed my stuff and followed him.

'Looks like it's going to stay a crater,' he said over his shoulder. 'Adel Abassi just threw his son to the wolves . . . He's gone public'

And those same wolves would tear Blackstone to pieces.

Chapter Fifty-Eight

Tuesday afternoon

As I drove out of Fordley, I rang Edge's number.

'I'm on my way over to you now,' I said when he finally picked up. 'They've identified Sandra's body.'

'I heard – on local radio.'

I told him about Abassi and the Crater. 'Hopefully Blackstone will be too preoccupied dealing with that shit-storm to worry about Nique.'

Edge didn't sound convinced. 'Or it might be the final straw. Bankrupt and in the hole for two-hundred million. Jesus! The most dangerous opponent is the one with nothing to lose.'

It was a good point, but one I didn't dare consider.

'Blackstone's a corporate animal,' I said. Unsure whether I was trying to convince him or myself. 'The investments – that'll be his only concern right now.'

'He's losing more than money though. There's the scandal. Putting people's lives at risk by building on contaminated land . . . attempted murder. Bloody hell, princess!'

He had a point. Now the news was out, it wouldn't take long for the press to uncover the rest, and even the Crater wasn't a deep enough hole to bury this poison. The fact that Blackstone had been willing to sanction murder was testimony to what he felt he had to lose if this didn't go ahead.

The corruption leaching out from what he'd done to protect his investment would contaminate it all. Stripping away everything he held most dear.

'He can't catch and kill *this* one,' I said almost to myself

'What time's your boy due back?' Edge asked.

I glanced at the clock. 'Jen should be picking him up from the station about now.'

'OK. We'll see you soon.'

* * *

Ten minutes later I parked my car a few streets from the office.

The air was heavy with the scent of summer flowers and I realised that May had somehow slipped into June.

Finally turning the corner, I crossed the avenue of laburnums, carefully stepping over cracked paving slabs that had been lifted by gnarled tree roots, their interlacing brown tendrils coiling out of the earth like benign serpents searching out the heat of the sun.

I was fishing for the office keys when my mobile rang.

'McCready,' I answered distractedly, cradling the phone under my chin as I fumbled with the lock.

'Jo!' Jen screamed.

I dropped the keys.

I could hear a commotion at the other end. People shouting. Jen sobbing. 'What's wrong?'

'Jo . . . it's Alex. Oh my God.'

Her words sent a surge of electricity through my body.

'Jen, take a breath.'

'Alex . . .' Ragged gasps were tearing the words away from her.

'What about him? What's happened?' I'd never heard her sound like this. The primitive rawness of her panic rocketed my own heart rate. 'Jen!' I shouted, in a desperate attempt to halt her mounting hysteria. 'Talk to me!'

'He's gone!' she wailed. 'They crashed into my car, they dragged him out – they've taken Alex.'

Chapter Fifty-Nine

In that moment, everything stopped. My peripheral vision shrank, as if I was looking down the wrong end of a telescope.

I was dimly aware of Jen crying. Voices raised above the sound of traffic – car horns blaring. Auditory clues from a scene I couldn't see.

'*Your door won't open . . .*' More shouting, the sound of metal on metal. '*Undo your seatbelt . . . Climb over into the passenger seat, we'll get you out. Here, love, hand me your phone.*'

'Hello?' A male voice spoke to me directly.

The firmness of his tone defibrillated my senses.

'Who's this?' I finally managed.

'Andy. We're working on the building site opposite. Saw the crash – ran over to help. Is this lady your mum?'

'Friend, she's my friend.' My legs suddenly felt as though they were going to give way. I leaned heavily against the door. 'What's happened?'

'A white Transit van T-boned the car – driver's door's buckled, so we can't get her out that way . . .'

'My son . . .' my voice croaked – I had no saliva. 'She said someone dragged him out?'

Please God – let this just be an accident – they've pulled Alex out of the car because of the crash . . . Please don't let this be more serious . . .

'Two men got out of the van.' Andy was talking fast. 'Wearing balaclavas – we were halfway across the road when we saw the guns . . .'

'Guns!' It felt like my heart stopped – black dots began to appear in front of my eyes. I leaned more heavily against the door, resting my cheek against the warm wood panels.

'We couldn't believe it – right in front of us. Your boy must be involved in some serious shit, lady.'

'What did they do . . . to my son?'

'One held us off at gunpoint, while the other one bundled the kid into the back of the van, then they drove off.'

He broke off – obviously shouting over to someone else. 'Yeah, mate – police and ambulance on their way. Sit her down, over here.'

'Hello?' I raised my voice – bringing him back to me. 'Is she OK? My friend?'

I could hear sirens in the distance.

'Hang on, I'll put her back on . . . Just a minute.'

My office door was suddenly yanked open from the other side, causing me to fall in. I'd have landed face first, if strong arms hadn't caught me.

'What the fuck?' Edge pulled me inside – kicking the door shut as he led me down the corridor to the kitchen.

Somewhere I registered Nique, sitting at the table – watching us with wide eyes as I held on to Edge, trying to focus on what was happening just a few short miles away.

'She's OK, I think.' Andy sounded out of breath. 'It's your friend,' he said to Jen as he returned the phone.

'Jo?' She sounded a little calmer.

'Are you OK?' I asked.

Edge pulled out a chair and sat me down opposite Nique. I could hear him at the sink behind me.

'Yes . . . I think so. I couldn't stop them, Jo. I'm sorry . . .'

Nique was watching me – mouthing questions. I closed my eyes to her. I had to concentrate on what was unfolding down the phone.

'It's not your fault.' I sounded calmer than I felt. 'Listen to me, Jen. When the police get there, they'll question you. You're a key witness.' I hesitated, knowing she wouldn't be able to process all this, not yet. But I needed to explain – and I knew she wouldn't like it. 'Once they get there, I won't be able to speak to you for a while . . .'

'What? But why?'

I took a ragged breath. 'It's just procedure. Once they know about the guns, it'll escalate.'

For once, I wished that I didn't have insider knowledge, that I didn't know how this would unfold. Because knowing made it all too real. And that my own son was in the middle of it was gnawing at my innards with reptilian terror.

'They'll seize your car and your phone for evidence—'

She leapt ahead of me. 'They can't believe that I'd . . .?'

'They have to be sure who's involved and who's a victim.'

I knew this would escalate to CID. 'They won't let you speak to anyone – they won't want any information leaking out.'

Crime in action was the phrase. I couldn't bring myself to say it out loud. It scared me to death.

The sound of a siren got louder, threatening to drown out everything else.

'Firearms cops are here.' Andy's voice, close to Jen.

'Why, Jo?' she finally managed. 'Who's taken him?' Before I could reply, I heard a police officer speaking to Jen. 'I've got to go,' she said, just before ending the call.

* * *

I stared at the phone in my hand. My mind was racing a million miles an hour.

Edge put a mug down in front of me, sloshing tea onto the table.

'Jesus, princess. Is that what it sounded like?'

I opened my mouth, then closed it again, just nodding.

Nique came round and crouched down beside my chair, putting her arms round me. A gesture of kindness that would normally have unravelled me – but my emotions felt fossilised, a lump of granite hanging heavily under my breastbone.

We all jumped when the phone rang. The screen flashed – 'Alex'.

'Alex! Thank God . . .'

'Jo McCready?' A male voice I didn't recognise slashed through my relief.

'Yes.' My heart pounded out of my chest.

'We have your son . . .' The tinge of a foreign accent that I couldn't quite place.

I put the call on loudspeaker, so they could listen.

A dozen questions screamed in my mind. *Is he OK? Who are you? What do you want?* But none of them made pole position. I was trying to form words but my jaw wouldn't work.

'If you tell the police we've contacted you, he's dead.' The voice was as unemotional as the speaking clock.

An icy hand squeezed my innards – until I couldn't move, couldn't breathe.

Edge was scribbling something on the corner of that morning's newspaper. He pushed it in front of me. *'Proof of life?'*

I cleared my throat. 'Let me speak to him . . . I need to know he's OK.'

'We'll call you with instructions. Don't speak to anyone. Make sure you're alone and we can reach you on this number.' An unemotional litany of instructions.

'Let me speak—'

There was a rustling sound, people moving around, then . . .

'Mum.'

'Alex—'

'That's all you get for now,' the male voice said.

'Alex?' I screamed down an empty line.

'They've gone.' Nique slipped her hand over mine, prising the phone out of my frozen fingers.

Bile rose in my throat – I knocked the chair over as I stumbled towards the sink, making it just in time to throw up.

Chapter Sixty

I felt disassociated – as if watching the world through thick fog. This couldn't be happening.

'What do they want?' I asked numbly – as though my mind had to go through the motions of logically unravelling what my instincts already knew.

Nique looked at me across the table. 'That's easy, *ma copine*.' She raised an elegant eyebrow. 'They want me.'

'It's Blackstone.' Edge's voice penetrated the fog. His arm around my shoulders. 'Got to be.'

'Why?' I asked no one in particular. 'Why would he risk it?'

I felt Edge's shrug. 'The police are looking for him. He's wanted for corruption, fraud, attempted murder. He's going down – so what's to lose? Might as well get his money's worth.'

That made sickening sense. I knew that for a man like Blackstone, prison meant more than loss of freedom. It meant loss of wealth, status – respect. Everything that fed his narcissistic ego would be gone and that would destroy him in every way.

'He's right,' Nique said, rubbing her tired eyes. 'I'm unfinished business – he's pursued me from the shadows until now. Got other people to do his dirty work – like the fire.' She raised her shoulders. 'Now everything's in the open he wants to finish it while he has the chance.'

'Plus . . .' Edge added grimly, 'he knows you've been involved in the investigations, Jo. Turning over rocks he'd rather have left alone.' He got up and went back to the sink. 'Taking Alex hurts you, as well as getting to Nique.'

'He's probably made the connection to me and Abassi by now,' Nique added. 'He knows I was there when they met at his home.'

I remembered that moment in Blackstone's office – as I was leaving. *'You have a son . . . I hope you never feel the agony of losing him.'*

'Blackstone made a threat about me losing Alex,' I said quietly. 'He told me how he felt, knowing you were alive, when his own son was dead.'

'Bastard!' Nique spat, reaching across to take my hand. 'He keeps a mental score card. Anyone who crosses him, in business or his personal life, has to pay. It's the way he works. His son was the only thing he cared about, after his business. Oliver was his legacy, the future of everything he'd built. He'll risk everything to make me pay for his loss.'

'It's more about his ego than love,' I said, reflecting on how it felt so very different to me, knowing that Alex was paying a price for something I'd become involved with.

I jumped when my phone rang. The screen said: 'anonymous caller'.

'Answer it.' Edge squeezed my shoulders.

'Hello?'

'Doc?' Heslopp was the last person I expected.

'Frank?'

'Wanted to let you know, we looked into the other casualties at the Mela attack.' I heard the loud exhale as he smoked.

He obviously hadn't heard about the kidnapping yet. If he was out of the office, why would he?

'One of the victims, Mr Sadiq, owned a haulage company at the time . . .' He paused, expecting me to say something. When I didn't fill the silence, he carried on. 'His site occupied land obstructing a Blackstone Enterprises development. He wouldn't sell. They offered him well over the odds, but he held out. Delays on the job started to incur penalties . . . Then the Mela attack happened.'

'He was one of the pedestrians that was killed?' I hazarded a not-so-wild guess.

'You get a gold star, doc. His family inherited but didn't have the stomach for the fight – so they took the offer.'

'Blackstone used Nichols to get rid of the problem,' I said. 'Just like he used Stamford.'

'Looks like it.'

I didn't have the headspace for this conversation.

'You OK, doc?'

'I've got to go. Thanks for the update, Frank.' I ended the call.

'He'll smell a rat,' Edge said. 'When he finds out about the kidnap, he'll wonder why you didn't mention it. They'll suspect you've been contacted.'

'I know.' The pulse behind my eyes was banging in time to the rhythm of my headache. 'I should go down to the police station, but . . .'

Nique squeezed my hand. I looked into brown eyes that held mine with an intensity I couldn't ignore. 'He's your son, *ma copine*. Do what's best.'

'If you don't get out of the country, this has all been for nothing.' I swivelled round to look at Edge. 'Go, both of you. Leave now. Bring your plans forward and get out.'

'But Jo—' Nique protested.

'The kidnappers haven't made any demands yet,' I reasoned with a cold logic my fear fought against. 'If they call, I'll tell them you're out of the country already. There'll be no point holding Alex. I'll go to the police then, let them handle it.'

Edge didn't look convinced. 'The police play by the rules, princess. Kidnappers don't. If they believe we've gone, they'll just . . . cut and run.'

What he really meant was they'd kill Alex.

'They might not.' I was grasping at any hopeful straw I could.

Edge walked round to stand beside Nique. 'You know how this works, better than anyone. If Blackstone's behind this, there's no deal to be done. This is the last roll of the dice for him. He knows there's no way out for him now. *He* has nothing to lose. *You* on the other hand . . .'

'Of course, there *is* another option,' Nique said slowly, her eyes never leaving mine.

'What?' I almost daren't ask.

'We give him what he wants.'

My eyes widened. 'You can't be serious!'

'Deadly.'

Chapter Sixty-One

'We offer an exchange,' she said simply. 'Me for Alex.'

'Are you insane?' I stared at her – stunned she could even suggest such a thing.

'It gets me close to Blackstone . . .'

'Oh great. So you'll have him exactly where he wants you!' I said without humour.

'Close enough to get Alex out.'

'Not wanting to state the obvious,' I said – about to state the obvious – 'but do you think he'll just let Alex walk away once he has you? We just lose you both!'

'You're forgetting,' she said, smiling. 'I have an "edge".'

I looked at them both in disbelief. 'No!' I shook my head. 'This is mad!'

'It *could* work,' Edge offered.

'For God's sake!' I glared at him. 'I was counting on you to be the voice of reason! Think about this, Nique?' I implored. 'You and Edge could be out of the country in a few hours.'

'And what happens to Alex, then? If Blackstone *doesn't* get to me, he'll kill him, and you know it. Edge is right – there's no bargaining with Blackstone now.' Her tone was icy calm. 'If I hadn't asked for your help, Alex would be safe. You're in this mess because of me. How can I go and leave you with this? Besides, I'm tired of running. Tired of having Blackstone dictate the terms of my life . . .'

'You want him to dictate the terms of your death instead?'

She was calmer than she had any right to be. 'He's already tried, remember? Sandra died in my place.' She took my hand again – her skin felt warm against mine. 'How many more innocents do I sacrifice to him?'

'The police will get Alex back,' I reasoned, but I didn't sound convinced.

'Do you think it would end there? He blames *you* for exposing him.' She regarded me steadily. 'His reach is long. It's easy to conduct a business from prison.' She smiled. 'I should know.'

'Even if I agree to this, what's your endgame, Nique?'

I looked into steady brown eyes, the depths of which held an enigma. Saint or sinner? The capacity to be both – but unpredictable.

In desperation to do anything to save my son, I couldn't afford to delude myself.

'I know you,' I said. 'You're walking into the lion's den for your own reasons. I know how you feel about Lawson.' Even at the mention of his name, a micro expression flitted across her features. Expertly concealed, but not before I recognised it. 'I can't be a part of some twisted idea of revenge.'

'I don't need your agreement,' she said quietly. 'I can do this with or without you. Without me, Blackstone will kill Alex. He has vast resources, Jo. Enough to simply disappear – that's the worst-case scenario. In the time it takes the police to go through the motions, he can be long gone and you'll have lost everything you care for most in the world.' Her eyes penetrated my deepest fears. 'I know what that feels like, remember?' she almost whispered. 'Why do you care . . . as long as your son comes back to you?'

What lines would I cross to save my son?

'No, Nique . . .'

'I'll offer the exchange,' she pressed, unrelenting. 'Edge will have my back – if anyone can get Alex out it's him.' She held my gaze. 'He doesn't have to play by the rules. It gives us an advantage that Blackstone won't expect.'

Disjointed words echoed in my memory . . .

'*You're too much of a straight dealer, McCready,*' Blackstone had said. '*You work with Ferguson – you're firmly on the side of the law. Your moral code would never allow you to cross that line.*'

'All I ask is that you give us a head start,' she was saying. 'A couple of hours – that's all we need to get ahead of the police. Then you go to the police. Tell them I only contacted you today . . . After they realised I wasn't in the fire. That I was letting you know I was leaving the country. Insist that's all you know.' She made it sound so simple. 'Then let the police do whatever they need to.' She watched me as I processed it all, before adding, 'It can't hurt to let me give Blackstone what he wants.'

I ran a hand across my eyes. 'I must be mad, because this is actually starting to sound logical.'

She sat back – finally satisfied.

'This can't be about revenge, Nique,' I warned. 'I can't stop you if you're set on this, but if you go ahead, it has to be about getting Alex back.' I took a breath before adding coldly, 'Because you owe me.' I hated myself for saying it, but it was the only chip I had left to play. I looked into her eyes – holding them with a gravitas I knew she couldn't miss. 'You have to leave Lawson and Blackstone to the police.'

'Well'– Edge got up from the table, saving her from having to answer – 'we can't do anything till they ring back. I need to get organised for when they do.'

* * *

I'd never been good at waiting. I'd tried patience once and decided it was overrated.

'What was it you wanted to ask me about?' Nique suddenly said, dragging my focus away from the phone that stubbornly refused to ring.

'What?'

We were alone in the kitchen.

'You came here this afternoon to ask me something. About the interview with Lawson?'

As a distraction tactic, it was pretty transparent, but I was grateful for it.

'We asked him about that night at Boltby Hall.'

I picked up my phone and pulled up a publicity photo of Leo. I made sure I was studying her face for any signs of recognition before I turned the screen around.

'Recognise him?'

She shook her head. 'Should I?' I judged her reaction and believed her.

'Leo Fielding. He was at the party.'

'So?'

'He was murdered.' I watched her closely as I added, 'Tortured to death, two years ago.' Her body language revealed nothing.

'Yalena told you she was raped, by Oliver, Lawson and someone else?' She simply nodded. 'I believe Leo was the other

374

one.' I put my phone back on the table. 'We asked Lawson at the interview.'

'He wouldn't admit it, surely?'

'He didn't. But he was lying.'

She considered that for a second. 'Yalena had no reason to lie to me. If this Fielding was involved, then I'm glad he's dead.'

'What was Oliver's room like when you went in there?' I asked.

'In what way?' She frowned.

'The scene. Things that were there – on or around the bed?' I was trying not to lead her too much.

She drew a ragged breath, straightening in her chair, as if bracing herself to go back to the memory. 'As I went through the door, I saw the bed. It dominated the room.' Her brow creased. 'I was focused on Yalena.'

'Go on,' I said gently.

'She was unconscious – splayed out, like a broken doll.'

'Was she on her back or front?'

'Face down.' Her eyes were locked on a spot somewhere over my shoulder as she replayed the scenes.

'Picture the surroundings for me,' I said quietly. 'Bedside table, floor?'

'There were things scattered around . . . Bondage equipment, a riding crop.' Her knuckles blanched white as she clasped her fingers more tightly. 'I knew what Oliver was into,' she said tightly. 'When we organised events, we needed to know.' Her eyes suddenly moved to mine, glittering with barely supressed anger. 'All the girls I supplied that night consented to his fetishes. But that wasn't enough, was it?' Her words were pushed through gritted teeth. 'He wanted the real thing, someone who would resist for real, who would *really* suffer.'

I bit my bottom lip. 'What else?' I asked, hoping she could confirm what I already suspected.

'There was a bottle of poppers by the bed, it had burned her skin.' She took a long breath, her eyes refocusing on the present. 'Then I went to find Oliver . . . You know the rest.'

I'd been so immersed in the scene that I jumped when the phone rang.

The screen flashed– '*Callum Calling.*'

My hand hovered over it – finally I answered.

'Jo – where are you?'

I looked across the table at the reason I couldn't answer his question.

'You've heard . . . about Alex?' I deflected.

Nique got up and left the room.

'I was with the SIO on call when it got escalated,' he said.

'Are you . . . involved?'

'I had to declare an interest.' His breath escaped down the phone and I could imagine him raking frustrated fingers through his hair. 'Superintendent Charlotte Warner is heading it up. Because I know you and Alex, she thought I might be useful. I wanted to be the one to call you. You need to come in. We need to get you to a secure location – keep you safe until we know who's involved. I'll pick you up.'

'Is Jen OK?'

'Bit shaken, but fine. When they lifted her car, they found a tracker fixed underneath . . .'

'The broken lock on her garage . . .' I said almost to myself.

'What?'

I told him about Jen's prowlers.

'Maybe Jen was the target?' Callum said. 'Intended taking her, then got a bigger prize when she picked Alex up? They couldn't know he was arriving today.'

'Her bin was emptied out,' I said. 'He emailed his travel details to her. She prints things like that out – always wants a hard copy.'

'Old school,' he said with affection.

'Have they found anything else?' I wanted to get as much information from inside the investigation as I could, before I was potentially on the wrong side of it. 'A lead on the van?'

'Guys on the building site got the registration number. We're checking ANPR cameras to track it from the scene.'

'Can they track Alex's phone?'

'We're getting urgent authorisation for cell site data. The kidnappers will dump his phone, but if we recover it, it might give us their direction of travel.'

'Any sign of Blackstone or Lawson?'

'You think they're behind this?'

'Who else?'

His tone softened. Less businesslike. 'Are *you* OK?'

After days of tension and brittleness between us, hearing the tenderness in his voice again was more than I could take.

'I can't lose him Cal,' I choked.

'I know,' he said gently. 'We'll get him back, Jo. Let me come and get you.'

It was so tempting, to let myself be scooped up by him.

In an attempt to protect those I cared about from the horror of what was going on inside me, I'd inflicted a deeper internal wound. Appreciating only now how exhausting my self-imposed isolation had become. Building and maintaining the wall of ice and granite had drained me until I had nothing left.

I missed his tenderness.

'I needed to hear your voice,' I half-sobbed.

'Oh God, Jo . . .'

I knew he wasn't used to me being like this, but I had no reserves left to keep my defences up.

'Sorry.' I sniffed. 'Being pathetic.'

'No.' His reprimand was gentle. 'Not pathetic at all. I'm glad. Don't shut me out anymore, Jo, not now. Let me help . . . Please?' His tone was irresistibly coaxing.

I hesitated for less than a heartbeat, but he picked it up instantly. 'Have the kidnappers been in touch?'

My throat tightened – I didn't speak.

'For God's sake, Jo, let us handle this.'

'I've been told to wait for their call . . .'

'You can't deal with this alone. I'll come to you then, please? I need to know you're safe.'

'I'll let you pick me up after their call, once I know what they want.'

'No . . . please, Jo—'

'I'm sorry, Cal.'

Hanging up on him was one of the hardest things I'd ever done.

Chapter Sixty-Two

It almost took me by surprise when the call finally came. My hand shook as I snatched up the phone.

'Doctor?' The same male voice as before, but from an 'anonymous' number this time.

'What do you want?' I put it on loudspeaker.

'Dominique De Benoit – you know where she is?'

'Yes.'

'Where?'

Nique sat calmly across from me. We'd agreed the script, but I hesitated, hardly able to form the words. Once uttered, they couldn't be clawed back.

'I'm with her now.' I sounded steady, but my stomach was in knots.

Silence.

'Did you hear what I—'

'Put her on.'

Nique leaned over the phone – watching me the whole time. 'I'm here.' Her voice was disconcertingly calm. 'I'll come to you – in exchange for Alex.'

Silence.

'We do a straight exchange . . . but we choose where.'

'You're in no position to call the shots,' he said.

'A one-time offer.' She watched me as she spoke.

My heart was thundering against my ribs. I wanted to snatch the phone away and plead for Alex's life. I swallowed hard. Edge's hands squeezed my shoulders – a silent encouragement to hold my nerve.

'Do you want to reconsider, while his mother listens to me cutting off his fingers?'

'No!' My resolve crumbled. 'Please – don't hurt him.' I hated the pleading tone in my voice.

Edge's firm hands pressed down.

More silence then the phone went dead.

I stared at it in disbelief.

'That went well,' Edge said dryly.

* * *

I stared blindly at the table top as I tried to get my jumbled thoughts into some kind of order.

Think!

I'd lost my objectivity. I needed to use the only tools I had, to work a way through this. Do what I did best – get into their mindset. Try to unravel the elements at play and get some leverage.

'Alex wasn't with him,' I said finally, taking a long breath as I profiled the behaviours.

'What do you mean?' Nique asked.

'He would have used him to gain an advantage, made us listen while he hurt him.' The professional sound of my own voice was reassuring – even though the topic filled me with horror. 'He's not the decision-maker. He didn't expect the call to go that way . . . wasn't prepared for what you offered, Nique.' I finally looked up. 'He has to go back to whoever's in charge and get instructions.'

'So, he'll call back?' Edge said from behind me.

I nodded.

'If he doesn't?' Nique posed the question my mind shied away from.

The phone vibrated across the table as the call came through.

'Yes,' Nique answered.

'You come in McCready's car, we choose the location.' The disembodied voice crackled over the loudspeaker.

'OK,' Nique agreed.

'McCready drives —'

'No!' Nique snapped. 'I come alone.'

'No debate,' he said. 'McCready too – or it ends here and now.'

'OK,' I said. 'I'll drive.'

It wasn't the way we planned it, but I wasn't about to argue.

'You've got fifteen minutes to get to the car. I'll call with directions. I don't need to tell you what happens if you're followed.'

* * *

Edge dumped the Bergan onto the table.

'They know your car, it's two-seater – no room for passengers.' He shrugged on a dark jacket. 'If they're cute, they'll make you switch vehicles at some point. Your phone's the "communicator", Jo. They're using that to give you instructions, so you need to keep it free.' He handed Nique a burner phone. 'We can stay in touch on that. It's fully charged and the battery lasts a week.'

He produced a short, putty-coloured rifle – checking it before putting it into the rucksack.

'Edge! What the hell . . .?' I was horrified.

'SRS-A2 Covert sniper rifle,' he said, like it was an everyday item.

'I can see *what* it is! I meant what the hell are you thinking?'

He stroked it. 'Gives us a thousand-yard advantage in the game.' He saw the look on my face. 'A game with high stakes, princess.'

'No, this is insane!'

'*They're* armed,' he said, exasperated. 'How do you suppose we get your boy back if it all goes tits-up? I'm not about to take a knife to a gunfight!'

Nique squeezed my arm. 'Trust him, Jo.'

'Edge' – I made him look at me – 'promise me that's a last resort?'

He studied me for a second, his jaw bunching. Then finally nodded. 'The trail bike's in the back of the Defender. I'll follow you on that.'

'If they spot you . . .' I shot him an anxious look.

'Trust me.' He grinned. 'This isn't my first rodeo.' He turned to Nique. 'I'll hang well back. You can relay directions to me on the burner phone, then I can follow from a distance.'

I reluctantly dragged my attention away from what he was doing – mindful that the clock was ticking.

Chapter Sixty-Three

'This must be it,' I said, pulling the Roadster slowly down a rough track.

We'd been following directions for forty-five minutes, until we arrived somewhere near the border between North and West Yorkshire.

The area had become more and more rural as we'd driven.

'Easier for Edge to stay inconspicuous when we were in the city,' I said, negotiating a deep rut. 'He'll stick out like a boil on a bare bum out here.'

'We've relayed all the directions,' Nique said. 'He doesn't have to have eyes on us to know where we are.' She sounded more confident than I felt.

A few minutes down the secluded track, the route was blocked by heavy steel gates in a metal fence, marking the perimeter of an abandoned Victorian warehouse.

'You wait here,' I said, getting out of the car.

I was vaguely aware of the earthy scent of warm grass as I walked to the gate, which was held shut by a thick chain and rusty padlock.

Rising panic sent fluttering fingers through my stomach at the thought that we might have taken a wrong turn. Then I saw it – a length of loose chain dangling from the fence a few steps to my right. A smaller gate, not wide enough for a vehicle. A new padlock hanging open in the links.

I went back to the car. 'Looks like we're on foot from here,' I said.

Nique called Edge. 'We're having to leave the car by the gate – walking down to an old warehouse by the waterway.'

I could hear his brief reply. 'OK. I'm five minutes behind you.'

I locked the car, watching as Nique slipped the burner phone inside her pants. She saw my look.

'Might as well try, if I can hide it.' She gave me a half-smile that did nothing to reassure me.

'Don't think that's a good idea, Nique,' I said, but she was already walking away.

* * *

The windowless red-brick wall of the building towered above us as we walked along the narrow towpath beside a canal.

There was sudden movement as a familiar figure stepped out from the corner of the building.

Blondie.

We both stopped, unsure of the protocol when faced with a man pointing a handgun.

He gestured for us to keep walking, silently stepping aside to let us past. A door stood open on our left. He motioned us inside.

I took a few steps into the vast space, aware of Nique close behind me. There was a crunching of heavy footsteps on the broken concrete floor, then the runway of sunlight we were standing on narrowed and disappeared as the door slammed shut. I stood motionless for a second, allowing my eyes to adjust to the dimness.

Over the sound of the blood pounding in my ears, I could hear movement and was vaguely aware of Blondie making a wide arc to our right, before finally standing in front of us. Nique gently brushed my hand, giving my fingers a brief squeeze.

'Where's my son?' I didn't recognise my own voice. I felt disassociated – as if watching the scene happening to someone else.

His thin smile was humourless. 'First things first.'

He looked pointedly at the phone in my hand. 'Throw it over.'

It skittered across the floor.

'Now yours.' He nodded towards Nique. She fished her usual mobile out of a pocket and sent it to join mine.

He motioned with the gun for us to walk into the middle of the room to an iron stanchion supporting what remained of the floor above. 'Stand either side – facing each other.'

He tossed something towards us. There was a clatter of metal as it landed at Nique's feet. 'I'm sure you know how they work?' Nique picked up the handcuffs. 'Your left wrist to McCready's right,' he instructed, before tossing a second pair to me. 'On your other wrist.'

I fumbled, snapping the steel around my left wrist. He walked over and finished the job, shackling us together. It looked like we were holding hands around a rusty maypole.

I felt the heat of his body as he stepped up behind me. Tobacco-tainted breath against my neck as his hands began an expert search – running down each leg of my jeans, around my ankles, back up, into my crotch and around my middle. He pulled the car keys out of my jeans pocket and slipped them into his.

'What, no smile for me this time?' he whispered sarcastically as he leaned against me.

I gritted my teeth at the impersonal intrusion of his hands down my arms –between and beneath my breast and then under my hair, along the collar of my shirt. Finally satisfied, he stepped around to do the same to Nique.

I kept my eyes firmly locked on hers. Maybe she was used to body searches in prison; her expression remained impassive.

He leaned his head close to her ear as his hands ran down her body. 'That minder of yours, Brink,' he said quietly. 'Where is he?'

'He left this morning. Went on ahead to pick up our transport.' Her voice was steady, ice-calm, giving nothing away. One advantage of being a psychopath was the ability to lie so convincingly. 'I called Jo to say we were leaving. She'd just heard about Alex. So I went to her. I was there when you called.'

'And Brink?'

She shrugged. 'We agreed that if I wasn't at the rendezvous, he'd know something was wrong and he'd leave as planned. He's probably halfway to the south coast by now.'

His hands suddenly stilled. He paused, then fished the burner phone from its hiding place in her pants. With a flick of his wrist, it bounced across the floor.

He straightened up – then without a word, struck her hard across the face. The backhanded blow snapped her head back with a sickening crack and her legs buckled.

As she fell backwards, our bound wrists pulled me forwards. I turned my face just in time to avoid it being smashed against the pillar– hitting it with my shoulder instead, before we both fell in an ungainly tangle on the concrete floor, unwillingly hugging the post between us.

Blondie walked over and scooped up our phones, switching them off before slipping them into his jacket pocket.

His footsteps echoed around us and the outside door opened. A jagged shard of sunlight lit up the scene before the door slammed shut.

* * *

'How's your head?' I asked Nique. Our handcuffed wrists meant that her left hand rested against her chin as I wiped the blood from her torn lip with my thumb.

'I'm hard headed.' She attempted a wry smile. 'Besides, he hits like a girl.'

'This isn't quite the way I expected things to go,' I said, wiping her blood on my jeans.

She shrugged. 'At least Edge is out there somewhere.'

'Think he bought your story, about Edge?'

She shrugged. 'He'll have checked to make sure we weren't followed. If he'd spotted him, we'd know by now.'

I shifted my position, wincing as the rigid cuffs bit into my wrists. My thigh ached and I tried to get more comfortable by resting my leg across Nique's.

She tilted her head to look up at the partial floor above us. Higher in the lofty space, a chink of dull sky was just visible through broken grey slates – the exposed timbers bleached by relentless weather that deposited puddles of rust-coloured water onto the stone floor around us.

'Blondie's the middle man,' I said. 'He's gone to tell Blackstone he has us – has *you* – and get instructions.'

'If he works for Blackstone, he'll know the plan, surely?' she reasoned

I recalled Heslopp's comment about the fraud. That Blackstone stayed at arm's length – making sure no paper trails led back to him. Why would this be any different?

I studied Nique, hesitating to voice my worst fears.

'What?' She read my expression.

"You thought this would get you close to Blackstone and Lawson. But it might not go that way, Nique. He gets other people to do his dirty work . . . protecting him from the fallout.'

'In which case?' she asked quietly.

'In which case – Blondie just executes us both right here.'

She shifted her position, arching her cramped shoulders. 'Do *you* think that's likely?' She studied my face.

I weighed it up. 'Depends. If he just wants you dead, that's the easiest way to do it. He didn't feel the need to be there in person when they firebombed your apartment.'

'Then why insist on you coming too?' she reasoned.

'Two birds . . . one bullet,' I ventured, without humour.

'He's up to his neck in it. They'll throw away the key. He's lost everything and he knows it. But the last thing he did was arrange for Alex to be taken. What does that tell you?'

'That as a malignant narcissist he wants his pound of flesh, wants the end to be on *his* terms.' I took a long breath. Maybe he *wanted* it to be personal this time. 'He's had an unhealthy hatred for you that's fed his anger and bitterness for years. He said from the beginning that if you ever came out of prison, he'd see that "justice" was done. His sense of identity is so wrapped up in the hatred he's carried for you that he probably can't let it go.'

She nodded. 'You're responsible for uncovering the fraud and corruption with Abassi and the way he's been using Sangar. I cost him his son, you cost him two-hundred million and probably his knighthood. On balance, he probably wants *you* dead more than me right now.'

'Thanks for sugaring it up, Nique. That makes me feel *so* much better.'

* * *

The only sound was the dripping of water from the roof, plopping in unseen puddles in the darkening space.

Nique was shifting – pulling my hand towards hers as she put her palms flat on the debris-littered floor to lift herself into a more comfortable position. Her fingers closed around something. She held it up to the narrow shaft of weak late-afternoon light. A thin sliver of jagged metal, the width of a thumb, running out to a needle point at the end.

'Here.' She offered it to me.

'What am I supposed to do with that?'

'Thought you might be able to open the cuffs with it or something.'

I stared at her. 'I'm a profiler – not a bloody locksmith!'

389

Her retort trailed off as a side door to what had been an office at the other end of the warehouse opened. As if we'd conjured him up, Blondie's silhouetted outline walked towards us.

My mouth went suddenly dry and my heart rate soared. I tried to gauge his body language for tell-tale signs of intent as he got closer.

Instinctively I found myself processing every movement, every nuance. His posture, his mannerisms. He exuded a certain energy unique to those with a background of discipline and uniformity. Security forces or ex-military.

He stood for a moment, then hunkered down beside us.

'Hope you ladies are comfortable? Only a few more hours till midnight,' he said in a faint Afrikaans accent.

'What happens at midnight?' I kept my voice even, trying to control my fear.

'I take a call giving me the next location.' He tutted quietly. 'You see, if you *were* foolish enough to involve the police and they crashed in here, all they'd get is me and I don't know where your son is. No one holds all the pieces.' I flinched as he patted my face. 'So, if I get arrested, or can't take that call, the police never find him and he gets a bullet in the back of the head.'

'We had a deal,' Nique said.

He ignored her, leaning in close to me. 'I've done my homework,' he whispered, running his hand across my thigh. 'I know where your weaknesses are.'

Nique's glare was one of pure defiance as he gripped her chin in his other hand – the pressure of his fingers pursing her lips as he spoke with his face an inch from hers. 'You need to learn,' he hissed. 'That *you* don't dictate terms. And until then, if you give me any more trouble, I won't hurt you . . .' He slid his palm across my leg. 'But your friend.'

Without warning, he dug his thumb into the scar tissue on my thigh.

I screamed at the sudden jolt of pain that sent electricity shooting through my entire body – exploding in my brain like red-hot shrapnel. My body convulsed, jerking my legs up in a reflex action, while my hands gripped the metal pillar for support.

The next seconds were a confusing blur of movement and sound as Blondie screamed. Throwing himself away from me, his body arched in a spasm of his own agony.

Confused, I watched him fall backwards, his head hitting the floor with a nauseating crack. He lay there, stunned for a second, sucking air in through gritted teeth, both hands clutching his left leg.

The jagged piece of metal protruded from his thigh, buried deep, where Nique had driven it in just above his knee. A dark stain slowly spread across his jeans.

He struggled to sit up, glaring at Nique. 'You bitch.' He reached for the gun on his waistband.

A shadow shifted suddenly behind him. There was a dull thud as a heavy boot slammed into the back of his head. Blondie grunted and toppled forward like a rag doll.

We both stared, unable to process what had just happened.

Edge stood over the unconscious man, grinning. 'Need a hand, ladies?'

Chapter Sixty-Four

'You took your time.' Nique stood in front of Edge, rubbing her wrists.

He unlocked my handcuffs with the key from Blondie's pocket.

'You're welcome.' He rolled his eyes, nudging the unconscious man with the toe of his boot. 'What do you want me to do with this?'

I looked down at the blood pooling around his head. 'Oh God, is he dead?'

Edge squatted down, feeling for a pulse at the side of his neck. 'Unfortunately, not.' He straightened up.

'We need him.' My mind was racing. 'He has to take a call at midnight.'

'Sorry, princess, but he was about to shoot Nique —'

'I know.' I couldn't take my eyes off the prone body. 'They're going to give him the next location – without that, Alex dies.'

'When he comes round' – Nique kicked him in the ribs – 'we hold him until he takes their call, *then* we kill him.'

'We're not killing anyone. Besides, it wouldn't work . . .'

'Jo's right,' Edge said as he crouched down, unclipping the pistol from Blondie's belt and checking the chamber before making the gun safe and tucking it into the waistband of his own combat pants. 'He wouldn't cooperate.'

'Give me ten minutes with him.' Nique's top lip curled back, like a feral animal scenting prey.

As she moved forward, I put a restraining hand on her shoulder. 'No – I've got a better idea. Our phones are in his pocket. We need his as well.' I watched as Edge frisked the limp body. 'How many burner phones do you have in the Bergan?'

'A couple.' He frowned up at me. 'Why?'

I turned to Nique.' You're better with technology than I am.'

'Isn't everyone?'

'I need you to do something.'

* * *

Retrieving my car keys, I reactivated my mobile, before walking along the darkening towpath. Almost tasting the cool air, relieved to be out of the damp, clawing atmosphere of the warehouse.

I shivered as the breeze ruffled the water, sending silver ripples sliding across the surface of the canal to slap gently against the bank.

I unlocked the boot and recovered my briefcase. Sitting in the driver's seat, I flicked on the interior light as my mobile came back to life. I looked at the screen. Dozens of missed calls from Callum.

I noticed some urgent email notifications. Two in particular caught my attention. One from Jen – the other from Callum. Both sent before the kidnapping.

Jen's was the report from the Tunisian police, with photographs taken on Dimitri Chernov's yacht. Stopping at one in

394

particular, I pinched my fingers over the image to enlarge it. The implications of what I was seeing were finally registering.

Callum's email had the crime scene photographs that I'd asked for at the briefing – the ones of Oliver's bedroom.

The room was neat and tidy. The only sign that anything unusual had happened was the bloodstained white sheet on the bed. No sign of anything Nique had described. Someone had obviously cleared the room, destroying as much evidence as possible before the police arrived. I thought about what that meant and, finally, it all came together.

I rummaged through the case on my knee, finding the bubble-wrapped vial Geoff Perrett had given me. My hand was shaking and despite the chill I could feel sweat beading my forehead. I rolled the small glass bottle around my palm. What I was contemplating went against every tenet of my profession. Breaking every moral principle my vocation demanded.

Then gentle images of my son moved in a shimmering collage through my mind. Holding him in my arms when he was born. Watching his wobbling first steps. Hearing his first laugh.

I pulled out a notebook and wrote down a list of instructions – cursing my lack of technical know-how, I worded it in layman's language and hoped it would be enough. I tore the page out and folded it into my pocket.

That done and with a new resolve, I closed my fingers around the glass vial, locked the car and walked back to the warehouse.

Chapter Sixty-Five

'So how do you want to do this?' Edge asked as he knelt at Blondie's head.

I crouched beside his body, feeling a strong pulse fluttering beneath my thumb. Thankfully the blood flow from the back of his head had slowed to a less alarming rate. He was starting to moan, rolling his head slightly.

'We've got to time this just right,' I said, taking the army issue water bottle from the Bergan and unscrewing the top. 'Let him regain consciousness fully and he could remember what we've done. Not enough and he won't be receptive.'

'Receptive to what?' Nique looked on dubiously from the upturned crate she was sitting on.

'When he comes round, we can't afford for him to remember Edge's little intervention,' I answered, distracted as I tried to decide how many milligrams of flunitrazepam were in the vial – and how much would be just enough. 'He has to take that call at midnight. In the meantime, I want to find out what he knows.'

Putting a few drops of the drug into the lid of the bottle, I topped it up with water, hoping the dilution was about right.

'What is it?' Edge asked.

'You'd know it as Rohypnol.'

He raised his eyebrows. 'Steady on, princess ... Time and place.'

'It has other uses apart from date-rape,' I explained. 'High doses induce narcosis and amnesia, but he'd be out until tomorrow. A smaller dose should wear off quicker. It'll break down his resistance, allowing him to respond but not be fully conscious and hopefully have no memory of what we've done.'

'How do you know the right dose?' Edge asked.

'By employing an exact science.'

'Which is?'

'A wild guess.'

Blondie's eyelids fluttered open and he groaned, making a weak effort to sit up. Edge gripped his arms, holding him down.

'Hold his head still, Nique.' I put the rim of the lid on his bottom teeth and tipped the liquid into his mouth.

I was praying the active ingredients would still work, recalling tests on military stockpiles of medication that found they remained effective for decades.

'It's not working.' Nique held his face between her palms as his eyes flickered open. 'Give him some more.'

'I daren't.' I watched as his biceps flexed uselessly in Edge's powerful hold. 'He could go under too deep.'

'How long before it kicks in?' Edge asked.

'A few minutes.' I checked my watch, resisting the temptation to give him any more.

Eventually his breathing slowed and became deeper. He was mumbling. I moved Nique's hands away and lifted one of his eyelids. 'OK,' I said, sitting back on my heels.

'Now what?' Edge asked – still not releasing his hold.

'I need you to leave me with him.'

'No chance!' he snorted.

'Edge, you have—'

'I'm not leaving you alone with this bastard, drugged or not.'

It was useless to argue, but I still didn't feel comfortable with it. Years of clinical practice had ingrained the habit of privacy – even if the patient was a killer.

I handed Nique the notes I'd written. 'Can you sort out the phones?'

Her eyes scanned down my notes.

'Pre-programming tasks,' she murmured. 'Impressed you even know about such things.'

'Got the idea from my publisher,' I confessed. 'Can you get them to do what I've written there?' I indicated Blondie. 'On his phone too?'

She nodded, picking up Blondie's mobile. 'It needs unlocking.' She took his hand and pressed his thumb onto the fingerprint scanner.

'Can you get his number?' I asked.

'It's first on the contact list on most phones,' she muttered, frowning in concentration as she scrolled through various screens. Finally shaking her head. 'But not this one . . .'

'Shit!'

We were failing at the first hurdle. I glanced down at Blondie; his face ashen under the effect of the drug. My mind was racing through various alternatives, when Nique's voice dragged me back.

'But Blackstone's number's here.'

'And Lawson?' I asked, hopefully.

'Last number on the call history.'

'He's the one Blondie's been checking-in with,' I muttered, almost to myself.

'Go through the messages,' Edge suggested. 'Might save us the trouble if they've said where Alex is being held.'

It was a nice thought, but I didn't expect it to be so easy.

Predictably, Nique frowned. 'Nothing.'

I squeezed my eyes shut against the pounding headache that had its own marching band. 'We *need* his number.'

'Dial star, hash, 100, hash,' Edge said. 'The USSD code. Works on most phones.'

Nique's thumbs typed. 'Bingo!' She grinned.

I shot Edge a look. 'I'm impressed.'

He shrugged. 'Not just a pretty face.'

I watched as Nique read my notes. 'Can you do it?'

She nodded, taking all the phones, including mine, and dropping them into the Bergan. 'I'll go down there' – she indicated the office – 'where it's quiet, so I can concentrate.' Edge handed her a torch as she hefted the pack onto her shoulder.

As the sound of her footsteps echoed across the floor, I turned to look down at Blondie, grateful there wasn't much light.

Some activities were better shrouded in darkness.

Chapter Sixty-Six

'Are you sure about this?' Edge didn't look convinced.

'No,' I confessed as he replaced the handcuffs, shackling me and Nique around the post, in the same sitting position we'd been in before.

The torch propped on the packing case created a surreal arena of light.

'I just watched you do some weird shit to him,' he said uneasily, 'and I didn't understand most of it. But when he comes round, what's to stop him picking up where he left off and shooting you both?'

'*You* . . . if necessary.' I shifted my aching thigh. 'Hopefully it won't come to that.'

We'd left Blondie where he'd originally fallen. Hopefully he'd come round, believing he'd been knocked unconscious when his head hit the concrete floor. Bad enough, but preferable to him realising we hadn't come alone as instructed.

I still thought of him as 'Blondie'. Even though under the effects of the drug, we'd discovered his real name – Dan Bellew. Formerly of the South African army and now a mercenary, hired with a colleague he simply called Kriel. They'd arrived in the UK just before Nique's release, for what he worryingly called a 'short-term contract'. Kriel was holding Alex at the final location. If they were compromised and the scheduled calls weren't made, Kriel's instructions were to execute Alex, then everyone would make their own way out.

Edge was removing his green shemagh, which we'd used as a makeshift dressing to stem the flow of blood around the metal still protruding from Blondie's thigh. Unconcerned by the bloodstains, he tied it back around his neck and hunkered down – reluctantly clipping the pistol back onto Blondie's belt and replacing his mobile. He switched our phones off and put them back in Blondie's pocket.

'Think it's best if I'm up there somewhere.' He nodded to the partial floor over our heads. 'Above you both. Best line of sight.'

His rifle was equipped with a night-sight, so darkness wouldn't present a problem.

Blondie moaned.

Edge looked down at him. 'Goes against the grain, leaving him in-play.' He lifted the rifle out of the Bergan and slung the strap over his shoulder.

'I know you said last resort, princess, but if this goes tits-up when he comes round, I'll happily clip him.' He prodded Blondie's thigh wound with his boot, making him groan.

'Don't,' I said, uncomfortable enough with what I'd done.

'I only inflict pain for one of the three Ps,' Edge reflected grimly. 'Pay, Practice or Pleasure.' He looked down. 'This bastard would definitely be a pleasure.'

'You've got the phones?' I asked.

He patted his pocket. 'Yes. When I get chance, I'll hide the burners up in the roof where they won't be found.'

'Be careful, *mon chéri*.' Nique's quiet voice drew both of us to look at her. Even in the dim light, her face looked pale, her eyes full of an emotion I hadn't expected to see.

402

Edge bent and quickly kissed the top of my head, doing the same to Nique before walking towards the twisted remains of a broken staircase at the other end of the warehouse.

The arc of torchlight swung across the floor, then as he reached the steps it disappeared with a snap, plunging us into darkness.

* * *

We listened as Edge climbed the few intact stairs, then clambered the rest of the way across twisted beams and torn metal. Sounds marked his progress across the sagging, partial floorboards above us, scattering a flutter of pigeons – their indignant trilling echoing alarmingly around the cavernous space. Eventually they roosted, but it served as a nervous reminder that the slightest movement would send them lifting in alarm to betray Edge's presence.

Silence slowly settled around us like a damp blanket. There was a scuttling sound and something soft ran across our feet.

'Shit!' Nique kicked out. 'Rats.'

'Maybe better if we stood up,' I suggested, uneasily scanning the thickening darkness in a vain attempt to see what we could only hear.

Together we clasped hands around the post and pulled ourselves up. Nique rested her forehead against mine. 'It'll be OK, *ma copine,*' she whispered, her breath reassuringly warm against my cold cheek.

We seemed to stand there for an eternity, shivering under the chill of a cloudless sky. Our heads together for comfort and warmth – trying not to listen to the scurrying that seemed to be coming from every dark corner.

Eventually we heard a heavier shuffling and a groan. Watery moonlight spilled through the fractured roof, returning some of my night vision. I could just make out a vague shape as it began to move

'What the fuck.' The heels of Blondie's boots rasped against the concrete as he tried to sit.

'You cracked your head on the floor as you fell backwards,' I said, repeating the words I'd hopefully embedded into his subconscious during the drug-induced hypnosis. My voice sounded suddenly loud in the echoing stillness. 'You've been out for a while.'

'Arghh – bloody hell.' He'd moved his leg too suddenly, rediscovering the metal in his thigh.

I could just make out Nique's face. She cast a glance heavenward, no doubt hoping our guardian angel was looking down as promised.

What if this doesn't work? my mind screamed. *Is he reaching for his gun?*

I squashed my rising anxiety by picturing Edge watching us from his sniper's eyrie. Certain he would have Blondie's forehead in the cross hairs of the night-sight's green glow.

Every muscle in my body tightened in anticipation of that bullet from above. A fatal punctuation that would mark the end of my son's life.

Nique and I held a collective breath as Blondie cursed, gingerly examining the wound with his fingers.

'If I didn't *have* to keep you alive . . .' He left the threat hanging.

I felt rather than saw him use the nearest pillar to pull himself upright. He stood behind me for what felt like forever, clinging onto the post for support. His breath drawn in through gritted teeth, then more cursing. Sounds of him hopping, trying not to put too much weight on his injured leg.

The pain in my own thigh resonated like a tuning fork.

Now you know how it feels, you bastard!

A light flicked on beside me as he activated his phone. His face looked ghostly, pale and glistening with sweat in the surreal blue glow of the screen. He limped unsteadily to the office, his wavering progress illuminated by the torch on his phone.

'He looks like shit,' Nique whispered with undisguised pleasure.

'He'll have the hangover from hell,' I said. 'Concussion and flunitrazepam – bloody lethal cocktail.'

The roll-call of side effects scrolled through my mind. Cognitive impairment, loss of motor function – not to mention vomiting and blinding headaches. As if I'd conjured it up, faint sounds of retching came from the office.

My body jumped a split second before my mind registered the distant sound of his phone ringing.

The midnight call.

Chapter Sixty-Seven

Tuesday Night

Time had lost all meaning since we'd been forced into a Range Rover parked behind the warehouse.

When Blondie came out of the office after taking the call, he had a field dressing strapped tightly around his thigh, obviously having removed the metal shard. I took some comfort in the knowledge that pulling it out would have hurt like hell.

Lying cramped in the footwell behind the driver's seat, my wrists handcuffed in front of me, I shifted my position with my legs across Blondie's feet as he sat in the rear nearside.

Nique was driving, her handcuffed wrists at an awkward angle on the steering wheel.

At first, listening to his directions, I'd tried to form a map in my head. But watching the passing silhouettes of trees in the darkness, with only an occasional glimpse of clouds scudding across a purple-black sky, it had become hopeless and I'd given up.

'Take the next right.' He gestured with the gun in his right hand, before resting it back on his knee, too close to my head for comfort.

As the Range Rover rumbled across a cattle grid, Nique spoke over her shoulder. 'I don't need any more directions. I know where we're going.' She twisted in her seat. 'It's Boltby Hall, Jo.'

Where else? I thought. *The landfall of an emotional tsunami that had changed the lives of all those involved – and ended some.*

* * *

From my position, I could just make out wrought-iron gates between high stone, moss-speckled pillars. An avenue of ancient oak trees marking the route through private parkland – sweeping up a gravel driveway to a stone fountain. A sentinel, guarding the entrance to the once imposing manor house.

Solid grey walls, which three centuries before withstood the onslaught of the English Civil War, were now bleak and silent. The tall sash windows flanking the partially open oak doors, stared with dead eyes as we were marched from the car into what had once been an impressive reception hall.

As Blondie roughly shoved us ahead of him, I was vaguely aware of a chequerboard marble floor with grand staircases on either side. I stumbled into Nique as he pushed us into a room that had once been a library. Panelled walls lined with bookcases – some still containing leather-bound volumes, others covered in dust and the random debris of a sad and neglected place.

The space was illuminated by a brass lamp on a desk facing the door. A figure behind the desk was reduced to a dark silhouette against un-curtained French doors.

'Any trouble?'

'No,' Blondie said from somewhere behind us.

A chair scraped back and the silhouette moved around the desk. When he stepped into the light, Lawson's face looked drawn with fatigue. He noticed the bloodied field dressing on Blondie's thigh but thought better of mentioning it.

'Where's my son?' I asked.

He leaned back against the desk, his arms folded. 'Somewhere safe.'

'Safe for who?' The words almost choked me. 'I need to know he's OK—'

He cut me off with a shake of his head. 'He's alive . . . for now.'

'How does hurting my son change anything?' A wave of hopeless exhaustion rolled all over me.

He nodded towards Nique. 'It got her here,' he said simply. 'Like the boss wants.'

'And once she's dead?' I couldn't help the callous sentiment. 'Then what? Blackstone's finished. The corruption. Murder of Mr Sadiq at the Mela. Attempted murder of Baahir Abassi.' I took a ragged breath. 'All to protect his jewel-in-the-crown development, his knighthood? He's finished, Myles, and he's taking you down with him.' It grated using his first name, but was worth it to reach something inside him that might give me some leverage.

'Adding more names to the death toll only digs you a deeper hole when this is done.' I tried to reason. 'Are you willing to throw *your* life away to help him? Do you really want to be part of his madness? Tell them to let Alex go.' I glanced at Blondie. 'Then you both get out while you can.'

'And of course you'll both agree not to tell the police about all this?' His lips twisted in that sardonic smile I hated so much. 'We have our exit strategy planned, McCready.'

Someone like Lawson would always have a backup strategy to save his own skin if things went wrong.

409

'Besides,' he continued, 'only one person knows where Alex is and that's Sir Neville. We can't be compromised if your friends from the police gate-crash the party. "Operational security" – courtesy of Bellew and Kriel.' He gestured to Blondie. 'Bellew will check, to make sure you weren't followed. Then I make a call to Sir Neville to say it's safe for him to come here and only he can make the call to Kriel to free Alex.' He smiled. 'So, you see, if you want your son to survive, you've got to let this play out exactly the way it was planned.'

Nique took a step forward – stopping short when Blondie raised the pistol. 'You have me – let Jo walk away.'

He pushed away from the desk and stood in front of her. 'Last time I stood face to face with you, you'd just murdered Oliver.' The muscles bunched in his jaw. 'If it was up to me, I'd kill you right now.'

'Do it then!' she spat, her eyes glittering with a contemptuous hatred she didn't even try to conceal. 'Grow a pair and get it over with.' She curled her lip. 'You hypocritical bastard! He'd have lived that night, if you'd—'

The blow he dealt sent her sprawling behind me. I moved to go to her, only stopping when Blondie's gun dug into my ribs.

Nique looked dazed as Lawson stood over her.

'When the time comes, I'm going to enjoy watching the life leak out of you.' He crouched beside her, dropping his voice to almost a whisper. 'And if I have my way, it'll be a slower death than the one you gave Oliver.' He stood up abruptly. 'Take them downstairs.'

Chapter Sixty-Eight

Boltby Hall – Wednesday

The windowless wine cellar probably looked the same as it had in the seventeenth century, except for the happy addition of electricity which made the candle sconces a redundant feature.

Thick stone walls, quarried out of solid bedrock, guaranteed a moderate temperature – but I couldn't help thinking, it also meant total soundproofing and no means of an easy escape.

I leaned against a cold lime-washed wall and looked at the wooden shelves, once stocked with the finest vintages from around the world. A few bottles remained, coated in cobwebs that clung to them like dirty lace.

Broken wooden crates and empty barrels made up the detritus in the stone warren which stretched to several rooms, separated by wrought iron gates secured with rusting padlocks.

I massaged my wrists, grateful at least that the handcuffs had been removed, and watched Nique lift a bottle from one of the shelves and wipe the dust from the label.

'Nineteen twenty-one.' She raised her eyebrows. 'Vintage Burgundy'. She began poking around the dusty wine rack.

'What are you looking for?'

'Bottle opener of course . . .'

'Really – at a time like this?'

'*Especially* at a time like this.' She turned, brandishing an old-fashioned corkscrew – 'Ta da!' – then frowned. 'Unfortunately, no glasses. But beggars can't be choosers, *ma copine*.'

She slid down the wall, to sit on the floor, gripping the bottle between her thighs as she ran the sharp point of the opener around the waxed seal.

A half-heard sound made me pause. I strained to hear – tilting my head to one side – trying to decide where it had come from. Nique stopped what she was doing. 'What's the matter?'

'That . . . did you hear it?'

We both fell silent – nothing.

'Probably rats,' she said, returning to the task at hand. '*Et voilà.*' She held the bottle up with a triumphant flourish. 'You first.' She handed it to me.

I took a sip of the brackish liquid and shuddered, handed it back.

She got to her feet and took the bottle, taking a long pull.

There it was again. A soft scraping sound. Nique stopped with the bottle to her lips. We both looked towards the sound coming from the wine racks against the far wall.

'Jesus, I'd forgotten,' she breathed. 'The priest hole . . .' She put the bottle on the floor, calling out, 'Edge?'

A shelving rack groaned as it grudgingly shifted another inch.

A hand appeared round the edge of the makeshift door.

'Come out, Yalena,' I called.

* * *

I'd never seen Yalena Vashchenko, but I knew who it was the moment she appeared.

Nique stared at the woman she called 'the love of her life', her face a pale mask of incredulity. 'Yalena?' she whispered.

412

'Or do you prefer Thana?' I asked.

Nique shot me a confused look, but I was gauging the responses of the woman in front of us – trying to read the mind that had coldly conceived and executed the deaths of at least two people, maybe more.

'Very clever,' she said in thickly accented English. 'Should I be impressed?'

'Oh, you're the impressive one,' I said without feeling. 'Your "death" on the yacht? Nice touch.'

I could feel the tension radiating from Nique as she stood rigid beside me, staring in disbelief.

'Tell me,' I continued. 'Was that Dimitri's idea . . . or yours?'

She considered it for a moment, then lifted a shoulder. 'He agreed to help me.'

'To take revenge on the men who raped you?' I ventured. 'But it proved useful, didn't it? For the Bratva to have a ghost on the payroll? Someone in their debt, doing whatever they needed. And in return, you used their resources.'

'It made things easier,' she said simply.

'Easier!' Nique finally found her voice. 'I thought you were *dead!* I grieved. It nearly destroyed me to think—'

Yalena snorted indignantly. 'You lost a possession that's all. You don't know grief . . . don't know pain . . . like I felt! The torture of what they did to me, what they took from me that night!'

Nique took a step forward, then stopped as we both saw the large black-bladed combat knife in Yalena's hand.

'Don't, *lyubovnik*,' Yalena warned.

'Lover?' Nique snorted. 'When you can hold a knife on me?'

413

'We stopped being lovers the night you sent me here.' The hatred in her voice was tangible.

'The body picked up by the Tunisian coastguard?' I asked, partly to diffuse the tension between them, but mainly because I needed to know.

She turned to me. 'A prostitute – same height and build as me. Died from a drugs overdose. Dimitri knew people who provided the corpse. They dropped her out at sea, after we arrived in Tunisia.'

'The ship's captain identified the body, paid by Dimitri?'

She nodded.

'And the passport Chernov gave the Tunisian authorities – it had the dead girl's photograph?' Fake passports after all, were his stock-in-trade.

Again, the silent nod.

'How did they manage the DNA match?' The report Jen had emailed over to me said the final ID had been confirmed by DNA.

'Her hairbrush and toothbrush, we left them in my cabin.'

She glanced up to the house above, her mind already turning to the reason she was here.

'Myles Lawson's next, isn't he?' I already knew. 'You've been following him for weeks, stalking him like you did Leo Fielding.' The look she gave me confirmed I was right. 'Leo didn't recognise you because the last time he'd seen you, you were being held face down on the bed. And anyway, he was too far gone on drink and drugs that night to remember you, wasn't he?'

She shifted uncomfortably; her eyes locked on mine as I took her back there, back to the night that had started it all.

'When he met Thana in the Munch Bunch, he didn't realise she was the woman they'd all gang-raped four years before.' Her breathing became shallower as her anxiety levels rose. 'He was the one who forced you to inhale the amyl nitrate.'

'It burned . . .' Her face crumpled at the memory and I realised how tenuous her hold on sanity really was.

'You planted the pornography and the bondage gear in Leo's wardrobe, to make it look like he'd consented to a BDSM scene?'

'His precious reputation would be ruined,' she said. 'I humiliated him, like he humiliated me.'

'He had to suffer the same,' I said softly. 'Face down, raped, made to breathe that drug. Tormented and beaten.'

Her eyes were glassy. The point of the knife lowered imperceptibly as her focus shifted down a tunnel of time.

'They drank wine as they watched you being brutalised, didn't they, Yalena? Just like you did in Leo's apartment. The wine bottle and glasses – your own private party.'

'He deserved it.' She ground the words out through gritted teeth. 'They all deserve it.'

'How did you know?' Nique looked at me.

I kept my eyes on Yalena, noticing her knuckles grow pale as her grip tightened on the knife.

'When I recreated the way Thana got back into Leo's apartment – I suspected it then. To climb the sculpture and get up into the garden, required two people when I did it. But an athlete – a gymnast – could have done it. Then I saw the crime scene photographs from Oliver's bedroom – that's when I knew for sure.'

415

'How?' Yalena asked.

'Nique described how the room was when she found you,' I said. 'The crop . . . the way you'd been beaten . . . the amyl nitrate bottle – they were all the "staged" elements in Leo's death.'

'But that didn't prove that Yalena was still alive.' Nique's voice was strained as she struggled to comprehend it.

'When the police photographed the scene here in Boltby Hall, it had been cleaned up before CSI arrived. Whoever choreographed Leo's death must have known what was done to Yalena and couldn't have staged it from police reports or photographs – it had to be someone present when the rape took place.'

'But I "died",' Yalena almost whispered, her eyes glassy as she stared at me.

'Crime-scene photographs from Dimitri's yacht.' I watched as she moved another step towards us. 'Your clothes, folded so precisely on the chair in your cabin. The suicide note they found was tucked inside your shoe. That's a habit of yours, isn't it?' She just watched me, silently. 'Did you do that in the changing rooms at the Olympic training camps in Russia, to protect the few valuables you had?'

'I don't understand . . .' Nique said to no one in particular.

'She did that with Leo's belongings, and Jacinta's.'

Nique gasped. 'You killed Jacinta? But . . . why?'

Yalena's eyes narrowed and she moved again – circling to our left. Instinctively we turned with her, keeping our distance.

'She saw you, didn't she, Yalena?' I said quietly.

I looked at the knife in her capable left hand and the forensic report flashed across my mind. *The ligature used to strangle Jacinta – tied by a left-handed killer.*

'You were following Lawson, stalking him to map his routines so you could kill him – like you did with Leo. You were there when he parked outside Blackstone's office. But Jacinta recognised you. She realised in that moment you weren't dead.'

Yalena sounded regretful. 'She called over to me. She thought she was seeing a ghost . . .'

'That night, did you go to her apartment to try to persuade her to keep your secret?'

She shook her head slowly. 'I thought maybe I could reason with her. But I was there, waiting outside her apartment when she got back with Blackstone. I was hiding in the shadow of the building opposite. They didn't see me. They were arguing in the street. I heard what she screamed at him—'

'About his ghosts coming back to haunt him . . . like his son?' I asked.

She nodded. 'I knew then that I had no choice. She almost told him then. She'd always drunk too much and when she did . . . Well, she talked too much. She had to die. But she was my friend,' she said softly. 'She was asleep – I made it painless.'

I remembered Jacinta's face, the swollen tongue protruding through purple lips. Terrified eyes, pleading from the other side of life. Nothing peaceful about the way she died – nothing.

I swallowed hard – trying to keep the revulsion out of my eyes. I couldn't let her kill Lawson.

'You don't need to do this, Yalena,' I said. 'If you go after Lawson here, tonight, they'll kill you. Then they win.'

She stared at me. 'I don't know who you are – or why you're here – but this has nothing to do with you.'

'It has *everything* to do with me.' My words were ragged. 'Lawson kidnapped my son. If you kill Lawson, my son dies too.'

417

'You've stumbled into something you don't understand, Yalena.' Nique's voice sounded hollow – as if it was coming from an empty place. 'Go back the way you came. Leave Lawson for another time.' She took a step forward, but stopped when the tip of the blade jerked. 'He's got armed protection up there. You won't get near him.'

'I'll get near him, even if they kill me.'

'Is this vendetta worth your life?' I pleaded.

The look she turned on me was ice cold. 'They took my life already.' Her eyes flicked upwards. 'Up there. I've died a thousand times since then . . . The final death would be easy by comparison.'

She moved towards Nique. 'And *you* . . .' she gritted her teeth – 'sent me here that night.'

Nique backed away as Yalena moved towards her. As she drew level with me, I could see the tension in her shoulder, her posture changing as the arm holding the knife drew back. Instinctively I reached out to deflect the blade.

'No!' I shouted.

Yalena spun towards me – I felt the whisper of air as the wide blade slashed past my face. Using both hands, I grabbed her wrist. Strong muscles flexed beneath my fingers and I knew she had a strength I couldn't match.

Her face was within an inch of mine as I tried to hold the knife away from me. I could feel her breath on my face, her eyes burning with a rage and hatred rooted so deeply that I knew nothing could reach it.

Suddenly she grunted, dropping all her weight against me. Despite her petite build, I strained to hold her. Her arm fell slack and the knife slipped from her hand, clattering uselessly to the floor

Her eyes registered momentary surprise as I felt her knees buckle. I was struggling to comprehend the sudden change, when her body began to slide down mine.

'She was right,' Nique said. 'The final death *was* easy.'

Confused, I lowered Yalena's limp body to the ground. It was as she rolled over that I saw it – the corkscrew embedded in the base of her skull.

Chapter Sixty-Nine

Neville Blackstone stood with Lawson, his back to the desk as he regarded us.

'It ends tonight,' he said, glaring at Nique as we entered the room. 'Upstairs . . . the same place Oliver died.'

'Very poetic,' Nique said, her face a mask of contempt. 'You got the balls to do it yourself this time – or are you using the hired help?'

Before he could answer, Blondie spoke from behind us. 'You've got a problem. There's a body in the cellar – a woman.'

We'd debated hiding Yalena's body before Blondie came to get us but decided against it. Letting them find her would escalate events, hopefully in our favour. Derail the convenient script they'd written. Distract them away from Alex, from Nique. Give them something much bigger to worry about – their own survival.

'What the hell . . . who?' Lawson looked at the mercenary who had a gun to our backs. 'How did she get in there?'

'Must have already been there before we arrived,' Blondie said.

I glanced at my watch – I'd set a clock of my own ticking and it was time to play my hand.

'You know her,' I said. All eyes turned to me. 'Yalena Vashchenko.'

'What?' Blackstone said.

'But Vashchenko's dead,' Lawson said in disbelief.

'She is now,' Nique said dryly.

'Her death was faked in 2016,' I said. 'She killed Leo the following year. Then Jacinta . . . and tonight she was coming after *you*, Myles.' I watched the colour drain from his face. 'She had no idea what was going on tonight. She just followed you here, must have hidden down in the cellar before we arrived.'

Blackstone shot him a look. 'What's she talking about?'

Lawson opened his mouth, then closed it again, his eyes never leaving mine.

'Ever since Leo died, you suspected his death was because of what you and your friends did on the night of Oliver's party, here, in this house. You didn't know *who* the killer was. But when Jacinta was murdered, you *really* started to sweat. It was all getting too close to home, wasn't it?'

Blackstone looked from Lawson to me – then back again. 'Myles?'

'He can't give you answers, Blackstone.' My voice sounded calmer than I felt. 'Without implicating himself.'

'Blackstone's eyes narrowed. 'In what?'

'Tell him, Myles.' It was a risky roll of the dice.

'Don't listen to her,' Lawson choked. 'She'll say anything to save her son.'

'Not very grateful, are you?' Nique piped up from beside me. 'After we saved your skin . . . down in that cellar.' She started to move towards him, but Blondie moved between them, the gun never wavering. 'I killed Yalena so you could make your call.' She jerked her head towards Blackstone. 'To get *him* here.'

Blackstone stared at me. 'Implicate himself . . . in what?'

I answered Blackstone, but my eyes never left Lawson. 'Leo Fielding was commissioned to paint your wife, Talia. That painting doubled in value after his death. The police wondered why you never collected it.'

He was staring at me in obvious bewilderment. 'You didn't collect it, because you didn't know it existed, did you?'

I turned to Lawson. '*You* commissioned it, as a present for your lover . . .'

'What!' Blackstone spun around, glaring at Lawson.

'I knew when I watched you being interviewed,' I continued. 'When you were asked about Talia – you said you didn't know her, but your body language said otherwise.'

Blackstone rounded on him. 'You and *Talia*!'

'He couldn't collect the painting. It would've come to your attention once it went public. He told Leo's family to destroy it.'

Silver beads of sweat coated Lawson's top lip – he swallowed hard. 'This is mad. You can't believe this!'

'Speaking of madness,' I said to Blackstone. 'What you did at Sangar—'

'I fund the charity – that's all!'

'You weren't hands-on. You never are. But you *knew* about the mind control. Used it to remove people who got in your way.' He stared at me in silence. 'Why not just use Bellew here to eliminate the problems?' I asked – genuinely curious. 'Why something so elaborate as the assassinations triggered by mobile phone calls?'

'They were expendable,' he said simply. 'Their backgrounds made it look like something political, racially motivated. There was no investigation because they were always meant to stay at

423

the scene – like Nichols did – get arrested but have no memory of it, no defence.'

The callousness of it was frigidly logical.

'That's why you believed Stamford could have killed Jacinta. You thought he was coming after you and anyone close to you because of what was done to him. It didn't work quite as well with him, did it? He snapped out of it at the train station. You didn't have the imagination to come up with that, Blackstone. Was it Briggs? Did she tell you about the techniques she could use if you paid her enough?'

'She said she could use the therapy sessions to do it. Myles organised it all.'

'Lawson and your wife used it against *you*,' I said.

His eyes narrowed as he looked at his protégé.

'To avoid paying tax. Everything's registered in your wife's name, that's a matter of public record. The fact that you avoid paying UK taxes gets raked up every time they try to get your knighthood stripped away,' I said. 'Lawson and Talia had it all worked out – an exit strategy for when they were ready to get rid of you. Obviously, they'd have alibis.' Blackstone's eyes widened in disbelief. 'This method of remote killing that you all came up with means they wouldn't even have to be in the same country when you died.'

'Kill me?'

'Lawson and Talia got Briggs to do some extracurricular conditioning of their own.' I looked at Blondie. 'They arranged to meet you and Kriel in the Caymans didn't they – before you came to the UK?'

Blondie's brow knitted slightly. 'What makes you think—'

'You told me – at the warehouse.' I couldn't resist a smile – the same smile I'd given him on the bridge that day. 'But you don't remember, do you? Any more than you remember the conditioning Briggs subjected you to in the Caymans. Probably after a heavy night of drinking at the villa – a party maybe? Did you wake up with the mother of all hangovers and not remember the night before?'

'What have you done?' Blondie rounded on Lawson. 'What's she talking about?'

'I've had burner phones programmed for when you got us all to the final handover,' I said.

I'd had to estimate the approximate time from the "midnight call" Blondie told us about, but, I'd reasoned, whatever circumstances we were in by this time, the result couldn't make things any worse.

'We knew you'd never let us walk away from this. So, they were a backup.' I thought about Edge in the roof of the warehouse. 'They're safely hidden where you'll never find them. They've had "tasks" set to make calls from one-thirty a.m. onwards. I have to send a coded text from my phone to abort. If you kill me, or Nique, there's no way you can stop them.'

'This is bullshit!' Blondie exploded, but he didn't look certain.

'You confiscated my phone,' I said quietly. 'And without it – I can't stop the first call, in' – I looked at my watch – 'fifteen seconds.'

'You're bluffing,' Lawson sputtered.

'You think so? Get Blackstone to make the call to free my son – or I'll demonstrate on you, what you and Talia had planned for him.'

425

Lawson's face contorted into a mask of rage. 'Kill her,' he ordered Blondie.

The mercenary looked at Blackstone for consent.

Blackstone shook his head. 'No. I want to see this.'

My heart was hammering as I took a breath – watching the second hand countdown.

What if this didn't work?

I felt Nique's hand squeeze my arm and I risked a quick glance at her. She nodded her head in a silent '*Trust me.*'

We all jumped as if activated by a single shock as a ringtone suddenly shattered the stillness.

No one moved.

Blondie pulled out his phone, staring at the screen. He seemed frozen, making no move to answer. But he didn't need to. If I'd done this correctly, hearing it would be enough.

My eyes were on the gun in his hand. I held my breath – feeling Nique step closer to my side as we watched transfixed.

Blondie's face seemed to freeze. I daren't move, daren't breathe, as he turned slowly towards Lawson.

'Shoot her!' Lawson screamed, his face reddening as a pulse throbbed on his forehead.

The deadly ringtone carried on playing and then – stopped.

The pistol jumped once in Blondie's hand, the gunshot deafening in the confines of the room.

Lawson screamed – seeming to lift into the air before crashing heavily against the desk, his hands clawing his knee. Blood seeped through his fingers as he rolled on the floor.

'Two calls programmed,' I said. 'Two minutes apart.' I tried to calm my breathing which was coming in adrenalin-fuelled gusts. 'The first one to wound. If the abort code isn't sent – the second is to kill. And the next target is *you*, Blackstone!'

It wasn't true. The 'kill code' was one I'd programmed only as a last resort and a separate code had to be sent to trigger it – but Blackstone didn't know that.

He staggered back behind the desk. 'What's happening?' He stared at Lawson as his blood crept across the dusty carpet like thick molasses.

'The same thing that happened to Nichols . . . and Stamford.' Surprisingly, I felt totally unmoved as I watched Lawson rolling in agony.

Blondie stood motionless. Expressionless, in the catatonic state I'd embedded, until I gave a verbal command to break it.

'Get our phones, Nique.'

She went over and gingerly slipped her hand into the mercenary's pocket, her eyes never leaving his face as she watched for any sign of awareness. There were none. She switched on our phones, cautiously backing away from him, and handed me mine.

Blackstone was staring at Blondie in stunned disbelief.

'He can't hear you . . . or see you,' I said, answering his unspoken question. 'Embedding the commands with him was easier than I imagined, because someone had been inside his head before me. It could only have been Briggs – and she was working for Lawson.'

He watched the man on the floor as if he'd never seen him before.

'They programmed him to kill me?' He sounded incredulous.

'Cheaper than a divorce.' My smile was devoid of humour. 'I removed the audible trigger they'd installed to kill you. Even

427

if Talia made that call now, it wouldn't work.' He opened his mouth, but I held up a hand. 'Don't rush to thank me. Because I replaced their trigger with my own.'

'Make the call to Kriel,' Nique said. 'Tell him to free Alex.'

'You!' He seemed to suddenly snap out of it. 'You think I've gone through all of this, lost everything – to just let you walk away now?' He glanced at Blondie, at the gun in his hand.

'Don't even think about it,' I warned. 'You'd never close the distance in time. And even if you did – I've conditioned him to kill anyone who tries to take the gun from him without the "break" command.' I glanced at my watch. 'There's a call scheduled in less than thirty seconds. If I don't send the abort message, the next one's for you.'

His eyes narrowed. 'You won't,' he said. 'That's murder, McCready.'

'And I'm such a "straight dealer", right?' My whole body was trembling. The phone I held in my outstretched hand, suddenly felt like a dead weight. 'This is my son's life in the balance, Blackstone . . . My son!' I shouted. 'You willing to put your life on the other side of those scales?'

He hesitated for a just a heartbeat, but it felt like eternity.

Then finally he sagged down into the chair, looking like a puppet with its strings cut.

He fished the phone out of his inside pocket and held it up so I could see. I wasn't sure how long was left to the next call, but couldn't risk taking my eyes off him to check, and I wasn't about to abort the call until he made his.

As if reading my mind, I heard Nique beside me. 'Fifteen seconds, Blackstone,' she said. 'Fourteen . . . thirteen . . .'

'Alright,' he snapped, dialling.

'Put it on loudspeaker so we can hear.'

I pressed the key – aborting the call.

'Kriel.' Blackstone's voice quivered. 'Let the boy go.'

'Now?'

'Yes. Now!' he shouted, flecks of spittle flying across the desk.

'Proof of life, Blackstone,' I said.

'Put him on the phone,' Blackstone ordered. There was the sound of shuffling – someone moving and then 'Mum?'

'Alex,' I almost sobbed. 'Have they hurt you?' The sound of blood rushing in my ears almost drowned out his reply.

'No . . . I'm OK.'

A man's voice came back on. 'Boss?'

'Leave him there – and get out.' Blackstone ran a hand across his forehead – his eyes closed and I imagined he was running scenarios already, calculating his position and his options.

'Where are they?' I almost screamed at Blackstone.

He looked at me for just a second, then his shoulders slumped. 'A Portakabin on the site of the Crater.'

'Give him a phone so he can call me as soon as he's safe.' I drew a deep breath, hardly daring to believe that this was working. 'Did you hear that, Alex?'

'Yes,' he said.

'When Kriel's gone and you're safe – ring me.'

Chapter Seventy

Ten minutes had passed since I'd heard Alex's voice. I watched the clock, with one hand on my phone, aborting each task as it came up to avoid triggering any more calls.

Blondie stood in the centre of the room, a deadly automaton. The gun held limply by his side – his unseeing eyes staring straight ahead.

I'd gambled that the catatonic state would hold until I released him from it, but I hadn't been sure. So far, so good.

Lawson was still lying in front of the desk, his face a deathly pallor. He groaned and gripped his shattered knee as Blackstone looked on – totally unmoved.

'What's your plan? Or don't you have one?' Blackstone's tone didn't carry its usual confidence.

I hated to admit it, but I hadn't thought beyond getting Alex to safety.

'I have arrangements – to get out of the country later tonight,' he continued. 'With Bellew.' He looked down at Lawson. 'Obviously now I know about him and Talia, he can take his chances with the police.' He looked at me. 'I take it they're your next call?'

I looked at him in amazement. 'What makes you think I'll let *you* walk out of here?'

He pursed his lips. 'Usually I'd pay,' he said thoughtfully. 'But that won't work with you, will it, McCready? Your friend on the other hand' – he pointed to Nique – 'just admitted to killing Vashchenko. In front of witnesses. We give evidence and she'll never see daylight again. Not to mention your part in all this. But if you let us walk out of here before the police arrive, those witnesses are gone.'

Lawson glared at him, his face contorted in a mixture of panic and pain.

'This piece of shit will say whatever I tell him to, in return for the best legal representation I can pay for. He's finished and he knows it. The paper trail leads to him. The payouts to Briggs and Abassi.' He glanced at me and actually smiled, traces of irritating arrogance returning. 'All communications between Nichols and Stamford went through him and Briggs . . . nothing comes back to me. Lawson will say Bellew killed Vashchenko when he found her hiding in the cellar.' He shrugged. 'He's got enough kills to his name – one more won't make a difference to him and he'll be long gone, with me.'

I opened my mouth to say something, when my phone rang – the vibrations in my palm were like volts of unexpected electricity, making me jump.

It was Alex.

'Where are you?'

'In a street, not sure where exactly. But Kriel's gone.'

'Call the police,' I said as waves of relief severed the tension down my spine, suddenly making my legs unsteady. 'They're looking for you – give them a landmark so they can pick you up.'

As I ended the call, Blackstone nodded to the phone in my hand. 'I've done what you want, McCready. Now abort the rest of the calls.'

432

I deleted the tasks scheduled and wiped it all from the call history. I saw him glance at Blondie.

'Aborting the tasks, doesn't affect the state he's in,' I said. 'Only I can do that.'

He pushed up from his chair and walked to stand beside the desk. Looking down at Lawson, he prodded him with the toe of his highly polished shoe.

'He'll do as he's told. You let Bellew walk out of here with me now and your friend doesn't do time for murder and you don't face any charges either.'

Just then Nique's phone rang.

'Edge?'

We could all hear the other side of the call.

His voice was low. 'MAST approaching the house.'

'MAST?'

'Mobile Armed Surveillance Team. Armed police. They've been on you since you left the warehouse. I followed. Hung well back, took parallel routes. Bastard of a job not to be spotted.'

'What do we do?'

'I'm covering you from high ground, but I'm half a mile away. They're on your doorstep, girl. I can't see a clear exit for you; they'll have it totally contained in less than a minute.'

She looked at me, her teeth catching her bottom lip.

'The priest hole,' I said. 'Where does that come out?'

Her eyes widened. 'Outside the grounds,' she said into the phone. 'Ruined chapel just beyond the village, Edge. Is that outside the police perimeter?'

'Dunno. Maybe, but not for long. You'll have to get out now!'

'I'll meet you there. If it's too late, leave me and get out.' She ended the call. 'Come with us, Jo.'

I looked at her, my mind suddenly frozen with the enormity of what we'd done – what I'd done.

'I can't.'

'Jo, they'll know what you did. Helping me.' She looked around us. 'All this. What you did to Blondie . . . Lawson.'

'Very touching.' Blackstone's tone was caustic.

She regarded him with dead eyes. '*He'll* tell them, Jo.'

'Oh, not just her,' he said. 'You too. I'll make sure they know who killed Vashchenko. Maybe they'll let you two share a cell?'

She looked at me with a silent plea. I shook my head. 'Go on . . . Alex is safe. The rest doesn't matter. I'll take whatever comes.' She hesitated. 'Go!' I pushed her gently.

She hugged me and pressed her lips against my cheek.

Before getting to the door, she stopped in front of Lawson, crouching over him. I hadn't realised she'd picked up Yalena's combat knife and concealed it beneath her jacket, until the instant I saw her pull it from the waistband of her jeans.

'Nique – no!'

Her arm swung in a precise arc and Lawson's legs jerked in a final spasm. As she stepped away, I could see him clasping his neck. Gurgling and thrashing, his eyes staring wildly in disbelief as the life drained from his severed throat.

'One less witness for the prosecution, Blackstone,' she called as she pulled open the door and started across the hallway, glancing back to blow me a kiss.

I ran to Lawson's side, dropping to my knees with some vague notion of stemming the bleeding, but even as my hands closed over the slippery lips of the gaping wound, it was obvious he was already dead.

I sat back on my heels, with his blood pooling around me, the warmth of it soaking into my jeans.

'Looks like it's just you, me and the zombie then.' Blackstone's voice was devoid of emotion. I looked up at him as he leaned against the edge of the desk. 'We've got less than a minute before the police surround the place – what story do you want to tell them?'

'What?' I was struggling to take it in.

His lips pulled into a mocking half-smile. 'You're in as much shit as me now, McCready.' He leaned back, folding his arms. 'We're the only people who can tell them what happened here and I'm sure they'll be interested to know about your part in all this.' His eyes narrowed slightly. 'Unless we agree . . .'

'Agree?'

He shrugged. 'If we *both* tell them this was all down to Lawson, they'll believe it.' He glanced at the body beside me. 'Everything leads back to him anyway.'

'You think I'd even consider for one minute, doing *any* kind of a deal with someone like you, Blackstone?'

'Someone like me?' He raised his eyebrows. 'You can hardly claim the moral high ground here, McCready. From where I'm standing, you've got as much blood on your hands as me—'

A phone began to ring.

I looked up, confused. Not recognising the ringtone.

Blackstone was staring at me. We both looked at my phone, lying in the pool of blood. The screen was blank – it wasn't activated.

There was a movement in my peripheral vision. It took less than a heartbeat for me to realise it was Blondie.

He raised the gun.

'No!' Blackstone began to back away. 'Call him off, McCready!'

'It isn't me.' My mind raced in horrified panic. Had I missed one of the task settings? I knew I hadn't.

Nique! She programmed the phones back at the warehouse. She must have installed a trigger on hers and activated it as she made her way down to the priest hole.

'McCready!' Blackstone screamed.

'Stand down!' I shouted the command to break the hypnotic state – just as Blondie fired.

The shot hit Blackstone in the middle of his forehead. He fell, landing on his back, his arms splayed out like a man crucified.

Blondie's arm dropped to his side and the gun slipped from his fingers, clattering onto the floor. He turned slowly to look at me.

'Stand down,' I said again, quietly. But it was unnecessary – there was clarity in his eyes.

His jaw slackened as his mouth opened, but no sound came out.

He looked down at his arm as a red dot moved along it, across his chest to hover over his heart. Another red dot appeared on his forehead. It took a second for me to realise I was looking at laser sights marking their target.

A similar red dot swept across my knee and stopped above my left breast.

'Armed police! Move slowly towards the door with your hands on your head.'

Blondie's expression was one of total confusion. I knew he had no recollection of what had just happened or why.

I stayed on the ground – frozen.

Blondie moved as directed, pushing the unlocked doors open. A draught of cold air cut through the room, shifting the metallic smell of warm blood away. I watched him step out onto the dark stone patio, his hands clasped behind his head.

An officer barked instructions for him to get down on the ground. But before he could comply, his head snapped back as if punched by some invisible fist.

A split second later, the sound of a single shot rang out. It was still echoing in the night air as his lifeless body hit the ground, the black circle of a perfect shot clearly visible in the centre of his forehead.

Chapter Seventy-One

Kingsberry Farm – Saturday morning – Two weeks later

Harvey uncurled from his spot by the Aga and padded over for his morning hug. I lifted the lid on the hotplate and set the kettle to boil, opening the porch door to let him out.

The air was already warm. I shooed a bumble bee away from the post box, scooped the letters out and took them back to the kitchen.

Skimming through the usual junk, I stopped at an unexpected postcard from Venezuela – the picture on the front showed a cobalt sea and cloudless sky. I flipped it over to read the elegant copperplate handwriting.

"Wish you were here, my darling Yorkshire Rose"
Xx

I took my tea, along with the post, into the office.

Early-morning sunlight streamed through the huge arched windows and I inhaled the comforting smell of books and polished wood as I switched on the shredder. Feeding the postcard into the slot, I watched as the glossy image turned into azure serpents, coiling noisily into the bin.

I'd been promised more postcards. Just occasionally – to let me know what part of the world Nique and Edge were in – and I'd promised to shred them all.

I sipped my tea. Jen would be here soon, moving in to look after business and Harvey while I went away for a while.

Not a holiday. More of a decompression.

I felt as if my spirit had been drained – the gauge on my emotional tank hovered over 'empty' and I knew I was digging deep into depleted reserves.

After events at Boltby Hall, I'd been interviewed over several days. Walking the fine line between a truthful account and not incriminating myself had proved mentally and emotionally exhausting.

I'd later learned, that on the day of the kidnapping, the police had tracked my phone but lost me when Blondie switched it off at the warehouse. They tracked cell signals across various masts around Fordley, picking it up again when it came back to life as I'd downloaded my emails while sitting in my car outside the warehouse.

By the time the MAST had reached the place, Blondie was moving us to Boltby Hall and they'd followed the Range Rover from a safe distance.

I'd stuck to the story Nique and I had agreed. That I'd believed she'd died in the fire and only knew otherwise when she'd contacted me to say she was leaving the country, found out about Alex and agreed to go with me to meet the kidnapper's demands.

They wanted to know about Edge's role that night. I said that Nique had told him to follow their agreed plan to leave the country. Then she'd come with me – and I had no way of knowing what he'd done after that.

The bullet that killed Blondie hadn't come from any police firearm but was an expert shot, fired from outside the police cordon. Which meant Edge was a serious person of interest. Arrest warrants were issued for him and Nique in connection with at least two murders.

Prison officer Penny Harland had finally been picked up. It transpired she was nothing more than a jealous lover, drawn to the scene of the fire out of a desperate need to trace Nique. She *had* sent me the warning letter, but it had nothing to do with the rest of the case. She was currently suspended, awaiting an investigation into misconduct in public office.

The police had tracked the Mini seen on CCTV outside Blackstone's building and managed to get a number plate from ANPR cameras. That had proved to be Yalena's car, registered to one of Dimitri Chernov's UK companies.

On the day of the kidnapping, when she followed Myles, they were tracking the car. They'd followed her as far as ANPR coverage allowed – just to the edge of the Yorkshire Dales – but from there, Callum had realised the only location of interest in that area was Boltby Hall and had directed the team there.

I'd given a truthful account of the rest of that night – pretty much.

Yalena's appearance and subsequent death, just as it had happened. She *had* followed Lawson there with the intention of killing him, not realising what else was unfolding.

The investigating team were happy that Blackstone had ordered Blondie to shoot Lawson after finding out about his affair with his wife and that Nique had cut his throat in a final act of revenge.

The armed response team had witnessed Blondie killing Blackstone and accepted my version of events.

I'd said Blackstone had refused to pay Blondie because he felt the contract hadn't been fulfilled and Blondie killed him – just as the armed officers had seen for themselves.

The deception that haunted me most, though, was what I'd done to Blondie. The post-mortem found traces of flunitrazepam in his system, which I denied all knowledge of, and without the vial – which was at the bottom of the canal by the warehouse – there was no evidence connecting me to that.

Geoff Perrett had agreed, as I'd known he would, to never mention his gift of the flunitrazepam. 'You did what you had to do to save Alex,' he said when I told him. 'And sometimes doing what's right means breaking a few laws – I can sleep nights with that. What's important, is that *you* can too.'

Which was why my sabbatical was going to be in a rented cottage in the Highlands with Geoff, battling the demons in my psyche and outmanoeuvring me in a game of cerebral chess. I needed counselling from him. More than that, he was the only person I trusted to unpack the horrors I was carrying inside.

I consoled myself in part that the triggers I'd set and the conditioning I'd carried out on Blondie had been to wound – with only one trigger code set to be fatal. I'd struggled with that initially, but Nique persuaded me that, as a last resort, we might need it.

Could I ever have used it? Even to save Alex's life? Thankfully I would never have to find out.

Nique had installed the 'kill code' on her own phone without my knowledge. But I knew I'd created the mechanism she'd used to kill Blackstone.

Was that as bad as pulling the trigger myself? I was haunted by the belief that it was.

Fortunately, the theory would never be tested before a jury. But I would serve a life sentence of my own.

Had Nique guessed that Blackstone would try to do a deal with me after she'd gone and then undoubtedly betray me anyway?

Is that why she triggered the call to kill him – to protect me? Or would she have done it anyway, to settle her own scores?

I would never know.

'You made the weapon,' Geoff had said. 'But you didn't use it and you didn't tell *her* to either.'

But it was a fine distinction and one I knew he'd have to wrestle from the tortured corners of my mind once we were in our secluded Highland retreat. I didn't envy him the battle.

That dark abyss that continued to haunt me – maybe it would be with me forever now.

As the only surviving witness from that night, there was no one who could contradict my evidence. I knew Callum had his suspicions but nothing he could prove. It was only the currency I held, in the credit column of our previous relationship, that meant he was giving me the benefit of the doubt.

There had been times when I'd wanted to tell him everything. To share the burden with him. But knowing him the way I did, I knew he would feel compelled to let the law take its course, despite his feelings. The value system he lived by was too strong to break, even for me.

My secret would forever rob us of the kind of future we might have had. An emotional isolation from the only man, I now realised, I had ever loved since my husband's death, was the price I paid to save my son and protect my friends.

I walked into the kitchen and poured a cup of tea for Alex.

He'd come out of this physically whole, but like me, he was emotionally exhausted and I'd been grateful to have him at home with me for the past couple of weeks.

I carried the tea upstairs and quietly pushed open his bedroom door. His tousled hair poked out from beneath the duvet – his breathing was deep and slow. I put the cup on his bedside table and gently touched his hair. Sleep hadn't come easily for him lately, I didn't want to wake him.

As I went back downstairs, I could hear car tyres crunching down the gravel drive. By the time I'd walked into the kitchen, Callum was coming through the door with Harvey fussing excitedly round his feet. His face was obscured by the huge bouquet of flowers he was holding.

'Going away present,' he said as he laid them on the kitchen table. 'Thought they'd cheer up your Highland hovel.' His hands felt warm against my skin as he pulled me to him. 'And remind you of me when you look at them.'

I stood in the reassuring circle of his arms, my head on his chest, listening to the comforting thud of his heart. He tilted my face up to look at him, his breath warm against my lips.

'Please come back to me whole again, Jo,' he said softly.

I nodded and buried my face in his neck. 'I will,' I said with more than a little hope.

Author's Note

MK-Ultra – Programming an Assassin

It's said that, in life, truth is stranger than fiction. The occasions when I stumble across those strange truths often trigger 'what-if' moments that lead to the idea for a plot – and that's exactly what happened when I was training to become a hypnotherapist.

During my studies, I met a retired psychiatrist who told me that as a student he had been an assistant to William Sargant, a British psychiatrist famous for his work with shell-shocked servicemen during World War Two, and later for his book, *Battle for the Mind: A Physiology of Conversion and Brainwashing*, published in 1957.

Sargant established a research unit in the basement of St Thomas' Hospital, London, to conduct controversial experiments into 'biological psychiatry'. That was where my psychiatrist friend observed covert experiments into mind control, which were code-named MK-Ultra. Sargant was apparently associated with British Intelligence and the CIA, who began MK-Ultra during the Korean war. My source said that the experiments involved 'attempts to create a potential assassin'.

It was this encounter that gave me the idea for Jo McCready's mentor, Professor Geoff Perrett. In this book, I gave him the same backstory as that retired psychiatrist, making him one of Sargant's students and a first-hand witness to the experiments carried out all those decades ago.

A quick search on the internet brings up dozens of articles about MK-Ultra, which was sanctioned in 1953 and officially ended in 1973. Most famous, is the assertion by Sirhan Sirhan – the man convicted for the assassination of Bobby Kennedy in 1968 – that he was programmed by the CIA using MK-Ultra techniques, to commit the assassination but have no memory of it.

MK-Ultra used numerous methods to manipulate behaviour, including administering psychoactive substances, such as LSD, which resulted in the death of some of the unfortunate guineapigs. They discovered that a combination of drugs and hypnosis produced the most successful results – allowing behaviours to be implanted and then 'triggered' by an audible or visual signal, while leaving the subject with no memory of the event.

In hypnotherapy, amnesia scripts are commonly used to implant suggestion deeper into the subconscious and increase the effectiveness of treatment by leaving the patient with no memory of the procedure. But I was shocked to learn about the abuse of this technique during Cold War experiments – carried out by both sides.

My chance encounter with that old psychiatrist had a profound effect on me, and throughout my studies I was intrigued by the whole subject of conditioning, false-memory implantation and 'brainwashing'.

As a therapist, most of my work involved helping clients eliminate behaviours and negative thought patterns that were creating problems in their lives. But I couldn't help thinking back to that early conversation, about how those same techniques had been reversed, often with unwitting subjects, to actually *install* destructive behaviours.

The 'moral maze' questions that posed, horrified and fascinated me in equal measure and the 'what-ifs' began.

What-if an individual used those techniques to advance their own agenda? What-if that agenda involved committing murder? Or, like MK-Ultra's original aim, to have an individual set up to become an unwitting assassin and then take the blame for the crime but have no memory of it, to be unable to mount a credible defence, just as Sirhan claimed?

To make that work, I needed to know whether it would be possible to replicate those techniques today? Could the modern drugs now available, facilitate that process and make it even faster, and would it be possible to condition an individual to become an 'assassin'? Given the advances made in hypnosis and psychology, I believed it was and my research became the plot for this novel.

In 2011, Derren Brown tested Sirhan's claims in the television show, *The Assassin*. Using both hypnosis and conditioning (but no drugs, obviously), he succeeded in having the subject 'assassinate' Stephen Fry while he performed on stage in front of an audience. Afterwards, the 'shooter' had no recollection of what he had done.

In 1973, the CIA ordered the destruction of all files relating to MK-Ultra – but some documents survived and came to light when they were declassified in 2001.

In 1975, the presidential 'Rockefeller Commission Report' revealed to the public for the first time that the CIA and the Department of Defence *'had conducted experiments on both*

*unwitting and cognizant human subjects, as part of an exten-
sive program, to find out how to influence and control human
behaviour through the use of psychoactive drugs and other psychological means.*' Given the CIA's destruction of most records,
the full impact of MK-Ultra, including the number of deaths,
may never be known.

Acknowledgements

I would like to thank everyone at RCW Literary Agency. In particular, my brilliant agent Jon Wood for all his support. Without you – none of this would have been possible.

Thank you to Zaffre, for giving Jo McCready a bright new future. The whole team are amazing and work tirelessly on my behalf. Especially, my editor Ben Willis, who has the patience of a saint. Thanks Ben, for holding my hand and making my work so much better.

Huge thanks must go to my police advisor, retired Detective Superintendent Stu Spencer for his advice on the procedural aspects of the book and for great suggestions that added to the storyline. You have now become a partner in crime! Any errors on police procedure, were made in the name of dramatic licence and are entirely mine.

To the author Mike (M.W.) Craven for his advice on issues around probation and for putting me in touch with his great friend, Crawford Bunney who filled in the finer details of parole. Thank you both for giving your time with such good humour and patience.

My friend and fellow author, Kate Bendelow, for her expert advice on all things CSI related. Our conversations about strangulation and other methods of murder are priceless, if a little scary at times.

Ray Freeman, Psychologist and friend is the real-life inspiration for the curmudgeonly Geoff Perrett. Thanks for exploring with me, on this occasion, methods of mind-control and brainwashing and for your help and advice in developing the psychological theories I use in my books, even if it does mean I always have to pay for lunch.

Inspiration for the character 'Edge' came from my friend, 'Biff', who is actually larger than life than his fictional persona. Thank you for trusting me with your stories and allowing me to weave some of them into my fiction. I promise, I'll never tell it all.

Sandra Hayton kindly donated to a charity auction to become a character in the book. It goes without saying that she bears no resemblance to the fictional Sandra.

I am eternally grateful to the family and friends who encourage me along the way in what is, by nature, a solitary pursuit. My sons, Adam and Kyle, are always on hand to help their technophobe mother with the 'techie' stuff. Thank you for your ingenious solutions to all things cyber-crime related. I knew I'd given birth to you both for a reason.

Thanks to my step-daughter, Katie, for helping me brainstorm ideas. If ever you take to a life of crime – we're all in trouble.

To the good friends, who read my books before I dare send them to anyone else and whose honest feedback is invaluable, Maria Sigley, Sharon Beddoes and Alison Barnes. I couldn't do it without you cheering me on from the side-lines. Your constant faith and support, mean the world to me.

To my boxer dog, Bruce, the real Harvey. For keeping me company in the she-shed. I can't say your snoring is helpful – but it has become the sound-track to my working day.

Finally, to my best friend and partner Ian, who built me an amazing space in which to write and gives me the emotional support to do it. Thank you for all your love and encouragement. I simply couldn't do any of this without you.

If you enjoyed *The Killing Song*,
why not join the
LESLEY MCEVOY READERS' CLUB?

When you sign up, you'll be the first to know about
updates on the Dr Jo McCready series, plus you'll gain
access to exclusive content, offers and giveaways.
To sign up, simply visit:
bit.ly/LesleyMcEvoy

Keep reading for a letter from the author . . .

Hello!

Thank you for picking up *The Killing Song*, the second book in the Jo McCready crime series. I hope you enjoyed reading the book as much as I enjoyed writing it.

It's said that in life, truth is stranger than fiction. The occasions when I stumble across those strange truths often trigger 'what-if' moments that lead to the idea for a plot, and that's exactly what happened when I was training to become a hypnotherapist. During my studies, I met a retired psychiatrist who told me that as a student he had been an assistant to William Sargant, a British psychiatrist famous for his work with shell-shocked servicemen during World War Two. Sargant established a research unit in the basement of St. Thomas's Hospital, London, to conduct controversial experiments into biological psychiatry, which is where my psychiatrist friend observed these covert experiments. The subject fascinated me and we discussed various ways in which these methods might be replicated today.

That conversation, and the research it inspired, gave me the backstory for Jo McCready's mentor, Professor Geoff Perrett, who was introduced to readers in just one very brief line in *The Murder Mile*. In this book, I wanted to flesh out his character and develop his story and so I made him one of Sargant's assistants, just like my retired psychiatrist friend.

In the second book in the series, I also wanted to dig deeper into Jo's character and introduce some 'moral maze' questions around friendship, loyalty and family, by presenting her with the dilemma of just what boundaries she might cross to protect those she cares about.

If you enjoyed *The Killing Song*, then please do keep an eye out for news about the next book in the series, which will be coming out towards the end of the year – in fact, you can keep reading for an exclusive extract.

If you would like to hear more about my books, you can visit **bit.ly/LesleyMcEvoy** where you can become part of the Lesley McEvoy's Readers' Club. It only takes a few moments to sign up, there are no catches or costs.

Bonnier Zaffre will keep your data private and confidential, and it will never be passed on to a third party. We won't spam you with loads of emails, just get in touch now and again with news about my books, and you can unsubscribe any time you want.

And if you would like to get involved in a wider conversation about my books, please do review *The Killing Song* on Amazon, on Goodreads, on any other e-store, on your own blog and social media accounts, or talk about it with friends, family or reader groups! Sharing your thoughts helps other readers, and I always enjoy hearing about what people experience from my writing.

Thank you again for reading *The Killing Song*.

All the best,
Lesley McEvoy

Don't miss the thrilling next instalment
in the Dr Jo McCready series

Coming Winter 2022

Keep reading for an exclusive extract . . .

An apex predator is, by definition, at the very top of the food chain. In its natural habitat, nothing preys upon it.

Therefore, many would say that we are apex predators.

I know that's not true.

I know beyond doubt, we have predators out there, ones that don't hunt and kill us in order to survive.

They do it because they can.

But the most terrifying of all . . .

They do it because they like it.

Chapter One

Thursday morning – Late November – Kingsberry Farm

I threw a stick for my boxer dog, Harvey, and watched as he bounded across the frozen field after it.

We were lucky to live in a place like this, with six acres of my own land to walk across without seeing another living soul. The isolation up here on the Yorkshire moors suited me, given what I did for a living. But it was easy to get complacent about the scenery when it was an everyday companion.

I stopped and turned my face into the watery morning sun, breathing in the crisp air. Jamming my hands into the pockets of my heavy Barbour jacket, I turned down the well-worn track to the woods that bordered my land. Harvey was already out of sight – leading the way as usual.

I felt the mobile vibrate against my palm a second before its shrill tone shattered the rural tranquillity.

'McCready.'

'Finally dragged yourself out of bed then?' I could hear the smile in Callum's voice, beneath his barely discernible Scottish accent.

'Been up for hours – already out walking.' I climbed a stile which Harvey took in one leap. 'How come you left so early?'

'Got an early call. You were out for the count – seemed a shame to wake you.' I heard the shuffling of papers and could picture him at his desk in the CID office in Fordley police station. 'Charlotte picked up a murder case overnight.'

Detective Superintendent Charlotte Warner headed up a team of specialist detectives in HMET, West Yorkshire Police's Homicide and Major Enquiry Team.

'I'm DCI on it. Going to be putting in all the hours for a while, Jo. This is a bad one.'

I thought about the shockwave from sudden death – destroying everything in its path. 'Aren't they all?'

'Hmm, well this one has extras that I really don't like . . .' He paused but I sensed there was more to come. 'Was hoping you could come and take a look? I really need you to see this.'

'What is it this time? Sick, sadistic or just plain deviant?'

'How did you guess?'

'Because I *only* get called if there's an element of sick or sadistic–'

'Or just plain deviant,' he finished helpfully.

'So . . . which is it?'

'Thought that's what you did? Read minds.'

'I'm a forensic profiler, not Mystic Meg.' I scooped up the stick Harvey had dropped at my feet and launched it for him.

'I know you don't want to get involved in police investigations anymore–'

'I don't.'

'I wouldn't ask if it wasn't important.'

'They're *all* important, Cal – it's not a matter of degree.' Harvey ran back and danced around my legs as I tried to ignore him. 'It's a matter of balance – for me, anyway.'

'I know. Last year was a tough one, Jo. Stress wise. I under-stand that–'

'My caseload is full. The Crown Prosecution Service are keeping me busy. I've got offender assessments to do for two upcoming trials.'

'We don't want you in this all the way,' he pressed, 'just need you to come out today and take a look. To give me your opinion. Please?'

'Just today?'

'Absolutely.'

His answer came too fast to be true.

'Charlotte's authorised your involvement – got a budget code for your time.'

'Already?'

It was unusual for a profiler to be called in at such an early stage, which compounded my uneasy feeling that there was a lot more he wasn't telling me.

He hesitated for just a heartbeat. 'I know you hate seeing them in-situ, Jo . . . but it's important for this one.'

Seeing the bodies had never been something I found easy. Even though 'walking the scene' was a process I employed to get into the mind of an offender, to map the events that had led up to whatever atrocity we were dealing with. But usually it was long after all the physical evidence had been removed. I preferred it that way – for all kinds of reasons.

'I can meet you at the scene,' he pushed again.

Pre-empting my agreement. Nice tactic.

'I don't know, Cal . . .'

'Please, Jo.' His tone was coaxing. 'It's on the Kenley Estate in Fordley. Do you know it?'

I let out a long breath. 'Okay,' I said finally, 'I'm walking Harvey, so give me time to go back and get changed.' I glanced at my watch. 'Can be there in about an hour?' I still wasn't sure I wanted to do this.

'Don't get changed on my account.' I pictured his schoolboy grin. 'Quite like the wellies and jeans look.'

'An hour, Ferguson.'

'Okay. I'll send you the address.'

Chapter Two

Thursday morning – Fordley

I drove past rows of identically neat semi-detached houses on the Kenley estate. The one I was looking for was in a quiet cul-de-sac of well-maintained gardens, separated by tidy privet hedges.

I remembered the estate being built when I was a teenager. My mother – known to everyone simply as 'Mamma' – dragged me and my father into the show-home one Sunday morning.

As an Italian immigrant, arriving in England with my grandparents not long after the second World War, Mamma had always aspired to live in what she referred to as 'the posh part of town'. My father, a typical Irish-Yorkshireman, was totally unimpressed by the vision of suburbia the salesman painted, and by lunchtime we were in the local pub, my dad telling his pals about the 'bloody extortionate price' of a new life on the other side of town. Needless to say, we didn't relocate.

I spotted Callum as soon as I turned into the street, even though he was wearing the anonymising white scene suit. The head of thick, silver hair was unmistakeable as he leaned against the bonnet of his unmarked BMW, with the obligatory face mask pulled down and dangling around his neck.

The women at Fordley nicknamed him 'The Silver Fox' – though never to his face. In his mid-forties, his hair was an unusual feature which only made his good looks more striking.

Blue-and-white police tape marked the outer cordon at the end of the cul-de-sac. A uniformed officer stood guard outside one of the houses about halfway down, as Crime Scene Investigators came and went from their van parked further along the road.

This unassuming home had once been the same as all the others. But not anymore. It would now forever be known as the place where a murder occurred. Tainted. Different. Changed forever, like everything that's touched by sudden and violent death.

In a neighbourhood that was just beginning the tentative process of putting up Christmas decorations; festive tinsel and fairly lights incongruous against the harsh formality of police tape and paraphernalia surrounding a crime scene.

Callum strolled over as I locked my Roadster.

'People will think you're a hairdresser driving around in that,' he teased.

'Still beats yours out of a bend, any day of the week.'

'Emasculating a man by insulting his car.'

'Then get a decent car,' I said with humour.

'It's the new body shape.'

'You can put lipstick on a pig . . . but it's still a pig.'

Our usual petrol-head banter – much more fun than a mundane 'good morning'.

We stood apart, feeling suddenly awkward about not touching. But this was work and we'd always kept that distinctly separate from our personal lives.

Everyone in Fordley nick speculated about our on/off relationship, with no one ever quite sure whether we were 'on' or 'off'. After almost two years of dancing around it, I don't think we knew ourselves. Then, just a few short months before, I'd decided to stop holding DCI Callum Ferguson at arm's length. Weighing up the risks of becoming vulnerable against the need to end my self-imposed emotional isolation. But it was still early days for both of us, so we were taking it one step at a time, until we'd worked it out.

'Can see I'm going to have to distract you with work, before this gets totally out of hand,' Callum grinned.

'So – what've you got?' I asked.

'Barbara Thorpe. Fifty-two years old. Lives alone. Apparently she let the cat out every night and was up around five every morning to let it in and feed it . . . but not today. Next-door neighbour heard the cat crying to get inside the house and knocked on.' He gestured to the house next door with a nod of his head. 'She had a key and let herself in around seven o'clock. Found her friend with her throat cut. No sign of forced entry or a struggle, and doesn't look like anything's been taken.'

We both paused as an officer guarding the outer cordon handed me a paper scene suit, gloves, mask and overshoes. Callum leaned against my car and watched as I began to pull them on.

'Still not sure why you need me for this,' I said as I ducked under the cordon tape.

'Looks like it might be connected to the Stephen Jones murder,' he said, by way of an explanation.

Stephen Jones had been murdered the previous month, at his home in a quiet suburb of Leeds. He'd had his throat cut as he sat watching TV. I'd only read about the Jones case in the newspapers, same as everyone else.

We both stopped to pull up our hoods and slip the masks over our faces, before ducking under the blue-and-white tape that marked the inner cordon around the house and its small garden.

'That's the connection? They both had their throats cut?' I asked. 'Not *that* sick, sadistic or deviant in the grand scheme of things.'

'Not just that.'

'What then?'

His expelled breath was muffled by the mask as he opened the gate and walked me down the path. 'After Jones's murder, we held back certain details.'

'Like what?'

'As well as having his throat cut, he'd had a body part amputated.'

'Has that happened here?'

'Not exactly.'

My legendary lack of patience was being sorely tested. This was like pulling teeth.

'What then?'

'You'll see.'